THE HIGH-HEELED ECO-WORRIER

Debbie Bourne

Eco Romance Series Book 2

MALCHIK MEDIA

Published by
Malchik Media
www.richardlynttonbooks.com

Softcover ISBN: 978-1-959755-05-0
Hardcover ISBN: 978-1-959755-12-8
eBook ISBN: 978-1-959755-04-3

Cover design: Elisabetta Giordana
Interior layout: Gary A. Rosenberg

For further adventures
in the Eco Romance Series:
Book 3: High-Heels & Tight Briefs

For all book enquires:
richard@richardlynttonbooks.com

The High-Heeled Eco-Worrier
Confessions of an Eco-Worrier

*'Yesterday I was clever,
so I wanted to change the world.
Today I am wise,
so I am changing myself.'*

—RUMI

Contents

THE CHARACTERS

Deborah: The High-Heeled Eco-Worrier

Nat: Debs BF. Future Prime Minister

Father Guy: Local priest. Known as GG—Gorgeous Guy. But is he?

Rich: He may be living without money for a year, but he's rich in spirit

Nahal: Chef of the Abundance Cafe (not Café!)

Jafar: Nahal's son, age seven

Pippa: Studying to become an environmental lawyer

Sacha: Pestival organiser. She's simply the pest!

Margaret: Septuagenarian meat campaigner: From squeals to meals. Carer of Old Spot

Old Spot: Pet with built in apple sauce

Thomas Montjoy: Property Developer. Owns the unlikely named Greener Properties

Greg (Peck): Bird conservationist. Great bustard lover

Henry Smythe: aka Henry Smarmy Smythe. Single dad from Daddy Day share. Or is he?

Henry Junior: His son

Michael: Single dad from Daddy Day share. Founder of the Knit Wits

Chloe: Michael's daughter

Leroy: Ten-year-old inventor

Francis: Leroy's dad

John: Ex-legal student

Fretting Frederik: Danish investigative journalist

Lucia and Mouse: The Chip Fat Travellers

Boxing-Bradley: Ex-boxer. Lidl area manager. Nat's political campaign manager

Benji bard: Shakespearean herb/seed grower

Mr Pang: Owner of the local Chinese takeaway

Father Bill: Bishop of Edmonton

Anousha & the Power rangers: Singing-and-hammering Iranian women's carpentry group

Fliff/Phoebe: Deb's (so-called) best friends

Sir Keir Stammer: Politician

Barry Sheen: Furniture polish

Wangari Maathai: Inspiring historical environmental campaigner

Joke: Runs battery hen adoption company

Peung: Beautician from Cute-i-cles

Mr Rentokil: Does what is says in the name

Chef Chang: Internationally renowned celebrity chef

Clive Garney: Director of Bank of England

Harold: Senior Economist at the Bank of England.

Hari: Proprietor of local dry cleaners

Miss 'Jam Tart' Stuart: Year 2 teacher at Kentish Town primary school.

Stu: Deb's brainy husbondage

James: Deb and Stu's 18-year-old son

Sophia Lorhen and Brutus: Ex-bats. Battery hens. Live at Cluckingham Palace

Fireman Sam: Fireman from the fire station across the road

Joe Swift: Gardening TV Presenter

Marjorie and Glynis: Twitchers and testes

Jim: Food critic

Mikey Gove: Politician (or maybe ex-politician be-time you are reading this!)

T.U.R.D: Town, urban, river, diviner's

Annuciata: Read on to find out!

Let There Be Light...

'Welcome to your second home, Deb.'

'Second home? What are you talking about?' I ask Nat as the smudged outline of an old Gothic church appears through the misty September morning.

I look up along the crumbling stone walls and up the spire. While I must have walked past this church in the middle of Kentish Town Road hundreds of times, I realise I've never stopped to look at the rather ornate, rundown building.

'This deconsecrated church was meant to be turned into a posh block of flats,' says Nat. 'But I've met with the Bishop of Edmonton, and he's agreed to lease it to us.'

'Bishop of who?' I laugh. 'The only bishop you know is Bishop's Stortford, where your mum was born!'

'Oh, ye of little faith,' Nat says, pointing up at the cross above the entrance. 'All I had to do was contact the Diocese of London and point out to the bishop that this empty church would make a great base for a climate action group, like ours. Amen. The bishop agreed to lease it to us free of charge for a year!'

'What climate action group? I look at the cross, several loose nails clearly responsible for its unfortunate flexure. 'And more importantly, what on earth would we want to do with it?'

'Exactly, Deb!' Nat thumps me on the back. 'It's all about the Earth and saving it. 'This church is going to be the base for our inspiring new community eco project. The bishop loved our idea!'

Our eco project? *Our* idea? The only idea I have is to end this outing, get out of the damp, and retreat to Café Espresso for a steaming cup of hazelnut latte.

Probably best to pause here and explain something about us two. While Nat is my new best friend, we come from completely different backgrounds. I'm a fashion designer who for many years worked for top international fashion brands, although if I'm honest, I haven't had a job for a couple of years. But this is hopefully about to change. Nat is a dab hand at power machinery and works part time at Charles Wilson tool hire down the road. The tools of my trade are chiffon and lace; for Nat, it's grinders and planers. We met three years ago, when we turned a disused patch of land that surrounded my house and Nat's flat into a thriving community garden—a garden that now grows more than fifty varieties of fruit and veg, and even supplies produce to a local veg box scheme.

'I know it's probably just some tax avoidance scam to prove that the diocese is doing their bit for the environment and not just selling off properties,' says Nat, grabbing my hand and pulling me along the uneven cobbled path to the front door. 'But as the guv here once said, knock and the door will be opened. So, I just knocked, and, hey presto, this church is ours, gratis, with phones and internet all thrown in until September next year. If it's a success, maybe we'll get it for good.'

I stare at the front door, it's once-intricate wooden panels now inlaid with wood lice and beetle grubs. Instead of the door being opened to us, it's more like the door is just about hanging on from rusty hinges. Above the door, my eyes fix on a rather grotesque looking gargoyle, its menacing features adorned with lichen.

'A God life soon to be turned into our very own Good Life! Just add a vowel—another "o." Get it?' Nat, the would-be grammarian, bursts out laughing. 'Remember that telly series from the seventies? I'll be Margot and you can be Barbara!'

My mind flashes back to the TV show, *The Good Life*. Margot? wasn't she the posh one?

'But instead of one family's go at self-sufficiency,' Nat interrupts my musing on social status, 'our narrative will be all about creating community climate action, and co-efficiency.'

Climate action? Co-efficiency? I listen to Nat spout out her newly swotted-up, bishop-impressing eco terms, while my only narrative remains to go to the cafe. Never mind adding or dropping an "o," I want to pick up an "a"—for almond croissant.

'The Good Life! That's what we'll call our project!' Nat excitedly races on. 'It's going to be all about supporting the environment, creating enterprise, and helping our community flourish from this church. Our very own Good Life hub.'

'No, I'm sorry Nat—creating a community garden was one thing, but a community eco hub is a complete other thing. And not one I have any interest in pursuing.' I turn and start to walk away.

'Deb!' Nat calls out. 'Can't you just picture a hub full of handsome conservationists and environmental do-gooders? All doing good here. We'll cook local food, develop projects to protect nature, generate our own energy. It's all about sharing ...'

Sharing handsome conservationists? I'm suddenly thinking Ben Fogle ... not such a bad premise. And Bear Grylls's recent TV series definitely had an eco-slant to it. Maybe I could just take a quick peek inside the church ...

Nat lifts a large antique key from her carrier bag and inserts it in the lock. With a creak, just like in a horror movie, the door opens. In front of us, a cavernous room stretches into the dim distance. A nasty dank smell pervades the air. Fumbling in my purple leather Chloe bag, with its well-ordered compartments, I locate my mobile in the pitch black and manage to switch on the phone's torch. I shine it up onto the pointed arches and wooden beams that hold up vaulted ceiling. A balcony overlooks the rows of askew pews. I look around what once must have been a very grand room, its walls stuccoed and painted in a curious shade of peach. Several huge stone arches loom above diamond paned windows decorated with richly coloured stained glass. Although I'm not religious in the slightest, I'm struck by the display of skill in the architecture, the tarnished grandeur.

'But we don't know anything about climate, er...action, Nat.' I take a deep breath. 'We are just two local mums who set up a community veg patch.'

I refrain from adding that I couldn't even spell the word environmentalism at a pub quiz last week; or mention the alarming chat

I had on the phone last night with my husbondage, Stu, who is on yet another business trip in the US. Stu told me about a potential job offer that would mean him leaving the Bank of England, where he is a micro—or is it macro? -economist for a prestigious teaching post at Yale University in Connecticut. I may not be the brainiest of people—more at home with a needle, than a pen—but even I've heard of Yale. Stu didn't laugh when I told him I didn't see myself as a Stepford wife.

I sigh, take a deep breath, and share the one bit of info Nat does know about. 'Anyhow, I'm really hoping that I'm going to be offered a styling job at Selfridges. I know it's a bit vacuous and all about encouraging people to buy more clothes—the opposite of what you're talking about creating here—but ...'

'Well, you can style this church now!' Nat chuckles. 'Look, I agree with you, perhaps we don't know much yet about environmental campaigning, but we'll soon learn. After all, as you are always saying, we've all got to do our bit to help combat global warming.'

Yes, but I meant more along the lines of buying a scarf made of recycled cashmere. I keep this less than altruistic thought to myself.

'Anyway,' Nat persists, 'we are going to invite an assortment of worthy causes to come and help us get down and dirty sprucing up this space, at the same time trying to convince us why we should give them free desk space and shared comms.'

As I look around the room, a ray of daylight steals in through a window, illuminating layers of thick dust and cobwebs. Could this sad, damp space really be returned into a thriving hub of community? My eyes alight on a beautiful stained-glass window of a man with his indigo cloak wrapped around a baby, his arm pointing along the panels of browns and ochre. Perhaps symbols of a desert. I look at the next panel and its now neglected story of struggle and hope. My musings are interrupted as I feel something unpleasant suddenly brush past my ankles. I shine my phone torch down to see a rat scamper its way through the aisles. As I let out a shriek, my phone and bag fall to the floor, plunging the room back into near darkness.

'Hello, is everything OK?' A voice of concern pierces the gloom. 'Hold on a moment, I'll turn on the lights.'

I hear the flick of a switch, and the church is flooded with light. A gorgeous man is standing there. Let there be light indeed!

'Allow me to introduce myself. I'm Father Guy Mowbray. So sorry you didn't realise the electricity was still turned on. I do hate to hear a damsel in distress.' He rifles his hand through waves of golden hair.

Hold on a mo, indeed. Did this guy say Father Guy Mowbray? Mowbray as in the pork pie and Father as in ...'

'You must be Deborah?' He hurries up to me.

And you must be ... a vicar? I look at his low-slung jeans, his T-shirt hugging his muscled arms in just the right places. Surely it wasn't possible.

He crouches down to help me pick up the scattered contents of my bag. Close enough that I can almost feel the silken hairs on his bare arm brush against my own arm right through my double-down parka jacket.

'I see you like Doritos, too!' He scoops up a handful of chips— my other guilty pleasure. 'So, tell me, Dorito-Deborah, are you a zesty-salsa or chilli-heatwave girl?' He smiles at me through eyes as intensely blue as the Indian Ocean I swam in only last month.

@NTS: strike all non-eco-friendly similes from mind.

'Deb's favourite flavour is sour cream. I'm the flamin' hot lover,' Nat butts in, brushing past me. 'And of course Deb's OK. It was just a brush with one of God's little creatures who have made this fine building their home over the past year! Good to see you again, Father Guy.' She shakes his hand as he stands up.

'Ah yes, this little problem of the rodent infestation *has* been bought to my attention, but I gather you have plans to deal with it straight away. Anyway, good to meet you Dorito ... er, Deborah. I've heard so much about you.' Father Guy takes my hand and holds it. I feel my body flood with warmth (spiritual warmth, of course), while an unpleasant chill settles over my brain at the mention of rats. The biggest rat being Natalie, with her latest less-than-consulted-upon eco shenanigans.

'I believe everyone was terribly upset when the diocese decided to deconsecrate this church, only to have it remain unused, and unloved for a year while plans for its future were finalised.' Father Guy shakes his head. 'Terrible how quickly deterioration sets in.' He pauses to wipe a layer of thick dust off one of the pews. 'You must be pleased that the bishop has decided to assign a short-term lease to you ladies. I'm newly appointed to run the parish in this area, but the bishop has asked me to oversee this project alongside my other church, St Margaret's. Quite frankly, while I'm not sure this place can ever be made good, we will need to be in close contact.' He smiles at me. 'Natalie has told me that you're interested in holding unofficial multi-faith services here. Are you practising, Deborah?'

Practising what? My eyes run down his body.

'She's Jewish,' Nat interjects, 'but has always been very interested in learning more about the New Testament. After all, as she's always telling me, it is the most famous book in the history of the world!'

My protestations remain unvoiced, as Nat's steel-tipped boot nudges my ankle.

'How wonderful,' says Father Guy. 'That is certainly something we can explore together. Anyway, talking about exploring, do let me give you a tour of the church. Our new shared home. For now. And do call me Guy.'

Gorgeous Guy—GG—it is, I decide, as we follow him back towards what he tells me was the vestibule at the church entrance.

'This church was built in the style of Gothic Revival in the second half of the 19th century,' GG explains. 'At the time, England saw an unprecedented expansion in the number of churches being erected in response to a growing population. I do find it ironic that the so-called "enlightened" Industrial Revolution has led us to a point in history where anthropogenic climate change is now a grave threat to us all. Don't you agree, Deborah?'

'Jesus, just look at this!' Nat's outburst prevents me from having to answer GG.

@NTS: Anthropo what?

'It's disgusting,' Nat says. 'This is the first thing we are gonna clean up.' She stares into a large white marble font—the assorted invertebrates lying prostrate inside are clearly not there to be baptised.

GG nods in agreement and leads us to the nave, the main area of the church. I look up at the cornice work decorated with ribbon motifs. All the walls, in fact the whole church, look quite frankly in need of a jolly good coat of paint—and not peach.

GG pauses besides a rather grand wooden dais, a small winding staircase leading up to a booth with badly chipped gilt paint.

'And here is the pulpit—the sacred desk!' As GG starts to ascend the stairs, I can't help but notice the way his taut buttocks press against his jeans. This guy totally works out.

Nat whispers: 'Bet you're praying Father Guy will be up there delivering his sermon on the mount. Like mount me!'

'Be quiet, Natalie,' I hiss. 'As you well know, I'm a … happily married woman.'

I imagine husbondage Stu and me at our lovely home, roaring fire illuminating our Farrow & Ball-painted walls; Stu sipping claret and sampling the cheese plate while reading his *FT*. Me, well into the latest edition of *Grazia*. Mind you, Stu has been away rather a lot recently with work. Best replace that vignette with me on my own tucking into a cheese and pickle sarnie.

'Wow, look at this!' Nat dives into an ornately carved wooden cubicle and pulls the curtain behind her. 'This must have been the confession box,' says her muffled voice from inside.

I touch what must have been once a wonderful velvet curtain in a deep shade of carmine. It's now just a mouldering piece of fabric. This certainly could do with a good dry-clean. I stare at the intricate carved lattice work, a *Fleur de Lis* carved into the confessional window, which casts a shadow on the facing wall.

'And through here, ladies, is the vestry,' GG leads on.

We follow him into a small room at the back of the church. 'This will be my office,' Nat says. Then she raises her voice, 'Wait a minute, what's going on? There's a bed in here!'

It's a blow-up plastic mattress laid on the floor. But I must admit it does look rather cosy with its Thomas the Tank Engine duvet cover, pillows, and a pink floral bedside lamp complete with tassels. There's also a bedside book, '*The Moneyless Manifesto*.' It's lying open at a chapter headed: '*How I started to live without money and thrive with the local gift economy.*'

'Hmm, I'm sure there's a very simple explanation,' GG murmurs as we follow him back into the church. 'But I'm sure it will be the first of many challenges that might make this place untenable.'

'Just imagine this fantastic space filled with desks, people brimming with energy and ideas.' Nat, ever the optimist, ignores GG's gloomy comment and turns round and grins. 'The pews can be used to create seating around tables made from pallets, and recycled wood could be sourced for our cafe.'

Nat has a questionable concept of recycling. I remember that when we were creating our community garden, all sorts of suspiciously new pieces of furniture started appearing, including a bathtub in which Nat grew herbs—a bath from a very expensive bathroom boutique in Primrose Hill that apparently had just been left outside the shop in the street.'

'This space is a wonderful canvas, Deb.' Nat tosses her arm around me. 'You're a designer, so design this.'

'I gather you may set up a microbrewery in the crypt?' GG adds.

'You want to brew beer in a church?' I blurt out.

'We certainly do, Deb,' says Nat. 'And we'll grow the hops ourselves. We could call it: "Land of Hop and Glory!"'

We all burst out laughing.

'What I don't understand, Father, er, Guy, is how come we've been given this space?' My unplanned question pops out.

'To be frank, the bishop has been approached by a developer who's keen to turn this church into a block of flats.' GG clears his throat. 'But the diocese, in conjunction with the local council, have decided to take time some time to consider what's best for, er ... the whole parish. Increasingly cash-strapped ecclesiastical bodies are having to sell off more and more churches.'

'But if it's all about financial turnover, how on earth could anything *we* do compete with a block of flats?'

GG sighs, 'I believe a successful parish project is one that benefits, and pays homage to, the history of the community. The Bishop and I are therefore keen to hear your plan, which Natalie told him you have both been working very hard on.'

'Er, plenty of time for that, Father Guy. Why don't we go and look outside?' Nat grabs my hand, and charges towards the door at the back of the church.

'Deb was very interested to take a look at the flying buttresses.'

We go outside into the back garden. In front of us, the trunks of apple trees, from what would have once been a wonderful orchard, lean over despondently; their gnarled branches look like they hadn't been pruned since the Creation. A garden of Eden, *pas exactment*. I look around at the compacted clay soil, the only evidence of life being a profusion of bindweed and brambles now covering everything.

'Jesus never promised us a rose garden, but he'll go through the thorns with us,' Nat adds her spiritual offering, as she starts to pull up the weeds.

I walk on along the rather uneven cobbled path and let out a yelp as I stub my toe on something hard. I bend down and brush aside weeds to uncover the start of a lovely old brick wall.

'I wonder if this garden is a vegetable potager based on the four-bed cross design?' I ask GG. (Who says watching *Pointless* on daytime TV has no benefits?)

'Well, wouldn't that be wonderful,' GG smiles at me. 'I have visited many monastic gardens, and always find it marvellous to look out from a window and see the garden in the shape of a cross. I look forward to uncovering the secrets of this garden with you … and more, Dorito-Deborah. As it is said: "I am the vine, you are the branches; he who abides in Me and I in him, will bear much fruit."'

I look away as my face flushes a ripe shade of blackberry to match the bramble clawing against my parka.

'I want to get down and dirty and build a cob pizza oven here.' Nat gives a wry smile. 'It's the only down and dirty coming my way in the foreseeable future,'—she pauses—'seeing that my old man left me last night.'

'What? Pete's left you?' I blurt out. Talk about jaw hitting floor …

'Yeah, he's run off with Di, the opera singer who lives in our block. They've gone on a classical tour of Italy.'

Pete? Nat's meek hubby who wouldn't say boo to a goose. A man whose idea of culture is a karaoke night at the Bull and Gate pub? Running off with an opera singer and touring coliseums?

'I'm soo sorry, Nat. I don't know what to say.' I wrap my arms around her.

She smiles sadly. 'Well, we need all the time we can get to concentrate on this project, don't we, Deb? Then there's the launch of my political career to think of.'

Political career? The nearest political sentiment Nat has ever expressed was when the council tried to close her beloved Lidl, next door to this church, over an infestation of rats.

All thoughts of politics—Nat's sad news about absconding Pete, plus her *fait accompli* statement about us needing time to concentrate on a project that two hours ago didn't exist—are lost when we hear a rustling in a tree at the far end of the garden. We all turn to see a squirrel dart down the tree trunk and disappear over the fence to the Lidl car park. A head—a human one—appears through the branches.

'Hi, down there! I'm just doing a bit of scrumping. This is the one tree that seems to have borne fruit this year. I blame the wet spring.' A man in his early forties climbs down from the tree, carefully balancing a circle of apples in a battered, upturned fedora hat. He's wearing khaki shirt and trousers, and I can't help but chuckle at what looks like a botanical Indiana Jones: no whip but holding an apple picker, and no gun in his holster but instead a rusty pair of secateurs.

'My name is Richard. My friends call me Rich.' He has a broad Geordie accent. 'I'm picking fruit and apples that would have gone to waste. Are you the ladies starting up the project here?' He walks up to us. 'I'm embarking on a project where I'm going to live for one year without any money. I'm going to teach folks to rethink their reliance on money's divisive power and show them how to escape its grip.'

'Is that your bed in the vestry?' Nat snaps.

'I'm here to introduce you to the sharing and gift economy. With the challenges of the climate emergency and global inequality, we've got to find new ways to live successful lives. Resource depletion is rife,' Rich sighs. 'And yes, that *is* my bed,' he says blushing, as he tries not to stare at her body. Nat may be petite in height, but she is generously built in other departments. And not even her works jacket with its Charles Wilson Tool-Hire branding can hide this fact.

'Well, I'm not having you depleting our resources,' Nat says, raising her voice.

'Nice duvet cover on your bed, Richard,' I observe, changing the subject. 'Did you get it from IKEA? I love popping in there, everything is so cheap.'

'IKEA?' Richard snaps. 'That's a typical example of a corporation that has used the economies-of-scale model to create the problems that the world faces today.' Well, that's telling *us* ...

'Ah! There you are, Father Guy,' a much-calmer voice interrupts us. It belongs to a very smartly dressed man who has just walked into the garden. 'So sorry for being a little early.'

'Ladies, this is Thomas Montjoy. He runs a company called Greener Properties,' GG mumbles in an embarrassed tone. 'I, er ... wasn't expecting to meet you here, Thomas.'

'Greener *what*?' Nat directs her less than placatory tone to Thomas Montjoy.

I stare at his Savile Row suit and highly polished shoes, which are outshone by an even more polished smile.

'Father Guy, I just wanted to give you a sneak preview of the brochure before it goes to print.' Montjoy scrolls down on his phone to show Father Guy various pictures. 'You can see the flats will have off-street parking here and ...'

I push aside a bramble and walk over to Montjoy. I peer over GG's shoulder to see the picture of a gleaming, new, boutique apartment block—one that is to be built on the site of this church.

'Of course, I understand it's entirely speculative right now,' Montjoy laughs. 'Look, I've got a driver parked outside who can whisk us off to the new gastropub down the road. I can fill you in on the details there.'

'Yoo-hoo!' There's another new voice. We turn to see a woman come strolling into the garden. Wondering how this day could get any stranger, I stare at the woman's tweed braid-trimmed Chanel jacket. An Alice band scoops back a bob of perfectly groomed blonde hair. 'I'm Sacha,' she says in a very plummy voice. 'I got a tweet saying that you're inviting folks to be involved in a new eco project. My pitch is this: Does anyone fancy a cricket burger? After all, edible insects are going to play a big part in the future of our food security.'

The stunned silence that follows is broken only by the sound of another apple falling to the ground. Did we hear her correctly? Cricket burger?

'Anyway, Father Guy, shall we go?' Montjoy points to the door.

'Some lovely apples you could eat right here.' Rich picks one up and offers it to GG. 'And they're free.'

GG looks at the green apple, which, like his face, is flushed with crimson. He runs his hand along its lovely waxy skin.

'I mean, I'm not offering you a cricket burger right away,' Sacha says hopefully. 'It's more like …?'

GG pops the apple into his hoodie pocket and turns to follow Montjoy out of the garden. I wave at GG who gives me a slightly flustered look and waves back. I hear a crunch—and not of the apple kind. I bend down to see that the heel of my new Jimmy Choo has snapped on a cobble stone.

'Well, I think that went brilliantly!' says Nat, ignoring the fact that I'm now holding a broken designer shoe and am about to refer to GG's boss in a less than devotional manner.

'Apart from that Thomas Montjoy.'

Nat takes the apple Rich hands to her, and bites into it. She links my arm. 'Look around Deb. Imagine chickens and bees, wildflowers and communal meals.' She points to my shoe. 'It's our new story of High Heels to Small Holdings: our very own Good Life.'

OCTOBER

CHAPTER 1

Old Spot & the
Chip-Fat Travellers

'So here we go once again Deb—the big clear out day for our second project together!' Nat links my arm as we walk up to the church entrance. 'Reminds me of the day we met at that big dig three years ago, when we cleared out the derelict patch of land and went on to create our wonderful communal garden. I remember you digging away in your posh raincoat, holding an umbrella in the rain to stop your hair from going frizzy.'

@NTS: First—I can't believe I've only known Nat for three years; three years of being swept up in her life-changing, crazy exploits. Second, I don't have 'frizzy' hair, just well-defined curls.

'I wonder if we will attract as big a crowd of volunteers today?' Nat grins. 'We had at least fifty folk last time, led by Toby. Shame he buggered off to Devon to start a permaculture farm. You were gutted when he left. Do you ever hear from him?'

'I don't know what you're talking about. Of course, I don't hear from him.' I push the door open, and we walk into the church.

It's empty inside. And hushed—except for a loud snoring coming from the vestry. No crowd of volunteers here. It's less of a community turn-out, more like a community turn-off.

'Oh well, Nat,' I'm relieved, but trying to hide it, as I return to fantasising about the delightful prospects of the couture department at Selfridges, 'not every plan can work. Tell you what, I'll treat you to a nice café macchiato at Starbucks.'

'Starbucks, surely not.' We turn round to see a little old lady in a raincoat and patterned headscarf who has come tottering in. 'I couldn't possibly work with a team who support tax avoiders.' She introduces herself, 'My name is Margaret Lyntton. My sister—she lived in Cheltenham, you know—just passed on. God rest her soul. She left me her treasured pet, Old Spot.'

Old Spot? I watch as Margaret, who must be in her seventies, takes off her raincoat to reveal what looks like an original 1950's floral pinny.

'She looks just like the late queen,' Nat whispers, as she pokes me in the ribs.

'Me, I've lived in Kentish Town all my life,' Margaret goes on. 'I've only got a small flat and there's no room to keep Old Spot. But then I saw the advert in the library for the big clear-out day for your Good Life community project, and I thought I'd come and get involved. Old Spot is very good at weeding, very sociable, and loves a tummy rub.'

I picture a cute little dog. I love dogs and have always felt slightly sad that we have never had a pup at home. No, Deborah, I remind myself, stick to visualising the Burberry fur bolero accessorised with a cute pom-pom hat in the Selfridges winter coat department.

'Well, nice to make your acquaintance, Marg. I'm Nat and this is Deb.' They shake hands. 'Deb's an ethical fashion designer and I'm campaigning to become a new eco-councillor.'

Ethical designer? Hmmm! Best replace all thoughts of fur bolero with a hemp trench coat.

'I'm a campaigner too!' Margaret takes a pair of rubber gloves from her handbag. 'Old Spot and I want to campaign against meat. You know, meat production is one of the greatest causes of environmental degradation in the world.' She pulls an old photo out of her bag. It shows her standing next to an African woman dressed in a wonderful cerulean blue head- dress and wrap. 'Here's me in Kenya with my dear friend, Wangari Maathai, also now sadly passed.'

'Wang who?' asks Nat.

'My dear, for an aspiring eco-warrior, you have an awful lot to learn.' Margaret dips back into her bag and pulls out several more pairs of rubber gloves and hands them to us. 'Anyway, thought I'd bring a few spare pairs.'

She's interrupted by a voice behind us: 'Oh my god, you know Wangari Maathai?' It's spoken in a lovely soft Irish brogue. A girl in her early twenties, her ponytail as bouncy as her walk, is heading towards us. 'I'm Pippa. I'm a law student, and I'm hoping to specialise in environmental law—that's why I'm here. I'm so excited to hear you talking about Wangari Maathai.'

It turns out that this Wangari woman is an internationally renowned Kenyan environmental political activist and Nobel laureate.

'She's one of my is one all time heroines!' Pippa walks over to Margaret. 'You must be in charge here? How do you know her?'

'She was a very good friend, dear.' Margaret hands Pippa the photo. 'This was taken in Nairobi in 1973 when we both worked for the Red Cross. But that's a long story for another day. And no, I am not in charge here, these ladies are.' She points to us.

'So, what's your pitch?' asks Nat, shaking Pippa's hand.

'As part of my degree,' Pippa eagerly races on, 'I have to do some work placement, so I'd like to set up a desk here to investigate environmental legal cases for a potential new law called "ecocide."'

'What's ecocide when it's at home then?'

'At home's the right word for it,' Pippa laughs. 'Eco is from the ancient Greek word for home. Ecocide will be a new law to protect our home—our planet, from the killer of exploitation and corporate abuse. This brilliant lawyer called Polly Higgins spent her life trying to establish ecocide as a crime against humanity at the International Criminal Court. It's up there with genocide and war crimes. After all, nature should have rights, don't you agree?'

Can nature have rights? I ponder the philosophical question.

'You mean, like, do trees have feelings?' Nat chuckles.

'Well, I think your ideas are wonderful,' Margaret tells Pippa. 'Welcome aboard.'

Ignoring Nat's mutter that it wasn't Margaret's call to decide who is accepted into the Good Life Project, Margaret takes Pippa's hand, and whisks her over to the pulpit.

'Well, we had better get on cleaning up this place or we will never get round to saving the world!' She wipes her hand along the grimy wood. 'Nothing I haven't done before. You should have seen the state of the Red Cross building we took over in Nairobi. Just as well I've bought along Mr Sheen to give us a hand.'

'Mr Sheen? Is he also a famous environmental activist?' Nat says, just as her eye is caught by a movement at the door. A man with a big case is walking in. 'See, I told you Deb,' she says turning back to me. 'Our project is going to attract some of the leading lights in the eco world.'

More like leading light in the dust mite world, I chuckle to myself, as I watch Margaret take out a can of Mr Sheen from her seemingly bottomless 'Mary Poppins' bag.

'Anyway, Pippa dear, why don't we start cleaning over here, and you can tell me all about it?' They get to work spraying and chatting.

The man with the big case walks over to Nat.

'Are you here to pitch for desk space?' asks Nat. 'If so, I have to tell you there's some strong competition; we already have a Nobel laureate associate.'

'No love, I'm from Rentokil,' he replies. The man opens his case. 'You've got rats.' He gets out an order form. 'Sign here.'

I'm just doubting I would ever see a deeper shade of red than Nat's blush of humiliation when Rich walks in carrying a tray of steaming cups of bright red liquid.

'Morning all, I've made us a nice brew of rosehip tea.' He walks over and offers cups to Pippa, Margaret, and Mr Rentokil. 'Fantastic crop of rose hips growing in the garden. Are you ladies and gent the first new members of our team? Welcome, I'm Rich, the caretaker. I live on-site.'

'Says who?' blurts out Nat.

'I'm living for one year without money to prove how this will lead to a path of wealth, not sacrifice.' Rich hands Nat a beautiful pink floral bone China cup. 'After all, money does not create things: we create money. Money is just a means of exchange and has no intrinsic value.'

'Well said, mate,' Mr Rentokil interrupts. 'But in the meantime, here's your sixty-pound invoice for the work I'm doing here today.' He hands Nat the invoice, walks over to the vestry, and starts unpacking his tools.

'I'll show you a path to wealth, Richy-Richey-Rich, or whatever your name is!' Nat points to the front door.

'Listen Nat, it does make sense for Rich to be caretaker here,' I say, taking the invoice from her. 'I'll settle this bill.'

'And I would like to pay half of it,' Margaret adds, as she takes a sip of tea. 'The council have just paid my winter fuel allowance, and now that Old Spot and I will be spending some of our time here, we shall be cutting down greatly on our energy usage.'

'And I could chip in a few coins,' Pippa pipes up.

'This tea is absolutely wonderful dear,' Margaret smiles at Rich. 'I remember how during the war, we children used to get paid to pick rosehips.'

'They have twenty times more vitamin C than an orange,' Rich beams, as he pours her another cup. 'At this time of year, they are all over the place, and yet no one picks them. If you ask me, it's a crime.'

'Well, as it happens,' Pippa smiles, 'I'm studying environmental crimes.'

@NTS: Ask husbondage Stu if he thinks money is simply a means of exchange and has no intrinsic value. Must admit I'm rather enjoying these questions of philosophy. In the unlikely event that I don't get the Selfridges job, and am whisked off to become a Stepford housewife, perhaps there's a Yale college for dummies I could join. I picture myself three years hence on graduation day from my philosophy degree clad in black robe, throwing my cap into the air. Although, on second thoughts, I'm not sure how flattering those hats are with their horizontal square board stuck on a skullcap—a design based on a tool used by bricklayers to hold mortar, as explained in Vogue mag's millinery review last month.

Who says fashion magazines don't have any academic content? And a third thought: I really don't want to move to the US.

'Anyhow, team, the crime here is the level of mess,' Margaret continues. 'Let's get cleaning!'

Two hours later, we are still dusting and cleaning: Margaret, with the energy of a teenager aided by Mr Sheen, busy on the font; Pippa and I scrubbing the floors. Our exertions are directed by Nat from the pulpit. She has taken off her jacket to reveal a rather fitting T-shirt sporting the logo, 'may contain prosecco.'

Rich, meanwhile, is dividing his attention between sampling

Nat's hooch and sawing the pews in half to create benches. He's helped by Mr Rentokil who has been persuaded to give a hand in return for some free nosh.

'Here's a great joke to chivvy you along, team,' Nat grins. 'What nationality is Mr Sheen? Or Barry, as I'm going to rename him?' I take in a deep breath, having been on the receiving end of many of Nat's less than well considered jokes. 'Polish!' Nat roars with laughter. 'Isn't that hilarious!'

'I don't think that's very PC,' Pippa mumbles.

The door opens and a Chinese man walks in. I pick up Nat's clipboard and pen and walk over to greet him. 'Welcome. Can I take you name?'

He gives me a bewildered look. 'Mr Pang.'

'Are you here to pitch for desk space, Mr Pang?' I ask in my most officious voice.

'No, to deliver a takeaway to someone, Kill?'

'Kill-someone? What?' I shriek.

'Oh, yeah, that's me.' Mr Rentokil calls out. 'After all, you did promise me free food if I helped out.'

'One portion number twenty-eight, spring rolls and chips.' Mr Pang opens his bag and takes out a polystyrene box, which he hands to him.

'You can't bring that bloody single-use packaging in here,' yells Rich. 'When I offered you free food, I was referring to a bag of apples.'

'And two portions of crispy beef with sticky rice,' Mr Pang proudly announces.

'I don't think we should have meat in here,' says Margaret. 'Do you know, Mr Pang, dear, that meat production produces fifteen per cent of all greenhouse gases—more than all the cars, trains, planes and ships combined.'

Pippa jumps in: 'Not forgetting how meat production is also responsible for poor animal welfare like the McDonalds McLibel court case.'

'We do very nice pork rolls,' Mr Pang offers. 'Who in charge here?'

'She is!' Nat points to me.

'That will be twenty-one fifty.' Mr Pang gives me a bill which I reluctantly pay, having got Mr Rentokil to take his food away.

'Excuse me, did you say chips?' The increasingly heated exchange is interrupted as a couple of teenagers—a girl and a guy—enter the church. 'Would you like us to take your used vegetable oil off you?'

Vegetable oil? Could this day get any stranger? I think.

'Don't look at us like that! We're serious,' says the girl. 'I'm Lucia and he's Mouse. We call ourselves the Chip Fat Travellers.'

'What's a Chip Fat Traveller? asks Nat.

'We're going to convert an ice-cream van equipped with a standard diesel engine to fuel it with leftover vegetable oil from fast food restaurants. Then we'll drive around London delivering workshops on both energy generation and conservation.'

'Yeah,' says Mouse. 'We wanna turn Kentucky and Dixy's fried-chicken places into a chain of low-cost fuel stations! We've already been offered chip fat from Nando's.'

Nat shoots me a quizzical look, clearly none the wiser to what they are talking about than I am … 'You don't look old enough to have passed your driving test. How old are you?' she demands.

'Eighteen,' says Mouse. 'Left school this summer. Fed up with it. All those bloody GCSEs, and then one-year boring A-Level course. Waste of time apart from the chemistry lessons when we learnt how to create biofuel out of chip fat. Now we plan to make a job out of it.'

'We wanted to do something radical to bring attention to at least one environmental problem,' adds Lucia.

'Diesel engines.' Rich appreciatively pats Mouse on the shoulder.

'And one solution: powering our van with home-made biofuel!' Lucia beams.

@NTS: Judging by the spots on Mouse's face, I'd say he's a regular customer of Dixy's. And what kind of name is Mouse? I've had more than enough of rodents for one day, I think, as I watch Mr Rentokil squirting an extra final spray of his acrid potion for good measure.

'You say you have an ice-cream van,' Nat asks. 'Where did you nick it from?'

'Joking aside, guys, I'm Deborah, and this is Natalie.' I shake their hands as I wonder whether husbondage Stu's car could be fuelled with chip fat. And whether the fuel would have stinky bits of old chips floating in it?

'I'm certain I speak for Nat and myself when I say we're really impressed with your vision.' I want to sound sincere and welcoming.

'My nan left me the ice-cream van ...' Is that a tear rolling down Lucia's cheek? 'My nan sold ice-creams in it for forty years until she died earlier this year. In honour of her memory, we want to turn Nan's van into our Chip Fat Traveller project.'

'Biofuel is not a new idea,' Mouse says. 'It all started back in 1911, in Germany, with a bloke called Rudolph Diesel. But ... look, before we carry on, why don't you come outside and look at the van? We've parked it in your drive. We'll leave it there.'

'Leave it where?' snaps Nat.

We follow them outside, mesmerised by their idea, even if I don't really understand it. Mesmerised by their enthusiasm, and quite frankly, entrepreneurship. I think of my son James, only a year older than them, in his first year of studying economics at Exeter University—in complete contrast to these kids, who are taking a completely different road, pun intended. I reflect on my own studying days, which I really hated. Who is to say where success will fall for any of us? And what does 'success' really mean? I look around at the assorted group we've managed to gather and realise that, although this day has been rather odd, and Nat's Good Life plan, is doubtlessly confused, I have learnt an awful lot today, and feel a strange sense of communal wellbeing.

My sense of wellbeing is immediately enhanced when I see the Mr Whippy van in the driveway. It's pink and white stripes with, *'Yippee! It's Mr Whippy!'* blazed across the front of it. I am immediately transported back to the 1970's—to my teenage years of flicked-back Farah Fawcett hair. My years of carefully licking a lolly while trying not to disturb my lip gloss, to keep my pucker lips fresh in case our local David Cassidy look-a-like deigned to ask me for a snog.

'So, what do you think?' Lucia asks.

'Go on, Deb, climb into the back. You know you want to!' Nat laughs. 'Bet you spent your teenage years behind ice-cream vans sucking 69's. Or was it 99's!?'

'I don't know what you're talking about, Natalie.' I feel myself blush a shade of Raspberry Mivvi, but eagerly climb into the van. I open the glass serving booth. 'Enjoy a Sundae today!' I look around at the pictures of 1970s ice-lollies. Gosh how well I remember Fabs, my fave, with their smattering of hundreds and thousands. There's a good old 99 machine—no longer spewing out what I now know to be reams of whipped fat. Judging from the state of the rusty paint-work, the last time an ice-cream was sold in this van was probably when the last Zoom bar was in production.

'Excuse me, missus.' There's a knock on the window. 'I'll have a Coola lolly.' I look out to see a little girl on a scooter.

'Er, I'm afraid we don't have any ...'

'Mummy, mummy! This lady is being mean to me.' The girl bursts into tears and yells at her harassed looking mother, who comes running into the drive pushing a double buggy.

Around me, Lucia, Mouse, Pippa, Margaret, and Rich roar with laughter.

'So have we got a deal then?' asks Mouse. 'Can we park here, and be part of your hub?'

'Well, I'm really pleased with our first campaigners, aren't you, Deb?' Nat has joined me in the van, and she throws her arms around me. I find myself nodding in agreement without meaning to. Nodding in agreement, that is, until we look out to see a pig saunter up to the van.

'Ah, there you are,' says Margaret. She goes up to the pig and hugs it. 'I was wondering where you had got to.' She gets a lead out of her bag and attaches it to the pig's collar.

'Girls, meet Old Spot!'

'Old Spot?' Nat and I yelp in unison. 'We thought he was a dog.'

'Oh no, girls, Old Spot is a pig. A very special pig, with built-in apple sauce.'

CHAPTER 2

The Great Bustard

'Two weeks to go until we are open for business, and I would say that we have a good half of our hub filled,' Nat proudly announces to me, as a week later we stroll up to the church entrance. We pause to look up at a new carved wooden sign: 'The Good Life.' Someone has tied it round the gargoyle's neck, causing it to look like it is being throttled.

We enter the church and look around. I'm not sure if we are really half-filled or set up for any kind of business at all but the place is looking good. After a week of cleaning, which I chipped in with despite having no intention of seriously getting involved in the project, the church is spotless. The font sparkles with clean water, the polished woodwork gleams, and the late October sunlight streams in through the stained glass and casts shades of copper and greens around the room.

To the right, a pop-up cafe has been set up, with long tables made from railway sleepers and pews arranged either side of them. A dresser has been made from a pallet, its hooks awaiting a display of cutlery and plates. Even old desks have suddenly appeared, and now lay scattered around the room with an odd assortment of chairs.

On one of the former school desks, there's a sign: 'Meatless Marg.' There's another sign on the crumpled blanket next to it: 'Reserved for Old Spot.' In contrast, its neighbour is a huge, ornate desk with the label: 'The Good Life'.

'Ah great, this is mine!' Nat sits down and swivels around on the chair behind the desk. 'This is where I'll welcome the community and introduce them to the Good Life. It's also going to be where I launch my career to become a Good Life councillor at next July's local election. I don't know where Rich got this desk, but I must say you were right about him.' Nat slides her hand along the mahogany. 'He works wonders.'

To our left we see a giant tree made from chipboard, onto which the words: 'Ecocide: Climate Justice' have been painted in green. On the plasterers table in front of it, Pippa has placed a collection of resource sheets and literature.

Onto the next desk. This one is called: 'Pestival.'

'I've reserved this for Sacha. You know, the posh one who came to tell us about cricket burgers,' says Nat. 'Do you remember her? She's coming back in this week to pitch to us her idea for a setting up a 'Pestival.' After all, you've been telling me for ages that you'd like to go to a festival next summer.'

Yes, but I meant a festival of love in the bucolic countryside, not a festival of bugs in Kentish Town. I refrain from voicing my thoughts and concentrate on visualising my Stella McCartney dress floating down over Punter wellies, dirty martinis and cleansing hot tubs.

Nat pauses besides the final desk positioned in front of the pulpit. 'And this is yours, Deb.' She leads me to the chair behind the desk.

I smile at the 'Debo Designs' sign she has created from letters cut out of magazines.

@NTS: Must check my new copy of *Harpers* to see if it's still intact.

'Look, Nat,' I link her arm, 'you know that I'm hoping for the contract from Selfridges. I've been waiting for a job like this for ages. Being let loose among the gossamer fabrics, bustiers, peplums and polonaise.'

'Sounds like a posh dinner to me, but I do know what you mean, Deb!' Nat chuckles. 'When I'm at Charles Wilson, that's exactly how I feel being surrounded by the rotavators and tile cutters, wood strippers and angle grinders. It's like being a kid let loose in a candy shop.'

I smile at the thought of how different Nat and I are. Such unlikely, but jolly good, friends. 'And anyway,' I sit down behind my desk, 'what real work could I do here?'

'The Lord works in mysterious ways, Deb.' Nat looks up at wonky cross which tilts on the wall behind us. 'Must ask Rich to fix that. Where is he by the way?'

'Interested in his whereabouts, eh?' I wink. 'Anything you want to tell me?' I get up and give her a hug. 'I also wanted to ask if are you really OK about Pete? I feel we haven't really talked about it.'

'I'm sort of OK.' Nat gives a sad smile. 'After all, the Lord doesn't close one door without opening an another. But as to that Richie Rich, he's a right pain in the arse. I want to meet a rich man. In fact, I might ask your Stu to hook me up with an economist chum at the Bank, then we can all go to those boring Bank of England dinners you're always moaning about. I'd be sure to liven things up!'

I chuckle. I can just imagine Nat, with economist partner in tow, cracking a joke at dinner, about how bankers never die, just lose interest. I take a deep breath. 'Listen Nat, there's something I need to tell you about Stu. He's thinking of taking a jo -'

My admission is interrupted by the sound of several loud snorts followed a series of snores which seem to be coming from the vestry.

Eyebrows raised; we push open the vestry door to find Rich in bed. He's not alone. Old Spot is curled up asleep next to him.

'Morning, ladies,' Rich says, sitting up in bed, while Old Spot snores on.

'Hardly morning! It's 1 p.m.,' Nat snaps.

Rich yawns, 'I was up till 2 a.m. last night, skipping.'

Skipping? Wasn't that a bit late for exercise? More importantly, is that pig really in bed with him? I didn't know pigs snore.

'And what is this bloody pig doing here?' barks Nat.

'Yes, shouldn't we call the council or something?' I add. 'Is it even legal to keep a pig?'

'I'm sure it's legal, dear,' says Marg, walking into the room with Pippa. 'Potbellied micro pigs make good companions. They are smart, clean, charming, and inexpensive to feed. They're also extremely social. Give their tummies a rub and they're yours for life!'

'Not forgetting to mention that Old Spot will be very good at weeding the garden,' adds Pippa. 'Talking of which, come on Marg, let's go out and check the garden.'

Rich scratches Old Spot's snout and takes up his story again. 'I went skip-diving last night. Lidl's dumpster which is just over our garden fence had some amazing ingredients. I've invited my friend, Nahal, to cook them up. She's in the kitchen now.'

'You got waste food out of a bin?' Nat snaps. 'Isn't it off, and all mouldy?'

'Sell-by dates are all part of the conspiracy of corporatocracy,' Rich sighs. 'A conspiracy to de-skill us as shoppers. In a supermarket, you can't be guided by texture or smell because the products are so heavily packaged. We are conned into throwing away perfectly good food, just because it has some spurious sell-by date, and we buy more, leading to more waste.' He stands up to reveal a pair of tight orange Y-fronts, which look as if they've been around since the 1970's. And a big erection.

I try to avert my eyes away from Rich, but talking of big things ...

@NTS: Corporatocracy! Now there's a big word. I must remember to use it at future dinner parties with Stu's economist colleagues. Might also have a little peek in the bin to check how much food we have thrown away at home. Probably very little, but then there was that amazing M&S offer last week of the buy two tapas, get two free.

'And who is this Nahal?' Nat stares openly at Rich's crotch.

'Come and meet her.' Rich reaches for a pair of trousers. 'She's done wonders cleaning up the kitchen this morning and wait till you taste her food.'

We follow Rich to the kitchen. As we open the door, a wonderful aroma of herbs with a hint of citrus, permeates the air. A woman in her early thirties wearing a beautiful lilac headscarf, a long skirt in a deep shade of violet, and a woolly jumper, stands at the stove. I look around the kitchen, the one room in the church none of our group had got around to cleaning yet. But someone has. The yellow Formica worktops are gleaming; a duck egg blue 1960's pantry is now brimming with all manner of jars filled with herbs and spices; the shiny white oven is misted up as a fragrant dish is cooking away in it.

Rich introduces us, 'Nahal, meet Nat and Deb.'

'Lovely to meet you. This smells delicious!' I smile at Nahal, and go over to look in the pot.

Nat hesitantly follows me. 'Hi, Nahal, what are you cooking? It looks, er, very green?'

'This dish is called *torshi-tareh*,' says Nahal. As she stirs the pot, we see a mélange of green veg and herbs simmering away. 'I awoke this morning to find a bag of ingredients on the mat outside my flat, with a note from Rich inviting me to come and cook for you here today. As soon I saw the spinach, coriander, lemon, and eggs, I knew that I would prepare a *torshi-tareh*.'

'*What?*' Nat asks, clearly less than convinced. 'You cooked this from food Rich got from a bin?'

'It is perfectly good food.' Nahal bends down to open the oven door, letting out a mouth-watering waft of sweet and savoury rice. 'All I had to do was bring some rice, onions, and add some mint I found in your garden. *Torshi-tareh* is a sour herb stew from the northern part of Iran, best served with a Persian rice. That's what I'm cooking in here.'

'You're from Iran?' I stare at the stew and its beautiful woodland colours.

'My family originated there.' Nahal smiles at me as she pushes back several wisps of glossy long black hair which has escaped from behind her scarf. 'I lived there until I was five, when we moved to London. My father was an academic. After the Cultural Revolution closed the universities, there was no work for him there.'

'Doesn't sound much of a cultural revolution to me, closing down universities!?' Nat laughs.

'Nahal's family fled the country in 1990 after the Iran/Iraq war.' Rich glares at Nat. 'Nahal, her husband Ahmad, and their son, Jafar, now live down the road in Peckwater Street. Nahal is the most amazing, undiscovered cook.'

Iran closed universities. As I listen to the banter, I'm ashamed to admit that I have never really given Iran much thought or know anything of its history. My attention returns to the cooking, as Nahal cracks six eggs into the middle of the herb stew. The eggs float into the dish like bursts of sunlight in a forest. I hear a rumble in my stomach and realise it's lunchtime and I am eager to try this food.

My thoughts are interrupted by a knock on the door.

'Excuse me, is this the Good Life project?' There's a man standing there with a camera hanging round his neck. The lens on the camera is as large as his stomach. 'Hello there, I'm Gregory.'

'Pleased to meet you?' Rich replies, offering his hand. 'How can we help?'

'I'm a lover of great bustards,' the newcomer chortles.

Nat bristles, 'If I wanted any more bastards in my life, I'd have taken my ex back.' She points to the door. 'The family mediation centre is above the Rio Spa across the road.'

'Sorry, let me start again. I'm from a bird conservation project.' Gregory takes a crumpled leaflet from his back pocket. 'We're developing a programme to reintroduce endangered bird species and investigate migration. The Great Bustard,'—he points to a picture of a rather large bird in the leaflet—'is one of the heaviest flying birds. It can be found across Europe and as far north as the

Russian Steppe, but its conservation status is listed as vulnerable. In fact, the species became extinct in the UK in 1832. But you can't keep a Great Bustard down! They've been released in small numbers in Wiltshire since 2004, so the population is growing. A real bustard breakthrough, so to speak.'

A right bustard breakthrough indeed, I can't help but chuckle to myself.

Our bird man hasn't finished. 'Bird conservation is crucial in maintaining the diversity of the planet.'

He gets help from the lesser spotted Pippa, who has just walked in. 'Did you know that globally, one in eight—more than thirteen hundred species are threatened with extinction?' she trills.

'And climatologists,' Gregory sticks his beak in again, 'who study bird migration patterns can gather insight on seasonal climate changes by noting behavioural changes.'

'How very interesting, Greg,' Nat stifles a yawn, then whispers in my ear, 'I'm going to call him Greg Peck!'

Rich calls us all back to order. 'Chef Nahal's meal is ready. Let's all eat while we talk!'

As Nahal chats with me about her nine-year-old son, Jafar, she lifts a covered bowl from the oven. Picking up the pot of *torshi* from the stove, we walk out to Rich's up-cycled table, where Marg is busy placing china plates. I put the pan down on a piece of slate, that's serving as a mat, and stare at the lovely green chinoiserie plates. They do look suspiciously new. 'Natalie,' I whisper, 'this has got your name stamped all over it.'

'Not *my* name, Deb, it's Wedgwood!' Nat turns over a plate to show me the logo.

'I *know* it's Wedgwood,' I glare at her. 'The question is, where did you get the plates?'

'Lovely plates, dear,' says Marg, as she sets the table. 'I do think that fine china really enhances a meal. When I was in Africa with my dear friend Wangari …'

My questioning of Nat's procurement is put on hold as Nahal asks me to help bring in more food. We return carrying another pot to find the table set with the Wedgwood—and plastic cutlery.

'I nicked this cutlery from Starbucks—the tax avoiders!' Nat announces proudly.

'Stealing is not part of the gift economy,' Rich glares at her.

'Well, this wonderful gift of rice reminds me of the pilau we used to have in Nairobi,' says Marg. She lifts a pomegranate from the bowl.

'I must say, it *does* look like a bowl of jewels.' I gaze at the rice adorned with turmeric yellows, ruby reds, ginger, and almonds.

'This is a typical Persian rice,' Nahal smiles. 'But obviously I have made it from the ingredients Richard gave to me. This dish will go perfectly with some flatbreads, which I will make next time.'

'Did you know that birds are also extremely efficient insect pest controllers?' says Greg, as he ladles himself out a large helping of food.

'Talking of insects, we have a woman called Sacha coming in tomorrow to talk to us about setting up a Pestival,' Nat announces. 'It's some event she wants to run here in Kentish Town, all about eating bugs. But anyway, *bon appetite* everyone.'

Nahal serves everyone a hearty plate of food, and we all tuck in.

'Look at this, Deb—a shared meal with new friends. Our Good Life project is really starting to come to life,' Nat whispers to me.

I look around at this disparate group of people, who I've only known for two weeks, enjoying the food, and must admit that it's a nice feeling. At the same time, though, I'm still none the wiser as to what the Good Life project is really going to achieve, or how it will be judged a success. As I listen to Nat telling a joke—'How you can tell if a bird is hungry? He's peckish!'—I somehow doubt that she has any clue either. Best remind her that Father Guy—GG, is coming in to review The Good Life's business plan tomorrow. It feels like a long two weeks since we met him. Perhaps I could quickly scribble down some ideas at the hairdresser's this afternoon.

'This doesn't taste off at all.' My attention is bought back to earth as I hear Nat voice another less-than-considered comment to the room. 'It really is yummy, even if the green stuff does look a little …'

'My mission is to eliminate food waste.' Rich helps himself to a second helping. 'When we waste food, we also waste land, water, embedded energy. Did you know that the average UK household wastes twenty-five percent of its food? What do you think are the food items most wasted, Deb?'

I'm about to risk an answer when Old Spot saunters in, his upturned snout in full sniff mode. I never thought I'd reach a point in my life when I would be so relieved to see a pig.

'The answer is bread,' Rich continues. 'An unbelievable twenty-four million slices of bread are thrown away in this country every day. Followed by almost six million whole potatoes and two million slices of ham.'

Old Spot snorts, lies down on the floor and rolls over.

'Go on, tickle his tummy, Deb. You know you want to!' Nat chuckles.

Rich won't be put off his stride: 'Followed by over one million tomatoes, bananas and eggs being thrown away each day.'

'It's a crime,' Pippa nods.

'I agree. I personally feel obliged to use every ounce of food we can,' says Greg, as he helps himself to a third portion.'

Don't forget to mention, dear, that half the world is undernourished.' Marg takes a Tupperware dish from her bag, spoons some rice into it, passes it down to Old Spot.

'That was delish,' Greg says, as he rubs his stomach. 'Can I donate to the chef? Here's a fiver, will that do?' He hands over a banknote to Nahal.

A donation, I hear.

'Nice one, mate.' Rich shakes Greg's hand.

'See that, Deb, it's the first earnings for anyone in the Good Life team,' Nat nudges me.

'Do you know, there are loads of pop-up cafés being set up all around the country turning food waste into wonderful meals which folk pay for by donation,' says Rich, looking at Nat, who in turn looks at me.

'All we would have to do is build some more tables and find chairs,' adds Marg.

'Maybe add posies of herbs and flowers in jam jars,' offers Pippa. 'There's the hugest rosemary bush I've ever seen growing in the garden.'

'And cover the tables with pretty floral tablecloths,' I suggest, finding myself caught up in the excitement.

'You could make them, Deb, you're the designer!' Nat laughs.

'So, what do you think Nahal?' asks Rich. 'Could you set up a cafe and keep the proceeds, perhaps giving a small percentage to Team Good Life?'

'We could also serve meals to rough sleepers,' Marg chips in again.

Rich agrees, 'It would also provide a great way of educating people about food waste.'

'I'd eat here all the time.' Greg pats his stomach. 'I could give lunchtime ornithology talks. Birds and butties! And while we're about conservation, I don't suppose any of you fancy joining me at a stag do in two weeks?'

'Stag do? Nat perks up. 'Sounds wonderful. It could be a team bonding outing.'

'So, what do you think?' Rich ignores Nat's comment and walks over to Nahal. 'You could serve Persian food?'

'I do love to cook,' Nahal smiles. 'My husband is at work all day, and now with my son, Jafar, at school, I have some spare time. But there is the question of after-school to think of, as I don't like to be away from Jafar.' She gets up from the table and walks round the church hall. Even with the motley assortment of desks scattered around, there's a giant empty space along the left- hand side, next to the door leading out to the garden. 'A couple of the fathers at my son's school are looking to set up an after-school club.' She opens the door. 'Would you have space here? The children could learn to grow vegetables and herbs in the garden which I could cook?'

'Wow, now that's what I call a plan,' Rich punches the air.

'What, have screaming brats here?' Nat shakes her head. 'No way.'

'I do love children,' Marg smiles.

'I could tell them stories of tufted titmice, smews and red billed oxpeckers,' Greg adds.

Nahal goes on, 'This after-school club ... as well as allowing me to be here, it would really help Michael, who is the father of Chloe, Jafar's school friend. Plus, some other dads at the school. It's hard for them being single dads.'

'Single dads?' Nat is interested now. She grins, 'Well, I think it would be most unneighbourly of us not to welcome them here with open arms.'

Open arms being just the start of it for Nat, I think, as I watch her face break out into a huge smile. 'What would we call the cafe?' I ask.

'*The Abundance Cafe,*' Rich grins as he wanders off. 'It's all about abundance.'

'It does make sense.' I turn to face Nat. 'As you said, it's all about sharing and community. This does seem to be evolving in a rather organic way.'

All thoughts of not getting enthusiastic about a project which I will not be around to get involved with are put on hold as Rich returns to the table carrying a suspicious-looking bottle.

'This is my homemade raspberry wine.' He uncorks the bottle. 'I thought we should open it to toast our new Good Life. I made it this summer, so it still might be a little ... how shall I put it?'

'Not quite *grand cru!*' I laugh.

Rich passes the bottle to Nat, who seems suddenly rather enthusiastic about the prospect of a 'sharing' community as she takes a large swig.

'Here's to abundance!' we all toast, as the bottle gets handed around the room.

CHAPTER 3

Daddy Day Share

The next day, my throat feels as rough as the oil I see Lucia pour into her nan's newly converted Chip Fat Travellers van. Crude, rather than cru, better describes Rich's raspberry wine which I now regret drinking so much of.

I wander into the church driveway to find Lucia fiddling away at the engine.

'Have you come to help?' She hands me a tool. 'Great, grab this.'

I look with horror at the greasy spanner thing Lucia puts into my freshly manicured hand. Car mechanic has never been on of one my 'must do' lists. But in the spirit of bonhomie, I try to sound interested.

'I'm very excited about this whole new bio-diesel idea.' I'm too embarrassed to admit I still don't really understand what biofuel is.

'Oh no, Deb, you are totally wrong.' Lucia gets up from the under the bonnet and shakes her head. 'Biofuel is not new, it's a hundred years old! It was first experimented with in 1893 by Rudolph Diesel, who used peanut and vegetable oils to power the internal combustion engine he had just invented.'

'Have you never heard the conspiracy surrounding the mysterious death of Rudolph Diesel?' Mouse walks up to us.

Diesel? Conspiracy theories? I wipe a bead of sweat from my brow.

'Biodiesel is made from any living matter, and it burns seventy-five percent cleaner than petroleum diesel fuel,' Mouse goes on. 'The problem for our Rudy, was that he wrote a book foretelling the dangers of petroleum engines—all that air pollution and the finite nature of the fossil fuels needed to run them. This set off alarm bells in the expanding international oil industry and they didn't like it one bit.

'And still don't,' Lucia tuts.

'Anyway, two years later,' Mouse lowers his voice, 'Diesel was on a trip across the English Channel when he disappeared. Mysteriously, his body was never found. Conspiracy theorists to this day suggest that he was bumped off by the big oil giants.'

Lucia picks up the story: 'After Diesel's death, the idea of fuelling engines with vegetable oil was quickly and quietly swept under the oily rug. Diesel engines were made to run on the expanding monopoly fuel—petroleum.'

Lucia puts down her tools, closes the bonnet, and turns around to reveal the flattering mechanics boiler suit she is wearing.

@NTS: *Auto*-couture—now *there's* an interesting idea!

'Throwing a spanner into the works, eh Deb?' Nat walks up to me looking at the tool still clenched in my fist.

'Anyway,' says Mouse, 'we believe that if Rudy could shock the scientific world in 1900 at the World Trade Fair in Paris, by pouring peanut oil directly into his new diesel engine, we could do the same using vegetable oil chip fat. Right here in Kentish Town!' He throws his arms around Lucia, and they start to snog.

'You're looking good, Deb.' Nat looks at me and chuckles.

'You too, Nat.' One couldn't help but notice her tight-fitting skirt and high heels, a wardrobe far removed from her usual branded outfit of Charles Wilson tool hire tracksuits. Ah, of course. Today's the day the single dads are coming to see us—so, in Nat's case, potential for a different kind of tool hire.

I contemplate on how spending so much time in Nat's company was even getting to my sense of humour. A loud shout in the street snaps me out of it.

'No, stop this right now. You can't chop this tree down! A tree has rights.' It's Pippa. She's climbed halfway up a large tree and is yelling at a man wearing a hard hat.

'Well, I have a council order here.' Hard Hat points to his clipboard.

'I'll have you know, young man, that this is the Good Life property.' Marg has rushed up and is swiping Hard Hat with her bag.

'A good life, minus one tree!' Another man, carrying a chainsaw and ropes and wearing protective clothing has arrived. He switches his chainsaw on.

'You need to get down from that tree right now, miss,' Hard Hat calls up to Pippa.

'Trees mitigate against flooding and cut down on pollution,' Pippa shouts back, her Irish brogue even more pronounced than usual. 'You'll have to come and drag me down.'

'Me too,' calls Marg who is being given a leg up by Greg.

'And birds roost in them,' Greg shouts.

'Plant each day and you will eat.' Nahal arrives to add her comment. She's closely followed by Old Spot, who waddles up to the tree and cocks a leg.

'Marg, you cannot climb that tree, it's not safe.' I rush over to try hold her back from climbing any further.

Across the street, a large black Range Rover pulls up. The driver opens his window, raises his mobile phone, and takes a picture.

'Oy, total shit! You can't do that!' Nat, clearly unused to wearing high heels and a tight skirt, staggers across the road to stop the driver from taking any more photos.

I look around to see that the traffic has begun to stop, and pedestrians are starting to point at the fracas. Old Spot is now sniffing up my skirt, and Pippa is screaming. The council man is shouting back, and Marg is hooking her leg onto the first branch of the tree. I hear laughter from the car, as the driver—it's Thomas Montjoy, the property developer—takes several photos, winds his window back up, and drives off.

'Hello, is everything OK out here?' I turn to see Father Guy striding out from the side entrance of the Church. 'I was just checking the garden.'

Rich rushes into action. He doesn't want GG to see the altercation going on in the street. He ushers him to the church's front door. 'I'm Rich, the Good Life's caretaker. You must be Father Guy,' he says briskly. 'It's a cold old day out there.'

He's hastily closing the door when I manage to squeeze through it, leaving Nat, as unlikely as it seems, to calm things down in the street. And with a bit of luck, to keep Old Spot out of sight from GG.

'As you can see, Father, we've been very busy,' I proudly announce, as Rich and I start to escort GG round the church.

'Gosh, I can't believe how much you've achieved.' He looks surprised.

'And with no money changing hands,' Rich adds. 'You see, I'm embarking on a project to live for a year with no money. At least not relying on it.'

We walk on, passing the desks and their project description placards. I have to smile at the mini wigwam made of tarpaulin in the left-hand corner, which has popped up overnight, clearly set up by Rich as a den for the single dads. (And their kids, of course.)

GG pauses to look at the confession box, its mouldy velvet curtain now spotlessly laundered. 'This curtain looks brand new! And the lattice is sparkling. How on earth did you manage that?'

'Potato water and mayonnaise,' Rich answers. @NTS: Potato water and mayonnaise? Wonder if I should have a go at polishing Stu's desk at home with last night's leftover potato dauphinoise?

'It's so easy to make household cleaning from natural products, isn't it, Deb?' Rich turns to me for support.

I nod in agreement, while pushing my new can of Barry Sheen firmly back into my Chloe bag.

'We're going to run workshops here on how to make natural cleaning products,' Rich continues. 'Wait till you see the toilet I cleaned with a can of Coke!'

'And here is the printer/scanner/photocopier which my hus ... and er, I have donated.' I move GG swiftly along, equally reluctant to discuss the merits of a Cola cleaner, and husbondage, Stu.

'What exactly is *your* role in the Good Life project, Deborah?' He smiles at me.

'I'm not quite sure,' I answer, sort of truthfully. I omit to tell him about my fashion background, where I worship the altar of conspicuous consumption.

'So, tell me more about your moneyless project.' GG turns to Rich. 'It sounds noble, but rather unlikely.'

'Of course, we *all* need money to survive.' Rich sits himself on the pulpit steps. 'But my aim is to encourage folk to lead a life of exchanging less actual money. I want to develop a localised gift economy: an economy that fosters the sharing of skills, time, and knowledge, as well as material goods. I want people to question whether all the extra stuff they are consuming is making them happy.'

I listen on, ashamed to admit that much of my happiness has been based around bagging a fabulous little extra pair of heels in the sales. But then, I am a great exponent of sharing, really, as proven last year when I leant my Manolos to my ex-best friend, Phoebe. I say 'ex' because there was that little matter of them being returned with a bent heel.

'As your boss, the Arch-bish of C recently said,' Rich continues, 'the problem with materialism is not that it exists, but that it dominates. I want people to re-evaluate their unhealthy relationship with money. Did you know that, as a recent Oxfam report high-lighted, the top twenty-six richest people in the world own the same wealth as the bottom half of the world's population.'

I'll be sure to repeat that at Stu's Bank of England staff cocktail party next week. On second thoughts, perhaps not ...

'I want to invite folk to join me in developing a different kind of wealth, one based on the connectedness with our community.' Rich pauses to smile at Nat as she totters in, clearly not used to wearing high heels. 'That's why I joined the Good Life project.'

'Ah, right.' GG sighs and crosses his arms only for his biceps to strain invitingly against the fabric of his black shirt. As he lifts his hand and caresses his dog collar, my middle-age hormones go into overdrive. I so empathise with Phoebe Waller-Bridge in Fleabag.

@NTS: Hot vicar's rule. Must watch re-runs.

'In our money-less, or at least, less-money world, we have to make use of everything,' says Rich, leading GG over to the new Abundance Cafe area.

'These plates are rather lovely.' GG picks up one of the chinoiserie dishes from the dresser. 'Where did you get them? Are they recycled?'

Nat jumps in, her face turning a shade of green to match the plates: 'And this is going to be our Abundance Cafe. It's where we will serve Persian dishes made from waste food. Come and meet our head chef, Nahal.' She whisks GG away to the kitchen.

'Yoo, hoo, anyone at home?' Rich and I turn around to see Sacha, the bug lover, walk into the church, carrying a tray covered with a Harrod's tea towel. I avert my eyes from the tray, dreading to see what lurks beneath, and concentrate on checking out her Chanel jacket and perfectly trimmed blonde hair, tucked behind her ears which are studded with pearls.

'Hello, Debo, hello Richard!' She gives us both a kiss on each cheek and places her tray on the table. 'I am here today to convince you all to let me host a Pestival next spring in Kentish Town, based here at the Good Life. We're aiming to redefine humankind's relationship with the insect world. Pestival will be a pop-up bug banquet to show folk that deep-fried locusts taste like popcorn. And the battered locusts are like prawns!'

As Sacha expounds upon the merits of critter cuisine, I remind myself to put the prawns for the gambas fettuccine for dinner tonight back in the freezer. Meanwhile, I busy myself setting the table as another delicious smell seeps from the kitchen.

'I've tried crickets,' Rich joins in. 'They really taste quite meaty.'

'My favourite is enchilada with fried garlic crickets and roast tomatoes.' Sacha licks her lips. 'Right now, I'm experimenting with how to process insects to get the tastiest results.'

'Is it true that some bugs, like crickets or grasshoppers, can be used as a main course, while others lend themselves to be more of a flavouring?' Rich asks.

'Yes, you're right. For example, mealworms taste just like tamarind.'

'Funny, I picked up a packet of tamarind from the bin in Tesco's last night,' Rich says. 'I'll give it to you later.'

Sacha is just asking me about my own culinary experience of eating bugs, when the kitchen door opens and Nahal walks in carrying a huge plate of food. 'This dish is *Koofteh Tabriz,*' she says, placing her platter on the table. 'It's named after the city of Tabriz in eastern Azerbaijan. Traditionally, it is a meatball dish mixed with dried berries, hard boiled eggs, and nuts, but I've made it with split peas and the ingredients Rich got for me from the bins.'

She is followed by GG with a tray of flatbreads which he almost drops as the shrill sound of a police siren wails from the street. I'm thinking I should go and check on the noise outside, and see what Pippa and Marg are up to, when Nahal ladles a scrumptious looking portion on a plate for me.

'Grubs up!' Nat winks at Sacha as we all start to tuck in. 'Do you know, I never laughed so much as when I saw Ant and Dec trying to eat locusts on, *I'm a Celebrity get me out of here*!'

'Look Natalie, despite all the jokes, there's a deeply serious message.' Sacha takes a bite out of the flatbread. 'Diversifying with insects will help make our food system more resilient. And more delicious.' She licks her Chanel-rouge painted lips appreciatively. 'The world's population is predicted to be nine billion by 2050, and a billion people are already not getting enough food. We need to think differently about how we feed the planet, and particularly the protein in our diets. Don't you agree, Father Guy?'

'Yes, yes, of course.' Father Guy turns to Nahal. 'I can't believe it's made from waste food. But you know you're going to have to get a health and safety licence to get your cafe started, and I believe that's a tricky thing to obtain.'

'Surely, Father Guy, as this ex-church is still part of the parish, you have special allowance for re-distribution of food in the community,' Rich urges.

'Yes, er … well, I will see what the bishops wants to do. But I wouldn't think it likely.' GG looks down and dips a piece of bread into the stew.

'It's estimated that insects form part of the traditional diets of about two billion people around the world, so why not us here in Kentish Town?' Sacha beams. She leans down to uncover her tray on the table. 'I've made dessert—a perfect ending to a perfect meal!'

I hear a collective sigh of relief when a plate of chocolate chip cookies is revealed. That's more like it …

'Excuse me, mister, could you give my dad a hand?' Any thoughts of dessert, just or otherwise, is put on hold as a little girl comes skipping up to Rich and taps him on the arm.

'What's your name?' I ask the pretty little girl.

'Chloe.'

'Doughy-Chloe!' A boy rushes in after her.

Chloe bursts into tears.

'Henry Junior! Stop calling Chloe, doughy, right now, or I will confiscate your phone. Chloe can't help it if she's a little on the chunky side. I'm sure when she grows up, she'll put herself on a diet!' A man saunters in, lugging a set of skis. 'Hello all.' He puts his skis down and wipes his hand across his perfectly slicked-back blond hair. 'My name's Henry. Senior, obviously.'

'Doughy!' Henry Junior spots the wigwam, and dives into it.

Pew! What's that smell? My nose recoils from the pong of over-liberal aftershave as Henry Senior walks past me and over to Nat.

'Welcome, Henry,' Natalie declares in her most ladylike voice as she gives him a kiss on each cheek. 'We've been so looking forward to meeting you and your lovely children.'

Sacha lifts the tray. 'Would you like a cookie, sweetheart? What a gorgeous pigtail you have.' Sacha points to Chloe's long brown hair swooped back into a pigtail. 'You look just like Pippi Longstocking.'

'That's my favourite book,' Chloe smiles through her tears.

'Are there any nuts in them? My daughter has a nut allergy?' A harassed-looking man carrying a lawn mower has come hurrying in behind the girl.

'No! I would never offer nuts in anything without getting parental permission!' Sacha looks shocked at the question. 'No, these cookies are just made from flour, butter, sugar, eggs, chocolate and half a cup of dry-roasted crickets. I call them my chocolate *chirp* cookies!'

'*Crickets*? As in insects? You *are* joking?' the man yells.

'I love bugs!' Henry Junior grabs a cookie.

'Yes, of course she's joking!' I take the tray from Sacha and head towards the kitchen. 'But do finish yours, Henry Junior,' I add rather meanly.

'I'd like one,' says Greg walking over to us.

'Sorry about yelling,' says the new man, introducing himself as Michael. 'I'm new to all this, and a little bit overwhelmed.'

'Time to man up, Michael.' Henry Senior pats him on the shoulder. He turns to the rest of us. 'Are there any more able-bodied men who can help Michael unload the van?'

'Empty the van of, er … what, Henry?' asks Nat.

'Oh, you know, all the equipment we've managed to gather—tents, trouser press, rowing machine, scythe, a chocolate fountain … just everyday stuff that people are happy to share.'

'Share for what?' I hesitantly ask Henry, who, I must say, I've taken rather a sudden dislike to.

'For Daddy Day Share, of course,' Henry replies in an overbearing tone.

'Sharing Dads? I think that sounds wonderful,' says Nat.

'But isn't Daddy Day Share an after-school kids club?' I ask.

'Of course it is, sweetheart.' Henry gives me a smug smile. 'Daddy Day Share will be open in the mornings as an equipment-sharing library which Michael will run, and in the afternoon the kids will come here after school, and Nahal will look after them. Talking of whom, where is she?'

'Well, I agree with Nat for once. It's a wonderful idea.' Rich walks up carrying a handful of gardening tools. The older generation might have led their lives prioritising private ownership, but young people today realise that it is not the DVD they want but the movie it carries. And it's not the drill they need, but the hole it creates. Talking of drills, do you know that the average drill is only used for eleven minutes in its lifetime? Most purchased drills sit around and rot in people's garages for years.'

Rich turns to Michael. 'Daddy Day Share is all about creating a trust economy.'

'Well, talking of sharing, you couldn't make me a cuppa, could you? I'm exhausted.' Henry Senior sits down and lets out a loud yawn.

I wouldn't trust this Henry farther than I could throw a cup of tea all over him, I'm thinking, when Father Guy walks in dragging a big plastic case. He's joined by Greg, also towing something that looks like a clothes mangle from a century ago.

'Yes, I've always been passionate about spreading the message of conservation,' he's saying to Michael. 'To that end, I've arranged to take the Good Life team to a re-wilding park for a night away next week.' He plops down and lets out a puff of exhaustion. 'October is a time of great excitement amongst us ornithologists. It's when migrants arrive from Siberia. I'm such a bird lover.'

'So is my dad,' Henry Junior pipes up. 'Sometimes on the week-ends when I stay with him, he comes back from the pub with ...' His words are drowned out by a sudden scream.

And it's come from me. 'No, not Chloe,' I shout.

'Oh God, has something happened to my Chloe?' Michael drops the box he is carrying and rushes up to me. 'I knew it would come to this. I just can't cope with being a single dad.' He bursts into tears. 'Since my darling Evie left us last year, I've done my very best, but I just can't manage. It's too hard,' he sobs.

'Michael,'—GG puts his arm around him—'I can't tell you how sorry I am to hear about your loss, but I want you to know that we are all here for you. Come and sit down, I'm sure your Chloe is just fine.'

'Daddy, I'm here.' Chloe skips in. 'I'm sorry if I worried you, but Nahal was showing me the garden.' She sits on Michael's lap. 'You're not upset with me are you, Daddy?'

'No, Chloe, I could never be upset with you. Daddy is just a little tired.' Michael smiles through his tears.

'I'm so, so sorry.' My own eyes well up. 'I'm afraid this little mis-understanding has all been my ridiculous, stupid fault. I didn't mean *your* Chloe; I meant my Chloe designer handbag. I point to Old Spot in the corner of the church. His snout is buried in my bag.'

Old Spot seems to get the message. He stops sniffing and wanders up to us.

'A pig?' GG looks shocked. 'And who does this pig belong to?'

'Oh, hello dear. Old Spot is mine,' says Marg, appearing on the scene. 'I wondered where he had got to! But don't you worry, we are obtaining county parish permission to keep him, as well a licence from the council to allow us to walk him in the street.' She pats GG reassuringly on the shoulder. 'But I'm afraid right now, we have a rather more pressing matter on our hands. Pippa has been arrested.'

'What? Pippa arrested?' Rich shouts.

'Yes, and the police have asked for someone from the Good Life team to come to the station.'

Marg valiantly leads Nat and Rich out of the church. Nat's muttering how she's sure there is a very simple explanation, and I'm left standing alone with GG. He takes a step closer to me. I feel my body erupt with goose pimples.

'What is going on?' His blue eyes widen with incredulity.

What's going on is that I have an over-active imagination going into over-drive with you standing so close to me—even with a pig now slumped down between us … A pig who is rooting out my secret stash of Doritos.

GG looks at his watch, trying to hide the odd smile that has broken out across his face. 'I'm afraid, Dorito-Deborah, we will have to continue this conversation at your team bonding meeting in Sussex next week. You *are* going to be there, aren't you?'

Shaking his head at the sight of Old Spot crunching a popping jalapeño, he turns round and dashes out of the room.

NOVEMBER

CHAPTER 4

Stag Do

'**I**'m so psyched about this team-bonding outing Greg Peck has arranged for us,' Nat chatters on one week later, as we walk out of the exit at Horsham Station. 'Although it does seem a bit odd going to a stag do in Sussex!'

I listen to Nat's descriptions of all the single blokes she is picturing, my own thoughts somewhat less elated—I still haven't received a job offer from Selfridges. I check my phone again. The HR department promised to update me today, but no joy. On the upside, there *is* that unfinished conversation with GG to be had.

We jump into a taxi, and I look out of the window as it drives out of Horsham Station and into the countryside on this granite-grey day. Around us, the last few leaves cling to the trees in a landscape that is starting to look noticeably wintery.

'It'll do you good to have a night away from home,' Nat says. 'I know you've been sitting around moping about the Selfridges job offer. I spoke to your Stu, and he agreed with me.'

'You spoke to Stu in the US?'

'Yep, on WhatsApp. BTW, what's he doing back there again so soon?'

'Oh, er … more meetings.' I'm not yet ready to admit to Nat that Stu is considering taking a job at Yale. What I do truthfully say is, 'I'd prefer to be in Horsham than New Haven any day!'

Nat lifts a brochure from her Lidl carrier bag to show me the pictures of a cute-looking shepherd's hut, a comfy bed draped with white bed linen, a wood-burning stove aglow. 'Anyway, you've always told me you wanted to try glamping,' she grins.

I have to admit, it does look rather cosy. I study the picture of the small wet room attached to the hut, with its proper flushing loo. The thought of a compost toilet is one step too far for me.

'Wasn't it nice of Mouse and Lucia to drive Marg and Sacha here in the Chip Fat Travellers van, as well as bringing our overnight bags,' I say.

Nat nods in agreement and looks at her watch. 'I'm sure they'll get here soon—they left an hour before us. Can't believe it's two o clock already.'

I check my phone again as the taxi turns into a long driveway and past a sign: 'Knepps Re-Wilding Park.' The driver pulls up beside a huge empty field.

'Hello, hello, welcome to Knepps!' a jolly woman greets us as we get out of the car. 'I'm Penny, the resident ecologist. You must be Natalie and Deborah?' She ticks our names off on her clipboard. 'A few of your group have already arrived. So let me show you to your accommodation and the facilities.'

Facilities, a word close to my heart, I think, as we follow her.

'This is our stylish new outdoor bath house. We do have running hot water, so you can take a bath in the open air.' Penny points to two cast-iron stand-alone vintage baths, which look rather inviting. I imagine bathing side by side with GG later under the stars, our bodies submerged under lashings of warm bubbly water. An invigorating rain shower would be sprinkling down on our heads and faces—raindrops threatening to pierce the stillness of our bath, to part the waters and expose …

'We also sell Cowshed bath gels made with natural oils to make your bath totally blissful.'

'I'm going to buy one of these!' Nat giggles as she picks up a tube labelled, 'Horny cow.'

Wondering what time GG is expected to arrive, I follow Penny to the communal fire pits, which are stacked with wood. I wince as I walk up to one and feel my Alexander Wang suede ankle boot—my little autumnal delight—sink into the mud.

'You'll need wellies, you know.' Penny looks down at my feet.

'My Hunters are coming in the van with the rest of our group,' I assure her.

'Hi, girls!' We turn to see Pippa hurrying up to us. 'So pleased you made it. But isn't it shame about the others?'

'What do you mean?' I ask.

'You haven't heard?' replies Pippa.

'Heard what?' Nat snaps.

'The van broke down, so they've had to be towed back to London.'

I'm wondering whether to be more upset for Lucia and Mouse over their van's failed trial run using biofuel, or for my lack of Hunters and overnight clothes when my phone rings. I quickly answer it, only for the signal to disappear. The call is ended. 'Shit, shit, shit!' I yell.

'You won't get a phone signal here, I'm afraid.' Penny shakes her head.

'Poor Lucia and Mouse. Such a terrible shame. But where,' Nat presses on, 'are the blokes from the stag do staying?'

'Stag do? Yes, we get that joke often!' says Penny. 'No, I'm afraid the only stags staying here are the red deer and fallow bucks. They're full of testosterone and you'll see them charging around the place. Tonight will be all about clashing antlers and gladiatorial battles.'

'What? You mean stags as in animals?' Nat asks in a shocked voice.

'Stags, as in doe, a deer ...' -Rich comes up to us with an amused look on his face- 'a female deer. Ray, a ...'

'The woods will certainly be ringing with a primeval roar tonight,' Penny laughs. 'Living in the middle of it, as you will be here, you may find it hard to sleep at night. But it is *very* thrilling!'

'Greg Peck and I are in the bell tent.' Rich points to a grand-looking structure next to the shepherds hut. 'We hitched a lift and got here in great time!'

'Where is ... er, Father Guy staying,' I ask Penny, while still trying to hold my phone in the air to get a signal.

'There's no one by that name on my list,' Penny checks her clipboard then shakes her head.

'He couldn't make it either.' Nat shrugs her shoulders.

Perfect. So, no overnight clothes, Hunters, phone signal, or GG. I keep my growing list of complaints—not necessarily in that order—to myself, and storm ahead to the shepherds hut. At least that looks lovely.

'Ahoy team! The door of the hut opens, and Henry Senior pokes his head out. 'It's really cosy in here. I know you weren't expecting me, but the family has a little country pile down the road and, well, having popped in to have lunch with the old pater, I thought I'd join you in a little team bonding.' He winks at Nat.

Country pile in Sussex? All at once I understand the wealthy background Henry comes from. The only unanswered question in my mind now is what is he doing with us at the Good Life?

'Brrr … It's a bit nippy out here, I'm just going to go for a quick power nap.' Henry closes the door to his shepherds hut behind him.

'Do come and see our tent. It's hidden in the woods.' Pippa catches up with me and links her arm around mine.

'Our *tent?*' Nat and I chime in unison.

'We'll be going on the rut at 7 p.m., after the sunset safari,' Penny announces. 'Why don't you settle in, and we'll meet at 4 p.m. where the taxi dropped you off.'

'But where's our shepherds hut?' I ask Penny.

Penny looks at her clipboard. 'No, we only have one shepherds hut, and it seems there was a change to the occupant details. Yes, look here.' She shows us the clipboard with a line scribbled through our names. They've been replaced with the name, Henry Smythe. 'Anyway, see you later.' She gives us a quick wave and dashes off.

'I'm not having this,' I shout. 'I'm going to get that Henry, henceforth to be known as Smarmy Smythe, out of our hut.' I storm back off towards Henry.

'Deb,' Nat calls after me. 'He's a poor single dad. You have to empathise with him. We single parents must stick together. I'm happy to let him keep our hut.'

Stick together, eh? That's probably something Nat would very much like to do with Henry in his hut tonight.

With my spirits as damp as the field we trudge through, I very much doubt that Henry could be judged as being poor in anything apart from trustworthiness. I reluctantly turn back and follow Pippa and Nat through a clearing in the woods.

Although it's not yet 3 p.m., the light is already sinking lower in the sky, particularly here under the woodland canopy. We walk along a path thick with decaying leaves, the rotting acorns and chestnuts only just providing my boots with some support to stop them sinking into the undergrowth.

'Listen girls, before we go and set up home in our tent, I just wanted to say how sorry I am about Tree-gate the other day.' Pippa turns to face us. 'It was silly of me to cause a fuss with the council when we are trying to establish ourselves as a good concern. I just get so overwhelmed with all the challenges facing the world, so I start with trees. Each tree has rights and a legal standing, and each tree should have someone act on its behalf.' She places her rucksack down, unties it, and pulls out a bottle of rum. 'I bought a gift by way of apology.'

'*You* are totally forgiven! Think nothing of it.' Nat grabs the bottle and disappears into the tent in front of us.

I bend down and follow her. The damp and dreary mottled green tarpaulin is stretched over a steel frame, and under it are three portable canvas camp beds and a threadbare mattress. I shiver. It's damp and absolutely freezing in here. My ruminations on the whereabouts of the nearest hotel are interrupted, as Rich walks in carrying a tote bag, a stack of sheepskin rugs, blankets, and an assortment of pillows.

'Most important of all,' says Rich, 'here's a torch. It's dark and totally off grid here in the woods. I've lit a campfire and procured some local sheep's milk. I have another bottle of rum and hot chocolate powder that Pippa gave me earlier. How about we meet in ten minutes around the campfire for a warming cuppa of rum and hot choc?' Another wink for Nat. He walks off.

'Well, I think this is fabulous,' says Nat. She busies herself making up the beds, while Pippa lines the floor with sheepskin rugs and wraps one round my shoulders.

I unpack the canvas tote bag to find a pair of giant wellies—at least three sizes too big for me—some chunky socks and a red beanie hat sporting the slogan: 'Men have big toolboxes.'

'Come on, Deb,' Nat says. 'It's an adventure. Just think of all the brownie points you'll get bragging to your posh friends about this.'

An hour later, wrapped in sheepskin, and looking more yeti than woman—or like 'a wolf in sheep's clothing,' as a grinning Nat insists—I've downed two, or possibly three fortifying rum choc-hocs, and am boarding a large open-sided safari truck.

'This Pinzgauer Austrian Troop Carrier is an all-terrain vehicle,' Penny explains. 'It's only a twelve-seater, but as there are fifteen of you, I'm afraid it is a bit of a squeeze.'

As the truck sets off, I find myself trapped between two very large German-speaking men, while Nat is conveniently nestled between Rich and Henry—hence-forth to be known as Henry 'Smarmy' Smythe—and she happily chatters away.

'We will stop at some of our wildlife refugia to look for grass snakes, toads, fieldmice and voles,' Penny tells us. 'We will also cross our fingers for a sighting of stoats, weasels, red kites, buzzards and ravens.'

With my fingers well and truly uncrossed, my rum-filled body bouncing up and down in the truck, I look around in a haze, as the truck starts to criss-cross land covered in animal tracks.

'At Knepps, 3,500 acres of land was taken out of conventional cultivation to re-wild. This has resulted in hedges growing out, meadows filling with wildflowers, young oaks, and sallow thickets,' Penny explains.

'Thousands of passage migrant birds arrive in the autumn: thrush, redwing and geese,' Greg adds. 'They have travelled thousands of miles from Siberia to stop off at Knepps. It's like their UK service station en route to …'

'Talking of fuel,' Nat interjects, 'did you know that some peeps claim that beer is soon going to be cheaper than petrol? I've got a great slogan for a new anti-pollution campaign: "Drink. Don't drive!"'

'I'm all for that!' Henry laughs as he takes a swig from the bottle of vino that Nat has snuck aboard.

Managing to find a space in between the over-arching arms of my fellow German travellers, who are enthusiastically taking photos, I look around as the truck turns off the road and starts to bump through a wild, scrub-like terrain. Above us the sun is setting, casting a Titian orange glow over the land which seems to stretch for miles. I can't believe I'm not in Africa, I think, summoning the spirit of Meryl Streep in my all-time fave film:'*Out of Africa.*'

'Ours is an ever-changing landscape,' Penny smiles. 'It's created by free-roaming, English, longhorn cattle, fallow deer, Exmoor ponies and Tamworth pigs who provide a mosaic of wild fecundity.'

While Penny continues with her observations on fecundity, I concentrate on mine. All that's missing here is Robert Redford look-a-like, Father Guy, to wash my hair, Streep-like, in the lake at dawn.

'This is also a breeding hotspot for turtle doves, the bird species most likely to go extinct in Britain in the next few years,' Greg says. 'Birds of prey not seen for half a century have reappeared here.'

'Well, I think that re-wilding the land is almost like letting it breath again,' Pippa adds, as the truck pulls up by a lake.

Having been handed a flapjack made with honey created by Knepps bees, I follow Pippa to a bench beside the lake where we sit and admire the sun, casting a wondrous copper glow on the still water.

Pippa smiles and asks me: 'Seeing all this beauty, doesn't it make you want to dedicate your life to fighting environmental degradation, like those fracking drills that discharge wastewater into lakes like this? They really contaminate rivers and create a toxic food web.'

'Did you know the UN predicts that by twenty thirty the world will have a global shortfall in drinking water?' Rich adds in a subdued voice, as he sits down next to us. 'As developing nations run short of water, economic growth will decline, and this will raise the risk of violent conflict.'

'All this talk of water has made my throat a little dry. Could you pass me another swig of the Chardonnay, please?' Nat inserts her more wry than dry comment.

'I think the Earth is in need of a good lawyer,' says Pippa, handing Nat the bottle. We finish our flapjacks and look up as a buzzard flies overhead.

Our thoughtful silence is suddenly interrupted by a shrill noise. 'Oh excellent, my detector has picked up the sound of a colony of bats,' Penny says excitedly. 'Bats use high frequency calls that are normally beyond the range of human hearing. This echolocation system enables them to wing their way through the dark night and pick out the tiniest of insects to hunt.'

We look up, as a group of giant bats flies unnervingly low over us. Like giant moths, they skim the water and then fly off into the inky sky.

'Look how free they are,' Pippa smiles. 'I don't want to be an *owner* of the natural world, just a steward for my kids and their kids. I'm fed up with the planet being treated as a commodity.'

I keep my cynical thoughts to myself about how this sounds all well and good, but how is a bunch of mismatched folks in Kentish Town going to be able to do much about it? I look up as the last vestiges of the sun disappear behind the lake. A swallow lands on the water, causing ripples, and the sound of roosting birds starts to echo from the trees. I take a large swig from the bottle that is handed to me and admit that it is all a very humbling sight.

'Now that the sun has set, it's time for the stag do!' Penny announces as she walks up to us. 'After which I'm guessing you will all be hungry for our sloe gin and venison bangers!'

We jump up, and in single file follow Penny, who shines a torch to illuminate the way along a dark path. After about fifteen minutes, we arrive at a corrugated hut covered in camouflage: our bird hide.

Having been told not to talk—that absolute silence is the only way we will experience the rut—we bundle into the hide, cheek by jowl, and Penny's torch is switched off.

The night is dark, all around is silent. Our ears alert to the calls of the wild—I hear rustling in the bushes; the wind in the leaves; a distant animal cry …

'You can almost smell the pungency of pheromones in the air, can't you?' Nat whispers into my ear. The only things I can smell is Henry, who is sitting too close to me. I sniff but keep quiet. We sit huddled in the pitch black in complete silence for what seems an eternity, until the sound of what I can only describe as a cross between a lion roaring, a cow bellowing and someone trying, unsuccessfully, to start a chainsaw, echoes around.

'Ah, the stags have starting bolving,' Penny whispers.

'What the bloody hell is "bolving?"' Nat bursts out laughing.

'Bolving is the stag's mating call. And do be quiet,' Penny pleads. 'The rut begins with two stags parallel walking and sizing each other up, before they clash together in pitched battle. If there is any noise at all from us, we'll put them off.'

'Wow, what was that?' I yell, as a white tail flashes out of the darkness in front of us.

'It was a rabbit, Deborah,' Penny tuts.

'Can someone tell these stupid women to be quiet,' one of the German men squashed next to me snaps.

The term *stuck in a rut*, totally comes to mind. The group falls silent, so great is our desire to see bucks locking horns out in the field, as opposed to the ones in this hide. In the distance, there's the odd guttural grunt, and I can just about make out the sound of what I guess is literally clashing antlers, but there is nothing to be seen.

Later, after what seems an interminable amount of time, Penny finally switches on her torch and announces, much to the displeasure of most of the group, that sadly the rut has not happened tonight.

'Never mind. I've got a joke that'll cheer you all up,' Nat says, as we head back into the safari truck. 'What did the doe say to the buck? "Boy, you're horny!"'

Stony silence.

An hour later, huddled around the campfire drinking sloe gin, the rest of the stag-seeking group sadly having chosen to forgo our company, our wildlife and ornithological conservation continues.

'What do you call a busy bird?' Henry Smarmy Smythe raises his eyebrow at Nat, as he turns the sausages which we are grilling on the campfire.

'A frequent flyer!' I answer, making a mental note to check how many air miles Stu has accrued on his trips. Not that I am at all considering any greenhouse-gas-creating air travel. But there was that talk of a little pre-Christmas shopping trip with the girls to New York …

'What do you call a bird that's out of breath?' asks Greg.

'A puffin!' Pippa giggles, as she takes a gulp out from the bottle of sloe gin.

'I must say, Pippa, I really felt your sadness besides the riverbank earlier,' Rich takes her hand. 'But take heart, no need for any ...' he pauses for effect, *'egrets!'*

'Do be quiet. You're now just chirping on,' I add my own quip, as I accept the bottle from Pippa.

'Anyway, I think we should toast the rest of our absent team?' Rich slurs.

'Yes, here's to Marg and Old Spot and the Chip Fat Travellers,' Pippa says. She tries to stand up, but finds herself toppling over, clearly having had a few swigs too many.

'Not forgetting Father Guy,' I add.

'As if you could!' Nat nudges me before going over to sit between Rich and Smarmy Smythe.

'Talking of absent team, where is Henry Junior?' I ask.

'Oh, I dropped him off at Michael's,' he replies in a nonchalant voice. 'Michael has to stay in to look after Chloe, so one more kid won't make a difference. After all, we are Daddy Day Share.'

'What a good idea!' Nat flutters her eyelashes at him.

'I don't see you pitching in with much sharing, mate,' Rich snaps.

Greg tries to get the talk back from ruffled feathers to another pecking order. 'Did you know that psychologists use bird courtship rituals to better understand complex group dynamics?' he says.

'Au contraire, I'm very good at sharing.' Smarmy Smythe prods a sausage with a fork and lifts it out of the fire. 'Fancy a banger, Nat?' He cuts the sausage in half and places one bit in Nat's mouth and the other half in his own.

'Or just poking it?' Rich stabs another sausage on the barbie with a stick.

The sausage oozes out fat causing a huge flame to erupt. We all jump up and back away from the fire. I notice Smarmy Smythe and Rich are each holding a sausage, glaring at each other. Sausages—rather than pistols—at dawn, eh? Nat, meanwhile, is clearly relishing the sausages as much as the attention.

'Just wait,' Greg slobbers on the bite he chews, 'until you see the courtship dance of the great crested glebe in February.'

'Anyone fancy a quick drink for the road?' I ask.

'Yes, but better make it a swift one,' laughs Pippa.

But swift one it wasn't to be, I realise, as I wake up the next morning, still fully dressed and shivering in our tent. My legs are reaching for the floor, while the upper half of my body is on our sorry excuse for a bed. I peel away the sheepskin rug covering my face to find Nat sitting in front of me looking flushed and well-rested.

'Did you hear that bloody tawny owl hooting all night? I didn't sleep a wink!' I moan.

'Talking of owls, this is going to make you laugh,' Nat chuckles. 'Why don't tawny owls mate in the rain? Because it's too wet to woo!'

'I'm so not in the mood for a joke, Nat.' I pull my hat further down over my ears to block out her hysterical laughter. 'Anyway, where have you been?' I lift out my phone to find there's still no signal. 'It's only 7 a.m.'

'Oh, you know, early birds and all that,' Nat winks.

Yes, but what worm did *she* catch? I decide to keep that pressing question till later as Natalie hands me two slices of cucumber.

'I've arranged a treat to help you recover. I've run us a bath in the outside bathhouse, and I'm just going to find us some towels. I'll meet you in the bath in a mo. You go ahead of me.' And with that, she dashes off.

A half hour later, laying outside in the bath, I'm taking in a deep contented breath as I listen to the birds. The Cowshed cream on my face is invigorating my pasty skin and the cucumber slices that Nat has placed on my eyes are having a wonderful soothing effect. I hear what sounds like Nat getting into the bath besides me and sliding under the delicious waters.

'It's very *hygge* in here, isn't it?' I let out a sigh of relief. 'So, tell me what happened last night? Where were you?'

'You speak Danish?' That's not Nat's voice, but a man with a Scandinavian accent. My cucumber eye patches almost fall off. 'I was asleep in my tent but would have been very happy to have had a knock on my tarp from you.'

I frantically peel off the remaining cucumber to see a rather handsome man who looks just like the actor, Michael Fassbender, reclining in the bath next to me. He's stroking his chiselled jaw and wiping the steam from his eyes to reveal an intense and brooding stare. I rub my over-tired eyes and wonder if I am in a movie, and it's not *Out of Africa,* or even, *Out of Horsham.*

'I'm Frederik.' He stares at me. 'I am an investigative journalist.'

'And I'm Nat.' Nat has just appeared wrapped in a Teletubbies towel. "Is there room in there for me?

CHAPTER 5

Stitch 'n Bitch

'Ciao, Debo darling! So, this is where you've been hiding ...'
I turn round to see my friend, Fliff, saunter into the church, the pitch in her heels as high as her voice. I wonder if she's here to give me the details of our next girls' night out, which my fashionista friends, Phoebe, Fliff and I, take turns to organise each month. Each outing is increasingly more glam than the previous months, and with that in mind, I whip off my pinny. Putting on my biggest smile, I try to hide my feelings of mortification that she has found me prepping food in the Abundance Cafe for our grand opening this lunchtime.

'I'm dying to hear about your little glamping trip, but you can give me all the details at our vegan dins at The Wolseley next week. I've just popped in here briefly to say how sorry I was to hear you didn't get the Selfridges job.' Fliff blows me an air kiss. 'You would have been fabulous there.

'What do you mean, didn't get the job?' The tray of beetroots I'm carrying starts to wobble.

'Oh God, you haven't heard?' Fliff places her hands to her lips in mock shock. 'Phoebe got it. But I *am* pleased you've managed to find something productive to occupy yourself with. Working in a café now, are you?'

I'm, er, just helping with the launch of our Abundance Cafe,' I mumble, trying to hide the tears welling up in my eyes. 'We're serving a Persian cuisine made from waste food. Did you know that UK households bin thirteen billion pounds worth of food per year, while four million people live in food poverty?' A string of words learned from goodness knows where tumble out from my dry mouth, but in my mind, I hear only three words: 'Phoebe, Selfridges, job.'

'And you must be the gorge vicar?' Fliff, who remains as oblivious to my tears as to my surprisingly well-informed words on food waste, turns to greet Father Guy as he walks out of the kitchen carrying another tray of food, followed by Nahal and Nat.

'Well, he is certainly gorging on Nahal's fantastic food!' says Nat, who is carrying several steaming cups of fresh mint tea.

GG, who has been in a quiet mood all morning, choosing not to share why he didn't turn up at Knepps, places plates of chopped tomatoes, walnuts, and yoghurt on the large sharing table that we've made from two pallets.

'What's this dish called, Nahal?' I look down and start to stir beetroots into the yoghurt. My cheeks are burning with the embarrassment after Fliff's comment about GG, as much as with the processing of her humiliating announcement: Phoebe got the Selfridges job.

'Why are you crying, Deb?' Nat asks.

'Oh, it's just the onions,' I reply, hoping that Fliff doesn't notice there are no onions in the dish I'm preparing.

'We are making this *Masto-laboo*, this tasty beetroot dip, to bring colour into our lives.' Nahal hands me a cup of mint tea and smiles. 'There is a wise old Iranian saying that when someone feels unappreciated or overlooked; and it goes like this: am I a beetroot leaf here? *Pas man inja barg-e choghondaram?*

I breathe in the lovely aroma of fresh mint, take a fortifying sip, and smile back at Nahal with gratitude.

'Anyway, I'm pleased you're taking it so well, Debo.' Fliff leans into her Prada bag and pulls out a newspaper. 'I'm also so delighted to see that your sweet little project has made the press. But this is not the best-looking pic of you, is it?' She passes me the copy of the *Camden New Journal*. There's the picture Thomas Montjoy, the property developer, took two weeks ago besides the threatened tree outside the church. It shows Pippa with her fists clenched atop the tree, Marg dangerously trying to hoist a leg up, and me, my face covered in grease, struggling to pull her down and shooing away Old Spot, who has his snout up my derrière.

GG looks at the photo and the headline: 'Good Life or Good

Laugh? Good use of church property, not!' Shaking his head, he puts the paper down and heads back towards the kitchen.

'Gosh, sorry darling! Not quite your day, is it?' Fliff gets up. 'Anyone care to give me a tour?'

'We are too busy to show you around, and Deb had no intention, anyway, of going to work at that Selfridges shite!' Rich, who has been earwigging our conversation while cleaning something in front of the pulpit, storms into view. 'The fashion industry causes environmental devastation with its unethical labour practices, just so you and your sparkly Selfridges shoppers can buy another showy hat.'

Fliff places her hand protectively on her purple sequin beret.

Rich barks, 'You don't remember that when buying a matching purple jumper that's too small. You don't mind because it's *cashmere*.' He stresses the word cashmere with a sneer. 'People like you buy without regard. When was the last time you assessed the likely lifespan of an item before you bought it? Good buy, bad buy, comfort buy, shag buy. Retail therapy, my arse. The fashion industry is nothing more than a giant glittery turd.'

'Er … that was quite a rousing speech.' Fliff takes off her beret and flutters her eyelashes at Rich. 'And you are?'

'Richard is our handyman.' Nat places a knife and another tray of boiled beetroots in front of Fliff. 'You might also need to remove your suede gloves to chop these.'

I forget my woes for a moment and stifle a giggle. And I've noticed that even though it's warm in here, Nat's jacket is now zipped up … surely nothing to do with hiding her Primark top. I can't believe Nat has just asked Fliff to chop beetroots!

'Very handy indeed.' Fliff eyes Rich up and down.

Now Pippa gets in on the eco-lecture. 'Don't forget to mention the waste,' she calls out from her desk. 'Did you know Oxfam claims that almost ten thousand garments are thrown into British landfill every five minutes?'

'And what about the way the fashion industry promotes overtly sexual advertising?' says Marg, coming into the church with a large stack of leaflets. 'It amplifies body issues and increases many young women's poor self-regard.'

'No, Deb doesn't need Selfridges. She's designing a range of re-fashioned clothes and accessories here,' Rich announces proudly.

'And the only models around here are going to be *re*-models!' Nat laughs.

'I *am?*' My remark is as much question as answer.

'It's outrageous that most folk today can't even use a needle and thread,' Rich says. 'Until we reconnect with the process of making clothes, we will have no respect for their value.'

'And that's no yoke!' Nat looks at me and laughs. 'Yoke—as in the fancy collar I saw on that new dress you were ogling in *Grazia* last week.'

'Well, Debo, I must say that's most *à la mode.*' Fliff seems lost for any more meaningful words.

'Fluff, isn't it?' Rich says to her. 'We'll leave you to get chopping, while Deb and I go and set up her design studio.'

As Fliff reluctantly starts chopping, Nat and I follow Rich to the desk in front of the pulpit, where a bulky item is covered in a length of aquamarine sari fabric. Rich removes the cloth to reveal a beautiful antique bentwood case with the words: 'Singer sewing machine' printed on it.

'This was made in Scotland in 1893. It's over one hundred years old and still working!' Rich lifts off the case to reveal a wonderful vintage sewing machine. 'I got it from a lovely lady on the Next-door website. She donated it free of charge when she heard what we would do with here with it. It's mechanically superb. I tried it out.'

'Here's to your Stitch 'n bitch label!' laughs Nat. 'Fluff is the bitch and you the …'

'It's beautiful, Rich.' I wipe my eyes clear of a few last tears and look at the black enamel, the wonderful contrasting gold decals, the very early Singer gold motif very much intact.

'It certainly is!' GG joins us. 'But Natalie and Deborah, we need to have a chat.' He looks at us in a serious manner. 'I'm afraid …'

His fears remain unspoken as Lucia comes dashing in. 'We are ready to start our workshop now guys. Are you coming outside? Isn't it exciting? The Good Life's first workshop!'

'Well, I suppose it can wait till after Lucia and Mouse's presentation,' GG mutters, as we head outside. 'Although we *do* need to talk.'

'Yes, and we want to tell you all about the fantastic team bonding event you missed last week in Sussex,' Nat tells GG, oblivious to the warning tone in his voice.

Wondering what his ominous sounding news is, we follow Lucia outside. I feel a sudden twinge in my body—a stitch of the wrong kind.

'Wow Deb, look at all the people who've turned up!' Nat cries, as we walk out to find folks of all ages standing around the ice-cream van. Above the van's slogan: 'Enjoy a Mr Whippy,' the words: 'The Chip Fat Travellers' have been painted on in navy blue. A giant loudspeaker has been rigged up on the roof of the van.

Marg is handing out leaflets promoting a film night she is going to host at the Good Life. It's called, 'Swine and Dine.' Unbelievably, a passing group of teenagers has stopped to listen to Greg describing the graphic details of the mating ritual of birds of prey. Pippa, meanwhile, stands in front of the now infamous tree, collecting signatures on a board inscribed with: 'The Tree Musketeers,' while Rich, who has attached a banner to the tree, scribbles the words: 'Pay as you feel—Abundance Cafe grand opening. One third of the world's food is thrown away, help us stop this today!'

I walk over to help Nahal, who is handing out slices of toasted French bread and beetroot dip garnished with beautiful pomegranate seeds. At first, the crowd are clearly suspicious of being offered food for free—in particular, the pink looking offering—but people soon tuck in.

Lucia and Mouse slide back the serving booth window on Nan's van, and the crowd falls quiet. 'From the fryer to the fuel tank,' Mouse announces loudly, leaning out of the window. 'Welcome everyone … we are here today to tell you all about our project. We call it "The Chip Fat Travellers." And we will soon be going out on our first expedition to spread the word on the streets around us.'

Lucia pitches in, 'For this project we have converted my nan's ice-cream van from a standard diesel engine to run it on biofuel and waste vegetable oil. That's WVO.'

'But does it run now after last week's unfortunate start—or rather, non-start—on the way down to the stag do?' I whisper to Nat, making sure that GG, who is standing nearby, does not overhear. While I don't know what he's going to talk to us about later, I do know that we cannot afford for anything else go wrong on this horrible day. I take a deep sigh and feel more tears welling up in my eyes, as I see Fliff sneak out from the church. Pulling her gloves up over her now red-stained hands, she disappears off down the street.

'The van's fine. In fact, everything's going to be fine.' Nat squeezes my hand in a surprising moment of reassurance. 'The reason the van wouldn't start was something to do with biodiesel being made from waste vegetable oil. It freezes in winter, and you remember how cold it was last week.'

As if I could ever forget that cold, I think wistfully, as I look over at GG, who is zipping his parka up as the sky turns a threatening shade of grey. A nice outdoor bath would have really warmed him up.

'But first, I hear you ask, what is wrong with diesel engines?' Mouse continues with his presentation. 'Diesel engines might once have been championed by the government as the solution for a cleaner environment, but they are really dirty, noxious and potentially deadly.'

Lucia spells it out: 'They emit high levels of nitrogen oxides—NO_2—and dioxides, which studies have proven cause health conditions such as lung and heart disease. And particulate matters, or PM as it's known, can also lead to cancers.' I listen to Lucia demonstrate her skilful knowledge of chemistry. Or is it biology? science not being my subject *sans pareil*.

'Did you know that London is reported to have pollution over twice the World Health Organisation legal limits?' Mouse adds. 'A recent study from the Department for Environment, Food and Rural Affairs claims that the total of premature deaths in Britain caused specifically by NO_2 could be as high as twenty-three thousand.'

'That's all very well, sonny boy, but did you know that biofuel is really bad for the environment as well?' asks a man with a broad Scottish accent in a very aggressive manner. 'It strips land away from food production, it drives up food prices, and it causes deforestation. You need to get your facts right, sonny boy, before you stand here in your tarted-up van.'

I see Rich approach the man and cross my fingers. I hope that Rich, who seems to have taken on the role as Good Life protector, does not lose his temper.

'You're right, sir,' Lucia's voice rings out loud and clear. 'And thank you for bringing it up. But the difference here is that we are not planning to use cultivated biofuel, but SVO—standard vegetable oil—and preferably, WVO, waste veg oil, instead.'

'To do this,' Mouse adds, 'we had to replace the fuel filter in the Chip Fat Travellers van, as WVO and SVO will only burn in a diesel engine if its viscosity is brought down to a level similar to pet-ro-diesel. In time, we will add a heating mechanism to the fuel tank, but now we are having to get our oils processed at a place in Kings Cross. I like to think of it in the same way as when you have leftovers in your fridge and the grease quickly coagulates and doesn't liquefy again unless it is heated.'

Listening to Lucia and Mouse answer away with authority and diffuse the situation, two thoughts come to mind. Firstly, I realise that I feel strangely proud of them, even though I have only known them for a month, and *that* perhaps is what community is all about? I can't believe school labelled them as dropouts. Second, I wonder what leftovers need to be re-used in my Smeg fridge.

@NTS: Coagulating. Yuck!

'I am going to give these chip fat travellers the leftover fat from my spring roll deep-fryer!' says Mr Pang, as he hands out leaflets offering a five per cent discount on Pang's Chinese takeaway across the road. 'We also specialise in very nice pork buns.' He pauses as Marg hands him a 'Swine and Dine' leaflet, inviting everyone to a film screening next month on the perils of the pig production industry.

Having finished their lecture, Lucia and Mouse close the hatch to a round of applause and get into the front of the van. 'Ban diesel, stop pollution,' Mouse's voice calls out through the Tannoy speaker, as the van drives off.

Suddenly the grey clouds burst and the rain that has been threatening for some time comes pouring down. The crowd quickly disperses, ignoring Rich and Nahal's plea to come and take shelter in the Abundance Cafe.

'Hope Lucia has a driving licence!' Nat laughs. GG doesn't look amused as he leads us indoors for our chat.

'I don't know how to tell you this, particularly after what I must admit has been a very stimulating morning,' GG says seriously. He, Nat, and I, are the only customers in the Abundance Cafe. 'It's not good news, I'm afraid. The bishop saw the picture and headline in the *Camden New Journal,* and I'm afraid he wants to close the Good Life.'

Close the Good Life? I glance over at Nat who looks totally crestfallen.

GG picks up the copy of the newspaper from the table. 'What was he meant to think when he saw a picture of a young woman committing an offence up a threatened tree? Or an old lady risking life and limb trying to climb up the tree behind her? And what about the reports of another woman walking up and down the high street handing out leaflets encouraging folk to eat bugs? Or the man ranting on about how we should protect great bustards? And it's all made worse by the rumour of a male escort sharing agency taking root on site. Then, of course, came the news of a man breaking into bins to get waste food and serving it in the cafe. And, worst of all, an unsupervised child was running down the road after your pig.' GG's deep blue eyes stare intensely into mine. He lowers his voice to a whisper: 'What was I meant to tell him, ladies?'

'You were meant to tell him to have faith.' The words slip out of my mouth. 'You were meant to tell him how wonderful Pippa and Marg, Sacha and Greg, Daddy Day Share and Rich are. How passionate and determined Nat is ...'

'How the Abundance Cafe is aiming to create local jobs and cut down on food waste,' Nat stands up and shouts.

'And our Chip Fat Travellers are out there right now encouraging people cut down on fossil fuels and lower pollution,' I, too, stand and cry out.

'Not forgetting to tell him about Deb's new Stitch and, err … re-fashioning label.'

'Excuse me, is this the Abundance Cafe?' The interruption comes from the elderly lady I had seen outside sampling the beetroot crostini. She taps GG on the shoulder. 'My husband and I would very much like to support this project. We've never eaten Persian food before, but we think it is very important, even at our age, to always try something new and meet new people.'

'Our first customers!' Nat grins. 'For as it says in the bible, "As ye sew, so shall ye …"'

DECEMBER

CHAPTER 6

Prada Power

'I was amazed when I heard that in the spirit of the season, the bishop had given the Good Life a two-month reprieve,' I admit to Nahal, as we sit in the Abundance Cafe a few days later, rummaging through a big box of fabric remnants that has appeared overnight in the church.

'Me too!' Nahal agrees. 'Although I am nervous about the outcome of the public meeting tomorrow night when that vile Thomas Montjoy will present his proposed plans for the church.'

I nod in agreement, as we continue to place the pile of fabrics, now separated into hues of wonderful colour to one side and take a break to tuck into a delicious brekkie of *laboo va mast*—walnuts, tomatoes, honey, and feta cheese.

'Mind you, I'm not sure realistically what can be accomplished at the Good Life, as everything goes so quiet over the festive season.' I take a bite of the freshly baked taftoon Persian bread, which is really warming on this bitterly cold first day of December. 'I've been meaning to ask you, Nahal—What do you and your family celebrate in December in Iran?'

'There is a sizeable Christian population in Iran who celebrate what is known as Little Feast—the equivalent of your Christmas.' Nahal pauses to sip her mint tea. 'My family here celebrate *Shab-e Yalda*, the longest and darkest night of the year. I think you call it the winter solstice.'

I look up at Nahal. 'Talking of your family, I hope you don't think I'm prying, but I've noticed that while Daddy Day Share has been open for several weeks here, your son, Jafar, has never visited. Why have we not yet met him?'

Nahal stares sadly into her cup. 'He has some, er … behavioural, I think you call it, problems at school. So he has to do some play counselling after school.' She is about to say something else but changes the subject. 'But *Shab-e Yalda* is always Jafar's favourite festival of the year!'

'Well then, we're going to arrange a Yalda—Solstice supper—here, and we can invite all the kids!' I excitedly suggest.

'That would be wonderful,' says Nahal.

'I know you left Iran when you were five,' I continue, 'but do you have any memories of growing up there? Where did you live?'

'My house in Tehran had the best view of the Alborz mountains. They're north of the city and are covered with snow most of the year,' Nahal smiles. 'I can still smell the *khamir*. It is a sourdough bread that is baked by our local *noonva* in tandoor open-fire ovens, and their aroma fills neighbourhood just after sunrise. But mainly, my memories are of my grandmother. I remember her taking me to buy steaming hot *laboo*, scalding hot tandoor-cooked beetroots. These were my grandmother's favourite! She would let the beets cool off, then peel off the skin and bite into the wonderful snack.' She pauses to take my hand. 'But tell me … what is going on in your life?'

'I haven't even told Nat yet …'—I look down at my wedding ring—'but Stu, my hubby, is considering taking a job at Yale University for the rest of the academic year starting from January. He said he wouldn't decide until I had heard about the Selfridges job, which he knew was important to me. But as you can gather from last week, I didn't get it. So, I guess there's nothing stopping us from moving there. He's even spoken to our son, James, at Exeter University, and he's excited about the prospects of spending holidays in the US.'

Nahal gets up and gestures for me to follow her. We walk over to my sewing machine. I sit down, wipe away my tears that are welling up, and trace my hand across the golden Singer logo. *Singing*, is something my machine has really done this morning! My guilty secret: I have been here since 8 a.m., busily sewing away. I lift the two tablecloths I've stitched together from the box of fabrics, and hand them to Nahal.

'They are beautiful, Deb,' she says, as she studies the patchwork of saffron sari, yellow gingham, and a red floral print. It's a mix of fabric and colour which shouldn't work but does.

I smile: could I really start a little local label making refashioned clothes and accessories? Something about Rich's words last week really resonated with me: '*Until we reconnect with the process of making clothes, we will have no respect for their value.*' I think back to my last fifteen years working in the international fashion industry, with its boundless global wardrobe, and realise I have lost that connection.

Lifting my bag, I take out an upholstered box, covered in a now faded blue and white vintage chinoiserie fabric ...

'This was *my* grandmother's sewing box.' I place my family treasure on the table and smile in recognition of the homage we are coincidentally paying our grandmothers—a shared connection.

'I haven't opened it in years.' With trepidation, I open the box that has been buried for years in the spare room among discarded videos and toys. There's a treasure trove of zips and buttons, beads, braid, and ribbon. I trace my hand across the offcuts of fringing and lace: the treasure trove of haberdashery. 'I remember as a little girl rifling through the box with my grandmother, my little fingers trying not to get snagged by the appliqué scissors; the nooks and crannies of sewing.'

Grabbing a huge piece of fabric from the remnant box, I take a pair of shears and start to cut it in two. The duckbill edge of the scissors glides across the material as gracefully as a swan across a river.

'This piece of cotton is lovely.' Nahal lifts a piece of the cut fabric and places it over the table.

'Yes, it's a paisley.' I look at the design featuring a repeat cluster of leaves.

'The leaf motif known as paisley in the West is taken from the ancient Aryan, *boteh*, motif,' Nahal smiles. '*Boteh* is a Persian word meaning shrub or thicket. Some say even a bramble!'

'Well, let's hope we don't get scratched on it!' It's a silly joke, but we both giggle.

'What isn't funny is that cotton used in fabric like that, uses more pesticides than almost any other crop in the world. It has a serious impact on our eco-systems, contaminating our water.' Our merriment has been interrupted by Rich, who appears carrying a clothes rail.

'Did you know that for every cotton T-shirt you buy, we use almost three thousand litres of water? As for this shite ...' Rich comes over the to the table and lifts a piece of synthetic fabric out of the box. 'I'm sure you know that the principal ingredient used in the manufacture of polyester is ethylene, which is derived from petroleum ... oil.'

Oil, I hear. Surely not?

@NTS: How can I have been a fashion designer for so long and not know that polyester is made from oil?

'But I must say that this tablecloth is great, Deb.' Rich picks up the tablecloth I have made. 'I'm so pleased you found the box of pre-loved fabrics that were donated. Let's hang it here along with anything else you make! This rail was given to us by Hari at the dry cleaners in return for my secret recipe for getting stains out of kids clothes—a milk bath.'

Never mind cleaning kids' clothes, I wouldn't say no to soaking in a nice latte lather, particularly after having been bent over my Singer for several hours. I keep my less than greener cleaner thought to myself.

'Excuse me, I'm sorry to interrupt ...' I return my attention to the room to see a man who looks vaguely familiar standing in front of me. 'I'm Frederik, do you remember we met a couple of weeks ago ...?'

As if I could forget. Here was the dashing Dane I had met in the bath on safari at Knepps. He looks rather different with his clothes on! I cast my eyes over his brown and ginger checked pullover and chunky cords. Not quite this season's sexy-Scandi look.

'Natalie invited me in here to take up some desk space.' He shakes my hand. 'As an investigative journalist, I'm here to expose the neo-liberal capitalist system, and the starting point for this should be redistribution of the commons.'

'How rude! My mother brought me up never to call anyone common,' Nat calls out, as she walks in carrying a board covered with a cloth.

'No, no … the *commons!* Our cultural and natural resources that should be accessible to us all and not owned privately—air, water, and a habitable earth.' Frederik is in full flow. 'I believe that the restoration of our shared *commons* has great potential not only to re-distribute wealth, but also to change society.'

'I couldn't agree more! Welcome, mate!' Rich slaps Frederik on the back. 'I mean, have any of you lot ever thought about who owns the air?'

In my case, hot air. I take a deep breath as a wave of sweltering heat suddenly erupts from the pit of my stomach and races up to my forehead. I feel my cheeks burn and take another deep breath. Whoever owns the air, can take it back.

'Another hot flush, Deb? Bloody menopause!' Nat's humiliating remark does little to quench my fire.

'Certainly not, Natalie. For your information, I'm intensely considering Rich's important philosophical question.'

'At the moment, most of these assets have been seized by corporate interests and treated like any other form of capital,' Frederik persists, clearly unaware of my torrid exchange with Nat.

Frederik might look like a Scandinavian god, but this guy does need to lighten up a bit. He's far more 'bore' than 'Thor.'

'I believe that the market or the state alone cannot meet our needs; we need a new kind of politics: a participatory governance that focuses on keeping democratic engagement through the participation of citizens in the process of governance.'

'Yes, I'm getting into politics,' Nat interrupts him. 'I'm going to stand for council election as an independent Good Life councillor next year. In fact, I'm just off to meet Bradley, my new campaign manager.' She checks the time on her phone. 'His shift finishes at Lidl in half an hour. You'll love him, Deb. He used to be a boxer.'

'So where does your political affiliation stand, Natalie? A new progressive alliance perhaps?' Frederik asks.

'Er, yes, well … we haven't got that far in our campaign planning yet.'

I stifle a laugh, as Nat, and her less than politically formed affiliations, turn a shade redder than the rose of the Labour Party.

Boxing-Bradley, eh? 'How long have you lived in the UK?' I quickly change the subject. 'I thought Denmark was the happiest place to live?'

'I am here for my work. I have important words to share.' Deep worry lines form across Frederik's face.

'Funnily enough, I too have sharing words.' Nat whips off the sheet from the board she was carrying. 'This is our Barter Board. We're going to offer skills to share on it.'

I read the first item on offer. 'Wanted—free plumber in return for shag!'

'That's my offer!' Nat bursts out laughing, as she nails the board to the wall next to the dresser in the Abundance Cafe. 'Hilarious, eh!? Swapping one type of plumbing for another!'

'I don't think Father Guy will be happy if he sees this,' I hiss. 'Remember you've only got eight weeks to turn the Good Life around.'

'Relax, Deb!' Nat walks over to the clothes rail and surveys my hanging tablecloth. 'Nice patchwork. Reminds me of a joke—How did the farmer mend his pants? With cabbage patches!'

Nat overdoes her laugh again, and rushes off, leaving Rich to show Fred his desk, which has been placed next to Pippa's. I sit down behind my singing Singer, and I smile as a shaft of sunlight beams down over my haberdashery box. Inserting the paisley fabric into the machine, I press my foot on the pedal and carry on spinning my own yarn. Nat's shenanigans aside, all feels good in the world.

Hours go by before I look up to find everyone quietly working away at their desks. Pippa has arrived and sits chatting to Fred. Marg is on the phone planning for her film show next week. There's even a scattering of folk tucking away in the Abundance Cafe. I've made six more tablecloths and don't know where the time has gone.

'Wait 'till you hear this!' Rich calls over. 'I placed the clothes rail outside with an honesty box and found twenty pounds in it. We have sold both tablecloths. It's official—you're in business!'

'I can't believe it.' I jump up.

'Unless you need all the money, Deb, I think we should donate half of your proceeds to the women's refugee centre down the road above that posh cocktail bar?'

A women's refuge centre here in Kentish Town, I hear, ashamed to admit I was totally unaware of its presence above the cocktail bar where I had whiled away many a frivolous night. The Good Life was really starting to make me aware of the bubble I've been living in.

'After all,' Rich continues, 'our project is meant to be all about co-operation, not competition.'

'I'm all for a bit of competition,' says Henry Senior, as he walks in. 'I'm exhausted.' He calls out to Nahal. 'What grub's up, love? Not beetroots again, I hope!'

But first he says he plans to have a quick lie down before Michael brings the kids in. And so he disappears off into the kids' tepee wigwam.

'I saw that Smarmy Smythe chatting to slimy Thomas Montjoy in the pub last night,' Rich whispers in my ear. 'I wonder what *they've* got to talk about?'

Wonder indeed, I think, as Rich's rather strange admission is interrupted by Marg, who comes rushing up. 'You've got to come out and see the BMX Bike Club rehearsing their presentation for later. They're quite wonderful!'

BMX what? The plot is certainly thickening as quickly as the clothes rail I see Rich filling with my tablecloths. I follow Marg outside to the front entrance. Strange, large batteries and metal objects are scattered around, while a man and a boy screw on a metal part to an upside-down bike.

'Electricity is invisible, so we don't really give it any thought.' The boy practises his speech to an imagined audience. 'I mean, which of you have your ever asked yourself, where does energy come from?'

Simple, I think. The plug socket. But what I say is: 'Great question! But who are you? And what are you up to?'

'Hi, I'm Leroy,' the boy smiles, 'and this is my dad, Francis. We're part of a new group called the BMX Bike Club, and we've invited my school class, Year 5, here later today to teach them how to use bike pedalling to generate electricity.' He points to a large battery stuck behind the back wheel on one of the bikes.'

'Francis is part of the Daddy Day Share,' Marg whispers to me. 'His particular interest is generating renewable energy. Isn't it wonderful! I'm trying to get them to generate enough energy to power our film showing next week.'

@NTS: Wheel to reel, eh? But can you really power a film by pedalling?

'That would be marvellous, Francis dear,' Marg says, giving Francis a hug. 'How much energy would we need to power a cinema screen?'

'We'd need to generate about six hundred watts of energy, and that would take about four to six bikes. I don't think we'll have them converted by then,' Leroy answers, instead of his dad. I'm amazed how a boy of ten can begin to comprehend any of this. I'm in my early forties, er … give or take, and don't understand a word. Creating energy by pedalling a bike? Whatever next? A device in my high heels to harvest power while walking around the shops? Prada power, now that has a nice ring to it. Or how about powering my hairdryer with an energy-generating bike? Coiffure-cutting calories!

'So how does it work, I hear you ask?' Leroy continues to rehearse his words while his dad puts his tools down and turns the bike back round. 'As people start pedalling, they spin the back wheel, turning a DC—direct current—motor backwards. The idea is that any motor you turn backwards becomes a generator.' He whirls the wheel round with his hand to illustrate his point. 'This transformer then converts the battery's DC current into an AC current.'

'In my day, someone who was AC/DC was a poofter,' an old man passing by calls out.

Francis carries swiftly on, 'We want to demonstrate the effort it takes to create the power needed behind a simple flick of a switch.' He flicks his finger to indicate a switch being turned on and encourages Marg and me to copy him. As we flick away, I spot Father Guy. He smiles at me and flicks his finger in my direction. I flick mine back. Have I just ignited at least a tiny spark between us? But the flame soon goes out, as GG turns around and disappears off inside.

'Fossil fuels are a non-renewable energy source which let off nasty carbon into the atmosphere, causing man made climate change,' Leroy's voice rises, as he reaches the finale of his presentation. 'We want to show you how valuable electricity is, and how not to waste it.' He takes a bow as Marg, and I burst out into rapturous applause.

'C'mon, Deb, hop on.' Marg urges me to climb onto one of the bikes.

'*Pig Business* … Come to our film screening at the Good Life, next Thursday December the 8th,' she calls out as she starts to pedal, attracting the attention of a few passers-by. 'Come and find out about the hidden costs in the pork industry to human health and the environment.'

I clamber on the bike and start pedalling. After a minute, beads of sweat erupt across my forehead. A minute later, my legs feel like lead.

'Come and find out how you can use your buying power and help create a more compassionate world,' Marg manages to call out as she pedals furiously.

I grip the handlebar, feel my body tense, droop my head, and let out an exasperated grunt.

'How lovely.' I look up, aghast, to see GG smiling at me.

Lovely? I try nonchalantly to raise my arm to wipe away the hair now glued to my face, but find my arm is as rigid as the handlebar. God no, did I just grunt in front of him?

'Really lovely.' GG is holding the paisley tablecloth I made and slowly caressing the lines of patchwork. 'As it says in Corinthians, "For the kingdom of God is not in word, but in power."' He winks at me and runs his eyes down my body. 'Although in this instance, I might add, "pedal power."'

CHAPTER 7

The Gargoyles

I t's the following night, and Rich and I are sitting squeezed behind small desks in the Year 2 classroom at Kentish Town Primary School—my old primary school.

Rich is tapping his hand nervously on the table, awaiting the start of the public meeting, whilst I am trying to adjust my derrière, which is more than a little bit sore after yesterday's cycling. Me not fitting comfortably in the tiny seat isn't the only thing that's changed since my day. The scratchy old blackboard of memory has been replaced by a whiteboard screen. And on it are the mysterious words: 'The Gargoyles.' And instead of the Miss Grey of my childhood, grey by name and grey by dress, the teacher now standing there is in a red dress. Her name, Miss Stuart, is on the badge pinned to her large bust. I run my eyes down her legs to see she is wearing black fishnet tights to go with the look.

I am also slightly alarmed by how packed the room is, with people I do not recognise. What I do recognise is how monied the crowd looks. The yummy mummies and alpha males of Camden are sporting designer jewellery and latest i-Phones which sparkle as brightly as the neon strip lights. They are people who look like they send their kids to the one of the plummy private schools in Hampstead (like the one Stu insisted we send our James to) and not to this state school in NW5. The question is, what are they doing here? Among them I spot one of our local councillors, Councillor Thornton, a rather overweight man who looks like he dines out well, and often.

'Ladies and gentlemen, welcome to Greener Properties,' Thomas Montjoy announces, standing up in front of the whiteboard. 'Before we start, I would like to thank Miss Stuart for allowing us to host this community public meeting here.'

Miss Stuart, in turn, blushes a shade more florid than her dress.

'It's hardly a community meeting, you bollix,' Rich yells out.

'Be quiet!' a man in the crowd shouts back.

I'm just wondering how Montjoy got permission to use this classroom, and where Nat and the rest of team Good Life are, when the whiteboard springs to life with a message: 'Welcome to The Gargoyles. *Your* luxury home in the heart of Kentish Town.' The words morph into the image of what I must admit looks like a fabulous block of flats made from Corten steel and smoked glass—but these flats are covering the site of our own Good Life church.

The murmurs of approval that break out around the room are silenced by Rich smashing his fist on the desk. For according to the on-screen computer image, all that remains of our church is the brick wall of the building now clad in steel, the steeple, and the stone gargoyle over the front door. And even its hideous features and lichen covered body have been spruced up into object d'art: a grand entrance sign for the luxury flats.

Montjoy continues, 'This sumptuous block will comprise of eight New York City style penthouse apartments. But this is just the first phase in a development, which will continue along Kentish Town High Road, transforming the empty shops into apartments and shops for luxury living.' He presses a key on his laptop and another image appears. It shows an artist's impression of a chunk of the high street turned into similar styled apartment blocks, all steel and smoked glass. No Lidl or library in sight.

'How bloody fantastic! Certainly puts a whole new spin on the term 'boutique!" a man with a pair of Ray-Bans perched on his head calls out. A titter of amusement breaks out, along with mutters of assent.

'This is no feckin' joke,' Rich shouts angrily. 'We should be discussing how education can create a moneyless system. Instead of this bollix, public meetings should be a forum for how to regenerate our high street, *not* destroy it.' He's now fired up and standing up. 'All this smoked glass is just a feckin' smoke screen for the accumulation of private wealth leading to further inequality. We should be brain-storming how to create community, not bribe a school to use its classroom to support another money-making scheme to line …'

'Thank you so much for mentioning community, sir,' Montjoy interrupts. 'At Greener Properties, and The Gargoyles, it is very much about *the community*. So just for starters, we will be donating ten i-Pads to this very school.'

I look at Miss Stuart and notice that Henry Senior has snuck into the room and is sitting next to her. I place my hand on Rich's arm to try to calm him, and gesture for him to sit back down. I know shouting abuse is not going to do the Good Life project any favours. But then, what will? I sigh, realising that there's no point me getting upset, when I most likely won't be here to witness the closure of the Good Life, anyway. I look around. Where the hell is Nat?

'As I was explaining,' Montjoy persists. 'The apartments will all have state-of-the-art smart systems, and will all be fully air conditioned …'

'You idiot!' Rich jumps up again. 'Hydrofluorocarbons accounts for a huge part of global warming.' He strides menacingly over towards Montjoy. 'They trap heat in the atmosphere at levels a thousand times higher than carbon dioxide. We don't need air-conditioning, we need …'

'Again, sir, many thanks for mentioning environmental issues. They are close to our heart,' Montjoy continues calmly. 'We will also have an electric charging point in the underground garage to encourage …'

Rich splutters outrage, 'Underground garage!? We are meant to be encouraging less car usage, not more. Haven't you heard that this little issue of pollution is killing ten thousand people a year? And we can't all afford electric cars, can we folks?' Rich looks hopefully around the crowd.

'Well, we are *very* happy with our new Tesla,' a man retorts.

'Getting back to the subject we are really passionate about,' Montjoy smiles smugly, 'it's all about the reinvigoration of the high street.' He points to the screen. 'And it starts right here with this defunct church, the site of our new apartments bringing …'

'Excuse me, young man, this church is not defunct,' Marg cries out, as she bursts into the room followed by Pippa, Fred, Nahal and Nat. 'It's simply deconsecrated.'

I smile in relief. The cavalry has arrived.

Montjoy continues, a smile glued to his face. 'As I was saying … at Greener Properties, our aim is for Kentish Town to become the new "go to" destination. On the ground floor of the flats next to The Gargoyles there will be an upmarket fusion restaurant …'

At this, Nahal speaks out, in her calm but firm way, 'But we have already got our Abundance Cafe in the church where we are serving Persian food, as part of our Good Life project.' While she is talking, Pippa and Fred unravel a long banner which reads: "Vote Nat! A Good Life vote!" 'And it uses surplus food from the neighbourhood that otherwise would have been chucked into landfill.'

Nat stands in front of the banner. 'Good evening, everyone. My name is Natalie. I'm here tonight to announce that next summer I will be standing as an independent candidate to become a Good Life councillor. I'm here to say that we don't want more posh flats in the area—we *need* more affordable and social housing.' She pauses to stare at the local councillor. The councillor stifles a yawn.

'We want more community amenities,' Nat carries on. 'We want our underused spaces to become inclusive community hubs—like our Good Life project—not more exclusive blocks of flats.' She points to a large poster that Pippa and Fred have placed in front of the white board. It's a visualisation of the front of the Good Life church: a bustling scene of folk digging around a vegetable potager; the Chip Fat Travellers van selling fresh veg; children enjoying slices of pizza around a cob oven. A sign points to the post office indoors. There's even a group of teens carving wood with some elderly folk …

It's an artist's impression far removed—if I'm honest—from the current broken-down chip fat travellers van, scattered bike parts, and wandering pig.

Nat raises her voice, 'We demand community services that are needed locally but are currently vanishing from the map. We've lost our post office and several banks, and there's even talk of the library being shut down …'

'Who needs a library when there's Amazon kindle!' a woman in front of me snorts as she taps away on her mobile.

'At the Good Life we plan to set up a community bank,' Nat continues, unflustered. 'We want to help disenfranchised youth start their own businesses. We have so many ideas for encouraging community cohesion, such as a shared exercise class between toddlers and older folk suffering with dementia. We even plan to host several champing evenings ...'

I'm wondering what on earth 'champing' is, as my eyes well up. I feel so proud of Nat and her unflinching optimism and ideas. Who knew she was such a great public speaker! I look at Rich. Surely that can't be a tear drop falling down his cheek too. He stares at Nat; his usual angry blinking eyes are now calm and full of tenderness. I wonder if he's developing feelings for her.

Nat's voice rises in urgency. 'I therefore urge you good people of Kentish Town together, let's concentrate on building community wealth, and reject this plan for ...' Fred, meanwhile, clearly the author of this inspiring speech, continues to mouth every word Nat is saying.

Montjoy interrupts, 'I would like to thank Natalie for her speech and wish her good luck in next year's elections. As they say, may the best man win!' He winks at the local councillor. 'But tonight is not a platform for political self-promotion.' He removes the easel from the front of the white board. 'The fact remains that on-line shopping has resulted in the closure of many high street shops. At Greener Properties, we believe that the best way to protect our high street and our essentials is to build sexy properties. Why have empty buildings when you could have this?' He presses another key on his laptop and a virtual tour of an apartment in The Gargoyles appears on screen. We see large bright rooms with smart systems, marble kitchens, crystal chandeliers and hardwood floors. There is even a huge walk-in shower.

'Those are the kind of essentials I'm interested in!' a lady giggles, as she points to the essential oil shower products on display in the bathroom.'

Montjoy grins and continues, 'In this rainforest shower room, which every apartment will have, you will be showering as if in you are in a jungle ...'

That's a red, if soggy, rag to Pippa. 'That's deforestation! Cutting down tropical hardwood trees to build your rooms is at the heart of inequality and environmental degradation,' she shouts. 'Land ownership in Britain is one of the most unequal in the world, with under one per cent of the population owning over seventy per cent of the land.'

'Anyway, thanks for coming folks. Do come and look at these pictures, and I'm here to answer any questions.' As Montjoy ends his presentation, he is swiftly surrounded by a group of folk eager to look through *The Gargoyles* mood boards. One woman asks him to sign her up for a flat.

My head starts to pound as I walk around the room trying to make sense of it all. I pass Miss Stuart, who has her hand on Smarmy Smythe's shoulder as he helps unpack the new iPads. She is whispering to him, 'Your son is a lovely boy, such a testament to good parenting—unlike others, who can't stop their badly behaved, out of control child from making silly bird noises in class.' She points at Nahal.

I sigh as I realise that she is talking about Jafar. I can't believe how unprofessional and downright unethical she is being, commenting on another pupil's behaviour. It was clearly Smarmy Smythe's relationship with Miss Stuart—in all senses of the word—that allowed this meeting to take place at the school.

As I walk out of the room, two and a half unanswered questions rattle through my mind: Firstly, just what does Smarmy Smythe have to gain from helping Thomas Montjoy, unless he's involved in Greener Properties? And if so, why is he setting up Daddy Day Share at the Good Life. And a second question: do I tell Nahal what I overheard? And the half question which makes me smile: What's so wrong with making bird noises? I think it sounds a rather lovely thing to do!

CHAPTER 8

Swine and Dine

I rush into the room, relieved to see that I have not missed the start of the film because of my emergency doctor's appointment. The chairs are all occupied with folk chatting away. Several new benches have been knocked together from reclaimed lengths of wood. In front of the altar, a giant screen has been erected. I feel a surge of pride as I look around at what really does look like a pop-up cinema. The room is full to the brim with people, the buzzing atmosphere only slightly tainted by a powerful aroma of something sour and briny.

I look around for husbondage Stu, who has promised to pop along after his meeting. I know an eco-film night in an ex-church in crusty Camden could never compete with the lofty academic heights of Yale, but against all odds, I'm hoping that if I could show Stu the potential of the Good Life, he might be persuaded not to take the job. Or perhaps not ... I study the offer Rich is scribbling on the Barter board: 'Jars of sauerkraut offered in return for thick male winter socks.'

'Ah, Deb, there you are,' says Rich, pointing to the stack of jars piled up on the ground. 'Nahal and I have made loads of sauerkraut. As I'm sure you know, preserved foods are important for filling the hunger gap in the winter months. Lacto-fermenting contributes to a healthy digestive system thanks to the good bacteria. Here, try some.' He hands me a jar.

'Thanks ... er, so sorry I missed the workshop.' I refrain from enquiring about the contents of the pulsing, fizzing jar of green matter. It's festering with enough bacterial matter to power the movie projector. I look up at him. 'Rich, I wanted to talk to you about the meeting the other night. Do you think Henry Smarmy Smythe is in cahoots with …?'

'I don't care about those rich tossers,' he interjects. 'What I care about is this cinema screen I made, isn't it great?' He points to the screen. 'I made it from a few metres of white Spandex I found in your remnant box. I built a frame out of wood and stretched and nailed the Spandex to it.'

Agreeing with him, I clutch my jar of pickles, and walk round the room looking for Nat. I pass Francis, Leroy, and Michael, who seem to be deep in conversation about the pros and cons of making renewable energy out of cheese. Next to them, Mr Pang from the local Chinese takeaway, is trying to prise apart Mouse and Lucia, who are snogging. I stop for a second to listen to Greg regaling Pippa and the lovely old couple, who now seem to come to the Abundance Cafe every lunchtime, about how not all birds migrate during winter. It seems a few, such as partridges, never move more than a kilometre or so from where they were born.

'Birds who don't migrate are called sedentary birds,' Greg continues.

'Deb, you're finally here! Come and meet my colleagues from Charles Wilson.' Nat, the living personification of an un-sedentary bird, rushes up to me and leads me over to a bench where a row of blokes wearing identical Charles Wilson hoodies are seated.

'We've only come for the free grub!' laughs one of the men.

'Only joking,' one of his mates says, poking him in the ribs. 'Anything to support our Nat!'

Nahal interrupts politely, 'And Deb, these are *my* friends.' Nahal is sitting on the bench behind, surrounded by several ladies whose bright hijab headscarves bring a wonderful blaze of colour to this otherwise drab December evening.

'And, of course, this is Jafar.' Nahal hugs the little boy next to her.

I smile at Jafar, but he doesn't look up, and sits clinging to Nahal. Probably just shy, I guess.

'Some of my friends do not speak good English, but we are really excited about setting up a weekly sewing group.' The ladies nod, and smile.

'Come and sit down, Deb, and we can talk about it,' Nahal urges.

'I'd love to, but …'

'She can't sit down,' Nat says loudly. 'Deb's got piles. She's saddle-sore! She got them from cycling on Leroy's bike!

I glare at her. I'm just as horrified by the sight of Nat's bulbous pink Christmas bauble earrings, as by her unwelcome announcement of my current predicament. 'Natalie has such a hilarious sense of humour!' I say, sarcastically.

'Persian lilac and hemp are good cures for haemorrhoids,' one of Nahal's friends suggests.

'Bakain leaves and bhang also give good relief from piles,' another lady adds. 'You simply make a paste out of …'

My humour is lifted by the cheery chorus of advice from these women, who, far from Nahal's description, seem to talk perfectly good English. 'I'm fine, honestly,' I say, 'Natalie's just joking.' I sit down carefully as Nat walks off.

'Welcome, everyone, to the Good Life's first festive film night. We'll be starting in ten minutes,' Nat announces a few minutes later, as she sashays her way up to the pulpit, her posterior squashed into what looks suspiciously like the Stella McCartney skirt I donated last week to Mary's Living and Giving in Highgate. 'This film focuses on Smitherfields Foods of America,' Nat continues, 'An organisation that processes twenty-seven million pigs in fifteen countries. It tells the story of how, when excreta from ten thousand pigs is sprayed over surrounding fields, local families report their kids having headaches, coughing, nausea, and asthma. But before we begin, do help yourself to food from our Abundance Cafe! *Bon appetit* and do donate generously.' She ends her message to a muted round of applause.

'Are you sure this film is suitable for kids?' I ask Nat.

By now, I've noted Chloe, Henry Junior and several other Daddy Day Share kids fidgeting in the front row. I mustn't forget to ask Nahal why Jafar isn't sitting with them?

'Deb, you've not yet met Bradley, have you?' Nat's attention is suddenly focused on a muscular man, the wrong side of his forties, who has appeared by her side. His biceps bulge through his rather tight-fitting, double-breasted, pinstriped suit as she links his arm.

'As I've mentioned before, Bradley, by day, is a trainee assistant manager at Lidl's, but by night he and I are going to be changing the face of local politics.'

He might first consider changing his own face, I rather ungraciously think, as I find myself staring at the jet-black stain coating his forehead. It seems to be coming from his dyed hairline.

'All right?' Bradley says in a deadpan voice.

'Bradley used to be a TV boxer, and an actor,' Nat beams.

'How wonderful. Been in anything I would know?' I ask.

'Dunno,' Bradley shrugs uninterested.

There seems to be more luminosity in his polyester suit, than his conversation.

'Bradley was in the TV show, 'Lights Out,'' Nat says. She hands him a bowl. 'You've got to try this Persian legume soup. It was made by our very own Nahal.'

'All right.' Bradley lifts a spoonful of soup to his mouth.

'It's called, *Asheh Hooboobaat*. It's made from split peas and turmeric.' This from Rich, who has come up to us, wholeheartedly tucking into his own bowl.

'Try saying that when you've had a few!' Nat chuckles.

'Actually, I got the split peas from your bins, mate.' Rich slaps Bradley on the back.

'Yer what?' Bradley spits the soup out onto the floor.

Rich's joke about how every Lidl helps—food waste and all—goes down just as badly as the soup with Bradley. He throws his bowl down on the table and raises his fist. But he's beaten to the punch by the film, which chooses this moment to start. On screen, the image bursts into life of thousands of pigs squealing in distress. They are in sheds crammed into steel crates too small for them to turn around in.

'Fellow anti-meat campaigners, this is Pig Business,' the voice-over announces. 'Junk-food chains, including KFC and Pizza Hut, are under attack from major activist groups because of their environmental impact.'

'Quite right! It's disgusting,' Mr Pang says loudly. 'That's why I offer duck spring rolls. Two for the price of one.'

'Intensive breeding of livestock and poultry for such chains leads to deforestation, land degradation, and contamination of water sources and other natural resources.' The screen voice goes on.

'It's Farmaggedon,' Rich shouts. 'The true cost of cheap meat.'

'Let's not jump to conclusions. Not all meat is cheap.' A man in the crowd jumps up and calls out, 'I'm the owner of the tasty, new "Lord of the Wings" restaurant opening down the road next month. Our burgers are …'

'These tormented animals gnaw on the steel bars in their cage until their gums bleed.' Rich cuts him off by turning up the volume on the film's voiceover. A horrific image of a pig chewing off its neighbour's tail appears on the screen.

'Pulled pork—not!' Nat whispers. She's almost drowned out by the sound of little Chloe who is sobbing. Michael rushes over to her.

Thank goodness Old Spot isn't here. There's another tap on my shoulder. 'Have I missed anything?' I turn to see Henry Smarmy Smythe standing behind me. 'I had a bit of business to attend to,' he chuckles. 'I see Rich has got his harem here!' He points to Nahal's friends, who are huddled together trying to shield Jafar's eyes from the screen.

'Animal agriculture has an enormous ecological footprint. The total cattle population for the world occupies around twenty-four per cent of all the land on the planet …' The voiceover is now competing in volume with the sobs of more and more children. 'The greenhouse gas emissions of the meat industry are greater than from all transport put together. Rearing cattle causes more damage to the atmosphere than owning a car.'

'Not *our* van!' Mouse calls out.

'It runs on vegetable oil!' Lucia adds.

The voiceover continues: 'British people eat double the global average of meat a year, while in the US they eat triple.'

'Blimey!' says one of the Charles Wilson group. 'This is putting me right off that doner kebab I was gonna get across the road later!'

The screen suddenly goes black, and the room plunges into darkness. Several children scream.

'I think we can all agree that that is enough of the film for now,'

Marg's voice pierces the darkness. 'Can someone please put the lights on?'

There's a pause while the kids are calmed down with the crisps which Nahal has made from surplus sweet potato peelings and the adults are fortified by cups of Nahal's sweet fennel tea. After the shocking images in the film, I would even have resorted to drinking Rich's homemade raspberry wine. After about fifteen minutes, Marg announces that it is time for the advertised 'meaty debate.'

She poses the first question: 'Don't you agree it's horrifying that the water necessary for breeding meat amounts to ten times more than what a normal Indian family is supposed to exist on in one day?'

'And that half the water consumed in the US is used to grow grain for cattle feed.' Greg cries out with such fervour that as he stands up, he lets out a loud fart.

The kids all burst out laughing. I'm happy to see that even Jafar is giggling.

'Sorry kids, it's the split peas!' Greg contentedly pats his stomach.

'Children, it's the same with humans,' Marg grins. 'When animals eat, gas builds up inside their tummies, and this must be got rid of. So, cows … er, fart and burp. The result is a large amount of methane heating up our atmosphere.'

'Isn't that sweet?' Nat points at Henry Senior and Junior who have kicked off a burping competition.

'Smarmy Smythe, sweet? Hardly,' I reply, still smarting from Henry's earlier offensive comment about a harem.

'It's estimated that every cow lets out over thirty gallons of methane per day. With an estimated one and a half billion cattle in the world today, that's a lot of gas!' Marg continues.

'But I don't understand? How does a fart or a burp heat our planet?' Leroy raises his voice to be heard above the sound of the gunshot burps being loudly fired across the room by the two Henrys.

'What a clever question!' Marg claps her hands. 'The answer is quite simple. Cows burp and fart a greenhouse gas called methane; methane in turn traps in heat; and trapped heat increases the Earth's surface temperature, and that leads to Global Warming.'

Talking about trapped heat, I feel a sudden shooting pain as a burping Henry Junior hurtles past me, accidentally smacking me on my backside.

'I don't know whether to start laughin' or barfin!' one of the Charles Wilson chaps chips in, as he watches the rest of the children start to crawl around like animals to demonstrate the story of creation—methane creation.

'So, in summary, everyone …' Marg looks a bit crestfallen over the hilarity that has erupted. 'We either become vegetarians, ignore meat production issues and their impact on the environment; or do something else. The question is, what is that something else?'

'*You hoo!* Gosh, sorry I'm so late.' Sacha bustles into the room. With great aplomb, she opens her burgundy Chanel bag—hello, is that the lambskin one featured in Vogue this month?—and takes out a picture of what looks like a Big Mac.

'Dad, *I* want a Big Mac,' Henry Junior shouts. 'You said we could have one later.'

'Here's a pic of the world's first lab-grown beef burger.' Sacha passes her picture around the room. 'This five-ounce patty was grown from cow stem cells and costs two hundred thousand pounds to create. It is the world's first truly cultured burger!'

Culture, eh? I can't help also noticing Sacha's pearl earrings. I bet they're far from cultured.

'Some scientists estimate that by growing meat in a lab, land, water usage and deforestation will be reduced by ninety per cent,' Sacha explains.

'A real happy meal then!' Nat laughs.

'More like a Frankenburger,' says Rich, glaring at Nat.

'Talking of happy meals.' The man from the new 'Lord of the Wings' restaurant stands up. 'The meat from our new restaurant comes from grass-fed cows.'

'Oh, shut it, Gandolph,' Rich shouts back. 'That's just meaningless platitude used to market your restaurant to more gullible consumers. What about the added antibiotics, the GMOs?'

'Also, the mayo in our relish is made from free range eggs,' Gandolph persists.

Nat pokes me in the ribs. 'Nice to meat u, let's ketchup soon. There must be a groundhog joke in this somewhere!' Nat chuckles.

'I forgot to mention that our buns are also gluten free,' adds Gandolph.

'You highfalutin' gluten bollix!' Rich raises his fist towards him.

'Some movie night this is!' Bradley mutters as Rich brushes past him.

'You are no better, buddy. Where's this Lidl meat from?' He lifts a packet of grey meat. 'I found this in Lidl bins.' He rips off the plastic wrapper and there's a reek of decayed meat.

'Well, er, perhaps that's enough of this particular debate,' Marg cries out as the adults jump up to shield the children from Bradley, Rich and Gandolph, who are starting to push each other around. 'Here's one you will like, children.' The image of a group of animated pigs in an episode of Peppa Pig comes on screen. The voice-over picks up: 'Peppa is a loveable, cheeky, little piggy, who lives with her little brother, George, Mummy pig, and Daddy pig. Peppa's favourite things include playing games, dressing up, days out and jumping in muddy puddles ...'

'Oi, who's in charge here?' A security guard in orange high-vis vest, who has walked into the room unnoticed by everyone, prises Rich and Bradley apart.

'I am.' Nat walks over to him.

The voice-over continues: 'Peppa and George are playing hide and seek. Peppa is very good at hiding, but George is too easy to find ...'

'Are you missing a pig?' the newcomer demands.

'Oh no! What's happened to Old Spot?' Marg bursts into tears.

'I'm from the Forum next door,' says Mr High-Vis. 'I'm in charge of club security. There's a pig charging around our auditorium. You've got ten minutes to reclaim him before we call the police.'

'Daddy, we need to find Peppa Pig,' sobs Chloe.

'The council's health and safety team will have us—and you lot—shut down,' Mr Hi-Vis shouts. 'Aerosmith are on stage in twenty minutes.'

'I used to love them.' Bradley has spoken. It's his first enthusiastic comment of the night.

'Daddy sings Peppa Pig's favourite song. Bong bing, boo, bing ...'

'Will someone turn that bloody film off?' yells Rich.

In the ensuing chaos, as people start rounding up their kids and clearing up, Nat makes an announcement that the Good Life film night is over. She hopes everyone has enjoyed it, and will come again next month ... I notice Smarmy Smythe trying but failing to suppress a rather delighted grin.

'Michael, take the kids home,' he barks an instruction whilst trying to sound mortified as he puts his arm around Marg.

I watch Nat, Mr Pang, Bradley, Henry, and Marg follow Mr Hi-Vis out of the room, before walking over to Rich. I'm joined by Greg, Nahal and Jafar. 'Follow me,' Rich whispers. 'I know a way in through the back door that will get us in more quickly.'

Out in the back garden, we are guided by a moon that gleams like the balls of mozzarella I have ordered as Christmas pressies from a local cheesemaker in Tottenham. Rich has suggested we proceed with stealth, and that means without using the torchlight from my mobile phone. Following Rich into our journey of the unknown, we walk slowly on. Around us, the trees are like watchful, shadowy presences, their silhouetted shapes shifting in the night breeze.

'Isn't nature different at night?' Rich's soft voice pierces the darkness.

'The ominous sky looks just like molasses,' Nahal whispers, as she wraps an arm around tightly around Jafar.

A ripple of icy wind whips across my face. It feels rather exhilarating, as I put my best foot forward, determined to help save Old Spot; that same best foot encased in my new Ugg boot. It immediately sinks into a morass of mud. My yelp of despair is immediately silenced by Rich, who comes to a stop, listening intently to a rustle in a branch on the tree in front of us.

'*Twit, twoo ...*'

I'm astonished to hear Jafar imitate the hooting owl—the first sound I've heard from him all evening.

'*Kewick, kewick.*' There's a bewitching response from among the branches. It's followed by a mournful '*Hoo, hoo.*'

'Omg! Was that a barn owl?' I cry out in surprise.

'No Deb, that was a pair of tawny owls,' Greg laughs. 'They've replied to your call, Jafar. Isn't that fantastic! We have our very own tawny owls. We'll have to look after them during winter, won't we Jafar?'

'I've read that bare branches provide perches and roosting spots,' Jafar says shyly. 'And that owls are crepuscular.'

'That's right, young man. How clever you are.' Greg pats Jafar on the shoulder. 'It's their silent flight, large eyes and nocturnal behaviour that makes owls both magical and mysterious.'

'Jafar loves nature, don't you?' Nahal kisses her son on the forehead. 'Jafar,' she tells us, 'means spring, growth and renewal in our language.'

Jafar is really coming out of his shell now, as he strokes a branch. 'Nature, like us humans, must rest before it can renew. That's why I love winter.'

I smile as I listen to Jafar speak. What a lovely, bright boy. He couldn't be further from the 'out of control' child of Miss Stuart's ascription.

I'm still wondering about the word 'crepuscular' and 'rapturous raptors' when Rich suddenly looms out of the dark. It seems he'd gone ahead to check out the clearing from our garden and now back to report.

'It's easy to get into the back entrance of the Forum through that unmanned door.' Rich points to a distant makeshift door made from a panel of corrugated steel. *My* question of how we are going to get through the thicket of brambles to reach the door, remains unasked, as the loud sound of a guitar bellows out.

'Quick, the band are on!' Rich races ahead, immediately followed by us intrepid travellers. Remarkably, we reach the door unscathed. And stop. Rich wants to do something before we go in. He lifts two jars of fermented pickles from a bag over his shoulder and places them at the foot of the door.

'I might be trying to go moneyless, but I still like to pay for my entertainment,' he says. 'It's the gift economy in action. I went to see Brian Eno here last week. And this is my way of saying thanks.'

The artist henceforth to be known as Brine Eno, I think. But I know better than to say it out loud. Someone inside the Forum is saying something out loud: 'Ladies and gents, we have joining us on stage tonight a very special guest ...'

We hear a drum roll followed by a roar from the crowd, as we follow Rich through the door and along a dark corridor to arrive behind the stage. Peering through a gap in the curtain, I see a rock band walk on stage, strobe lights flashing. And waddling in behind them is ... Old spot, his head covered in tinsel. There's another roar from crowd. I look out horrified to see Nat playing air guitar, surrounded by Bradley, Henry Senior, and Mr Pang. Bashing her way through the crowd with a brolly is Marg for goodness sake!

'Let's hope our special guest doesn't squeal the show!' the band's guitarist shouts, to the delight of the audience, as he turns up the volume on his guitar and the band starts to play ...

CHAPTER 9

A Wild Goose Chase

'A shadow casts across a closing sky,
where crowds meet to bid the night goodbye.
Yalda triumphant, light our darkened plain,
bring forth new life; our sun is born again.'

Nahal finishes reciting her poem to the sound of a hearty round of applause. 'In Iran, the winter solstice, which has been celebrated for centuries is called Shab-e yalda,' she smiles. 'Yalda is the Syriac word for birth. Shab-e yalda means the re-birth of the sun.'

'Well, thank you, Nahal, for sharing this. That was a most uplifting poem.' Father Guy, apparently newly returned from a retreat, looks up into the solitary ray of light shining from a waning moon that is shrouded in mist.

Nat nudges me in the ribs and says, 'Bet three months ago you never would've imagined that at six p.m. on Monday 18th of December, you'd be bundled up in your puffer jacket outside in the garden of a deconsecrated church, hugging a pear tree at an Iranian festival!'

'You're right. You've no idea how thrilled I am to be here!' I hug Nat tightly. She yelps as one of the red sequins on her tight red dress press against her body.

'What's got into you, Deb? You seem bloody cheerful for a change!'

'Don't shout at me, Nat, but there's something I haven't told you …' I turn round to look at Nahal, who gives me a smile of support. I take a deep breath and continue. 'Stu was offered a prestigious job at Yale University. We were going to move to the US from, er … early next year. But he told me last night he's not going to take the job.'

'What, you almost moved and didn't tell me?!' Nat shouts.

GG blushes a brighter shade of pink than the tinsel Nat unwraps from round her neck and threatens to throttle me with.

'I'm really sorry I didn't tell you; I just didn't know how.' I squeeze her hand. 'But I'm here now, and ready to get stuck into the Good Life for as long as, er … we have it …' I look questioningly at GG.

GG coughs and changes the subject. 'Why don't we share this blessing by praying in silence.' GG looks down.

Wondering which blessing he is referring to, I smile as Greg points out a robin to Jafar that has just landed on a branch, apparently keen to join in the prayer. I imagine I can even hear the '*kewick*' of our tawny owl. Yes, I realise, it does feel really good to be standing here with this lovely group of new friends—Nat's dagger looks aside—not only listing to crepuscular wildlife, but understanding what the word means!

'It is now traditional to share sweet nuts mixed with dried berries to bring us prosperity in the days to come.' Nahal breaks the silence to hand round a bejewelled bowl.

'And do try my homemade perry—or pear juice—for you, Nahal, and the kids, of course!' Rich adds. 'I hear that bloody Sacha has jetted off to Barbados for Christmas.' He sniggers as he swills the perry into his mouth. 'Where are you going Deb?'

'I think it's amazing that our intrepid Chip Fat Travellers, Mouse and Lucia, are driving the van to a sustainable travel rally in Bristol.' I quickly change the subject, ashamed to admit that I too am flying abroad on a skiing trip. I stare at Nat and hope she won't spill the beans. Beans being the operative word. It took three packs of my special hazelnut coffee beans to induce Nat not to share the news of my travel plans. I take a swig of the perry that is handed to me.

'I also hope Marg will be OK travelling to Norwich to see her older sister.'

'And don't forget Pippa's attendance at an Earth Law conference. We need a law that recognises humanity's dependence on a healthy …'

Fred takes a large gulp of the perry I practically force into his mouth.

'This is delicious, as well as healthy.' Nahal sips the pear juice.

'I must say I was surprised to hear how busy the Abundance Cafe has been over the last couple of weeks.' GG scoops a handful of Nahal's dried fruit. 'But in order for it to continue, you will need to get a trading licence which I'm afraid I haven't been able to help with.'

'We've even made enough extra money to buy balls of wool for the 'Knit Wit' club we are launching in January,' says Rich, ignoring GG's reminder.

'Knit Wits?' I ask, as I swallow a mouthful of dried fruit to alleviate the burning sensation of the perry.

'The all-male knitting comedy club that Michael is going to run!' Rich explains.

'*That* I've got to see!' Nat murmurs, as we watch Michael dash off to comfort Chloe, who has burst into tears over a drip of pear juice on her princess dress. 'Mournful Michael does comedy? I've never even seen the bloke smile!'

I take another sip of the perry, and hand the bottle to GG. 'Yes, it's been a productive week.' I fail to mention the disastrous film night.

'Henry and I had great fun in the mosh pit!' Nat smiles sardonically at Rich.

'Mosh pit?' GG raises an eyebrow.

'She means, er … the pit we have started digging in the back garden,' Rich hedges.

'I can't believe Old Spot's gone viral!' Nat continues, oblivious to the fact we're trying to hide the details of last week's piggy hijinks from GG. Thankfully, it hasn't made the press.

Father Guy gulps back his perry.

'Yes, Old Spot has got a bit of a cold. He's resting in my bed,' says Rich, trying to cover up the real story of Old Spot's stage act, as photographed by someone, and tweeted, and has now been retweeted hundreds of times. 'Talking of colds,' he continues, 'I've just finished making my elderberry cough syrup. I don't want to ruin the surprises in your Christmas pressies but …'

'Perhaps, as we are standing around a pear tree, it's time for a song the children will like?' GG smiles at the youngsters and starts to sing. 'On the first day of Christmas, my true love bought for me, a partridge in a ...'

I'm lost in his glorious voice which shines out as brightly as the star that has just appeared through a chink in the clouds. I gaze at his body wrapped up in a chunky Aran jumper and jeans, his legs as long, rugged, and strong as the trunk of the pear tree. As he runs his hand through his blond hair, a solitary golden strand falls on his face. He not only looks like an angel, but he sings like one.

'Hold on a moment ...' My reverie is broken by Rich's unwelcome intrusion. 'I think we should change the lyrics from "bought" to "shared."'

'Well, that's a novel idea, Rich.' GG pauses for reflection for a second or two, then carries on singing. 'On the second day of Christmas, my true love *shared* with me, two turtle doves and a ...'

'I hope you all know that turtle doves are faced with extinction,' Greg sighs, downing the last dregs of the perry. 'According to the latest official survey, their numbers have hit a new low. They've declined by ninety-three per cent since 1994.'

'No, Daddy, no! I love doves,' Chloe sobs.

'On the third day of Christmas, my true love sent to me, three French hens ...'

We all burst into song to try to keep the festive spirit going.

'And why *French* hens? I've never understood that?' Rich cries out above the sound of our less than harmonious carolling. 'It should be British hens—local chicks.'

'My dad likes local chicks,' Henry Junior pipes up.

'On the fourth day of Christmas, my true love sent to me, four calling birds ...' GG sings even louder. 'On second thoughts,' he pauses, 'perhaps it's best we miss this verse out.'

'Talking about birds, December is a quiet month for passage migrant birds,' says Greg, as he opens the second bottle of perry and hands it around.

'My dad doesn't like migrants.' Henry Junior shares another illuminating observation on his father's sensibilities.

'Where *is* your dad?' I ask, quickly changing the subject.

'He's gone shopping in New York for the weekend.'

'On the fifth day of Christmas, my true love shared with me …'—GG grabs the perry from Greg and takes a large gulp—'Five maids a-milking …'

'Sharing milk maids, now that sounds a plan!' Rich laughs and punches the air.

He gets a filthy look from Nat, and a shake of the head from Fred, who says, 'Do you know that because of agri-business, the number of UK dairy farmers has dropped from over thirty-five thousand in 1995 to fourteen thou in 2011. Another example of neo-liberal takeover.'

As I listen to Fred drone on, I have to bite my tongue and stop myself from asking about the five gold rings. Rich and Fred were sure to make painful observations on ethical mining. At the rate we were going, the twelve days of Christmas would have to be completely rewritten.

'Going back to the turtle doves,' Greg says, 'losing six out of ten of our turtle doves, and three out of ten grey partridges in five years, is nothing short of an unsustainable wildlife disaster.'

'Right, that's enough from you three *not* so wise men!' Nat shouts. She grabs Rich, Greg, and Fred by the scruff of their tinsel-less necks. 'This is meant to be a *Yalda* celebration. Now sing after me: On the ninth day of Christmas, my true love sent to me, nine ladies dancing … Let's go inside, eat, and get the disco on!'

I look at Nahal, and we burst out laughing at the sight of Nat frogmarching Rich, Greg, and Fred, while we, the merry perry flock, follow a wobbling GG, our sozzled shepherd, indoors. I gasp as I walk into the candlelit room and see what Nahal has created. Around us, red candles of all shapes and sizes flicker away. The long table has been covered in one of my red and gold tablecloths, and laid with cutlery and Nat's doubtfully procured green chinoiserie plates. A selection of cranberries, figs and pomegranates adorns the table, and a large watermelon graces its centre. To the right of the table, someone has even installed a Christmas tree in a pot. Its unadorned green branches look simply beautiful and bare fronds emit a glorious aroma of pine laced with cinnamon. Around the base of the tree, I spy the array of presents wrapped in … newspaper.

'The table looks stunning,' I enthuse to Nahal, who comes back carrying a large bowl of saffron flavoured rice. She's followed by Greg, bearing a steaming bowl of eggplant stew.

'I must admit, it does look tempting.' GG looks on, misty eyed at the sumptuous spread.

I look at GG and sigh. Certainly does.

'The red colour in these fruits symbolises the crimson hues of dawn and glow of life,' says Nahal, placing her bowl amid the pomegranates.

'And these are my pina-*kale*-adas. I made them from waste kale.' Rich offers a tray of thick green drinks. 'Great, aren't they?' He hands the glasses round. 'Equally great that everyone took in my message on the notice board about wrapping all the pressies in newspaper. It's unbelievable that the British use two hundred and twenty-seven thousand miles of wrapping paper each Christmas. That's enough to stretch nine times around the world.'

I clutch my Chloe bag firmly. It contains the pressies I'd wrapped in fetching Liberty print paper, and which I'd better now keep out of sight. Nahal asks everyone to sit down and then tells us, 'On *Shab-e-yalda*, it is traditional for the oldest member of the family to start the meal by slicing the watermelon. That is to thank God for the previous year's blessings and pray for prosperity in the coming year.'

'That's you, Deb, isn't it?' Nat laughs.

'Isn't she a hoot?' I smile across the table at GG and knock back my pina-*kale*-ada. Well, you know what they say about getting your five a day.

'Let me do the honours.' GG leans forward and takes the knife from Nahal. Cupping the fruit, I watch him slice into the taut green skin to expose the soft pink flesh. A rivulet of juice trickles down onto my hand as he hands me the first slice. The rest is shared around the table.

'I do love watermelon. It's so sweet and juicy, yet cool on the tongue.' He stares at me as he takes a bite out of his slice. I have to look away from the droplets of juice glistening on his lips, as red and luscious as the fruit's flesh.

'Next,' says Nahal, 'we always break open the pomegranates.'

Jafar jumps up, grabs a pomegranate, and starts to tear it apart with his hands. 'This is my favourite bit!'

'The breaking apart of the fruit is meant to symbolise rebirth and bring joy to people's lives.' Nahal laughs as a myriad of pips burst from Jafar's pomegranate and fly across the table.

'If we want more joy, why don't we try the appetiser Sacha made for us as her gift?' Rich suggests, while unveiling a large plate of crudités with soft cheese and what looks like caviar. I feel a rumbling in my tummy. 'Critter canapés,' says Greg. 'These look tasty.'

'Wild black ants are a traditional edible insect species in China.' Fred picks up the note from the top of the plate and reads it out loud: 'They are rich in nutrients, helping to regulate the immune system, and are anti-fatigue and anti-ageing …'

'Anti-ageing? Did you hear that, Deb?' Nat hands me the plate. 'Try a celery stick topped with goats cheese and wild black ant sprinklings.'

'Er … in a minute. I've got to retrieve my pressies I've stored in the confession box.' I jump up.

'Chefs say that ants taste like seared lemon rind.' Rich tucks into one.

'I love crunchy things.' Henry Junior licks his lips, which are covered in a residue of green drink. He scoops up a handful and stuffs them into his mouth.

'I'm, er, sure the children would love another song,' offers GG, having also declined the canapés, starts handing out song lyrics.

I walk over to the confession box and pull back the curtain. Quickly starting to unwrap my pressies from their lovely Liberty's wrapping, I'm relieved when a loud singing starts to drown out the sound of ripping paper.

'While shepherds washed their socks by night …' I hear Nat bellow out her version of the Christmas carol before she stops and apologises to GG.

But having also shared a good deal of the festive spirit—in all senses of the word—he just sings the same words back to her. I quickly hide my wrapping paper under the seat, and stuff the pressies back into my bag. 'Glad tidings of great joy I bring, to you and all mankind … Thus spake the seraph, and forthwith appeared a shining thong …'

'That's a bit rude, isn't it?' Nat puts an arm around me as I return to her side. 'An angel wearing a thong?'

'I don't think that's what he sang …'

A round of applause breaks out in the room, as Nahal appears at the table carrying a large, cooked bird. 'Our celebration goose,' she announces proudly.

'Seven geese a-laying,' Nat chortles. 'I wouldn't mind a bit of …'

'That goose reminds me,' Greg says. 'Over Christmas, I'm staying in Snettisham, where the mudflats are a roosting site for forty thousand pink-footed geese.' He tucks a napkin into the neck of his shirt. 'It's incredible seeing their feeding forays into the hinterland of rough grazing fields against a technicolour sunrise.'

'Is that a dead goose? No, Daddy, no!' Chloe sobs, looking at the dish.

'And this is my special rump of venison,' says Rich, carrying a haunch of cooked meat to table. 'And not just any old venison, but it's a roadkill. It was found off the A406. I swapped it for …'

'Dear God!' GG downs his kale cocktail in one.

'Doe, a deer …' Henry Junior pops out from under the table. His whole face is now smeared with green.

'Rudolph has been run over! No Daddy!' Chloe screams.

'Done right, the traditional hunting and killing of wild game is as natural and moral as having sex.' Rich shrugs his shoulders. 'Roadkill is a depressing by-product of our modern high-speed travel, but cooking it means the animal didn't die in vain.'

'What's sex, Daddy?' asks Chloe.

I change the subject away from roadkill cuisine. 'Why don't we let the birds, er, rest, and start to open some pressies?' I walk over to the tree.

'Rudolph doesn't need to rest; he's dead!' Henry Junior laughs hysterically.

'Henry Junior's pissed!' Nat, ever, the diplomat, shares her observation.

I pick up a present. 'Oh look, Chloe, here's one with *your* name on it!'

A few minutes later, Rich starts handing out *his* presents: a handmade owl-nesting box for Jafar, and jars of homemade fennel seed toothpaste, rosemary mint mouthwash and elderberry cough medicine for the adults. GG walks up to me. 'I'm so sorry Deborah, I didn't realise we were exchanging gifts.' He takes my hand.

'All we want from you, Father Guy, is your blessing for our Good Life project,' I hear myself mutter the words, but my body belies them by erupting in a strange heat, at his soft touch.

'And here's my present to you.' Nat begrudgingly shoves a present in my hand, forcing GG to remove his.

My present is wrapped in a page of the Daily Mail. I tear off the paper to find a roll of purple labels, on which the words 'Stitch 'n bitch' have been screen printed in white. Nat says, 'Doubtless a waste of time, but I had the name of your new clothes brand printed on these hemp labels. Great name, isn't it?'

GG knocks back the glass of homemade blackberry wine Rich has handed to him.

'Oh Nat, I love the idea of the labels.' I refrain from commenting on the name. 'Again, I'm so sorry for not telling you about Yale. I can't wait to get sewing, and, er, use these.'

'Alright, I forgive you. Now, talking of sewing, I've seen you hard at it. Time for you to hand out your pressies!' Nat laughs and grabs my bag. She hands out my gifts, as Nahal calls us back to the table to eat, and Rich starts carving up the meat, which, after all the festive spirit, we are all surprisingly ravenous for. Having filled our plates with saffron rice, aubergine stew, and what I hate to admit is very juicy, tender meat, we all tuck in.

I smile when a while later, Nahal puts on the pinny I made for her and does a twirl. Nat seems less than thrilled with hers. Everyone laughs at the snug I have made for Old Spot, while Greg looks chuffed with his silky cravat, printed with images of birds made from a recycled curtain I found in the local Oxfam shop.

'What a wonderful and thoughtful gift.' Rich hugs me, as he looks at the winter coat I've made him from the body of a yellow 1970's ski jacket and the sleeves of a chunky jumper. 'In the old days, gifts were objects that carried stories, just like this.'

'My Dad's giving me a fifty-pound note!' Henry Junior shouts out. Instead of joining us at the table, he's practising with the bow and arrow that Rich, in perhaps not the most well considered of gifts, has made for him.

'The modern numerical manifestation of our ideas about money: credit and debt, is no less of a made-up story than that of Father Christmas,' Fred tuts. 'In short, money—like Santa—is just a myth that's been made up.'

'Daddy, that horrible man says Santa's not real,' Chloe sobs again, and is quickly given a big hug by a fraught looking Michael.

'Who bloody asked Furrowed Fred to our Christmas party?' Nat mutters to me.

'My dad told me Santa wasn't real when I was three!' shouts Henry Junior, running up to the table and firing an arrow. A splattering of pomegranate pips flies up and hits GG in the face.

'Of course there's a Santa,' GG sighs and wipes his face. 'Santa exists as certainly as love and devotion. The most real things in the world are those that none of us can see, just believe in. It's all a question of faith.' He looks across the table to Nahal, who smiles and nods her head in agreement. Chloe, seemingly mollified, jumps up and goes to try on the woodland fairy costume I made her.

'Amen to that,' says Rich. 'I want to live in a world where you give for no other reason than to help someone, to make them happy.' He lifts up the coat I've made for him and smiles at me. 'Instead of seeing the world through the current lens of how much can I get,' Rich continues, 'let's change it to how much can I *give*.'

GG stands and walks over to the pulpit. 'Mother Nature, help us transcend the world of things …' He sighs and shakes his head.

'Right, you lot,' Nat jumps up. 'The only transcending we are going to be doing from now on is on the dance floor.' She grabs a startled Fred, and drags him over to centre of the room, where all the desks have been pushed aside. She presses a button on a laptop, and Rod Stewart's Christmas album bursts into life.

'He knows if you've been good or bad, so be bad for goodness sake,' Nat sings out as she forces Fred to dance.

'Before dancing, do you fancy a spot of fresh air, Dorito-Deborah?' GG says, looking slightly embarrassed. He knocks back another glass of wine in one gulp.

'On the first day of January, my true love threw out for me …'—Rich has thrown his arms around us and is singing loudly—'one billion Christmas cards, two million turkeys, packaging from twenty-five million Christmas puddings, seventy-four million mince pies, and six million sparkle-less Christmas trees!' Swigging back his homemade cherry brandy, he laughs and disappears off.

GG leads me to the front door across the pop-up dance floor, where Nat is twirling a still startled Fred around in a length of pink tinsel. We pass Nahal and Jafar doing the twist with Greg. Even Michael and Chloe are joining in the fun, while trying to avoid Henry Junior's arrows, which are zipping around all over the place.

We walk outside. Opposite the church, the faded neon lights from the Kentish Town Delight flicker on an off with their promise of doner kebabs and chips. A solitary car snakes its way down the high street, already bringing that Christmas promise of stillness, what some would call, melancholy. I smile as I see that someone has wrapped a recycled paper chain around our gargoyle, and likewise our enchanted, threatened tree. Thanks to Pippa and the Tree Musketeers, it has still been saved from the axe. For the moment.

'Well, that certainly was an interesting meal, wasn't it?' says GG, slightly slurring his words. He bends down to pick up a wet leaf. 'I love it when the air is ripe with a dewy petri-chor, don't you?' He lifts the leaf to my nose; I breathe in the lovely petri-what not -something, sweet and aromatic, anyway. I look up and him and smile.

'I, er, think you've got something green stuck between your teeth.' He points to my mouth.

Mortified, I lift my hand and pull out a messy lump that has wedge itself in my teeth. More holy kale than holy grail, I can't help but punning to myself even while so embarrassed.

'So, Deborah …' Our eyes meet, and simultaneously look up at the sprig of carrot and beetroot top that's standing in for mistletoe above the entrance to the church.

My uncontrollable mind tries to remind my racing heart that I am a completely drunk, married woman whose husbondage has just given up a job at Yale for me … Well, when I say given it up for me, Stu did admit that the real reason he didn't take the job was he that thought Yale would be too Ivy League for him. And didn't laugh when I replied that I was more of an ivy leaf, than Ivy League, gal!

As GG leans towards me, I once again remind myself that this is not a Netflix movie, or a chick-lit kindle read. Surely, it's just a wild goose chase, another example of my over-active mind, but …

JANUARY

CHAPTER 10

The Big Freeze(e)r

New Year resolution numero uno: I will never watch or read rom-coms again. I am a highly intelligent woman who henceforth will only watch highbrow documentaries.

It turned out that the only thing Father Guy wanted to share with me under the carrot-top mistletoe, was the fact that he had heard all about Old Spot being on stage at the Forum the other week, and he had seen all three thousand photo retweets on his Twitter feed. Furthermore, he had received a less than salutary health-and-safety letter from the CEO of the mega company that owns the Forum, and a complaint from the Lidl's manager about Rich's 'repatriation' of food from their bins. It's a knock-out punch with Nat's dubious campaign manager, Bradley's fists all over it. GG then informed me that the bishop was due to visit in two weeks' time, and the fate of the Good Life project rested in what he considered to be my sensible hands. Sensible is not the word my amatory mind had longed to hear.

In any case, my hands—sensible or not—are busy with some-thing else. A beautician at 'Cute-icles,' the newly opened nail parlour in Kentish Town, is filing my nails. Their varying, broken lengths are the result of a rather un-ladylike fall on the slopes, during what was otherwise a blissful New Year's skiing break with husbondage, Stu, and son, James, from which we had returned late last night. In hindsight, perhaps the rose-tinted Ray-Ban sunglasses—my Christ-mas pressie from Stu—might have contributed just a tiny bit to me mistaking a red run for a blue run. Hereafter, they will only be used for off-piste activities.

'Isn't this place fab? I can so identify with that poster on the wall!' A woman having her nails polished at the next table bursts out laughing as she points up at a poster. It reads: 'I knew I was a nail addict when my phone auto-corrected man to "mani!"'

My neighbour returns to a conversation she is having with a friend sitting on the other side of her. 'Anyway, isn't it sweet of darling Hen to put my name on top of the waiting list. There are only two penthouses in the property plans.'

'I hear there's even going to be an underground car park. God knows it's impossible to park in this high street,' her friend says.

'And I've heard there is talk of an indoor swimming pool.'

'Yes, it's about time Kentish Town high street had a makeover. It's so grotty.'

A frivolous thought: I must try that cerulean polish the women are having their nails painted with. Then a serious one: surely just a coincidence but sounds as if the women are talking about a penthouse in a new block of flats planned for this very high street. And 'Hen' couldn't be short for 'Henry,' could it? The very same Henry Smarmy Smythe who had been spotted talking in the pub with Thomas Montjoy, the property developer, before Christmas?

'Anyway, there's another public meeting about it in March. So, newly polished fingers crossed.' The women laugh and continue to chatter away about which gloss finish to choose. A short while later, having asked Pueng, the beautician, to quickly apply one coat of the blue polish, I pay my bill, and hurry out into the street.

I feel an overwhelming sense of protectiveness as I look down the road and see the spire of the Good Life church appear out from a leaden skyline. Wondering if I should tell Nat and Rich about the conversation I have just overheard, I realise I have missed my new friends over the past two weeks.

I walk briskly on, shivering as I look around the empty high street, which I must admit does look rather run-down. At least a quarter of the shops are closed, their shutters down, never to reopen. The word 'Hopeless' has even been graffitied on one wall. The card and gift shop that had been there forever has now gone, the local fishmonger is up for sale and even the local library has closed. What,

I wonder, is the purpose of a high street in these click-bait online shopping days? It certainly needs some new imagining. What I do know is that another new luxury apartment block is not the answer.

I smile as I see a flurry of activity outside the Good Life. The church's stone walls may be crumbling, and it may be absolutely freezing outside, but there is a real sense of animation in the air. I walk up to read a painted sign: 'Banish those new year's blues and go green.' I rub my eyes as I stare at what appears to be a fridge standing in the middle of the driveway, surrounded by a yellow fence.

'Ah, here you are, Deb.' Rich, wearing a snorkel mask and the orange ski jacket I made for him for Christmas, comes up and gives me a bear hug.

'What on earth is this fridge doing here?'

'It's our People's Fridge, Deb. A public fridge in which local residents and businesses can leave spare food for those who need it. And those who need it take the food for free! We're quickly finishing getting it all set up as snow is forecast.' He looks up to the grey sky, which is now flecked with a pink hue.

'But where on earth did you get the fridge from? And what will Father Guy and the bishop have to say about it?' I open the gate of the fence around the fridge and go through to look in the fridge. It's empty, apart from one cheese roll.

'Here are some stats that'll leave a bad taste in your mouth.' Rich lifts a bright orange wooden sign saying, "People's Fridge," and starts to nail it to the fence. 'UK households discard an average of twenty-four edible meals a month, but at the same time, eight and a half million people in the UK live in food insecurity. With this fridge, we are doing our bit to stop this in Kentish Town. Anyway, how was your Christmas?'

'Er, you know, quiet and …'

'I know you when you've knocked back a few glasses of glüh-wein, Deb, and you're anything but quiet!' Nat strides over to us. She bends down to slowly wipe off a speck of dust off *my* Ugg boots—the very same boots I had to also 'loan' her in return for her not mentioning to Rich and the team about my flyaway New Year's break.

'Isn't our People's Fridge amazing, Deb? I've put you down on the rota to clean it twice a week.'

Clean another fridge every other week, I hear. Well, forget that thought I had only half an hour a go about missing my friends.

'And don't you just love this yellow picket fence? Our new women's carpentry group made it out of pallet scaff boards?' Nat pats the fence proprietarily.

'It's great because it makes it look like the fridge isn't just some white goods discarded in the street,' adds Rich.

Unnoticeable white goods? Hardly. As well as the fridge and yellow picket fence, there's a bright blue plastic cable tubing attached to the back of the fridge and trailing on the ground all the way to the side door entrance of the church.

'I can see you've spotted the power cable supply into the church,' says Rich. 'Of course, it's only a temporary measure until we work out how to bring little Leroy's solar panel design to life.'

'Sorry you missed the women's carpentry workshop today.' Nat lifts my hand. 'But I see you've swapped one kind of nail for another!' She laughs at my newly manicured cerulean nails. 'Got those January blues, eh?' She links my arm. 'Anyway, you've gotta come and see the chicken coop we've made for our adopted battery chicks in the back garden. Me and the girls from our new singing-and-hammering power rangers group are building it all. You've arrived just in time to start digging. Hope you bought your gloves?'

Little Leroy's solar panel, singing power rangers, adopted ex-battery chickens, and least likely of all, me digging with newly manicured nails? Am I really hearing this fantasy?

'Yoo hoo, gang!' Sacha has arrived, pushing a shopping trolley laden with goodies.

My worries about council approval, health and safety, and the fridge's provenance—which I hope is not the result of Nat's more questionable appropriation resources—will have to wait.

'Happy New Year to you, Debo! Isn't our peeps' fridge fab?' She blows me an extravagant air kiss. 'It was such a kind donation from my parents. They got the idea after they heard about the similar community fridges in Japan and Brixton, and the solidarity fridge in Spain.' She starts to load her haul of sandwiches and bags of fruit and veg into our fridge.

'After all, it's human nature to want to share food,' says Marg who is following behind, lugging two heavy Tesco's carrier bags full of food.

'This way, everybody can give.' Sacha lifts out two punnets of soft strawberries, which are clearly on the turn, from her trolley.

'And everybody from food insecure families to peckish builders can receive!' Marg chuckles. 'But seriously, it's not about charity, but fighting against food waste and recovering the value of food products.'

'These bollix strawbs are from Egypt.' Rich grabs the fruit. 'What a shameful waste of resources to produce these and ship them over.' He shakes his head. 'I mean who needs feckin' strawberries from Egypt in January?'

I feel my cheeks blush an unseasonable strawberry shade as I recall the two-for-one punnets I bought from M&S this morning.

'Look what Gregg's the bakers have given us!' Michael rushes up to us carrying a box of croissants and other goodies.

He's immediately joined by Pippa, toting two Sainsbury's shopping bags. 'Great news, Sainsburys are willing to supply us with regular surplus food, so you won't have to go skip-diving, Rich,' she says.

Now Mr Pang arrives on scene. 'This all helps build trust in an area.' He adds his appraisal, before walking up to the fridge and removing a cheese roll. 'It's great that everybody can help themselves.'

'So, what can go in the fridge?' I ask.

'Folks can donate vegetables, bread and packaged goods, but no raw meat, fish or eggs,' says Sacha. 'I won't add any critter cuisine until after our Pestival later this year! But there again, I have been making some very nice ...'

'No!' we all shout in unison and burst out laughing.

'Anyway, Mr Pang, dear, I am so happy you're enjoying your second helping.' Marg raises an eyebrow, as Mr Pang helps himself to an armful of iced buns. 'I do hope you're going to reciprocate?'

Our attention is diverted from Mr Pang's offering of the glace cherry from atop his bun when the serving hatch window on the Chip Fat Traveller's van slides open and Lucia pops her head out. 'We're well chuffed! Loads a shops have agreed to donate surplus food every week for our "Saturday souper van."'

'Yeah, it's our next Good Life enterprise. We'll be launching it the week after next.' Mouse appears behind her.

'Every Saturday, we're gonna park up behind Kentish Town station, and serve free hot soup made by Nahal at our Abundance Cafe. Anyone can have some.' Lucia lifts a painted sign.

'Get it? Souper as in soup!' Mouse points to the sign.

'I've put you down on this rota too. You'll be volunteering every two weeks!' Nat nudges me in the ribs and whispers none too quietly, 'Yes, we've been busy while you were on the slippery slopes— slippery in more ways than one, according to your Stu. He told me all about your bruised derrière!'

'And do read this,' says Marg, thrusting a leaflet in my hand. "It will tell you all about why we are adopting battery chickens.'

'Make a new feathered friend and show a factory-farmed animal just how great life can be,' I read on the leaflet. It goes on: 'Each year, millions of hens are condemned to a short, miserable existence in battery cages for the sake of cheap eggs. These hens, who are social and affectionate, have no quality of life, their world restricted to the size of an A4 sheet of paper.'

'As well as finding homes for hens, we need to educate the public on how to make a difference to hen welfare by checking food labels,' Marg continues to explain, as we all watch Mr Pang tuck into an egg-mayo sarnie.

'For example, did you know that increased consumer pressure has led to supermarkets switching to selling free-range eggs, and brands such as *Hellman's* now use free-range eggs in their mayonnaise,' Pippa says. 'We need more legal policy and questions that ...'

'Talking about questions, here's a good 'un: What did the mayonnaise say to the Peoples Fridge?' Nat interjects. 'Shut the door, I'm dressing!' She roars with laughter. 'Isn't that hilarious?'

At the delivery of her punchline, Mr Pang also explodes with laughter—*and* with an eruption of egg mayo that dribbles down his chin.

'By the way, Deb, you'll be pleased to hear I've also put your name down on the rota to clean the chicken coop twice a week!' Nat grins at me.

So now I've been put down to clean the Peoples Fridge once a week, to become a hen humanitarian cleaning out a coop twice a week, and to serve soup in a souper-van every other Saturday! Is there any point in me going home at all, or should I just move in here with Rich and … er…GG? No, stop it, Deb. I remind myself of my New Year's resolve to leave all fantasies and schemes to Nat.

'One more important question about the fridge.' My attention is drawn back to the fridge by Sacha. 'Can we put avocados in it?'

Nat shakes her head. 'I've heard that plastic surgeons are now claiming that the middle-class must-have brunch, avocado on sourdough, has led to a growth in knife injuries called, "avocado hand." Bet you've had it, Deb?'

'Talking of avocados, you know that we can't feed them to the chickens because they contain persin, which is toxic,' says Marg, as she walks past us to go inside the church.

Toxic is the very word that comes to mind when I follow Marg inside and bump into Henry Smarmy Smythe. 'Good break, Debo? Mine was marvellous. Me and some of the boys flew to Cancun for a long weekend. Very relaxing.'

'Ciao, Henry,' says Nat, rushing in behind me.

'Ciao, Bella.' Henry kisses her on the lips. 'I just popped in to see how things were going. Perhaps meet you in that nice little cocktail bar for a catch-up, Natalie, eh?' He winks at her.

'That would be lovely, Henry.' Nat flutters her eyelashes, which I can't help but notice have been tinted.

'Time you started calling me "Hen." All my girls do!' He laughs.

I bet they do, just like the two ladies I overhead in Cute-icles.

Nat continues to giggle and flirt with Henry, and I can hardly criticise her. Despite all her bravado, I know she has really been down in the dumps recently and very much missed Pete over Christmas.

Somehow, I don't have the heart to tell her about the conversation I overheard. Anyway, I've probably misinterpreted.

'Great news, everyone. The hens are arriving next Tuesday,' Marg calls out from her desk.

'Which are the only feckin' hens we want round here.' Rich, who is busily stirring a barrel of onions, which he is pickling, raises his swimming goggles to add his comment.

I breathe in the pungent smell and walk over to the Abundance Cafe. The usual old couple and a good smattering of other people sit sipping vegetable soup and snacking on Nahal's delicious taftoon bread, while listening to Greg give a talk on bird migration.

'One of the highlights of my twitching year is when the almighty swallows migrate back here in April,' Greg says. 'British swallows spend their winter in South Africa. They travel through western France, across the Pyrenees, down through eastern Spain into Morocco, and across the Sahara.'

I walk on over to look at the noticeboard, and giggle at the suggested activity: 'Interested in taking part in a world porridge-making championship? Winner to take home the golden spurtle.'

'Interested in sowing your oats, eh, Deb?' I squirm as Henry sneaks up and pats me on the shoulder.

'I notice that your name is not down here on the cleaning rotes for the coop or People's Fridge, Henry? Shall I lend you a pen?' I smirk, and head over to my sewing machine.

Sitting down behind my Singing singer, I remove the azure sari covering, and run my hand along the cast-iron body of the machine. I'm excited by the thought that it's time to get sewing. A new year, a new inspiration. I smile over all the goodwill and positivity surrounding me. Such a marked contrast to the downbeat feeling in the high street. Of course, as yet, the Good Life project is not earning any real money and is heavily subsidised and totally reliant on the largesse of the church. But as I lift a pair of jeans out from my remnants box and start to unstitch the back pockets, I have a hunch that there *is* a profitable, ethical business idea out there waiting for us—a business with what Nat would doubtless call a new bottom line.

As if on cue, Nat appears by my side. 'Ah, here you are, Deb. It's time for a couple of hours of gardening before the laughter yoga session. While we're talking downward dog,' she laughs, 'you've gotta come outside and look at the chicken coop.'

I put the jeans and their de-stitched derrières to one side, along with any notion of participating in gardening or laughter yoga, put on my coat, and follow Nat outside.

In the rather bleak looking garden, we're greeted by the lovely sound of a group of women mid song: *'Goole, goole, barf, miad …'* At the far end of the garden, beyond the overgrown beds, Nahal and several women wearing trousers, long coats and brightly coloured headscarves are singing whilst hammering nails into lengths of wood. Next to them, several blokes in Charles Wilson hats and high-vis vests, pour concrete into wooden frames to form the shape of an outhouse: our chicken coop.

'Deb, how lovely to see you.' Nahal puts down her hammer and gives me a hug. 'These are my friends. They have come to help build our chicken coop.'

'Meet our singing Power Rangers, I told you about.' Nat lifts a giant mallet and with brute force hammers a length of wood into the ground.

'Sarde hava, zemestoone …' the women continue to sing.

'What are you singing about?' I ask one of the women who is called Anousha.

'It is a famous Iranian children's song: "Ball, ball, snowball, it snows, it is winter. The boundless cold, makes our bodies tremble …" *Zemestoone* is the Iranian word for winter.' She smiles and takes my hand.

'OMG, it *is* starting to snow!' Nat shrieks with joy. We all look up, transfixed by the enchanting, delicate snowflakes that, sure enough, are falling from the sky. Large, downy snowflakes land on the beds, soft white powder coats the bare branches, and a thick blanket of white paints the paths. We watch in silence as the snow gets heavier. Within moments, our derelict garden has been transformed into a winter wonderland.

'Snowflakes are dancing, as they come spiralling down, like tiny ballerinas all dressed in white gowns,' Anousha breaks the silence by singing out in the sweetest voice.

'Sorry team, the garden clearance will have to wait,' Nat shrugs. 'Unless we all think it's a good idea to clear away the snow?' She grins at me, and bends down to pick up a snowball. With great precision, she aims the snowball at Rich, who has come outside and now stands in front of me. He ducks down—and the snowball hits me straight in the face.

'Nat, I'll get you for that ...'

I wipe the freezing snow from my face and listen to Anousha and the Power Rangers continue to sing their catchy chorus joined in by the chaps from Charles Wilson. I can't help but smile at how today, from launching the People's Fridge to frolicking in the snow, has certainly been a case of defrosting in many more ways than one. I roll a snowball, aim at Nat, and throw.

CHAPTER 11

New Pecking Order

I t's a week later, and the snow has magically disappeared, as quickly as it arrived. We are in the garden for the second day, labouring away. All visions of spending a day steaming over cups of coffee with GG, while designing the garden have vanished like, well, steam.

Instead, we're bent over, weeding on all fours. The beads of sweat I wipe away are caused not only by the hours of physical exertion, but also my dismay of not having worn a long coat to hide my generous January-comfort-food-engorged-derrière. I'm all too aware of it as I turn to watch GG digging the bed behind me.

'Why did the chicken cross the path?' asks Nat.

'Because it could!' chuckles Marg, as she effortlessly weeds the pathway, while I stab away at unbudging weeds from the impenetrable soil.

'Keep diggin', girls,' Nat continues, barking out orders as she sips her tea. 'We've got to clear the pathway before the chickens arrive, and the garden has to look perfect for the bishop's visit the week after next.'

With a very stiff back, I stand up cautiously and look around. I must admit we *have* made good progress in two days: the garden has been cleared, beds have been dug over, and we've finished the impressive wooden chicken coop built by our singing power rangers—aided by the Chas Wilson chaps. There's even a nesting box for small birds attached to the tree made from an old boot glued onto a piece of wood. I smile as I hear our tawny owl hoots, clearly in approval.

At the other end of the garden, Michael, aided by Anousha,

Nahal's friend with the lovely voice, are nailing the final length of chicken wire that surrounds half of the chicken coop. Jafar lifts a wooden sign on which the words: 'Cluckingham Palace' have been painted in green, and nails it to the entrance. Downing tools, we all break out in a round of applause.

'What on earth are you doing, Rich?' The clapping is stopped abruptly by the sound of Nat's holler. Rich is waving his infamous orange underpants up in the air.

'I'm burying my pants,' he explains nonchalantly, as he digs a hole in the soil.

'Burying your *what*?' I blurt out.

'Surprised you managed to prise them off your arse,' Nat chuckles. 'Bet it's the first time those pants have seen the light of day for months!'

'I'll have you know that the best way to test soil is to bury a pair of underpants for two months. If the pants are exhumed intact, then the soil is sterile and lifeless. But if only the elastic waistband remains, the soil is thriving.' So saying, Rich places his pants in the hole, and fills it with soil.

I place all thoughts of ants in orange pants to the back of my mind.

'Gonna bury one of your thongs, Deb?' Nat winks at me.

'I do not know what you're talking about, Nat, I certainly don't wear …'

But I do see GG blush. My new year's resolution of not indulging in romantic, sexy GG daydreams are now as uprooted as the garden. What adorable pink cheeks he has, I sigh to myself.

'So, Father Guy, apart from a monastic four-bed potager based on the cross, what else to we have to incorporate into our design?' I ask, trying to change the subject to more ascetic considerations.

'Oh, is that the time?' GG, his cheeks still aflame, looks desperately at his watch. 'Must dash.' And so he does.

Marg pipes up, 'Well, you've got to leave room for Old Spot to wallow. Pigs do like to wallow, you know.'

That sets me off on another daydream … wallowing in the mud with GG, my wispy chiffon thong the lone element protecting me from the sticky, warm, terra-not-so-firma. I feel a hot flush envelop me.

'I discovered a rhubarb plant growing at the back of the garden and I have turned it into a cordial,' Nahal announces, as she appears carrying a tray of drinks. '*Shavat-e- rivas-* rhubarb sherbet—is a popular sweet drink in Iran.'

'This will cool you down, Deb!' Mind-reader Nat winks at me.

'Hallo, hallo …' This authoritative voice certainly cools me down and brings me back firmly to earth. A sturdy-looking woman in a navy-blue anorak is striding purposefully into the garden, pushing a large, covered wire container on wheels.

'My name is Yoke, and I am here with your chickens.' She walks up to us. 'But first I will need to inspect your coop.'

'Chicken? Yolk? What kind of name is that?' Nat whispers in my ear. 'What about "Egg?"'

'Behave, Nat!' I give her a gentle kick.

'Welcome, Yoke.' I shake the newcomer's hand. 'Where are you from?'

'The Netherlands. My name might be pronounced: "Yoke," but it's spelled with a "J" -Joke!' She pauses, obviously used to hearing a punchline.

'Oh, good joke, Joke!' Nat bursts out laughing. 'The yoke's on us! Have you heard this one? Why did the chicken join the band? Coz it had drumsticks!'

Is that a … er, 'fowl' look Rich is giving Nat? No pun intended! He's certainly glaring as he grabs her hand and drags her to the end of the garden, leaving Marg and me to guide Joke around the coop.

Some twenty minutes later, Joke, having ticked off the requisite requirements on the first page on her clipboard, looks up at us. 'Well done, this is most acceptable. You have given each chicken four square feet to roam, so your coop of six feet by twelve feet will accommodate all three of the chickens I have bought with me today. I am also pleased to see you have surrounded one half of your coop with chicken wire for ventilation, and, of course, you have laid straw for laying eggs. You will next need to build a perch for the chickens to sleep on. We now need to consider their emotional requirements.'

@NTS: Emotional requirements. Wonder where GG disappeared off to so quickly?

'You may not know,' Joke continues, 'but there are sixteen million caged hens in the UK. Each chicken has a personality that you can build a relationship with, just as with any other pet.'

'How about setting up a website to match battery chickens with new loving families,' Nat grins. 'We could call it *Thatch-dot-com?*'

'Not to be confused with Match-dot-com, your favourite website!' Rich scoffs. 'Any old cock will do for you, eh, Nat? I've seen you with that Henry Smarmy Smythe.'

'If you are ready for me to continue,' Joke eyes Nat and Rich sternly, 'when the chickens are first let out you may need to encourage them, as they have been in artificial light for up to eighteen hours a day. Your hens will be slightly shell shocked.'

'Shell shocked?—great pun!' Nat chuckles, displaying little emotional maturity.

Rich tuts, 'I doubt that the doctor who coined the term "shell shock" during the First World War would appreciate you turning the disorder into a laughing matter.'

'As I was saying,' Joke sighs, 'chickens form strong social groups and establish a pecking order within a few days of being introduced to each other. Once each chicken knows its place in the flock, they should all get on fine.'

Bit like the pecking order here, I think. I can see Nat look at Rich hatefully, as she continues to order everyone about, while Rich grins derisively back at her. Marg, meanwhile, quickly finishes weeding the final bit of pathway, aided by Nahal and Jafar, as Michael and Anousha stand chatting beside the tree with the nesting boot attached to it.

'I think the most important thing in establishing our new chicken society, as indeed with society in general, is that it is egalitarian.' This philosophical observation comes from Fred, his hand placed on his chin.

'*Egg-alitarian!* That's the first time I've ever heard you crack a joke, Fred!' Nat nudges him in the ribs.

'So, team Good Life, time to meet your new comrades.' Joke

whips off the cover from the wire container she has wheeled into the garden. She opens the door, and three flummoxed-looking chickens stumble out.

'Meet the flockers! As in "Meet the Fockers," the Robert De Niro film! Get it?' Nat laughs.

I look at feather bare chickens and feel my eyes well up with tears.

'Don't worry,' Joke smiles, 'after a couple of weeks their feathers will quickly blossom.'

'Oh, the magic of seeing a caged hen look up to the sky for the first time,' Marg cries out, dabbing her eyes. 'The joy of watching them feel the grass beneath their feet, of seeing their pallid bodies catch the first rays of sun ...'

Mmm ... Marg might be getting carried away over the thread-bare chicks who stand rooted to the spot besides their cage, but I'm left wondering about the lack of grass in the garden, and sun in the sky. It doesn't stop Nahal rushing over and cuddling one of the chickens, or Jafar joining in with a stroke.

Rich smiles, 'It's amazing how quickly the chicken's instincts return. They'll be scratching around and sunbathing with their wings stretched out before you know it!'

'This is Brutus. Unfortunately, he's a rooster who's been trau-matised, and has a habit of jabbing anyone who gets too close in the back of the legs with his spurs.' Joke points to one of the chickens.'

@NTS: Et tu Brute, I look down at the sharp horn-like protru-sions on the chicken's legs.

'This is all so exciting, eh, children? What do you want to call these two chickens?' Marg asks Jafar and Chloe.

'How about Yolko Ono!' suggests Rich. 'That's Yoko with an "L" of course?'

'That's quite a good one from you, Rich!' Nat chuckles.

'I would like to call this one Sophie, after my best friend at school.' Chloe points to one of the confused looking chickens.

'Would that be Sophie Lor-hen?' asks Nat. She and Rich burst out laughing.

'Sophie, that is a lovely name. It was also the name of *my* best friend at school,' Anousha smiles at Michael.

Chloe is also smiling—for the first time, as she strokes Sophie.

'Here's a question for you, children?' Joke asks. 'What is the difference between a hen and a chicken?'

Funny, I'd been dying to ask that question myself.

'A hen is an adult female chicken; chicken being the general term for the bird,' Joke continues. 'Male chickens are known as roosters, cocks, or cockerels, and castrated roosters are called capons.'

@NTS: Reconsider the capon in Armagnac sauce I was planning for next Sat's dinner party I'm hosting for Stu's colleagues and their perfect wives. The idea of castrated rooster suddenly makes my gourmet recipe sound less than appealing.

'Of course, hens do love to have a cock around,' Rich gibes at Nat, 'if only for a sense of protection and leadership.'

'And they love to bloody crow,' Nat snaps back.

'Yes, a rooster can crow at any time of the day, depending on his personality,' Joke adds.

Just then, my attention is diverted by another personality. It's Old Spot, who has wandered out into the garden, and is now sniffing madly around the base of the oak tree in the corner next to where Jafar is standing. He burrows his snout deep into the soil and his front legs kicks wildly at the loosened earth.

'What on earth's wrong with Old Spot?' I cry out. 'Is he on heat?'

'He looks like he's trying to exhume something,' says Rich, intrigued, as Old Spot's flap in a frenzy and his snout tunnels a foot deep into the soil.

Nat joins us. 'What's that black knobbly thing he's rooting out?'

Black and knobbly?

'It's only an old, shrivelled acorn, but I must say it's a giant one.' Nat lifts it up and goes to throw it into our makeshift compost bin.

'Oh my god, stop!' I rush over and grab the item from Nat. I lift it to my nose and breathe in its pungent aroma. Its earthy bouquet is so intense that I'm transported to a dank green wood; a forest populated with ancient trees, nymphs, and mythical creatures. The strangely hypnotic smell is not, I realise, from a shrivelled acorn.

'This is a truffle!' I look up at everyone. 'It all makes sense: the pig sniffing like mad, the truffle buried so deep.

'But truffles don't grow in bloody England,' Nat jeers.

'Yes, yes, they do. These days it's mostly in Wiltshire, but wild ones were once common in Britain. Trouble is, they're now rare because of modern farming methods, and loss of ancient woodland.' The words tumble out of my mouth. 'The finest black truffles come from France, particularly the Dordogne in the south, where they're called Diamonds of Périgord. They're exquisite from December to March.'

'Well spotted, Deb!' Nat slaps me on the back. 'I so knew our subscription to Country Life magazine would pay off one day!'

Our subscription? Oh, why did she have to mention my guilty pleasure—my secret subscription to the landed-gentry-land-grab-bing mag—just as GG, walks back into the garden? What will he think of me? I glare at Nat.

'In case you don't realise it, I get the magazine out of your recy-cling bin after you throw it away every week!' Nat says, noncha-lantly. 'I must have missed the week that truffles were featured. But as I said, well done, Deb, your aspirations of grandeur have paid off for once!'

I hiss, 'Natalie, you have no right to go through my bins. We need to talk.' I grit my teeth as GG walks up to us. 'But right now, what's important is *this* little beauty.' I cusp the diamond of truffle carefully in my palm, as Nahal, Michael and Chloe gather round. 'Just smell it everyone. The aroma is totally unique.' I pass it round.

Nahal takes the truffle and places it to her nose. 'It smells of exotic flowers.'

'I think it has the scent of warm velvety earth,' says Rich.

'Daddy, this smells like that dark chocolate you like,' Chloe giggles.

'I think it smells a bit like old socks,' Nat says, taking her turn. 'And Rich's pants are more than enough of a bad aroma for me for one day.'

'Let me tell you what it really smells of …' I look at them all. 'And that is *cash*! Truffles are one of the most expensive fungi on the planet. They are highly prized by top chefs for their exquisite flavour. The wholesale prices for winter truffles -' I go on, excited, 'can exceed a thousand pounds a kilo!'

'Did you hear that?—one thousand quid!' Nat shrieks and jumps up and down. The flummoxed chickens are suddenly jolted into action. Brutus, Sophie, and Yolko Ono race towards us, with their heads bobbing and wings flapping. They are closely followed by a startled Joke.

'The question is how the hell did we grow this truffle here? And how can we grow more?' asks Nat. Then she looks over to Old Spot and notices he has uprooted another two truffles. She runs across and picks them up.

I shake my head. 'All I know is that a truffle is the fruiting body of fungus that grows on the root systems of trees—particularly oak, like this one.' I point to the tree. 'They take years to grow and are absolutely incredible.'

'Well, it seems that my Old Spot is a bit of a hero!' Marg exclaims. The hero, Old Spot, having had enough truffle digging, waddles over to one of the beds and lays down in the soil. 'He is our very own truffle hog.'

'What's all the excitement about?' asks GG, coming over to us.

'Oh my God, we've discovered truffles growing in our garden!' Without realising what I'm doing, I throw my arms around him. 'They're probably worth over five hundred pounds each. That's fifteen hundred pounds already. With the bishop's visit in two weeks, this bounty could not have come at a better time. I, er ...' Mortified by my inappropriate, spontaneous gesture, I quickly remove my arms, which seem to be clenched around his strong shoulders, and hand him the truffle.

'As I have always said, the Lord will always guide you; he will satisfy your needs.' GG holds the truffle to his nose, closes his eyes, and takes a languid sniff.

'Did you hear that, Deb?' Nat winks at me. 'The lord will always satisfy your needs.'

'Talking of which, it's well known that truffles are the culinary counterpart of sex—they're an aphrodisiac!' Rich raises his eyebrows and winks back at Nat. 'Let me have another sniff.' He grabs one of the truffles from her.

Short gasps of pleasure are coming from GG as he breathes in the aroma, his eyes still closed. I feel a warm sensation building in the pit of my stomach.

'According to researchers in West Germany ...'—Fred starts to read some internet info from his phone—'truffles contain large quantities of a substance also synthesised in the testes of boars, which is secreted into their saliva when they court females. The same musky odour which is related to human sexual attractiveness.'

I lift a truffle to my nose, breathe in, and join GG in closing my eyes. I don't want to break the spell. I try to ignore furrowed Fred's prosaic banter and Joke's odd comment that I should look behind me.

Suddenly, I feel a sharp pain in the back of my leg. I open my eyes to see Brutus digging his spurs into me—and adding a vicious bite. The garden seems to spin round. I topple over. The last sound I hear is Nat's giggling that there was certainly a new pecking order in the garden.

All goes black—as black as the finest Diamond of Perigord.

CHAPTER 12

Give Us Our Daily Bread ...

While it is said that caring for others leaves a warm glow in your heart, it doesn't mention anything about shielding the rest of your body from the perishing cold.

Feeling the icy wind forcing its way through my several layers of thermals, I hopelessly pull the green 'Souper Van' cape Mouse and Lucia gave me to wear, tightly around my puffer jacket. I'm desperate to take a break after hours of washing up soup bowls.

It all started at freezing-o-clock this morn, when Mouse and Lucia parked up the Chip Fat Travellers van behind Kentish Town station and turned it into a 'Souper Van.' We've been giving out bowls of soup ever since.

Looking out from the hatch, I'm amazed to see people still sitting in the freezing cold, sipping bowls of steaming vegetable soup. Mouse and Lucia continue to chat away with them on the benches covered with coloured cushions I made from recycled fabrics.

'Where's your wife then, Jim?' Mouse asks, as he sits playing chess with the elderly gent who is normally to be found at the Abundance Cafe with his wife.

'She's come down with a bad case of flu.' Jim moves a pawn.

'I'm sorry to hear that,' Lucia says, pausing from clearing up the table next to him. 'Why don't you take her a bowl of Nahal's soup?'

'Yeah, it's got more restorative power than a bowl of kryptonite!' Mouse laughs.

'That's a grand idea,' Jim smiles. With a triumphant move of his knight, he swipes Mouse's queen from the chess board. 'You've always got to protect your queen, my lad.'

'Excuse me, but is this Kentish Town?' An old gent in a thread-bare, torn, raincoat walks up to us. 'I seem to be a bit confused and lost.' He's shivering. His wrongly buttoned up, powder blue raincoat does very little to protect him from the elements.

'Yes, it is. Where are you looking for?' I ask, leaning out of the serving hatch.

'You know what, I can't quite remember the address. I thought it was Kentish Town High Street. My brain just doesn't seem to work in this cold.' He rubs his head, which must be frozen without a hat.

'The High Street is just round the corner over there, sir.' Mouse points to the end of the road. 'But why don't you sit down first and have a warm bowl of soup?'

'I'm afraid I don't have any money on me, young man.' The man rifles through his pockets. 'I must have left home without my wallet.'

'There's no charge here, sir. It's all free,' Lucia says, as I hand over a bowl of soup, which she takes for the old man, who doesn't look too steady on his feet.

'Try some of this crispy flatbread with it.' I hand out the last portion of flatbread, which has been going like hotcakes—every pun intended.

'Free! But how can this all be free?' The newcomer sits down on one of the benches.

'It's part of our community project up the road. We call it the Good Life. Our Abundance Cafe based there makes meals from sur-plus food—ingredients that might otherwise have gone to waste and been thrown away.'

'The cafe is marvellous. Me and the wife go there most days,' Jim says. 'And we do give donations.'

'Souper Van! Tossers!' This is shouted by one of a gang of teen-agers as they go by. 'Is it a bird? Is it a plane? No, it's a shitty old ice cream van. Some Souper Van that is!'

'Never mind them, my lovely. What's your name?' asks Lucia.

'It's Bill,' he tells us. Bill, oblivious to everything apart from the warming bowl of soup, shovels a spoonful into his mouth, and lets out a deep, satisfied sigh. 'This is *delicious*. So, is this your Saturday job then?'

'No, we do this for free!' Mouse shrugs cheerfully.

'We believe that life can't all be about just taking ... but back giving too. Our motto is: how many people can we make smile today,' Lucia beams.

'For my job, I'm a food critic for *The Times*,' Jim chirps up.

'That's great Jim, but I think you've got more pressing matters to consider. Like, what your next move is now I've got your bishop!' Mouse laughs as he swipes Jim's bishop from the board.

'Oh dear, another lost bishop,' the old man mutters. 'Now what was I asking? Oh yes, do you go to school, young man?'

'Nah. Boring. We dropped out halfway through A-levels,' Mouse says. 'We've got a better plan. We think that preventing climate change is one of the most important lessons our generation need to do something about right away.'

'That starts with cutting down fossil fuel usage and carbon emissions,' Lucia adds. 'So we have turned my nan's van into a bio-fuel Chip Fat Travellers Van. We drive it around and talk to people about it. I do have a part-time job at Sports Direct to earn some dosh, though.'

'Well, you are most impressive young people. It's been lovely chatting to you, but I think I should be heading off now. I do have an engagement to go to.' Bill stands up. 'That kryptonite soup—is that what you said it was—was extremely tasty?'

His empty soup bowl threatens to fall from his shaky hand. As I take it from him, I say, 'Listen, Bill, if you're going up to the high street, why don't you pop into the Good Life project. I've made some up-cycled chunky scarves and I'd love to give you one as a gift.'

'No, I think I'm too old to cycle. Sorry my dear, but thank you anyway.' He starts to walk off, clearly a bit wobbly. 'Cheerio to you good folk now.'

'Yeah, may the Force be with you,' Mouse calls out, as he watches Bill tottering his way down the road.

There's a tap on my shoulder. I turn round to see Mr Pang. 'I just saw the Father Guy talking to that nasty man, Montjoy. He clearly swings both ways.'

'What? Father Guy is gay?' I blurt out.

'Father Guy … he says "yes" to both Team Good Life, and Montjoy, the developer,' Mr Pang confides. 'They are in pub down the road.'

'That Thomas Montjoy is totally the Lex Luthor of Kentish Town.' Mouse shakes his head.

'Anyway, tasty looking soup, I quite fancy some myself.' Mr Pang takes a bowl and sits next to Jim. 'All this detective work makes me very hungry.'

'Actually guys, do you mind if I dash?' I ask Lucia and Mouse. 'I do have a chore to do before the bishop's visit later today.' A little chore appertaining to getting my nails manicured after all those hours of washing up, I fail to add, as I head for the High Street and 'Cute-icles.' The only chips I intend to serve at my girls' lunch at the Abundance Cafe tomorrow will not be on my nails, but in the delicious roasted veg chips—part of the menu Nahal and I have planned to impress my fashionista friends: Fliff and Phoebe.

As Pueng the beautician speedily works on my nails, my mind casts over the idea of GG and Thomas Montjoy meeting in the pub. Surely, there was nothing suspicious about it, just a courtesy catch up? Looking around the salon, I think back to the conversation I overheard here between two women three weeks ago. I seem to recall there was talk of a public meeting to discuss a proposed new block of flats. I wonder when? Leaving all ideas of conspiracy to the makers of Netflix movies, I concentrate on choosing a luscious shade of brown for my nails.

An hour later, my nails as dark as the bark of the tree I once again find Pippa starting to climb, I arrive outside the Good Life.

'Trees like this are our lungs; the air is our breath, its earth our body,' Pippa yells out through the megaphone she is gripping. 'If trees didn't breathe, nor would we. If we kill trees like this, it's our body that we are killing, and that is why we need to make it a crime. I will not let this innocent tree be cut down. Look, Deb …' she calls out to me. 'The council have stuck a note here saying they are coming to chop down our enchanted apple tree tomorrow. I won't let it happen.'

I walk over to read the notice of intended destruction pinned to tree.

'Establishing the law of ecocide would signal a major break-through in the way we deal with crimes against the natural world,' Pippa bellows through her loudspeaker, as she reaches the top branch of the tree. 'I say let's make ecocide the fifth global crime against peace. Let's hold the companies to account—whether it's oil drilling in the Arctic, deforestation in the Amazon, or overfishing in the Atlantic. Activities like these that have a severe impact on global ecosystems should be brought under far closer scrutiny. I see the world in a grain of sand, and heaven in a wildflower ...'

'Amen, dear.' I turn round. Bill, the old gent from the soup stall is standing there listening to Pippa and looking rather confused.

Pippa has heard him too. 'Would you like to join me up this tree, sir? I am planning to chain myself to it and stay here all night.'

'Er, hello there. It's Bill, isn't it?' I say to him. 'We met at the Souper Van. I guess you have come here to take up my offer of a free scarf?' I link his arm and guide him away from Pippa towards the entrance.

'Today, we're going to start building our tandoor oven ...' We pause to listen to Rich, who is standing around a huge mountain of sand and clay, surrounded by the power ranger girls. They're wearing headscarves in citrus colours to match the orange high-vis vests over their coats. I smile at how they are brightening up a dull, grey day. 'As you ladies all know, a tandoor is a Middle-Eastern clay oven used for baking breads,' Rich explains.

'When I was growing up in Iran, I used to love running each morning to the tandoor for our daily *barbari*—that's thick and crusty bread,' says Anousha.

The lady next to her adds, 'my favourite was *lavash*. It's a soft, thin flatbread.'

'To build a cob oven, we simply have to get the perfect mix of clay, sand and straw.' Rich lifts up a handful of clay, and, rolling it about in his palm, adds a scoop of sand to it. 'To check if this mix is thick enough, you have to roll the ingredients into a large sausage.' Rich proceeds to do so. 'You can tell if it's firm by ...'

All around, the girls burst out into a round of giggles, as Rich continues to demonstrate how to make a large clay sausage.

'We all like a nice firm sausage, don't we, Deb?' Rich calls out after me. 'Care to join us with your new friend?'

I walk on swiftly past them, pausing by the fridge, which apparently unnoticed by Rich, is surrounded a group of men singing and swigging cans of beer.

'Wanna beer, old chum?' one of the men calls out. 'We are sailing, cross the ocean …'

Leading Bill, who is looking more confused than ever, swiftly into the church, I almost trip over Leroy, who has pieces of paper scattered all over the floor.

'What are you doing, young man?' Bill asks.

'I'm working on an invention to turn dog poo into renewable energy,' Leroy replies. 'As you can see from my picture here,' he lifts a sheet of paper, 'all people have to do is pop their dog poop into a biodegradable corn starch bag. Then it goes into this little box, which is attached to a streetlight. They turn the handle on the box and this in turn powers the streetlight. I think poop could even power a vehicle.'

From souper van to pooper van … could this day get any stranger?

Yes, a dart suddenly skims past my nose and lands smack bang in the centre of the cross nailed to the wall behind us. Had Bill not been bent down looking at Marg's table of meat-free information, the dart would've surely scored a bull's-eye on Bill's eye!

Henry Junior runs past me and starts to laugh. He's clearly the thrower.

But Bill's eye has now been caught by Michael and Francis who are sitting knitting. 'What are you gentlemen doing?' he asks.

'We are the Knit Wits club,' Michael laughs. 'We're a group of men who like to knit while we crack jokes.'

'We're knitting a long scarf to tie around the threatened tree outside, to help our friend Pippa,' Francis explains.

'Oh yes, the tree that the rather demonstrative young lady was chaining herself to?' says Bill. 'I do hope she'll be safe.'

'She'll be fine!' Francis chuckles. 'But listen—what did one Dalek say to the other?'

'Ex-ter-mi-knit!' The men all burst out laughing.

'Perhaps we should go and sit down and have a nice cup of tea,' I say, leading Bill to the cafe.

'No thank you, dear. As I've been trying to tell you, I'm here for the service,' Bill says. 'My full name is Father William. I am the Bishop of Edmonton.'

'But, but … you can't be.' I stare at him, aghast. 'And your service isn't meant to start until six p.m.. It's only four now.'

'Oh dear, I do seem to get my times muddled up these days.' Father William strokes his chin in confusion. He unbuttons his old blue coat to reveal a rather smart suit and black shirt with a white dog collar. 'Now where can I put my coat?' he asks. 'This was my grandfather's coat, so it's a rather precious family heirloom.'

My immediate feelings of panic as to the whereabouts of Nat and GG, followed by a quick rewind of the disarray Father William had witnessed over the past hour, are put on hold as, in what I can only describe as the opposite of a lightbulb moment, all the lights go out and the church is plunged into complete darkness. The sound of Chloe sobbing is drowned out only by the shrill squawk of Brutus who starts to crow. It seems to herald doom for the Good Life project. I'm just thinking things can't get any worse when a torch shines out of the darkness.

'Everything all right here?' The light beams into my face. 'I've had a report that you've got rats back.' Mr Rentokil is standing in front of me, clutching his case.

'Talking of rats, I met a very charming young couple in the high street who served delicious soup and homemade bread. I believe they were called Rat and Lucia. Are they your friends, and part of this project?' Bishop William asks, as Nahal, Greg, Michael and Anousha quickly light candles and place them on the tables and desks around the room, creating a rather lovely atmosphere.

'Yeah, I suppose we are all old friends here, mate,' Mr Rentokil chuckles.

All further rodent exchange is thankfully silenced, as Rich comes storming in, carrying a large torch. 'Someone's flipped the switch in the feckin' fuse box—that's why the power's gone off,' he shouts. 'I think we have an in-house spy, and when I find out who it is, I'm going to kill the wanker.' He eyes Father William with suspicion. 'Not only has all the power gone out, but you know that sign on the tree outside stating it was due to be demolished, the one that sent Pippa off on one of her nutty publicity antics—well, it's a fake.' He hands me the note. 'And now, this talk about rats coming back?' He glares at Mr Rentokil.

'I would be pleased if they came back here, I would love to meet them again,' Father William adds falteringly.

'Someone is out to get us, but I'm going to sodding well get *them* before they do,' Rich ends his rant, as the lights suddenly come back on in the room.

'Er, Rich, I would like to introduce you to Father William,' I say as calmly as I can.

'What?' Rich looks wide-eyed at the cleric.

'Father William is the Bishop of Edmonton,' I explain.

'Bishop of feckin' …?'

'Welcome, Father William! Welcome to the God life project!' We all turn round as Nat approaches. 'What a great, great honour it is to meet you once again.' She bows.

I stifle a giggle, as I stare at the big fat silver cross she's sporting around her neck. She's also wearing a pure white polo neck and sensible long skirt.

'I am the brains behind the God Life project.' She clasps Father William's hand. 'I wanted to let you know how much solace I've found here since my husband left me last autumn.' She points to the figure of Jesus on the cross on the wall. I squirm at the dart protruding from it. 'How much comfort the teachings of the Bible have given me.'

@NTS: OMG … she's actually clutching—and stroking—a Bible!

'Bless you, my child.' Father William kisses her hand.

'My favourite passage: *May he who is without sin cast the first stone, do not judge lest ye be judged yourself*—I believe is from Matthew, chapter seven, verses one to two, or is it three?' Nat beams at him.

We all look dumbfounded as Nat, contrition incarnate, continues to spout from the holy book. 'I feel like I am one of your lost flock who has returned.' She dabs away the tears in her eyes.

As if on cue, although I suspect not perhaps the cue—nor indeed the flock Nat was hoping for—Old Spot waddles into the church and lays down on the floor in front of us letting out a loud grunt.

'Is this really a pig?' Father William looks horrified.

'Oh yes, Father William. But he's not just any pig. He's one who has really bought home the bacon!' says Michael, clearly still in knit-wit, comedy rehearsal mode. 'This is Old Spot. The clever thing dug up some truffles in the back garden two weeks ago and we managed to sell them for fifteen hundred pounds to a fancy new Michelin-starred restaurant. It's called: "The Truffle Hog."'

'The Truffle Hog? Do you mean the Marylebone restaurant that all the celebrities and everyone in the know are talking about? It has a waiting list as long as the Bible.' Father William continues, 'But is the pig sanitary? Who gave you permission for him to be here?'

'Dear Father William,' Nat flicks open her bible. '*Ask the animals and they will teach you, the birds in the sky and they will tell you, the fish in the sea will inform you ...*'

'Yeah, you've definitely got rats. I can see a little bugger in here,' Mr Rentokil interrupts Nat's Bible recital to call out from the confession box.

'The hand of the Lord has created all of this.' Nat points to Old Spot who is now snoring under one of the desks. She closes her Bible. 'That passage, which I believe explains the importance of animals, was from Job chapter twelve.'

'Talking about jobs,' Rich pitches. 'We've decided, Father Bill, to give the truffle money to, er, Rat and Lucia, to modernise their cooking equipment in the van that served you the soup and bread today.'

'Well, that *is* wonderful,' Father William sighs. 'But as you know, I am here today to review your project, and considerations such as animal welfare are paramount to ...'

His words are interrupted by a loud shriek from the garden. 'Daddy, daddy, there's a fox trying to bite Sophie's head off, Chloe comes running in, sobbing, hotly followed by Greg—and Brutus, who makes a run up to Father William.

'Dear God, no!' the bishop cries.

'Father William, while we doubtless have a few teething problems here …' In more ways than you realise, Nat, I think with horror, as I watch Brutus sneak up behind Father William, lift a claw and open his beak. 'The aspect we haven't spoken about yet,' Nat continues, 'is how our community can help develop ecumenical projects with the church.'

@NTS: Ecumenical—I think for a minute she's saying economical, but then the only thing Nat's ever economical with is the truth.

'Yes, my dear.' Father William holds his chin, clearly lost in thought. 'You are right. It's vital that churches find new ways to engage with local communities.' He looks around the room as Greg shoos away the chickens. 'It's vital that diverse congregations, like, er … yours, work with churches to develop the four ecumenical C's: That's congregation, compassion, culture, and commerce.'

'Well, we certainly have "congregation" here! This project is a central resource at the heart of the community,' Greg adds as he tries to put his hands around Brutus's mouth to silence him.

Rich shouts above the cacophony from Brutus: 'And as for compassion and outreach that addresses local needs and social justice, I'm sure you will agree that Rat and Lucia's Souper Van, and Nahal's Abundance Cafe more than tick that box.'

'In terms of culture, just look around at the ideas here.' Nahal hands Father William a copy of Leroy's sketches.

'And I'm a single Dad who's just learned how to knit,' Francis laughs, as he lifts his knitting needles to display the multi coloured three-metre-long scarf draped on the floor.

'Don't forget Marg, septuagenarian activist,' says Michael. 'She's organised an inspiring film night last month. It was a real exposé of the meat industry.'

'I've told my Dad I don't want to eat meat anymore.' Leroy shakes his head. 'You should have seen them pigs stuffed into cages.'

'While on the subject of food … this spring, one of our team, Sacha, is going to be curating a Pestival,' Nat adds. 'It's a celebration of, er, future food …'

'I must say I am partial to a nice hot dog at a festival.' Father William licks his lips.

'Getting back to your "C" list,' Nat butts in, 'when it comes to commerce, our Deb here has got a great money-making idea for a big fashion brand.' She walks over to my sewing machine and whips its cover off. 'Just you wait and see, Father William, we are going to be self-sufficient in no time!'

I look at my singing sewer. Who is Nat kidding? Truth be known—tablecloths and scarves aside—I haven't yet managed to create anything I think has potential.

'There's another "C" here,' Rich glowers. 'It's the expletive-deleted so-and-so who tried to shaft us here today by switching off the *lecce*. Mark my words, I'm going to get'em!'

'Friends, all your sentiments are truly inspiring.' Father William looks around at us. 'In all honesty, I was here today to close you down. But now I just don't know what to do. There seem to be so many challenges, so many reasons against letting you and your rather un-conventional project continue.' He sighs as he looks around at: Old Spot asleep on the floor; chickens running round the church chased by children; the vociferous confession box echoing with loud swearing; the kitchen door, behind which comes the racket of crashing objects. 'And yet my mind keeps returning to the one phrase I heard today at your wonderful soup van,' he continues. 'The phrase that lovely young lady, Lucia, used about how she felt her job today was to make people smile. And smiling is very much what we need in these days more than ever.' He pauses to look around at all of us, as we stand wide eyed, staring anxiously at him. Nat tenderly caresses her crucifix, and it gleams in the candlelight.

'If you can make folk smile, and indeed yourself smile, while going through a period of personal upset,'—he takes Nat's hand—'well then, I think you're halfway there. You have also done a very good job at cleaning out what was a rather sad, neglected church, apart from that big fridge outside in the entrance. Were those men sitting and singing there drunk?'

'Er, no, dear Father William, they're practising for our weekly choir,' Nat blushes. 'The drink they were referring to was Rich's homemade raspberry communion wine.'

'Talking of which, would you like to taste it?' Rich, his hands caked in wet clay, picks up a tray with a bottle of wine and several glasses on it.

'I don't think the bishop wants any of this.' I shake my head at Rich.

Father William smiles, 'Well, maybe just a tipple to toast your project. I have decided to give you the go-ahead for another six months until the end of August. God bless you and your God Life project.' He walks over to my sewing machine and places a hand on it. 'But I must stress that this is on the proviso that you do start to create an income to pay for the utilities and the upkeep of this church.' A large glass of wine is handed to him, and he knocks it back with little trouble.

'Oh, thank you, dearest Father William.' Nat kisses his hand. 'We will not let you down.'

A loud cheer erupts around the room, interrupted by Mr Rent-okil, who strides out from the confession box. 'Got'em!' He laughs menacingly. 'There's never an escape from my rodenticide cocktail! But I wouldn't go and do any confessing in the next few hours if I were you!'

'Now, let us gather round, and share a multi-faith prayer.' Father William smiles as our female power rangers walk into the room, giggling at the sight of each other's hands covered in mud. We all form a big circle around Father William. He begins: 'Our Father, who art in heaven …'

I stare at the man who only two hours ago I had mistaken for a down-and-out at our soup van. His battered blue coat really was a precious family heirloom; his faltering voice was now confident and unfaltering. I'm sure there must be a passage in the Bible about judging others—something that I'm aware that I'm rather prone to. Listening to his lovely mellifluous tone, watching his eyes sparkle as he smiles at everyone in the mesmerised circle, I resolve immediately to never judge others in the future.

'And in the name of Allah, the most gracious, the most merciful,' Anousha adds.

'I would like to welcome our new congregation to this living place of worship.' Father William smiles as he looks at the power ranger ladies, some of whom stand with their hands in a position of prayer.

'As the Qur'an says, 'Guide us to the straight path; the path of those whom thou have blessed: *Ihdina As Sirta Al Mustaqim,*' Anousha sings.

'And lead us not to temptation.' Nat looks at me and winks.

I blush as I look at the flickering candles that have cast beautiful shadows around the room, accentuating the stuccoed ceiling and the stone arches, alighting upon the stained-glass windows with their stories of redemption and hope.

The gentle patter of rain drumming on the stained glass continues to serenade us, along with Nat's incantation, which some might say was not quite in the spirit of things. Not that I'm judging … 'And also give us our daily bread, but preferably of the pound-note kind!'

FEBRUARY

CHAPTER 13

Boxing Day

Placing several jam jars filled with sprigs of rosemary on the table, I check the pretty floral cloth I had upcycled from a couple of skirts. Still feeling anxious about letting my fashionista friends talk me into hosting a lunch in the Abundance Cafe, I place the serviettes—newly made from some old white linen shirts—either side of our mismatched antique cutlery and Nat's dubiously appropriated Wedgwood chinoiserie plates. I stand back to admire the rather lovely overall vintage effect.

Since being unable to get another job in the fashion industry, I must admit that my confidence has taken a bit of a knock. I feel more and more intimidated by my monthly get together with the girls who are all so successful. There's Fliff, who is not only an interior designer, but the perfect mother to an accomplished son, Damien, who is the same age as my James. Then Phoebe, the newly promoted editor of the lifestyle magazine, *'Au Courant.'* It was Phoebe who had suggested we meet for lunch here. She had enthused about how surplus food restaurants were all the rage now and was so impressed to hear about the 'little café I was now working at.' Word is that she has a job going as a senior fashion stylist on the magazine, so impressing her is something I really needed to do today. Particularly after my unsettling phone call with Stu last night.

'I do so love February,' Greg murmurs sotto voce as he shuffles some papers around on his desk, providing a welcome distraction to my melancholy musings. 'Can't you just imagine the grouse moving about on the moors, buzzards performing their territorial displays, the white hares turning brown?'

'As opposed to your brown hairs, turning white!' Nat, who has promised me faithfully not to get up to any antics today, walks past me carrying a suspicious large rope over her shoulder. She walks out of the front door into the street.

I rifle my hands through my newly dyed hair and sigh. I've been sitting bent double over my sewing machine every day for the last week, but despite the growing stash of fabrics Rich has managed to procure—so much that we have had to turn the confession booth into a temporary fabric storage unit—I have absolutely no idea about what to design or make. No pressure, but there was that small point raised at the meeting with Father Bill last week of my supposed idea for a fashion brand. The only honest crust coming my way at the moment is the one Nahal is going to serve today.

I breathe in the lovely fragrant smell coming from the kitchen and smile at how much I have enjoyed experimenting with Nahal over the past couple of days while planning and cooking our tasting menu for today. I'm really starting to get a taste for all this spicy food. I even added harissa to an egg buttie at home last weekend—something James, who was back from Exeter Uni, was delighted with! Shame I can't say the same for husbondage Stu, but he's always been a traditional eggy-soldiers man.

'Oh yes, I can almost hear the lesser spotted woodpeckers drumming on the trees,' Greg continues. 'Even the shrill scream of vixens attracting mates …'

'What's all this talk of vixens attracting mates?' Fliff walks in, followed by Phoebe. 'It all sounds rather fun!'

'Hello, Devore, darling.' Phoebe blows me an air kiss and looks down at the pinny I'm wearing.

'Now where,' says Fliff, 'are all these dishy single dads I've been hearing hang out here?'

'Um, they don't come in until later.' I hastily take off my pinny and straighten out the Balmain T-shirt I'm wearing over my increasingly tight Ted Baker skinny jeans. My look is carefully selected to look effortless.

'I so love your boiler-suit.' Phoebe feels the loose folds of Fliff's grey flannel jumpsuit. 'So utilitarian, isn't it? No one is wearing tight-fitting designer labels anymore, are they?' Phoebe looks at my outfit and shrugs.

'Anyway, shall we have the grand tour before lunch?' Fliff leads the way past Greg who is standing in front of his desk.

'Welcome ladies, I'm Gregory, often referred to by the girls as the movie star idol Gregory Peck, although personally I can't see the similarity!' He pulls in his protruding stomach. 'Would you like to sign up for a day trip to Woodberry Wetlands next month? We are hoping to see the mating dance of the great crested glebe.' He winks at Phoebe.

Reluctantly taking the leaflet on the reintroduction of Great Bustards that Greg forces into her hand, Phoebe turns away to Pippa.

'The snowdrop and primrose our woodlands adorn, and violets bathe in the wet o' the morn,' Pippa sings. 'Have you seen the snowy milk flowers that have burst into life today at the base of our enchanted tree? Such innocence compared to the ecocide that's destroying our planet. As you can see, I'm a conscientious protestor on justice for the earth.'

'I, too, am an eco-warrior.' Fliff nods her head in agreement.

'Is that a real fur bobble on your hat, dear?' Marg asks as she looks at the adornment atop Fliff's pom-pom hat.

I know for certain that the matching racoon fur bobble on Fliff's bag is real. According to *Vogue*, which obviously I still need to read for research purposes, furry pom-pom hats with matching key ring and charms, are this winter's 'must have' accessory. I stifle a giggle at how Fliff's frivolous balls of fluff are not perhaps the most sensitive item she could have chosen to wear today.

'Why don't we start outside? I really want to show you our People's Fridge and Chip Fat Travellers Van.' I swiftly guide the girls away from the threat of Marg and Pippa's chastisement over animal rights, or more likely, wrongs.

'And ladies, I do hope you will sign my campaign to commit to a meatless March,' Marg calls out, as we head to the front door. 'Over fifty per cent of global greenhouse gases are caused by animal agriculture.'

Walking outside, I can't believe my eyes. A boxing ring has been set up. Created on a platform of pallets covered with a tarpaulin, the three-metre square ring is surrounded by rope held aloft by wooden posts. Nat, standing in the centre of the ring wearing shorts and a T-shirt sporting the logo 'Nat: A Good Life vote,' raises her hands clad in large boxing gloves.

'I'm gonna deliver a knock-out blow to all the featherweight politicians; punch out all the below-the-belt lack of council funding.' Nat shouts as she throws punches at Bradley, who stands in the ring pretending to punch back.

'Doesn't he look just like the boxer who was on that TV show, "*Lights Out?*"' Phoebe nudges the girls.

I suppress a giggle at the thought of Phoebe watching late-night reality TV. Surely low- brow viewing was solely *my* guilty pleasure.

Nat is now in her pompous pomp, calling out, 'I believe that neither the state, nor the market alone can meet our needs. We need to weigh in with a new kind of politics; a participatory, co-operative governance that focuses on democratic engagement through the co-opting of citizens in the process of governance. I'm therefore going to be standing at the next local council election as an Independent for The Good Life. And Bradley here is going to be my campaign manager?

Good Life councillor, I hear. Even by Nat's standards, the transformation in one week from Bible-spouting lost sheep to boxing-clever co-opting politician, was something to behold. The only co-op in Nat's vocabulary prior to this week was when she was comparing the price of sausages at the Co-op and Lidl.

I very much doubt that Nat's campaign message has been devised by Bradley—not the most loquacious of folk. But while I should be angry at her for breaking her promise to not get up to any antics today, I can't help smiling as Nat takes off her gloves and lifts a stash of leaflets. Their message: 'Nat: A Good Life vote.'

She hands out the flyers and chats effusively to the people gathering around the boxing ring, while Bradley offers free boxing lessons to several teenagers.

'Ah, there you are, Deb.' I turn round to find Rich, Mouse and Lucia approaching in the most lurid green and red Christmas jumpers I've ever seen. Rich's woolly is emblazoned with a flashing image of Santa saying: 'I only get my baubles out once a year!' Mouse and Lucia sport the same logo: 'Totally on the naughty list!'

'Why are you wearing those jumpers? It's February?' I hiss, embarrassed in front of my fashionable friends.

'It's Boxing Day!' Nat calls out.

'I was given this job lot of sweaters in return for building a shelving unit in the new clothes shop down the road,' Rich explains. 'It's so cold today, it makes total sense to wear an extra jumper.' He looks up at the menacing clouds.

Lucia shakes her head: 'Did you know that one in four Christmas jumpers bought before Christmas are thrown away, or are unlikely to be worn ever again?'

'Or that thirty-five per cent of all under thirty-year-olds buys a new novelty Christmas jumper every year?' Mouse adds.

'And yet the UK spends eighty-five million pounds each year throwing away clothing and textiles into landfill.' This comment from Rich. He's sneering at Phoebe and Fliff as he eyes their clearly expensive new clothes.

I look nervously at the girls, but their indifferent expressions suggest that the only figures they're interested in, are still their own.

'Would you like one, ladies?' Rich bends down and pulls three more jumpers out of a box. He hands Fliff one decorated with the slogan: 'When I think about you, I touch my elf.'

'I certainly would not!' Phoebe hands the jumper back.

'Go on, put it on! It'll go well with your sweatpants,' Rich laughs.

'These are not sweatpants, they're cashmere capris,' Phoebe snaps back.

'Any of you ladies wanna learn how to box?' Bradley calls out his offering from the boxing ring. Saved by the bell! I never thought I would be so pleased to hear Bradley's voice.

'Ooh … yes, please!' Phoebe, sans pom-pom hat now, I notice, climbs into the ring, and puts on the boxing gloves Bradley hands her. 'Were you that boxer who was on that late-night TV show?' she flutters at him.

'He was,' Nat snarls. 'And I'm very happy to punch out your lights.'

I'm wondering how on earth I'm going to get through the next couple of hours, when Henry Smarmy Smythe strolls over to us. 'Hello, ladies. How very charming to meet you.' In turn, he kisses Fliff and Phoebe on the hand. 'So nice to have a different crowd here.'

'Talking about a different crowd,' Rich butts in, 'where the feck were you when Bishop Bill came to visit us last week? Someone cut our power and got up to all kinds of high jinks? He glares quizzically at Henry Smarmy Smythe. 'You were seen in the pub with that bollix Montjoy the other week. I don't suppose you two are in cahoots?'

'I don't know what you're talking about, Richard. How can you be so terribly offensive?' Henry Smarmy Smythe takes on a crestfallen look and smiles imploringly at Phoebe. 'As a single dad, I'm always rushed off my feet going to work, shopping, cleaning, and, of course, helping with our Daddy Day share. That's our shared tool hire project, you know?'

Would that be rushed off your Tod's suede loafers, I think, glancing down at Henry's shoes. His line of beleaguered woe somehow doesn't match with what appear to be four-hundred-pound shoes.

'Of course, I don't mind all that. My little Henry Junior is the most important thing in my life.' Henry (Senior) Smarmy Smythe beams as he takes Phoebe's hand. 'Are you a parent?'

'Not yet,' Phoebe flutters her eyelashes at him. 'But I do so love children.'

Like hell she does. I recall the one time she babysat for my James when he was six—how I came home at midnight to find her asleep on the sofa wearing earplugs and a cucumber eye- mask. Meanwhile, James was playing with the cutlery in the kitchen drawer.

'Talking of children, my Damian is going to apply to study for a master's in engineering at Oxford,' says Fliff. 'What does your James want to study post Uni?'

Apart from his new girlfriend's navel, I don't know. I'm saved from having to answer when Nahal pokes her head through the door to let us know that lunch is ready.

'Yes, Devore, I'm so looking forward to experiencing your latest job incarnation as a café proprietor.' Phoebe links my arm.

'Oh no, Phoebe, I'm not really working here. In fact, I wanted to talk to you about …'

'By the way, did I tell you that I'm gluten-free,' Phoebe interrupts. 'I'm also really trying to eat as much lacto-fermented food as possible. I was on a fabulous fermenting programme at the Champneys spa last week.'

'Ah, talking of spas!' says Henry Smarmy Smythe. 'That reminds me … I must dash. I don't want to be late for my massage down the road. All that playing with Henry Junior takes quite a toll on my muscles.' He stops to flex his fingers, fishing inside a pocket, and then producing a card that he presents to Phoebe. Do take this. It would be good to meet up and compare spa stories.'

'Fancy a turn in the boxing ring, Phoebe?' Nat mutters angrily, as Henry blows Phoebe an extravagant kiss and dashes off.

Accepting the fact that the only sparring I'm going to be doing any time soon is at this lunch with the girls, I lead them to the Abundance Cafe where the serving table is now laden with a sumptuous-looking array of food.

'This dish is "*Oozy*." It's popular in Syria.' Nahal points to a plate of filo pastry dumplings stuffed with almonds and peppers. 'Next to it on the next plate, we have a vegetable rice infused with orange and cardamom. It's a Persian dish called "*Shirin polo.*" It means sweet rice in Farsi.'

As Nahal stirs the rice, I breathe in the ambrosial aroma and smile. The dish is redolent with shades of ginger and cinnamon. Lifting a dumpling, I bite into the crunchiest of flaky pastry, which crumbles down my chin.

'No carbs for me at lunchtime, I'm afraid.' Phoebe pushes the plate away.

'Oh, what a shame,' says Nahal. 'Then you won't be wanting one of these flatbreads. They're filled with sunflower seeds and are fresh out of the oven.' She hovers the tempting plate of warm flatbreads in front of Phoebe.

Fliff points to the next dish. 'This reminds me of a wonderful tagine I had in Marrakesh last month when we were shooting at the La Mamounia hotel.'

'It's *Mast-o-Bademjan*,' I say, picking up the dish. 'Do try some.' I scoop up a portion of roasted aubergines with garlic and cumin onto Phoebe's plate. 'It's so delish, I can't eat enough of it!' I say.

'So I can see.' Phoebe looks disapprovingly at my tummy, which is peeking out from my skimpy T-shirt.

'This looks interesting,' Fliff says, as she tries a small bite of the *Omelette Khorma*. 'What on earth is in it?'

'It's a date and honey omelette,' I explain.

'Date, honey, and eggs? Oh no, darling, it's not good to mix food groups.' Fliff shakes her head.

A while later, with most of the dishes left untouched by my friends, but heartily appreciated by the other diners in the cafe, Nahal brings dessert to the table. 'This is a Persian love cake, but I have left off the frosting as I imagine you ladies like to watch your calories.' She smiles sweetly.

I suppress a giggle at Nahal's not-so-innocent comment, and look down at the enchanting cake. It's drizzled with rosewater, sprinkled with cardamon and the brightest of chopped pistachios, and it suggests what I imagine a Persian garden looks like in spring.

'This Cake, *Yazdi*, takes its name after the city of Yazd in central Iran where we serve it with fresh mint tea,' says Nahal, proceeding to pour the steaming mint tea.

'Nahal and I picked the mint from our garden this morning,' I add.

Phoebe spoils my moment of pride: 'Oh, tut, tut, I think there's a tiny piece of mud, or even a creature, stuck on my mint leaf.' She eyes a leaf that is floating in her glass cup and pushes it to one side. Then she perks up, 'But apart from that, the meal was absolutely marvellous!' She starts to clap. 'Middle Eastern menus are so *au courant*.'

'Bravo, Chef!' Fliff adds.

'Where are you from? Nahal, is it?' Phoebe asks.

'I am from Iran,' Nahal replies.

'Ah! We shot a marvellous fashion piece in Jordan last year.

Jordan, Iran … close enough, right! I've just had a wonderful idea.' Phoebe looks thoughtful. 'If you play your cards right, I might be able to get you a feature in my magazine,' she gushes. 'It's called *Au Courant,* and it features the hottest new food trends. Yes, I can just see the headline now: "Iraqi immigrant turned celebrity fusion Persian Chef in London."'

Eh? I wince at this geographical and grammatical mash-up. But Nahal is cool. She shakes her head. 'You are very kind, but no thank you.'

'Not that we're suggesting you're an immigrant,' Fliff says.

'If your hubby is a problem, I could always talk to him,' Phoebe presses.

'That's if she has one,' Fliff whispers none too quietly in Phoebe's ear.

'Yes, Nahal does have a very nice husband. He's called Ahmed,' I glare at Fliff. 'And she's from Iran, not Iraq.'

'Ahmed is very supportive of all my projects,' Nahal says calmly.

'If she says she doesn't want to be in your magazine, then she doesn't want to be in your bollix mag.' Rich storms up to us and says, 'She's played her hand.'

'I really appreciate your offer … Phoebe, is it?' Nahal smiles. 'But I am happy here being part of the Good Life team. Our Abundance Cafe is growing day by day, and it's rewarding to create tasty meals from surplus food.'

There's a moment of silence. This is my chance …

'Talking about *Au Courant Magazine,* Phoebs,' I say, 'I was hoping to talk to you about the styling job that's going. As you know, I do love styling and …'

'Oh, no, Devore! You're *far* too senior!' Phoebe bursts out laughing. 'The fashion girls are all in their twenties and thirties.'

I can see Fliff try to stifle their laughter, and I look down.

There's another awkward moment of silence. But then Nat reappears. 'Has Deb told you about our truffle harvest here in the back garden?' she says, still wearing boxing gloves and an over-sized Christmas jumper.

I had been on the point of tears in my misery, but these now turn into tears of laughter, as I take in the words on the jumper's two snowy peaks: "Tinsel tits!"'

'Truffles? Here?' Phoebe asks dubiously.

'Yes, we've sold them to that restaurant called, "The Truffle Hog,"' says Rich.

'What? as in The Truffle Hog that just opened in Marylebone?' replies a shocked Phoebe. 'The restaurant with the world-famous Chef Samuel Chang at its helm?'

'And best of all,' Nat gushes, 'Deb hasn't told you that in exchange for supplying our truffles to them on an exclusive basis, they've invited us, and Father Guy, for a free Valentine's Day dinner tomorrow night.'

I'm unsure whether to be happier about the prospect of a Valentine's dinner tomorrow night with GG—who we haven't seen for a few weeks—or the stupefied look on Phoebe's face.

'What? You've got *a table* at The Truffle Hog, Devore? That's impossible! There's a six-month waiting list. George and Amal were seen there last week. At *Au Courant,* we've tried to get Chef Samuel Chang to do an interview, but …'

'Ooh, what are you going to wear, Devore?' Fliff butts in. 'And what about Stu? Surely your husbondage won't be too pleased to hear you're having dins with the dishy vicar on Valentine's night?

'Stu's away in, er … Bristol, again this week,' I murmur, trying not to emphasise the word *again*. I stare at my wedding ring, and sigh as I recall my chat with Stu last night—how excited he told me he was, about a job interview at Bristol University to head a new Economic Futures programme. Whilst I'd assumed the job interview at Bristol was another red herring, like Yale, I was shocked to receive a series of WhatsApp pics showing details of a house he has found in nearby Bradford-on-Avon: A house with five bedrooms, a tennis court, and a formal garden; a house that he wants me to visit in a few weeks.

I look up, unable to meet Nat's sparkly eyes, as she continues to joke with Rich about his choice of outfit for tomorrow night. 'I bet since you buried your orange Y-fronts, you don't have any pants to wear!' she howls.

'Buried your *what?*' Phoebe almost chokes on an almond she's eating.

'I'm quite happy going commando style,' Rich says, giving a smug shrug.

'Well, no need to get your knickers in a twist,' Nat laughs. 'I'm sure Deb can quickly stitch you up a pair of boxers this afternoon from upcycled fabric.'

'Boxer shorts?' Rich asks.

'You obviously haven't bought underwear for thirty years. All men wear boxers now,' Nat chuckles.

'Yes, I'll stitch you up a pair this afternoon,' I absentmindedly offer.

Nahal adds, 'Yes, our Deb is designing a range of ethical boxer shorts from upcycled fabric.'

Oh, am I? I smile in appreciation of the show of encouragement from my Good Life chums.

'The brand is called "Box Clever,"' says Nat, putting an arm around me.

'I'm sure you will be featuring it in your magazine soon,' says Nahal pointedly.

Rich is less subtle. 'And they contain none of this nylon shite; none of that toxic mix of oil-based synthetics or emissions of nitrous oxide. And as for cotton manufactures …'—he's in full flow now—'they cover less than one per cent of the earth's land mass yet soak up twenty-five per cent of all pesticides and herbicides. I bet you didn't know that a single pair of cotton pants uses ten millilitres of pesticides.' He looks at his watch. 'Anyway, I hope you enjoyed your lunch, ladies. It's back to work for us all now.'

Phoebe and Fliff look stunned, as I escort them on their way after swapping air kisses and promises to do this again very soon. Then I get to work helping Nahal clear the table.

'Why do you feel the need to impress your so-called friends, Deb?' Nahal asks me as we wash the dishes. 'They are not kind women, and I do not think they are truly happy.'

'Well, individually, they *are* nice women, Nahal,' I sigh. 'It's just that when we get together, it all becomes so competitive. It's all about being seen to be successful. That's the culture I've grown up with, and that's how people like me are judged, and, I guess, judge others.'

'In Iran, we have a saying: *Always be yourself, express yourself, and have faith in yourself.'* Nahal puts down her tea towel and takes my hand. 'Do not go out and look for a successful personality and duplicate it. To me, a benchmark—I think you call it—of being successful, is to be kind and to share with others. Look at the community we are building here.'

She looks around the room and I follow her gaze. Marg and Pippa are beavering away at their desks; Greg is wearing paper bird wings that one of the kids has made for him and running after the giggling children; Michael is at the Daddy Day Share desk filling out a form and handing a set of skis to a woman who has come to borrow them. And there's Nat handing round her 'Nat: A Good Life Vote' leaflets in the Abundance Cafe, where Anousha serves steaming plates of food to more diners. Nahal smiles. 'I think this is what success looks and sounds and—for me, most importantly—smells like!'

Nat has heard her and, standing next to my singing sewing machine, calls over, 'But seriously, Deb, why don't you have a go at making boxer shorts?'

'I'm sure they wouldn't be good enough.' I join her.

'Oh, just have a go!' Nat slaps me on the back. 'After all, you are the one who is always saying that every dream …'

'Starts with a dreamer.' I sit down behind me singing sewer.

Nahal laughs, 'And don't forget to add a fly opening for tinkle winkle!'

'Or to allow room for movement,' Pippa pipes up. 'Wearing your boxers should feel as free as a breeze floating through branches on a tree.'

'Pick fabric that breathes,' Marg adds.

'And you may need this for the waistband.' Rich hands me a roll of shocking-pink elastic. 'As with everything in life, it's all a question of support,' he winks.

Bending down to sift through another pile of fabrics that has been placed besides my machine, I select various remnants, pick up my fabric shears and start to slice through the fabric. As I work, I think back over the day's exertions; thoughts of Bristol aside, I can't help but smile. Smile at how right Rich was in saying that it was all a matter of support. *Supported* is something my new, quirky community has really made me feel today. I muse over the horrid lunch with the girls, and Nahal's perceptive questioning of whether or not they are happy. And then there was Nat ... I giggle as I recall her in the boxing ring, coolly saying how she only needed a thousand votes to become a councillor and how hard could that be? And yes, I did know the answer to her joke: 'What is a boxer's favourite part of the joke? The punch line!' She could be a contender all right. The big champ—Prime Minister Nat!

A while later, lost in warm thought, it's a surprise when I look down to see that I have created several pairs of brightly coloured boxer shorts—all with a pink elastic waistband. From boxing gloves to boxer shorts, via Christmas jumpers ... and Bristol. It certainly has been a boxing day, in more ways than one.

CHAPTER 14

The Truffle Hog

'So this is what a restaurant that charges a feckin' ninety quid for a Valentine's tasting menu plus sixty for wine pairings looks like these days,' Rich scoffs, as we walk into the Truffle Hog restaurant the following evening.

Vases overspilling with florid red roses adorn the tables which are draped in violet tablecloths. As well as the exposed brick walls, there's wallpaper with what looks like abstract images of mushrooms and truffles in shades of burgundy and dark brown.

'That's six hundred quid for the four of us. We could pay all the Good Life bills for the rest of the year with that,' Rich sighs.

'Talking about four of us, where's Father Guy?' I ask, straightening the folds in my tight black satin skirt, as the serious looking maître d' escorts us to our table.

'Oh, didn't you hear? Father Guy can't make it,' Nat says, clearly trying to sound nonchalant. 'So Fred's jumped in at the last minute.'

'Good evening, comrades.' Speak of the devil. It's Fred bustling over to the table. We all sit down—reluctantly in my case.

'As Fred is going to be my political spin doctor, we thought we could kill two birds with one stone, and turn this meal into a campaign planning meeting,' Nat says.

The only bird I want to kill tonight is Natalie, and the only spinning is likely to involve my head. I swiftly gulp down the glass of rosé champagne cocktail a waiter places in front of me and raise my glass for a top-up. I can see only one way to soften the blow of my planned evening of Valentine's daydream being replaced by Fred's fretting; and *that* involves wine.

'After all, soundbites are the language of political marketing,' Fred, true to form, offers his first dictum of the evening.

'Well, the only bites I'm interested in tonight are in this capitalist over-priced shite restaurant.' Rich picks up a scarlet menu. 'I bet the food's not nearly as good as our Nahal's.'

'Oh, come on, guys,' Nat pleads. 'Can't we lighten up for once and have a bit of fun? I mean, this is meant to be a treat you know. Not everyone gets to eat nosh cooked by the famous Chef Chang. And it *is* Valentine's day.'

I nod in agreement and smile. Nat's completely right. And I must admit that she looks really good in the wraparound Diane Von Furstenberg dress I loaned her. Its jersey fabric clings to her in all the right places. Rich, to his credit, also looks rather handsome in a smart black suit that Hari from the dry cleaners lent him. Just don't tell the owner of said suit.

But if Rich is trying to keep his politics under wraps, Fred isn't. 'Bloody Valentine's day! It's just another capitalist conspiracy bowing to corporate greetings-card entities. Another billion-pound commercial construct.' Fred words are as dour as his fawn checked blazer, polo neck and cords. While I can forgive a man for his disagreeable comments, I can't overlook the elbow pads on his jacket.

'Come on, Freddy,' Nat tries to gee us up. 'So how many cards did you get?' She puts her arms around him. 'I didn't get any, but I'm single and proud.'

'Well said, Nat.' Rich jumps up and give her a surprising kiss on the cheek.

Well encouraged, Nat continues: 'Come on team—and that includes you, Deb, as we don't consider you to be a *smug* married— repeat after me: I'm single and I'm proud!'

We all stand up, and we all chant, 'I'm single and I'm proud'—in unison, much to the obvious disapproval of several of our fellow diners.

'Deborah, is that you?'

I turn around and am shocked to see Clive Garney standing there. The very same Clive Garney who is my Stu's boss at the Bank of England. Standing beside him is Harold, one of Stu's old colleagues. I recognise him from the occasional, insufferable, bonus-bragging dinners we had with him and his wife when he and my Stu used to work together. By the end of such evenings, the only bonus I was interested in was how to skip dessert and make an early night of it. But I smile as I look at Clive, his well-lunched torso hidden beneath an expensive Savile Row suit. Of all the economists Stu has worked with, I have always found Clive to be the most down-to-earth, and a good laugh.

'Clive, how wonderful to see you.' I kiss him politely on both cheeks. 'I was just sharing with my colleagues some thoughts on, er ...'

He eyes Rich, and Fred and laughs. 'So, this is what happens when your husband goes to Bristol for a ...' Clive says.

'So good to see you, Harold. How's Diana?' I swiftly change the subject away from Stu's interview at Bristol Uni (which I haven't told Nat about), to enquire after Harold's wife, whose appearance is as manicured as her behaviour. She certainly wouldn't have been caught inappropriately chanting in London's most fashionable restaurant about how she is single and proud.

'Diana's fine,' Harold replies, deadpan. 'She's helping the children prepare for a piano recital tomorrow night. 'Yes, I've just joined the bank as a Senior Economist.'

'We seem to be on the next table, Deborah. I can see I will have to keep an eye on you,' Clive chuckles, clearly happy to have an excuse not to focus on Harold and his children's arpeggios.

Our waiter walks up to the table holding a tray of crystal glasses filled with swirls of dark red and purple liquid. The floating crystallised pink rose petals complete the rubicund look. 'For your *premier amuse-bouche*, we present you with a cupid consommé,' says the waiter, getting us to sit down. 'This is a chilled plum and beet consommé with horseradish oil.'

Hmm ... The soup looks more putrid than cupid.

'*Amuse bouche?* What the hell is that?' Nat giggles.

'It's French. It literally means to amuse the mouth,' I explain.

'Bet you're good with *your* mouth Nat!' Rich leers at her.

'I see you're with a bit of a racy crowd tonight,' Clive laughs from the neighbouring table. 'But seriously, Deborah, Stu did tell me that you're working with some interesting environmentalists—a subject very close to our heart at the bank. Why don't we join tables together tonight, and share some ideas with our meals?'

'But don't you and Harold ...'

My hint that he had important business to discuss is ignored as Clive clicks his fingers and the waiters move our two tables together. Nat, who is delighted at being called an 'interesting environmentalist,' plonks herself down next to Clive, who I happen to know, recently separated from his wife.

'Well, here's a thought for you Clive ...'—a short while later, introductions and toasts having been made, amuse-bouches handed around, Fred picks a rose stem from the vase in the centre of the table—'Did you know that Kenya, one of the main exporter of roses, trucks blooms to Nairobi and flies them to Europe. The blooms stop off in Saudi where they might be cooled with a hosepipe. And they say that scarcity of water, and the battle for it, is going to be the driver of global conflict. What do you bankers have to say about that, eh, Clive?'

'Stopover in Saudi and cooling down with hosepipes? Gosh, that's a shocking fact.' Clive puts down the bottle of plastic mineral water he is about to open and drinks up his glass of cupid soup.

'Lovely weather today, wasn't it, Clive? Almost spring-like?' I try to change the subject, fearing that any opportunity for him to encourage Stu to stay at the Bank of England, would disperse with the spring blossom after eight more courses of Fred and Rich's critiques.

'Furthermore, the United Nations Environment Programme predicts that by 2030 almost half the world's population will face severe water conflict,' Fred continues. The only barometer he is interested in involves climate-change doom mongering. 'Unfortunately, many of the most fragile countries are also those with the greatest water stress ...'

'I do believe though, that the World Bank's water global practice has embarked on a programme to help tackle global water insecurity,' Rich interjects with an unexpected turn of allegiance. He looks strangely subdued. I never thought I'd see the day when Rich defended bankers. He usually calls them by rhyming slang beginning with the letter, 'W.'

Harold stares at him in a curious manner. 'You look familiar, old chum. Are you sure we haven't met or worked together?' Harold asks, fiddling with his gold embossed cufflinks.

Rich shakes his head and quickly looks away.

'Anyway, let's raise our glasses and journey back to ancient Rome,' says Clive. 'Imagine it's February the fourteenth in the pre-Christian era. A woman is woken up … but not to breakfast in bed and a rose, but by her naked husband spanking her repeatedly on the buttocks with a goatskin. This was a romantic gesture back then that was thought to increase fertility. Bet *you'd* like that, Natalie?' he grins.

A noticeably quiet Rich apart, everyone bursts out laughing. We enjoy another top-up of wine, as our plummy waiter places the next course in front of us.

'This is carpaccio of Maldivian long-line caught yellow fin tuna, fanning an island of Rio Grande avocado and Goan lime.' He points to a piece of tuna on the plate no larger than an Opal Fruit, or whatever the small fruity wrapped square is called these days.

'By the way, could you please tell Chef Chang that I'm in the house tonight,' Harold interrupts Plummy, the waiter. 'Chef Chang and I are old friends.' His words have more gloss than the fish sauce.

'Next, we have Pacific Ocean black cod fillet, hand-glazed with a Japanese tamari and manuka honey reduction,' Plummy continues, his tone suggesting he is clearly displeased with Harold's interruption. 'This is served on a bed of local kale.' He makes a little bow and walks off.

'Reminds me of a joke, Clive,' Nat chuckles. 'What kind of restaurant do rich people like to eat in?' Clive smiles, clearly charmed by Nat. 'The answer … is *ups-kale!*'

'Like you, Nat, tonight in that clinging dress.' The words pop out of my mouth, and I start to giggle.

'She's dressed to *kale*,' Clive chortles.

After a chorus of laughter, an amiable silence descends around the table as we tuck into the cornucopia of international offerings on our plates.

'Now, do tell me about your area of interest in environmental campaigning?' Clive addresses Rich.

'I'm living for a year without money, or, on as little as possible,' Rich explains in a low voice. 'I want to remind people that *money* does not create things, *we* create money. It's simply a means of exchange, and there are other possibilities, like the sharing and gift economy.'

'I'm sure,' Fred interjects, 'you are *all* well aware of the recent Oxfam report which stated that forty-two people hold as much wealth between them as the combined three and a half billion of the world's poorest.'

'Inequality is not an inevitable outcome of the economic laws of nature.' Rich drains his glass. 'It's a design failure and we could and should design it out of the system.'

I notice Harold curiously scrutinising Rich before saying, 'I know where we've met ...'

'Security in *your* financial context is a traceable financial asset that has monetary value collateralised in equity, stocks, bonds or debentures,' Rich continues. 'But the only security I'm interested in lies in the safeguard of my relationships with people, plants, and animals. *We* are mutually dependent.'

'Debentures! Sounds like a dental problem!' Nat taps her teeth and grins.

Clive looks thoughtful. 'Well, this is most fascinating, Rich. I think you should come in and present your theory to the chaps at the bank. Let's set up a date.'

'Oh, marvellous! Here are our lobster rolls.' Harold licks his lips, as the plate of lobster is placed before him.

'Did you know that scientists have determined that lobsters, like all animals, can feel pain?' Fred tuts. 'When lobsters are boiled alive by being dropped into scalding water, they whip around wildly and scrape the sides of the pot in a desperate attempt to escape.'

Clive places his lobster roll back on his plate. But Harold munches happily away on his, commenting on how juicy it is. 'And waiter,'— he clicks his fingers to summon Plummy—'I think we would like to replace this less than exemplary wine with Domaine Ramonet Montrachet Grand Cru.'

'I tell you what, Clive,' says Rich, glaring at Harold, 'I'll do a talk at the bank if, in return, you bring your team for a meal at our Abundance Cafe. *Our* Chef Nahal makes tasty Iranian street food from surplus food. Just look at this review in *The Times* today.' He takes a copy of the newspaper from his jacket pocket and hands it to Clive.

I lean over and scan the rave review. It's been written by Jim McGuire, the very same Jim who comes into the cafe every day with his wife; the same Jim I laughed at when he claimed at the Souper Van to be a food critic for *The Times*. I thought it was an elderly man's fantasy. What was that thought I had the other week about not judging people?

'Bloody hell! Show me that!' Nat startles Clive with a smacker on the lips. 'This is bloody amazing.' She jumps up, practically knocking the plates of foie gras and jam sandwiches off the table Plummy had just placed in front of us.

Fred pushes his plate away. 'This foie gras is not a sign of a thriving economy, but a symptom of a system that is failing hardworking people on poverty wages.'

'Well, I think it's bloody delish!' Nat bites into the sarnie and passes it to Clive to try. Clive licks his lips. Judging by the look in his eyes, it could be over Nat as much as the foie gras.

I try to get his attention again. 'Are you working on any interesting projects, Clive?'

'Yes, I've been asked to join a new parliamentary task force on the emerging drone delivery market. It's an interesting area. I predict there will soon not be a rooftop in London or any major city around the world that will not be bought up for the purpose of drone delivery.'

'Bloody online shopping is killing the high street,' Fred mutters.

'Our Good Life project is on the High Street in Kentish Town, you know. And as unbelievable as it sounds, we dug up truffles in the back garden last month?' I'm about to say more when a plate of what looks like pasta with cheese sauce is placed in front of me.

'Ricotta gnudi with wild mushroom and truffles,' Plummy announces.

'Oh look, Deb! These are *our* truffles,' Nat cries, as Plummy grates shavings of truffles onto our plate. 'That's why we're eating here for free tonight, Clive.' She lifts a shaving and lovingly cradles it in her palm. 'We supply our truffles exclusively to them.'

'That reminds me, Deb,' Rich says. 'We must go and give your pressie to Chef.'

I wince. Whilst I'm nervous about meeting the infamous Chef Chang and offering him the pressie Rich forced me to make, I'm pleased for an excuse to leave the table. Clive might return to the subject of Stu and his Bristol interview, which he clearly knows about at any time. We walk away from the table leaving Clive and Nat in raptures over what Plummy describes as Arctic char with fingerlings.

'Are you all right, Rich?' I ask, as we push open the swing doors to the kitchen. 'You seem a little down tonight. And what's with the weird looks Harold is giving you?'

Rich's answer is drowned out by a cacophony of clattering pots and pans, shouting sou-chefs, and general culinary creative mayhem. I look around the huge kitchen and suddenly duck, just managing to avoid a waiter who rushes past us carrying a loaded tray. While the heat is almost as oppressive as the noise, the atmosphere is totally intoxicating. For all the fancy dinners I have been to with Stu and friends, I've never actually been in a professional kitchen before.

'Ricardo, my friend! You're here!' An amazingly handsome Asian man in a chef's hat, his cheek bones as sharp as the knife he's carrying, strides up and gives Rich a big bear hug. 'It's been too long.'

'Good to see you, Changster,' says Rich, and hugs him back.

I stare at the world-famous Chef Chang, who I recognise from the profusion of magazines and TV shows he's regularly featured in. I'm no social media stalker, but I have to admit to following his recent exploits with a certain super model.

'Aren't you going to introduce me to your charming friend?' Chef Chang turns to me.

'Deb, meet the Changster.'

'Er, good evening, Chef Chang,' I manage to mutter, feeling rather starstruck.

'Bravo, Chef, for all the grub,' Rich beams.

'Oh, don't you of all people give me that old clap trap. You know me far better than that,' Chef Chang laughs. 'The food here's a load of pretentious bollocks.'

What? Rich knows Chef Chang better than …?

'I'm sure Rich told you about our adventures together at Citibank in New York. That's where I got my name "the Changster," because of my—some might say—less than scrupulous bond trading. Ricardo was the golden boy,' Chef Chang says. 'And now, some fifteen years later even with our change of careers, I'm still the racketeer, this time ripping off gullible fools with this so-called haute cuisine. But Ricardo, true to form, is the altruist campaigning for a new economic system.' He pats Rich on the back. 'I see that tosser, Harold's in the restaurant tonight.'

'What? You used to be a banker, Rich?' I hear the surprise in my own voice. 'But that's impossible. You absolutely hate …'

Rich turns to me: 'What the Changster says is true, Deb. For years, I was an investment banker in New York. I'm sorry I didn't tell you and Nat the truth. It's just not something I'm proud of.'

'But, but … when was this? And what happened? And is that how Harold knows you?'

'Our paths used to cross occasionally with Harold in the happy—or as I remember them, unhappy—hour bar circuit, where all of us investment bankers, including Harold, as I recall, hit the bars to gloat.'

'But then, I'm afraid it all went a little sour on me,' Rich continues.

'Sourer than this Meyer lemon.' Chef Chang lifts up a lemon and lobs it across the room to a sous-chef, who catches it, slices it, and tosses it onto a plate of fish.

'I'll tell you all about it later, Deb,' Rich sighs. 'But in the meantime, why don't you give Changster your gift?'

'I'm always up for a gift from a pretty lady,' Chef Chang grins at me.

'I, er, have made you a pair of boxer shorts.' I retrieve the boxer shorts from my bag and nervously hand them to Chef Chang. 'I made them by sewing several small patches of unused black and white silky fabric together. I've designed them in homage to the dog-tooth trousers you wear.'

'Yeah, it's way too feckin' hot in here, Changster,' says Rich, sympathetically. 'You and the boys should ditch the trousers and wear these dogtooth boxers. It's part of a new ethical brand we're launching called Box Clever. We upcycle fabrics and put them to sexy new use.'

Chef feels the lovely, airy fabric and traces his hand along the drawstring waist and little loops.

'I added the little loops so you can attach your ladles, spoons and other cooking utensils to them,' I clarify.

'Talking of utensils, just look how low the crotch is, mate.' Rich points at the boxers. 'Gives your "personal" tools room to breathe!'

'These boxers follow the A-B-C construction design principle.' I try to sound as professional as possible.

'She means *'anti-bollock crushing!'* Rich laughs.

'It's their wide panelled gusset ...' I continue to explain. Was I really standing in London's hippest restaurant talking *gussets* with one of the world's most revered chefs?

'These are great. Do you have any more?' asks Chef Chang

'Well, yes, I do.' I lift out several more pairs of boxers from my bag.

'Down your tools, team! Off with your britches and gather round,' Chef Chang calls out to the room, as he waves the boxers in the air.

At his command, and to my amazement, the all-male team strip off their trousers and pants. Not sure whether to be alarmed more by the sizzling pans now left unmanned, or by the range of dangling genitalia now left uncovered, I try to avert my eyes. Sort of.

The team put on the boxers and come together for a photo opp.

'Right ... selfie and video time,' Chef Chang calls out. 'What's your Instagram feed, Deb?'

Just as I am about to reply how I don't have one, Rich trundles off an Instagram address.

'"Box Clever," eh? Wow, these feel great, man. A real breath of fresh air.' Chef Chang enthuses, as Rich takes a short video to upload to Instagram.

The sous-chef and rest of the team agree.

'Right,' says Chef Chang, 'now back to your table and wait to see what pretentious rubbish I've come up with for dessert. It's hilarious the way all the punters love it. I'm going to make sure wanker banker Harold's dessert goes off with a *real* bang tonight.'

'If you don't mind, Changster, I'm going to split. I need to clear my head.' Rich spuds Chef Chang. 'Do you mind tagging along with me, Deb? I feel I've got some explaining to do.'

Seeing the solemn look in his eyes, I make a mental note to send Clive a short note of apology in the morning and follow Rich out through the back door.

'It's a gift to walk in the dark, don't you think?' Rich breaks the silence after fifteen minutes of strolling down Marylebone High Street with him lost in thought, perhaps reminiscing. 'Look at the moon reflected in this puddle. Listen to the faint rustle of the last few leaves on the branches. Our noses and ears become keener in the dark,' he smiles sadly at me.

I look down into the puddle, but the soft moon glow is replaced by the glare of shop lights that are now reflected in it.

'Just look at all these shops.' Rich shakes his head as we walk on. 'The street might be empty of shoppers, the shops closed, but still the lights remain on. It's so overbearing, that constant show of products and consumerism. Don't you ever think, Deb,' he says pointing, 'how goods like these in this fancy kitchen shop, are less about the things themselves, and more about the human desire to be part of a tribe?'

We pause besides the shop in question. It's called Divertimenti and it has a tempting display of copper pans, blue Le Creuset pots, olive chopping boards, and Bosch processing gadgets. I know it all too well. I'm a regular shopper here. *I* am part of this tribe.

'Well, that name says it all,' Rich continues. '"Divertimenti," eh? Consumerism is all about creating a diversion from what our real priorities in life should be, and that's sharing and caring. But we consumers continue to buy into the powerful corporate mythologies that have been carefully constructed to project meaning onto any object simply by stamping a brand on it.'

'Why did you leave banking, Rich?' I blurt out the question I had been dying to ask.

'It was all just spinning numbers, Deb.' Rich looks down. 'In the end, the numbers started spinning *me*.'

'I must admit that you being an ex-banker explains a lot to me,' I say. 'You always seem so good with numbers; you seem to know the stats on so many …'

'I was an investment banker for ten years. Then when I hit my mid-thirties, I just wanted my life to be worth more. I wanted it to have real value. It was time to give back. Can you understand that?'

'I understand it more than you realise.' I place my hand on his shoulder. Time to give back was exactly the same reason Stu gave me on the phone last night for him being so excited by the Bristol University job: A job that would be his chance to inspire the next generation of economic thinkers.

'Unfortunately, my decision led to the breakdown of my marriage, and left me drifting for many years.' He looks up at me and smiles. 'But suddenly, it's all changed. I now sleep so well at night, curled up under my Thomas the Tank Engine duvet cover in the crypt at the Good Life, because I've spent the day talking to local folk about things that have meaning to me.' He turns to me. 'And, of course, making new friends like you and Nat.'

'I feel exactly the same, and I'm sure Nat does too. Thanks for sharing your story with me, Rich.' I look down at my wedding ring. I so want to confide in him about Stu but can't take the risk of Nat finding out Stu's potential new job and the move it would entail. I'm not even sure how *I* really feel about it, or where I fit into Stu's giving back. I may not be an acclaimed academic like my brainy husband-age, and making blokes' boxer shorts may not be world changing, but it has meaning to *me*—and made *me* happy tonight.

I also I fail to say out loud how wonderful I think it is that we've turned an old, rundown church into a hub that serves scrumptious surplus Persian street food, even if it's only to a few people at a time; how trying to talk people into making more considered choices about consumption and resource use might be a drop in the anthropogenically plastic-polluted, plundered ocean, but it's our little puddle. Maybe it *is* all about changing the world one grain of rice, one new friend, and one shared tent peg at a time.

'By the way, Deb, please don't tell Nat yet about my banking background,' Rich says softly, interrupting my thoughts. 'I can imagine how much she'll take the piss. I'll never hear the end of it. Mind you, I wonder if she might not have a bit of a penchant for bankers. Did you see the way she was all over Clive tonight?'

I'm hit by two surprising thoughts.

@NTS: Anthropogenic? It's a word only used by serious environmental campaigners! I must remember to voice it at next month's girls lunch. The second lightbulb moment is the recognition that Rich seems to have feelings for Nat. What an interesting and lovely couple they would make.

Then Rich links my arm and we walk away from the altar of consumerism that is Marylebone High Street. Rich heads home towards his cosy chapel at a regenerated church in NW5, and me to an empty house, which I need to fill with some serious thoughts.

MARCH

CHAPTER 15

The Avian Funfair

7 a.m. One week later. Woodberry Wetlands in northeast London. And wet it certainly is.

In trepidation, I steal a look out from the musty bird hide where we are taking shelter from the incessant rain. Around me in the quarter light, the buff-coloured reed beds surrounding the wetland, lay prostrate, pummelled by the rain. The peppery sky is leaden with unbudging clouds. We have been here for an hour—Greg having had the bright idea to arrive at the wetlands early to catch the dawn chorus. But judging by the amount of sniffling to be heard in the hide, the only thing we have all caught is a cold. And the only sounds we have so far heard are from sneezing and wheezing children. The birds have wisely stayed tucked up in their cosy nests.

'Wonderful idea to bring the children to the Wetlands, don't you think?' says Father Guy. 'I do love going on school trips. Such fun.' I can't help noticing that even his head-to-toe waterproofs cling to his body in all the right places.

I nod in agreement. But fun, if I'm honest, is not the first word that comes to mind about the morning so far. I shiver as I try to wrap my inadequate coat around me. Yes, I know … there's no such thing as bad weather, just bad clothes. Perhaps in retrospect I should have worn the waterproofs offered to me by Rich; but, as they say, you can lead a horse to water, but you can't make it drink. At least I can fancifully drink in the sight of my reversible poncho and shapely (if soggy) black tights tucked into my purple wellies with just a hint of heel. And … hmm … I'm certain I caught GG having a good gander at them too.

'Mizzle, fiss, blunk and dibble!' Greg cries out. 'C'mon kids, repeat after me: *mizzle, fiss …*'

Jafar and Chloe giggle as they call out Greg's words, whilst Henry Junior, of course, substitutes 'piss' for 'fiss.' And as I try to flatten my hair, which has taken on its own miss and fizzle, I smile at GG and join in with the chorus of strange-sounding words.

Then Greg adds another enthusiastic note: 'Children, did you know that there is a huge repertoire of local words and regional dialects to describe rain?'

'I can't dial anything from my mobile,' says Henry Junior in a sulk. 'There's no signal and I'm bored.'

Greg tries to ignore this interruption. 'Words such as "blunk" for a sudden squall, or "dabbly," describe moist air that feels like wet linen on the skin.'

'I think it's a shame we no longer experience rain as closely as your poetic words suggest we once did,' Rich says.

'Well said!' says Pippa, as she pokes her head out from the hide into the pouring rain. 'My nan was from Scotland where I know "fiss" describes drizzle.'

'It's a really *clarty* day,' GG joins in. 'I think that's an expression from the Lake District where *my* family are from.'

The Lake District, I hear. My mind immediately conjures up images of exhilarating days hiking to the top of Scary Pike—or whatever it's called—and evenings with ... er, GG and I roasting around a log fire in a cosy ...

'It sure is raining *forks'tiyundown'ards* ...' Greg's guffaws of laughter spoil my daydream. Well, a girl's allowed to dream, isn't she?

'If you don't watch it, Pippa, you'll get *drookit* from this *smirr* ...' Greg goes on.

'Funnily enough, I'm due for one,' says Nat, much to the bewilderment of the men, while Nahal, Anousha, and I giggle. 'I only received a letter from the doc's surgery yesterday reminding me to book one.'

'Hold it, kids,' Rich butts in. 'Our lecture on the avian funfair is due to start in an hour when the rest of your class and your teacher arrive. Doesn't it sound fun?'

'No! I hate rain,' Henry Junior moans.

'Rain is vital and life-giving: it allows us to grow crops and create the lovely gardens for which this country is famed, you little shi ...'

GG cuts him off as he starts to sing, *'And did those feet in ancient time, walk upon England's mountains green ... Bring me my arrows of desire ...'* He looks at me and stops singing. 'Oh Deborah, you're shivering. Why don't you come and sit next to me, and I'll warm you up.'

'Listen everyone, as the rain seems to be set in all day, I say we just go out and enjoy it.' Rich stands up and gestures for us all to do the same. 'Let's go on a puddle walk. After all, every puddle tells a story. We just have to slow down and offer them our curiosity.'

No, let's sit here, I think. But I manage to restrain myself from shouting it out. Puddles? I'm a lot more curious about whether GG really did just offer to warm me up. Or is it just part of my daydream?

'Well, I agree with Rich,' says Pippa. She links my arm and pulls me up from my seat. 'Did you know, children, that our bodies are composed of seventy percent water? As two thirds of Earth is covered by water, each of us mirrors our global habitat.' It sounds like a dry statistic to me, but she gushes on. 'It follows therefore that turning the world's natural wealth into resources to be exploited can only lead to the destruction of our personal ecosystem.'

Taking my hand, Pippa leads me out of the hide and urges to me follow her example and open my arms out wide in some kind of rain salutation. As the drops trickle down her face and she continues to greet the rain, I bend down to grab an umbrella from my bag. I try to open it—but it droops downward-dog style, hopelessly around me.

'Money can't buy a splash in a puddle,' shouts Rich, as he jumps in a puddle next to me. He's swiftly followed by some of the children. It's a proper pool of pleasure.

'Oh Deb, you're getting soaked! Do put on this hat. And this sensible coat.' Nat pops an aptly named bucket hat on my head. 'I don't think bright pink is your colour!' she laughs, as she forces my sodden arms into what my grandmother would have described as a canary-yellow Pac-a-Mac ... Oh so far from the 'Mac' of today's ascription.

'Gather round, children,' Nahal calls out, saving my blushes and drawing attention away from my abject humiliation. 'Did you know that hundreds of years ago, Arab navigators had a name to describe someone who had the wisdom to read the physical signs in water? They were called the *Isharat*.'

'I'm an Isharat,' Jafar laughs, as he runs off pretending to sail his boat, darting in and out of the ever-increasing puddles.

'Look everyone, there's a duck swimming in the middle of the reservoir,' Rich shouts.

Sure enough, a lone duck has appeared on the murky water, doubtless on its search for brekkie. Oh, for a bacon sarnie, I sympathise with the duck. Vegan bacon, of course.

'Just take a look at the beautiful wake the duck is creating,' says Rich. 'The mix of ripples coming from the breeze. The shapes and rhythm of the water are in the signs all around us. It is so fascinating to "read' water. Who wants to come and learn?'

'We do,' chorus the children—well, all except Henry Junior.

I watch the would-be armada sail off with Rich, weaving in and out of the reed bank on the water's edge.

'You look like a translucent tropical fish—all pink and yellow,' says GG approaching me. 'The question is, are you a deep—or shallow-water fish?'

Deep, oh so deep, I want to reply. And full of steamy, warm water. Instead, I say, 'Fascinating this idea of reading water, don't you think?'

There's a sudden and unwelcome tug on my granny mac-cum-equatorial-mermaid coat. I turn round to see Chloe pointing up. 'Look at that red balloon in the sky.'

A red balloon has just appeared through the mist. A balloon perhaps hoisted free by the wind from a child's hand many miles away. Hovering high over the reservoir, its rosy glow casts a glimmer of colour on the otherwise sombre surround.

Nat joins us. 'That balloon reminds me of the dessert we had at The Truffle Hog last week. You missed a great meal, Father Guy.' She licks her lips and continues, 'It was an amazing edible balloon that Chef Chang had made from sugar. And it was tied with string made from apple peel. We had to suck the helium from the balloon, pop it, and then eat the balloon up. There was so much helium in one balloon that it blew up in some bloke's face! Harold, I think he was called.'

Even though I have heard Nat recount this story dozens of times over the last week, I still have to suppress remembering how Chef

Chang had promised Rich that Harold the wanker banker's just dessert would go off with a bang.

'You're probably too highbrow, Father Guy, but do you ever watch *MasterChef*?' Nat asks.

'Well, yes, occasionally,' he admits, with a guilty look. 'In-between choir practice and my many other parish commitments.'

'Well, you'll be thrilled to hear that Chef Chang, who was on the show the other week, is a friend of ours. He's heard all about our Abundance Cafe and is coming to share an Easter meal with us in a couple of weeks—so you'll get to meet him. Yes, I must say The Good Life is really becoming quite celebrated.' She turns round to face Chloe and Henry Junior, who have walked over to us. 'Isn't that exciting children?'

As Chloe replies how her dad doesn't allow her to watch TV, and Henry Junior says he only watches horror movies on Netflix, two thoughts come to my mind. First, I don't remember Nat meeting Chef Chang. And second, I wonder how good GG would look dressed only in a chef's hat and a pair of my dogtooth boxers.

@NTS: Almost good enough to eat.

The image dissolves, damn it, when Rich appears and says, 'Talking of Changster, I forgot to tell you, Deb, the Instagram picture of him and the boys wearing your boxers has gone viral. I've asked Little Leroy to set us up a PayPal account so we can take orders online. Your "Box Clever" brand is days away from going live.'

Viral? My amazed reaction to Rich's info is echoed loudly behind us. Two elderly ladies have walked up to us unnoticed. They're wearing the same sensible raincoats and hats, and they look exactly like each other. 'I hope there are no germs here?' one of them says sternly. 'My sister, Marjorie, has only just recovered from the flu, and she certainly can't afford to catch another viral infection.'

'Oh, stuff and nonsense, Glynis!' the other lady interjects. 'Good morning, all. We are Glynis and Marjorie. We're twins. Are you also here for the Avian fun fair talk?'

'You can't be twins, you're too old,' Henry Junior pipes up.

'I'm afraid the rain must have kept most folk away,' Glynis smiles. 'But it's stopped now, so it won't prevent us from having fun, will it?'

'How lovely to meet you,' I say. 'And yes, we are excited about taking part in the Avian funfair aren't we, children?' I look out towards the reservoir, relieved to see that while the rain hasn't completely stopped, it *has* eased to a dribble of droplets rippling upon the water.

'Where are the slot machines? I thought this was meant to be a funfair?' demands Henry Junior.

'What an amusing little fellow you are.' Glynis pats him on the head. 'So, children, even though it has been raining cats and dogs, have you got any twitches yet today?'

'No, I can't get online. I want to go home,' Henry Junior sulks.

Greg taps him on the head with his clipboard and says slowly and deliberately, 'Henry, as was mentioned during my ornithology talk at The Good Life yesterday, the main goal of twitching is to *identify* birds to add to our list.'

'Sister and I always agree on our favourite birding sight. It's the mass gatherings of swallows in autumn as they get ready to set off on one of the longest journeys.' Marjorie looks up to the sky. 'Do you realise, children, that migratory swallows travel south ten thousand kilometres to South Africa, and then, of course, fly back here again in spring?'

'I'm a bird too!' Jafar smiles at her, as he raises his arms and starts to soar in and out of a puddle.

'Yes, sister, swallows are undoubtedly our best-known migrants,' Glynis agrees.

'My dad doesn't like mig—'

Jafar continues, preventing Henry Junior from sharing anymore family information, 'I've been reading with my dad about how birds find their way. There are many navigational clues, like the direction of the setting sun, the stars in the night sky, even the earth's magnetic field.'

'Well said, Jafar,' says Greg. He grins at Nahal. 'Your son is such a bright lad.'

'But this is our favourite avian season,' Marjorie smiles. 'Sister and I love this mating time of year. Although with this cold start to spring, the mating season will probably be delayed. The only birds we see from our block down the road are the pigeons we watch canoodling on roof ridges over many months.'

'As they say, sister, any ridge and any female will do!' Glynis chuckles.

'Birds sing to attract a mate, children. Did you know?' Marjorie goes on.

'Shame it hasn't worked for you Nat!' Rich winks at Nat.

Glynis picks up from her sister, 'The dawn chorus that you hear from March to July is a signal that those feathered alarm clocks are at it again!'

'At *what* again, Father Guy?' Chloe tugs on GG's rain jacket.

'Er ...'

'Yes, we always look forward to hearing the resident robins—they're the first songsters of the season,' Glynis says hurriedly to save GG from having to answer Chloe. His face has turned a deeper shade of red than a robin's breast. Glynis continues, 'Then comes the song of the migrants like the chiffchaffs and blackcaps.'

'Oh, look, sister,' Marjorie says excitedly. 'There's a dunnock swimming in the reservoir.'

We all look out towards the reservoir to see a small and inconspicuous bird with brown plumage and a grey breast swimming along by the reeds.

'While the dunnock is normally such a very humble bird, what makes it stand out is his amorous behaviour,' says Glynis. 'The size of a male bird's testes can often have a bearing on its behaviour, and in the case of the dunnock ...'

'What is *testes*?' Chloe once again asks Father Guy. 'Is it like the maths one?'

'Er ...'

Marjorie has an answer of sorts. 'Sister and I have heard that the Argentine lake duck has the longest bird penis. It's corkscrew shaped and seventeen inches long.'

I turn away in embarrassment, unsure where to look. And I'm trying really hard not to listen to the sound of Nahal and Anoushka in full giggles.

'I do hope you are warm enough, Glynis.' Marjorie wraps a scarf more tightly around her sister's neck. 'But back to the dunnock. It might surprise you, but this amorous species can mate as often as a hundred times a day in a variety of liaisons—even a threesome.'

'Even two males with two females at the same time. Isn't that so, sister?' adds Glynis.

'And as the male wants his own efforts to prevail over those of other chaps, he then pecks at the female's cloaca to get her to reject a previous deposit.'

'What's a *cloaker*?' It's curious Chloe again, this time tugging at *my* coat. 'Is it like what you're wearing under your fish costume?'

My first reaction is to think, *No, it's not a cloak—it's a designer poncho.* The second is to wonder if we have misunderstood the theme of this morning's talk on the avian funfair. Just what kind of fun are we talking about? But if I'm not sure this is the most appropriate conversation for children to hear, somehow—like Nahal, Anousha, Nat, and Rich—I can't stop myself laughing. The unlikely patter from two elderly ladies is undeniably hilarious. However, GG, I notice, is looking rather uncomfortable.

'Yes, in this competition for fertilisation, the more sperm the better the prospects of success,' Marjorie beams.

'What's *sperm*?' Chloe asks.

'*I* know what it is,' Henry Junior pipes up eagerly. 'It's …

'Anyway, kids,' Greg interrupts, 'shall we move swiftly on to look more closely in the water?' His suggestion could not be timelier.

'Ah, swifts! They pair for life, you know,' Marjorie adds, as we all walk down to explore the water's edge. 'They meet each spring at the same nesting site.'

As we stand in front of the perimeter of reeds, which have started to sway in the not so gentle breeze, I see through the mist two birds with long elegant white necks, who rise from the water. Their long, maroon-coloured beaks touch as they face each other.

'Oh, I don't believe it!' Greg shouts in excitement. 'Two great-crested grebes. Look everyone. This was the one bird species I was hoping to see today. Their courtship ritual is so beautiful. And it's so rare to see.'

We watch as the grebes flick their heads from side to side,

crowned with elegant ruffled black and chestnut plumes. This is followed by mutual head shaking, each bird mimicking the other. We watch transfixed, as the birds lower their heads, swim low in the water like alligators, then swim apart. Turning round to face each other again, they continue with more head bobs and shakes whilst showing off the crest of feathers on their heads.

'Blimey! It's like a dance from *Strictly Come Dancing*,' Nat breaks the mesmerised silence.

The birds continue to perform their tango-like moves until suddenly after a series of what sounds like braying calls, they dive under the water. A short while later, they resurface several metres apart carrying weed in their beaks.

'Ah, this is the weed dance, the climax of their mating ritual,' Marjorie sighs.

'Yes,' says Greg with a smile. 'It's the part of the courtship when they give each other gifts of weeds.'

'How generous of them!' Nat laughs.

Back on the rippling water, the birds are racing inexorably across the surface towards each other. Half opening their wings to extend their feathers as they meet, they rear up out of the water, paddling like mad to stay afloat as they offer each other their weeds.

'And that is how they mate,' says Greg. 'Beautiful, isn't it?'

'It looks like fun. I want a go.' Chloe once again tugs on GG'S coat.

The pained expression on GG's face suggests he is regretting his in loco parentis offer.

'I'll do it with you,' offers Henry Junior.

'Why don't we sing a bird song?' GG suggests hurriedly. 'Two little blackbirds sitting on the hill, one named …'

Whether it's to help cover his embarrassment, or because we all enjoy recalling the words from childhood, we all join in the singing. But after a few minutes it starts to rain again, our cue to retreat into the hide.

As we all sit in a huddle, Greg tries to keep the kids amused. 'Bird song can be a funny thing. For example, the Yellowhammer's song sounds like he is saying, "a little bit of bread and no cheese." Whereas a Chiffchaff just repeats its own name.'

'I've heard that starlings can mimic everything, including car alarms,' Pippa laughs.

'Did you hear that bloody alarm going off in Kentish Town High Road last night?' asks Nat. 'It kept me awake for hours last night.'

I refrain from reminding Nat that she lives nowhere near the high street she's talking about. Unless of course she spent the night at The Good Life. But doesn't Henry Senior also live in a house just off the high street? Hmm ... I scan her and Rich's face to see if they're giving anything away.

'Well, my favourite birds are a flock of shags,' Rich shares his sole admission about shags in any form.

All further thoughts are put out of my mind, as with a sudden burst of light, the sun comes out. It is quickly followed by a glorious rainbow.

'Wow!' Jafar exclaims. 'Look at all the colours reflecting on the lake.'

We rush out to see the wetlands rippling with colour, the raindrops glistening through the sunshine. Above us, a perfect painterly arc decorates the sky.

'Children, here's something to think about,' says Rich. 'You can measure the size of raindrops by looking at the colours in the rainbow.' He opens his arms to try to catch a rain- drop. 'The redder they are, the bigger the drops.'

We all look up into the sky, but find that as quickly as the rainbow appeared, it had now disappeared, taking the sun with it.

Now Nahal has a go at diverting the children's attention. 'Would you like to hear a famous story from Iran, the country where I come from?' she asks. 'It is the story of a giant bird called Huma, who lives its entire life flying invisibly high above the earth, and never alighting on the ground?'

'Yes, please!' Jafar and Chloe call out in unison.

I grin as Marjorie and Glynis join the children in flapping their arms and pretending to be birds. They're quickly followed by Greg, Pippa, Nat, and Rich.

'Come on, Deborah.' I feel GG take my hand. *'He will cover you with His pinions. And under His wings you may seek refuge.'*

Too startled to question what on earth GG is talking about, I join in with the pretend feathered fun, and soar around with him relishing every second.

'Huma is considered to be the most compassionate bird, even a bird of fortune,' Anousha continues with the story. 'In the Sufi tradition, catching the Huma is beyond the wildest imagination, but even catching a glimpse of its shadow is sure to make one happy for the rest of one's life.'

'Those who don't believe in magic will never find it,' says Nahal, smiling at our flapping around.

I stop 'flying,' and look round. Not so long ago, I would never have been seen running in the rain, pretending to soar like a bird, laughing in the bleich dreich, soggy, clarty weather; or listening to rain pounding on story-telling puddles. Nor would I be standing and wearing a big grin and soggy boots, recalling Rich's news about how the photos of Chef Chang wearing my boxers had gone viral, *and* that Box Clever, an ethical fashion brand that hadn't even existed two weeks ago, was going to go live.

As the gentle rain continues to fall, blurring the wetlands and surrounding tower blocks into impressionistic brushstrokes of muted colour, I agree that perhaps there *is* a bit of magic in the air; a magic tempered only by the knowledge that Stu returned last night from a second interview at Bristol University even more excited by the prospect of the job which he claims could change the world of Economics' teaching.

Putting aside all dreaded thoughts of the house Stu was planning for us to view in Bradford-on-Avon, I look over at Nahal and smile. For as it was said by Rumi, the famous Persian poet who Nahal urged me to read: *'Yesterday I was clever, so I wanted to change the world. Today I am wise, so I am changing myself.'*

I walk over to a puddle, jump in, and laugh.

CHAPTER 16

Smoking Guns

'Love is a smoke raised with the fume of sighs.
Being purged, a fire sparkling in lovers' eyes.'

Ben pauses from reciting his Shakespearean quote to take a puff of his joint. 'I've missed hanging out with you guys.' He inhales, and smiles with satisfaction.

'Yes, it's great to see you too, Ben.' I hug the strapping 19-year-old I've not seen for two years, and sneeze.

Nat and I first met Ben—or, as we used to call him, 'Benjy-bard'—when we started developing our community garden together five years ago. Ben was as renowned for his love of Shakespeare as for the quantity, and, apparently, quality of the marijuana he grew.

@NTS: Is this a reefer I see before me …

We had always judged Ben as an unlikely candidate for university, but he surprised us all by getting an offer at Newcastle Uni to study agronomy.

'So, how's your degree going?' I ask as I sneeze again. I zip up my puffer jacket to ward off the chill that permeates through my body on this freezing-cold March afternoon.

'You got yon terrible cold there,' Ben says, as he hands me a perfectly laundered white handkerchief.

'I caught it at a birdwatching event last week. It turned out that it had been cancelled due to the rain, but we didn't find out till we got back here.' I wipe my nose and sigh. 'I thought it was meant to be spring by March.'

Ben shakes his head. 'You know what they say. *"Beware them ides of March."'*

'Benjy-bard!' Nat shrieks, as she rushes up and throws her arms around him. 'I'm so psyched you finally made it. I hope you're impressed with our Good Life project?' She points to the fridge that is being cleaned out by Pippa, and to the Chip Fat Travellers Van where Lucia is bent over the bonnet busily fixing something ...

'Who'd have thought when we started our small community garden that it would expand into a Good Life smallholding in a deconsecrated church!' she laughs. 'In the back garden we've got chickens and even a pet owl!'

'Yeah, you noble girls hast done good. It's almost as lit here as our campus,' says Ben. 'We've got a flock o' sheep, a dairy unit, even a modern pig finishing unit.'

'Did someone mention pigs?' Marg asks, as she walks up to us. She takes a lead from her bag. Old Spot grunts, clearly as unimpressed with Ben's comment as with the lead that Marg now places around his neck to take him for a walk.

Ben bends down to tickle Old Spot's nose. 'I'm loving agronomy. It's the science and tech of producing plants for food, fuel, and fibre. I'm currently studying strategies for sustainable agriculture. It's totally goat.'

'We've not got any goats yet.' Nat shakes her head. 'But it's a good idea.'

'No, he means G-O-A-T-, as in *Greatest of All Time*,' Marg explains. 'Don't you girls keep up with teenage vernacular?'

Ben winks at Marg. 'However, with molecular and genetics on the crop management horizon, there's some real shady stuff going on. In particular, the villainous Bayer and Monsanto companies. Sons of darkness ...'

Marg interjects, 'We know all about Bayer and its purchase of Monsanto, then relaunched Monsanto's evil GM products under a new brand name. Next month we are going to screen an exposé on them.'

'Talking about shady stuff,' says Nat. 'Although I'm totally thrilled you've finally popped in, we are just on our way to a public meeting to discuss the future of this very site.' She looks around. 'A nasty bastard called Thomas Montjoy wants to turn this land into a posh block of flats.'

'But we're not going to let that happen!' Pippa skips up to us. Her chestnut hair has been released from its ponytail and blows freely in the breeze.

'What, this amazing place filled with beautiful colleens? No way!' Ben blushes as he smiles at Pippa. 'I think I'd better come and help you damsels in distress. There's daggers in men's smirks. But I think you ladies may also have another small problem.' He points to a filing cabinet in the corner. It's something that seems to have been dumped overnight. And it now has smoke billowing out of it.

'Quick, Deb,' Nat yells. 'Run and get water. That cabinet is going to catch fire.'

'Relax, girls.' A hand is placed on my shoulder.' The reassurance comes from Rich. 'This is exactly what is meant to happen. It's a smoke house.'

'A smoking filing cabinet?' says Ben. 'That's totally Gucci!'

@NTS: Gucci? A smokehouse in a filing cabinet? I'm wondering if the flu pill I took this morning has hallucinogenic properties.

'Holy smoke!' laughs Nat.

'That's a good one from you, Nat!' Rich puts his arm around her. She pushes it away. 'That's what we should call our new smoke-house: *the Holy Smoke!* I'm so pleased it's working; I've been up all night building it. I was just out in the back garden collecting oak twigs to infuse in it.

'Yuck! Smoked food went out with the cavemen,' Nat grimaces.

'*Au contraire*, Nat,' I say. 'Smoked food is experiencing a huge revival right now. It's totally hip.'

I fail to mention the details of the swanky dinner I was obliged to go to with Phoebe last week to celebrate Fliff's birthday. The lapsang souchong smoked salmon was almost as satisfying as the expression on Phoebe's face when I shared with her the Box Clever insta feed showing Chef Chang wearing my boxers!

'And anyway, you can't build one in a grotty old filing cabinet. Nat persists.

'Yes, you can, and from one little hot dish to another, let me show you how!' Rich links Nat's arm and pulls her over to the smoking files. Ben and I follow in hot pursuit.

Rich dons an oven glove and opens the top drawer to reveal a tray of smoking fish. It gives me an idea: I wonder if I can file my credit card statement in the bottom drawer before Stu can see it!

Rich points to several holes on the side of the filing cabinet. 'To turn a filing cabinet into a smoke house, you just drill holes in the side of each drawer. In the bottom drawer you place a cooker.' He opens it to reveal a disposable barbecue. 'This is just for now. I am going to build a more sustainable cooker soon.' Leaning over, he adds several oak twigs to the charcoal. There's a lovely, woody aroma. Rich then closes the bottom drawer, and opens up the one above, where there's a stainless-steel rack sizzling with more fish. 'Nahal and I are dreaming of smoking with tea leaves and herbs,' he says. 'We're going to experiment with veg, and perhaps smoked cheese. We've been offered a regular supply of fish from that posh fishmonger in Tufnell Park in return for some of your Box Clever shorts, Deb. I hope that's OK?'

'Methinks there's a magical alchemy when smoke and wood chip combine,' says Ben. He closes his eyes and breathes in before I can agree.

'Talking of magical alchemies,'—Nat looks at her watch—'I hate to interrupt your latest fantasy, Richard, but the public meeting is due to start in fifteen minutes. If we don't go and stand our ground, it will be more a case of smoking guns, than smoking fish. It could be a showdown for the Good Life!

Having scuttled down the high street at breakneck speed, Nat, Rich, Marg, Ben, and I arrive at Kentish Town Primary School to find Michael pacing up and down.

'I … er, think we need to get inside.' He starts to shake as he gives Nat a multi-coloured, knitted rosette. The words: 'Vote Nat: A Good Life vote,' is sewed on a patch in the middle.

'We can't go in until Bradley arrives. He's bringing our secret weapon,' Nat replies, affixing the rosette to her tight-fitting lurid pink T-shirt.

Boxing Bradley armed with his secret weapon? I stifle a giggle as I imagine a giant pepperoni truncheon, or a frozen peashooter.

'Er, I'm afraid the meeting started half an hour ago,' Michael stutters. 'I tried to call you all, but none of you answered.'

Nat and I quickly check our phones to discover that Michael *did* call each of us several times, but in the rush to get here we missed his calls.

'What the fek!' shouts Rich. 'Someone's given us the wrong start time.'

We take a deep breath and dash into the Year 2 classroom. In the front row, Father Guy is sitting next to Councillor Thornton, whilst Miss Stuart is cosying up to Henry Smarmy Smythe. The room is filled with people transfixed by an image on the white screen of a swimming pool planned for the basement of The Gargoyles apartments.

Thomas Montjoy looks at his watch and smiles smugly as we enter the room. 'So, in summary, folks, the only decision you will need to make is crawl or breaststroke!' He leers at the rosette bouncing up and down on Nat's ample breasts, as she rushes up to the front to stand next to him.

'And that just about wraps it up,' he races on. 'Thank you all for coming. I hope you enjoyed the update.'

'What do you mean "that wraps it up?"' shouts Rich. 'We were told this meeting started at six-thirty.'

'So sorry, sir, you were misinformed. No, the start time was definitely six p.m., as it clearly states here.' Montjoy lifts a flyer with a start time of 6 p.m. printed on it.

'You deliberately misled us, you, feker! I'll get you ...' Rich strides over towards him, with raised fists.

He is blocked from reaching Montjoy by Nat, who steps in his way.

'Good evening, everyone. My name is Natalie.' She addresses the room in a gentle, butter-wouldn't-melt voice. 'As Richard is saying, we will get Mr Montjoy the facts as to why The Gargoyles apartments will not get planning consent.' She pauses to smile hopefully at Councillor Thornton. He's not listening, but busy scrolling through texts on his phone.

'Sorry we're late,' Nat continues undeterred, 'but we've been attending important community matters: and matters it does!' She grins at her wordplay. 'I'm here once more to say that we demand more affordable and social housing in the area, not another posh apartment block. We demand that our empty spaces become inclusive community hubs for mutual aid groups—like our Good Life project. We the community want a more equitable, caring Kentish Town where folk have a good life. That's why I'm standing as an independent Good Life candidate in this summer's local council elections.' She pats the knitted rosette she is wearing.

'My Knit Wits group made the rosette if anyone's interested!' Michael proudly calls out. 'We're a group of single dads who meet at the Good Life once a week to swop jokes and ...'

'We want to hear about the swimming pool in the flats, not another yarn!' a man calls from the back.

Thomas Montjoy does little to hide the snigger which breaks out on his face, whilst Councillor Thornton simply yawns. I look over to GG and smile. He looks down, refusing to meet my gaze.

Natalie continues, her voice rising with urgency, 'Just because our Good Life church is deconsecrated, it still is a valuable community meeting place. We the community need to stick together and ...'

'As I've already said,' Montjoy cuts her off, 'at Greener Properties we totally agree that our churches are at heart of our community. But whilst we all want exercise classes and knitting lessons ...'—he pauses to smile condescendingly at Michael—'electricity bills do have to be paid! That's why we will be donating twenty-thousand pounds to St Margaret's Church.'

St Margaret's? But isn't that Father Guy's other church? It's a disconcerting thought: what would Montjoy have to gain by placing a large donation there? I look over at GG, who coughs nervously.

'Smiling, damned villain ...' Ben mutters under his breath.

The question I'm wondering is just *who* is the villain here? It's a poser that must wait, as Boxing-Bradley, usually a man of few words, rushes into the room calling out, 'Nat also has a community offer to share!' He proceeds to walk around the room handing out his secret weapon: Lidl vouchers for lobsters priced at only ten pounds each—valid only for the next day. Attached to the voucher is a flyer: 'Nat: A Good Life vote.' While I must admit to being bowled over, once again, by Nat's speech, I'm not as convinced by her marketing ploy—or its legality.

'Well, er, perhaps now is the time to have another look at the literature and copies of the share offer I've laid out around the room.' Montjoy's words remain unheard as a swarm of people jump up and rush over to grab a voucher from Bradley. 'I do hope you enjoy reading about the porter and the exclusive gym for apartment owners.' He pauses, then adds, 'As they say, the devil's in the details.'

'There's only one feckin' devil here,' Rich shouts.

'Anyway, er, thanks for coming, everyone. Any questions ...?'

'I've got a question.' Marg walks up to Montjoy and whacks him on the arm with her large bag. 'If you were telling the truth about caring for community, you would also be donating to the local Somali centre, the Bengali community. Why are ...'

I don't hear the end of her question because I must admit, I too, am jumping up to claw one of Bradley's sought-after secret weapons. As I do so, I bump into GG. 'Oh, Father Guy, such good news about the donation for your *other* church. But why has it gone to ...' I pause to wipe away the stream of green phlegm—greener than the Rizla packet I spy Ben opening—which has started to trickle down my face.

'Oh, Guy, there you are!' Councillor Thornton would like to have a chat.' Montjoy whisks GG away before I can finish asking my question.

Ben comes up to me. Seeing my flushed cheeks, he offers to walk me home. As we head for the door, I notice folk looking eagerly through The Gargoyles share offer documents, whilst two women ask Henry Smarmy Smythe where to put their name down for a flat.

I walk down the road with Ben ruminating on the evening's machinations. For some reason, I'm unsettled by GG's St Margaret's church being offered so much money. I want to know who gave us the wrong meeting start time, and how Henry Smarmy Smythe is involved with Greener Properties? But right now, if I'm honest, I'm mostly unsettled by the prospect of going to Bradford-on-Avon tomorrow to visit a house—and not having confided it to Nat.

I turn to face Ben, who is smoking a joint, and take a deep breathe; for the one thing I *am* sure about, is that where there's smoke, there's fire!

CHAPTER 17

The Rites of Spring

'Don't you think that dawn is normally what the world does when no one is watching?' Rich muses as we stroll into the Good Life's back garden. 'Just look at the shadows shifting around the garden, the changing light sculptures across the sky.'

I look up from my phone's unwelcome reminder that it's only 6 a.m., to see the rays of early spring sunlight peeking through the still leafless branches on the oak tree, and the vegetable beds encrusted with a droplet of dew. The taupe and buff winter palette is now punctuated with specks of green.

Rich continues to wax lyrical: 'Only early risers, like us and the birds in spring know dawn's secrets.'

A secret I could do without knowing, I think, stifling a yawn. But then I remind myself how I had allowed Nat to coerce me into joining her and Rich at the crack of dawn to get the Good Life ready for today's lunch and workshop with Chef Chang after me being away for a few days with Stu.

I feel as conflicted about lying to Nat about the purpose of our trip as I do by the house we visited in Bradford-on-Avon. Stu, of course, loved it, calling it a rural idyll: a dream house. But the more he enthused about the spacious bedrooms and tennis court, the grand garden and potager—and all within a ninety-minute train journey of London—the more I realised how much I love our urban townhouse. Its rooms may be small and crammed with Stu's books and my ... er, accessories. The only sports area may be an old, dented basketball hoop affixed to a wall by the back door, but I'll take a communal garden over an empty striped lawn any day! Stu wants us to go back and visit the house again next week. The only thing I *am* sure about, is the need to talk to Nat, *today*.

I take a deep breath and look around. I'm amazed by the progress in the garden in my absence. On the right side, there is now a home-made polytunnel—one wall constructed from used plastic water bottles placed side by side in columns over bamboo canes—the other walls covered in stretched plastic. The four raised vegetable beds in the middle of the garden have been dug over and filled with a musky, sweet-smelling compost. The gnarled branches on the apple and pear trees have been pruned back, their limbs now uncrossed and reaching out to welcome spring. Inside the polytunnel, I find several trays of compost filled—according to the labels—with an assortment of tomato seeds and peas. Several cotyledons have already made their first appearance.

Funny how a word like 'cotyledon'—the first leaf to appear from a germinating seed—is now in my consciousness! Hmm … and thinking of germinating seeds, will I finally get to see Father Guy today to find out how his *other* church managed to bag a twen-ty-thousand-pound donation from Thomas Montjoy?

A voice from above brings me back down to … er, earth. But it's not GG. It's Rich.

'Most folks think that a brilliant sunset is one of nature's best spectacles, but I find the quiet dawn the most enchanting time of day. Don't you agree?' Rich is calling out from the pear tree which he has just climbed up. I watch him tie two chunky bits of rope around the tree, two feet apart, before climbing back down. Lifting a two-foot-wide plank of wood, he threads the other ends of the rope through holes at either end of the piece of wood and ties a knot in each part.

'Lo and behold! We now have a swing!' Rich gestures for me to come and have a go on it. So, I do.

And as I swing to and fro, the garden comes alive in the half light. Vivid pink rhubarb stems glow in one of the beds, and pale-yellow primroses are waking from their winter snooze. Beneath me, the prettiest of lightly violet flowers are wrapped around the pear tree like a necklace. How lovely—the violets match my new gardening bag! New season's colour, eh!

I am just reflecting on the old adage about how March comes in like a lion and goes out like a lamb, when Rich opens the door of the chicken coop to feed his charges. Brutus waddles out and heads purposefully towards me. Jumping off the swing, I pick up my bag and head to the other end of the garden. Time, I sigh, to get on with digging the weeds out of the pathway between the beds—the unappealing task I've been allocated today. Having been reminded by Rich to save any dandelion roots I dig up—for them to be added to one of the *delicious* dishes at today's seasonal feast—I put on my gardening gloves, and unenthusiastically begin to weed.

Two hours later, my back as stiff as the wooden boards, I'm kneeling on, I watch Rich bring out a long table for our alfresco lunch. That's my cue to stop. I clasp a bunch of freshly picked mint and head inside the church to the kitchen. There's a mouth-watering aroma.

'I hear you have earned brekkie, Deb!' Nahal grins. She takes the mint leaves from me, places them in a cup of hot water, and hands it to me. Then, opening the oven door, she brings out a steaming loaf of bread, pops it onto a plate, and places it on our newly built worktop.

Never one to decline a piece of Nahal's *taftoon*, I slump onto a stall and tuck in. 'I can't believe it was the spring equinox last Sunday and it's already Easter tomorrow,' I mumble between bites.

'And the equinox signifies the start of *Nowruz*—the Iranian new year,' Nahal smiles. 'I am so happy we are hosting a *Nowruz* feast here today, and Jafar is doubly excited about meeting a real-life TV celebrity. I can't believe I'm cooking for Chef Chang. I think he's very handsome!' she giggles.

I think back to dinner at the Truffle Hog restaurant, and Chef Chang's revelation about how both he and Rich are ex-bankers. If Rich revealed that to Nat today, how would she react?

Meanwhile, Nahal is explaining her menu: 'As it is a time of celebration and observance in many religions—Easter, the spring equinox, *Nowruz* and Passover in the Jewish faith—I thought we could make *Khoresh bademjan*—a rich aubergine and tomato stew served with *gondi*.'

'Sounds delicious,' I say, licking my lips. 'What are *gondi*?'

Nahal lifts the lid on a pan on the stove. 'Look,' she says, 'they're dumplings. They've been cooking in a turmeric and vegetable stock for several hours.' I stare at the simmering broth. Its vivid swirls of orange tinted with red are rather like this morning's sunrise.

Stirring the broth, Nahal continues, 'When I was growing up, my mama would cook *gondi* every Friday night. They were also traditionally eaten by Iranian Jews on Friday nights during their *Shabbat* dinner. It's a proud reminder of the Jewish community that's also been living in Iran since the start of the Persian empire.'

I smile as I remember the Sunday evening Chinese takeaways Stu and I used to share with James when he was younger; dumplings a favourite part of the meal, and the melt-in-the- mouth dough as sweet as the memory itself. I bet there's no Cantonese call-in within miles of the Bradford-on-Avon retreat.

Nahal puts her arm around me. 'For dessert, last night Jafar helped me make these *nan-e Nokhodchi* chickpea cookies. They'll sweeten any day! Try one, Deb …'

'Ah, here you are, Deb! Putting your feet up, as usual!' Nahal is interrupted by Nat who comes bustling in carrying a stack of posters. 'I need help putting these up to advertise Chef Chang's free pesto workshop this afternoon.'

Before I can protest about how Nat failed to turn up to this morning's gardening session, she hauls me out of the kitchen and reminds me that we only have three hours left to get the Good Life ready. She might have had a point … if the new golden highlights in her hair hadn't given away that she had been attending to roots of a more personal nature.

Nat slides a bundle of posters under my arm and unravel one that reads: 'Nifty nettle and wild garlic pesto workshop with celebrity Master Chef Chang. Today @ 3 p.m. The Good Life,' she grins. 'I hope there's not going to be a sting to this tale, and we get a big crowd here today!'

I'm grateful that Chef Chang is helping to promote The Good Life. But I'm less convinced by Rich's insistence on including nettles on the menu. More pest than pesto, I feel. I just hope Nat is right and folk do turn up. I smile as I recall a bitter-sweet memory of the nettle beer Nat's ex-hubby, Pete, used to brew in our communal garden, the evenings of laughter followed by mornings of sore heads.

I put my arm around Nat. 'I really do need to have an urgent chat with you. I've got some news ...'

'It'll have to wait, Deb,' Nat replies, slapping me on the back. 'I'm going to put some posters outside, but I'll leave you the small task of getting posters up all along the high road! You can tell me all the juicy details of your spa break later.'

Before I can counter that the only sparring we are likely to be sharing has nothing to do with any hotel, or protest that putting up posters along a whole high street is no *small* task, she dashes off.

I sigh, walk into the church, and look around the room: The solitude of dawn has given way to a frenzy of activity. On the left, Pippa and Greg are up ladders erecting a huge banner: *'Ecocide. Does nature have rights? Do trees have feelings?'* Beneath the banner, a forest has been constructed from chunks of fallen timber: a lattice-work of branches. The kids' tepee sits snuggly in the middle of the grotto, the giant rope spiderweb surrounding it creating a lair of mystery. Around the forest, fairy lights have been woven into the branches. I follow the trail and find that the lights are connected to an energy generator bike. Leroy, who has been tweaking the battery pack attached to it, jumps on the bike, and starts to pedal. The lights flicker on. Time to power up!

I pause to inspect the new desk next to the confession box. A sign above it reads: *'Post office coming soon.'* I chuckle at the framed picture of Chef Chang on which someone has scribbled: *'First-class male!'*

Then ... wow! In the centre of the church a huge desk has been positioned in a prime spot: *'Vote Nat: A Good Life vote.'* It's Nat's councillor campaign HQ. The desk is piled high with leaflets. Their messages: increase social housing and social reciprocity; build community wealth and amenity. Fretting Fred, dressed in a brown and paprika striped tank top worn over a denim shirt, sits behind the desk, his furrowed brow suggesting deep concentration. Whilst Nat's spin doctor might be single-handedly keeping 1970's male fashion alive, Fred certainly is on trend with current issues. I sigh, knowing that realistically Nat has little chance of winning. But then, don't they say that every great dream begins with a dreamer?

I try to shrug my doubts off as I walk round to the Daddy Day Share area. It's starting to look like a junk shop. Is it letting the rest of The Good Life down? The so-called items to share are now spread over a quarter of the church. That sun bed ... weren't they banned in the 1990s? I spot an old radiator, a VCR player and a typewriter with several keys missing. I am still wondering how much actual sharing takes place with these redundant-looking items, when there is a loud crash.

'Bugger!' Michael shouts. The plastic hood from a salon hairdryer he is dragging in through the back door has smashed to the ground.

'Where on earth does all this stuff come from?' I ask as I grab a broom and walk over to help sweep up the damaged pieces. 'This hairdryer looks like the type my grandmother would've used in the 1950s!'

'I've no idea, Deb,' Michael sighs. 'I come in and find items dumped here when I arrive in the morning. It's like someone is trying to fill this place up with stuff that *no-one* wants to use or borrow.

Somehow this makes me think back to the first Gargoyles meeting. For starters, who gave us the wrong start time? I have a nagging feeling about Henry being involved in Greener Properties ... But what would he have to gain? And, if he *was* involved in Greener Properties, why would he be part of Daddy Day Share? Unless he wanted it to fail?'

I stop sweeping. 'Michael, whose idea was Daddy Day Share?'

'It was Henry's.'

'When did Henry Junior join school?'

'Last September, at the start of the academic year.'

'So Henry Junior only joined school a month before the Good Life project started?'

'Yes. I was surprised when this new dad, who I hardly knew, approached me to tell me about an eco-project he'd heard about that was starting up in a local church. He suggested we set up a Daddy Day Share enterprise there.' Tears well up in Michael's eyes. 'Since my darling Evie passed on three years ago, I've not got involved with anything social, but Henry persuaded me that it would be good for me.' Michael looks up and smiles. 'And it has been. I'm happy here.'

'I'm so pleased you did.' I give him a peck on the cheek. 'I'm happy here too.'

Happy here more than I want to admit. Our shared moment is interrupted by another text alert from Michael's phone. 'I've got to pick up Chloe from school.' He grimaces as he shows me the text. 'She's not feeling well again.'

As Michael dashes off, Rich approaches carrying a dustpan! I ask him, 'Don't you think it's a bit of a coincidence that Thomas Montjoy got to use Henry Junior's school once again to host his Gargoyles public meeting?'

'I agree that Henry is a total smarm-ball, Deb, but don't forget that Jafar and Chloe go to the same school, and they're hardly in cahoots with Montjoy!' Rich gestures for me to brush my theory, along with the remaining bits of plastic, into the pan.

'But did you see how cosily Henry was sitting next to Miss Stuart at the meeting?' I continue. 'I just think it's so odd that …'

'What I think is odd is how excited Nat is about our Clive Garney talk at the Bank of England next week. She left her phone on a desk, and in passing I just happened to see a couple of texts she and feckin' Garney have been sending to each other.' Rich blushes. 'Also, look how psyched she is about the Changster coming here today. I'm not so sure about inviting him …'

I put my broom down. 'Well, *I* am! The pictures Chef Chang uploaded to Instagram of him wearing my boxers has gone viral. I've had over two hundred orders in, and Leroy is getting tons of followers on the insta account he set up.'

I give Rich a hug. It's quite sweet how clearly jealous he is of Nat's alleged suitors. I'm just thinking how he and Nat would make a lovely couple when Nat bursts in.

'Always saw you more of a room-than-broom-service girl, Deb! she laughs. 'Bet you ordered loads of goodies at your hotel last week?'

'About that … Nat. I really need to tell you something,' I speak hesitantly. 'Stu and I didn't actually go to a …'

'Jesus Christ! You haven't put those posters up yet,' Nat yells, spying the posters I've left on the decrepit Daddy Day Share radiator.

'Natalie,' I persist, 'Stu and I went to see ...'

'BTW, did you hear that Deb's going all Miss Marple on us!' Rich interjects, linking Nat's arm. 'She thinks that Henry Smarmy Smythe is in cahoots with Montjoy?'

I sigh and raise my voice to ensure they *do* listen to what I have to say.

'How are we going to question Father Guy today about the twenty-thousand pounds Montjoy offered his other church? He must realise it's a bribe aimed solely at getting the Good Life closed down?'

'Oh, come on, Deb! Father Guy's a man of the cloth,' Rich laughs. 'He's not that gullible. That money was just bollix greenwash talk.'

Nat studiously removes her arm from Rich's. In a sulky voice, he mutters something about helping Nahal lay the table, and walks off.

'But Nat,' I say, 'Father Guy couldn't look me in the eye at the meeting ...'

'Couldn't look you in the eye? I think you just fancy him rotten!' she grins. 'And he's not been giving you the kind of attention you're fantasising about. You need to admit it to yourself, Deb, it's your middle-aged hormones. And with Stu always away—now in Bristol—it's not like he's been giving you much attention either.' She stares at Rich, who is strolling out into the garden. 'Unlike the unwelcome attention I seem to be receiving from others!'

As Nat walks off to do the postering, I retreat to my sewing machine. Oh hell, there's a lot of threads to pick at. There's nothing wrong with my relationship, is there? Am I being selfish not wanting to move? Or would a move to 'Brat'ford-on-Avon give Stu and me the fresh start we need to combat our empty-nest phase. Then there's my hormones. Are they more unbalanced than my niggling feelings about Henry and the twenty thou offered to GG? who from this moment on, I resolve to no longer fancy. A ping on my phone cuts through my self-pitying, menopausal-princess thoughts. I look down, shocked to read a DM on Leroy's Box Clever Insta account. It's from Plant Shack, a new restaurant chain, which according to

Grazia Mag is soon to be set up by another celebrity chef. It's an enquiry for an order of two hundred and fifty pairs of boxers. My heart races. I can't wait to tell the others. Could I really start a viable social enterprise?

@NTS: Just what is a social enterprise?

I lift a pile of fabrics from the box besides my desk and bunch them into a makeshift pillow. I lay my head upon the silky yarn. I'm sure no-one will notice if I take a quick nap to recover from my early start in search for the light …

CHAPTER 18

The Wrongs and Rites of Spring

Hmm. A little nap ...What's that?! There's an unwelcome prodding on my arm. I sit bolt upright to find Jafar standing over me.

'Wake up, Deb. Chef Chang is here, and we're about to start lunch.' Jafar retrieves my phone from under the pile of fabric where it's buried, and points to the time. To my horror, I discover it's 1 p.m. ... As impossible as it seems, I've been asleep for two hours.

I jump up, and quickly follow Jafar into the garden. I squint, stunned by the glare of the sun. It may only be late March, but the temperature must be over twenty degrees. To my dismay, everyone is already seated around the table, dressed in their finest. Chef Chang looks devilishly handsome in a beige linen suit, as he chats to Rich, whose fedora has been decorated with a narcissus flower and sprig of rosemary. Leroy is helping Jafar decorate an egg—dribbles of yellow paint splashing all over his once pristine white school shirt. They are watched by Father Guy.

'Pleased you could join us, Deb!' Nat stands up, her cleavage in full display in the decolletage of *my* new charity-shop-best-find-ever Pucci floral dress—the very same I was planning to wear today. She grimaces, 'Before you sit down, you might want to fluff up your hair. It's got bits of cotton thread in it.'

'Allow me, O'Goddess Arachne,' says GG standing up. He walks over and, with the gentlest of touches, removes several wisps of cotton from my hair. My head instantly tingles from his touch. My mind reels. Did he just call me a goddess? I rack my brain. Wasn't

Arachne the younger sister of Aphrodite, the Roman goddess of love? I knew my Classics O-level wasn't a waste of time after all! But back to the here and now ... GG is taking off his jacket and revealing a tight-fitting black T-shirt. He links his muscular arm through mine and leads me to an empty seat he seems to have saved next to him. Hurrah for T-shirt weather! Then a less than joyous spring thought: I have bed head hair and am still wearing my gardening dungarees. Not exactly the look of a goddess of love.

I sit down and try to focus on the lovely spring vision laid out in front of me. The table is draped in the cloth I made from a fabric the colour of lemon sherbet. It matches the primroses placed in recycled jam jars. Rich is filling our pretty, mismatched, glasses with some kind of yellow home brew. The green chinoiserie plates gleam as they await a tempting portion of Nahal's aubergine stew and *gondi*. In the centre of the table there's a stunning indigo blue glass plate on which several items of food, as well as a purple hyacinth, have been placed.

'Welcome to our *Nowruz* meal,' Nahal announces proudly, as she approaches the table carrying a large dish. '*Nowruz* means "new day," and it is the name for the Iranian and Persian new year. It falls on the same day as the March equinox—the first day of spring.'

'Let me help you with that!' Chef Chang stands up and lends an expert hand to placing the heavy dish on the table. 'It's so good of you to invite me, Chef Nahal. Rich has told me all about you!'

Nahal blushes, clearly not used to being referred to as 'Chef.' 'The most important part of our *Nowruz* celebration is the ceremonial *Haft Sin* setting. It has been sacred in Persia since ancient times.' She smiles as she points to several items on the indigo glass plate. 'Our *Haft Sin* plate contains seven symbolic items, each one beginning with the Persian letter *Cinn*. In English, this is an "S." These will bring us luck for the new year.' She pauses and turns to her son. 'Jafar, help me explain them?'

Jafar jumps up and lifts an apple from the glass plate. 'This is *Sib*. It means apple in Farsi and it helps us stay healthy.' He takes a bite before handing the apple to Nahal, who cuts it into small pieces and hands around slices for us to eat. '*Sabze* means "rebirth."' Jafar grins as he lifts another item from the plate. It's a small clump of grass. 'This is as green as my mum's *hijab*!'

I smile as I look at Nahal's green headscarf. It really is a verdant shade.

Nahal bends over to give Jafar a kiss, then lifts a clove of garlic from the plate. 'This garlic, or *seer* as we call it, is a symbol of contentment. It is also a reminder not to invade the rights of others.'

Perhaps Nat could do with eating a few cloves. I glower at her as she flirts between Chef Chang and Rich. Nat giggles when she places a slice of apple into Chef Chang's mouth, tucking another piece into her cleavage which leaves little to the imagination. And in my dress! I feel my face reddening—which is appropriate, because Nahal is now pointing to a mound of red powder. 'Whereas *Somaq*—what you call sumac—is a symbol of patience and tolerance.' She looks over at me and smiles.

'It's like the colour of sunrise,' says Rich, managing to tear his eyes away from Nat and her apple antics.

Nahal cups the hyacinth petals on the *Haft Sin* plate. 'Our next symbolic item, this *Sonbol* plant, celebrates the coming of spring.'

'And *Sekkeh*, which means coin, is to bring us money!' Jafar picks up a pound coin from the plate.

Rich adds, 'Although real wealth is the friendship and humility we have around this table.'

'Well said, mate.' Chef Chang pats him on the shoulder.

I glance over at GG, who for some reason, has sighed and lowered his head.

Nahal takes a handful of dried fruit from the table. 'Finally, my favourite is this *Senjed*, the fruit of the Lotus tree. It will bring us love.' She smiles as she looks round the table. '*Nowruz Mobarak* everyone. It is now time for our blessing.' She claps her hands. 'Father Guy, as this is a mixed celebration, perhaps you would do the honours?'

'Er, yes, of course.' GG stands up and starts to speak falteringly. 'Dear Lord ... we ask that you renew our hearts and minds for the days ahead ... We ask your forgiveness, as the redeemer lives within you. Er ... Amen.' He sits back down and stares probingly into my eyes.

Forgiveness and redemption, I hear as I knock back my yellow drink in one gulp. I wonder what GG is planning that would need forgiveness? I blush at the thought whilst trying to remind myself of my earlier resolve not to indulge in any GG daydreams. I wonder if I've got time to nip inside and change into my rather shapely midnight blue velvet dress. Luckily, I hadn't yet taken it home after picking it up from the dry cleaners yesterday.

'I think it's time for a toast with my sorrel-plant mojito,' says Rich. He refills my glass and points to a scrubby-looking plant in one of the beds. 'I would like to add my own blessing.' He raises his glass: 'May the nourishment of the earth be yours.'

'Cheers!' we all call out, and savour the tangy, lemon flavoured cocktail. Its sugar crust does little to hide the potency of the rum that lurks beneath.

'This is delicious, Rich.' Nahal licks her lips as she and the children sip away at their sorrel mocktail. 'It's so exciting that spring is here, and we will be able to grow and cook with more herbs like this.'

'Talking of herbs,' says Rich, 'I would like to thank Chef Chang for coming here today and hosting our nettle and wild garlic workshop this afternoon. I don't think we'll get a big crowd, but cheers anyway, Changster!' He clinks Chef Chang's glass.

'My absolute pleasure,' says Chef Chang. And there's more pleasure for him as the piece of apple pops out of Nat's cleavage when she jumps up. He catches it and places it in his mouth.

Nat winks and says, 'To get us all in the mood, here's an Easter joke for you. How does the Easter bunny like to party? Around the *cluck!*'

As everyone bursts out laughing, and Rich refills our glasses, I notice how subdued GG seems. He's watching the bonhomie around the table but not participating.

'Did you know, Chef Chang, that this egg was made by my friend, Sophia?' Jafar, who has certainly come out of *his* shell, bends down to stroke the chicken that has waddled up to him. He lifts an egg from the table and hands it to Chef Chang.

'Meet our ex-bats, Changster!' says Nat. 'We rescued these ex-battery hens.'

'Young Jafar here does a great job looking after them,' says Rich, giving Sophia a tiny piece of bread.

Nahal lifts the lid off the large cast-iron pot in the centre of the table and agrees. 'Anyway, let's eat our first course before it gets cold! It's *Khorsesht-e bademjan* with *gondi*—aubergine stew with dumplings.'

Chef Chang leans over the pot. 'It smells divine. A heady mix of orange and ginger—as warm as your words.'

Nahal smiles as she ladles out the stew to everyone.

As we all tuck in, the only sound to be heard is the buzzing of a bee and a bird chirping. Summer always used to be my favourite season, with its days of sunbathing and sultry evenings under a Mediterranean sky, but since getting involved in community gardening, I must admit I'm now rather partial to spring. I twiddle my toes, certain that I can almost feel the earth coming back to life beneath my feet. My joy is tempered only by the realisation that said toes are still firmly encased in steel-tip boots—gardening—as opposed to the high-heeled Jimmy Choos I selected to match *my* Pucci dress. I look over at Nat who is still openly flirting with Chef Chang, much to the annoyance of Rich. But as outrageous as my enthusiastic, glass-always-full friend is, I will really miss her if or when I move.

'So how do you two know each other?' Nahal breaks the silence to question Rich and Chef Chang. 'Yes, do tell us, Changster,' says Nat. 'Rich has been very elusive on the subject.'

Chef Chang licks his lips after a final mouthful of stew before responding, 'Surely Rich told you how we met when we were both investment bankers in New York?'

'Rich, a banker? Pull the other one!' Nat bursts out laughing.

'It's true, Nat.' Rich puts his fork down. 'I lived and worked in New York at CitiBank for ten years. If you come out for a drink with me later, I'll spill the beans.'

'The only beans you're going to spill later are of the baked variety, and they'll be on your lonely piece of toast. Richey Rich, an ex-banker-wanker!' she sniggers. 'That's made my day! And as it happens, I'm going on a date tonight.'

Rich bows his head into his hands.

So who is Nat is going out with? And did I really hear Rich finally pluck up the courage to ask Nat on a date? My musing is interrupted by Nahal asking Chef Chang how he went from being a banker to a chef.

Chef Chang first responds by saying, 'This is absolutely delicious, Chef Nahal. You must give me the recipe.' Then he smiles and answers her question, 'Unlike Rich, I didn't become ethically and morally disillusioned with the world of finance, I was just bored. I had always loved good food, so on a whim I decided to train at a culinary college in New York. After two years I dropped out, and simply bought myself a fancy restaurant in the city with my ill-gotten banking gains. I scored a few lucky breaks—got some good press reviews, including a piece in the *New York Times*, and the requisite celebrity endorsements. After five years, I decided to come home to the UK, where, as you know, I've been on MasterChef and now set up The Truffle Hog ...'

'Whereas in complete contrast, I've just wasted the last ten years of my life dossing about trying to turn waste into wine,' Rich says in a crestfallen voice.

'But there's everything to be praised for saving the world one sorrel leaf, one home-made nettle pesto at a time,' Chef Chang insists. 'I totally believe in the butterfly effect.' He gets up, walks over to Rich, and pulls him into a bear hug. 'I take my *toque blanche* off, and bow down to you with respect, mate.'

I wouldn't mind Changster taking off his toque blanche—and every other piece of clothing—any day of the week! My sex life is currently all *toque* and no action. I glance at GG and blush. I kick myself under the table in self-punishment for having vapid thoughts when such a profound exchange is taking place. Just how many sorry daiquiris have I had? I mean sorrel wotsits. Or mojos. Or ...

'But aren't you going to tell Chef Chang how you've been invited by Clive Garney to address the Bank of England next week?' The right words of support finally pop out of my mouth.

'That's great, mate!' Chef Chang throws a fist into the air. 'What are you going to talk about?'

'Designing an economy that promotes human prosperity no matter if GDP is going up or down,' Rich answers quietly. 'Today we have economies that grow whether or not they make us thrive. I want to talk about creating an economic system that makes us thrive, whether or not it grows.'

'That's very impressive, mate,' Chef Chang applauds. 'Thanks for sharing. Sounds a million miles away from the talk of a dosser!'

'When I'm the Good Life councillor we are going to promote a sharing economy,' Nat butts in. 'But first we've got to make sure we keep hold of the Good Life site. This bastard Thomas Montjoy wants to buy the church and turn it into a private apartment block. Since the public meeting two weeks ago, he's coerced several local papers into running stories bigging up his role in the regeneration of the high street. It's all aimed at getting council planning permission.'

Chef Chang turns to Father Guy and asks, 'But, of course, *you* are doing everything you can to make sure this never happens, right, Father?

'Well, I'm new to this area, of course, but, er, the bishop has been supportive of the project.' So saying, GG swigs his mojito. 'Could I trouble you for a top-up, Rich, just to toast spring growth and all that?'

'While we're on the topic of spring growth, Father Guy, you must be overjoyed about the twenty-thousand pounds Thomas Montjoy told the meeting he was donating to your other church?' Fortified by drink, I, Miss-Martini-Marple, lift the coin from the *Haft sin* plate. 'Surely, it's just a blatant attempt to bribe ...'

'Oh, it's all, er, just speculative, at his stage,' Father Guy coughs, and looks away from me.

'That's enough serious talk!' Nahal berates us, as she walks up to the table carrying another large pot. 'It's time for our main course. This is *Ash-e-reshteh,* a thick vegetable and noodle soup we traditionally serve at *Nowruz.*' She places the pot on the table and starts to ladle out portions onto the plates we hand her.

'And what about you, Deb?' Chef Chang asks, leaning over his plate to breathe in the spicy aroma. 'What are your dreams for Good Life?'

I take a deep breath and realise that now is the perfect moment to tell Nat, and everyone else about the offer we are probably going to place on the house in Bradford-on-Avon next week. 'Listen everyone, I have some news to share,' I begin.

'Yes, Deb's Box Clever brand is really starting to take off,' Rich butts in. 'We have lots of orders in, and I believe an enquiry has just come in from Gordon Ramsey's new vegan restaurant chain.'

'Gordon Bennett!' Nat laughs, 'I'd give *him* one!'

'I haven't told you yet, Deb,' Rich glares at Nat, 'but I've just come to an arrangement with Hari at the dry cleaners. He's going to donate to us, on an ongoing basis, all the dry-cleaned clothes that are not picked up from his cousin's twenty-five branches across London. After six months, they get rid of the clothes as they don't have enough storage. You can start to expand your range, and you'll probably need to get more help with production. Isn't that amazing?'

'Well, er, yes, I guess it is,' I sigh. 'But the fact is that ...'

'And my boys love 'em,' says Chef Chang. 'I was going to suggest to the Celebrity Chef producers that next season we do a programme in which the contestants and talent wear a pair of your boxers. Can you imagine Greg Wallace wearing your pants? It would be a real ratings earner!'

'And bring countless sales,' adds Rich.

Leroy pitches in, 'Me and my dad are also going to set up a new online platform to help manage sales.'

'Certainly will be a new kind of platform for Deb!' Nat giggles. 'She's used to high-heeled wedged ones in the shoe variety!'

There's laughter all around. Except from me. And Nahal. She looks at me as she hands a portion of soup. 'The knot of noodles in this *Ash-e-reshteh*, represents the many possibilities for the coming year. Untangling them is thought to bring clarity ...'

I dig a fork in to scoop up the noodles, but they slide off, and plop back onto the plate in an even more congealed knot.

'I've got a dream!' Leroy jumps up. 'We should have solar panels here on the roof of the church.'

'Well, that's certainly a lightbulb moment!' says Nat.

'Do you know,' says Leroy, 'in the UK, renewable energy

accounts for just under thirty per cent of all electricity made—more than nuclear power. I've been reading all about nuclear waste and it sounds terrible.'

'I can't believe you're only ten, Leroy! You're so clever and you're going to change the world one day!' says Rich.

'Leroy was teaching me about energy earlier. It sounds fun,' Jafar says.

'What's pretty fundamental is that Leroy is right, and we no longer have to be passive consumers buying power from big and distant power stations,' Rich continues. 'In our new local economy, we can change the world's age-old power systems by setting up our own micro-grid. So yes, Leroy, let's talk about having solar panels here.' He leans over to shake Leroy's hand.

'Talking of light, I've just realised that the clocks go forward tonight. As a result of the longer evenings, we'll be able to work more in the garden.' Nat winks at me. 'You'll like that Deb, won't you?'

Before I can say anything, Greg bursts through the back door. His face is blackened with soot, his stomach bulging out of the suit I made for him from an upcycled red Chinese kimono.

'*Hajii Firuz!*' Jafar jumps up and shrieks with joy. He rushes over to Greg who dances round with a tambourine.

'*Hajii Firuz* is like an Iranian Santa Claus!' Nahal explains to us. 'He traditionally appears in Iran as part of our Nowruz celebration.

'*Hāji firuz e, sāl-i ye ruz e. Eyd e Nowruz e, sāl-i ye ruz e.*' Nahal stands up and starts to sing loudly in time to the banging of Greg's tambourine. 'It's *Haji Firuz*, it's only one day a year. It's *Nowruz*, it's only one day a year.' Jafar joins in, as she repeats the lyrics in English.

A round of applause breaks out around the table. Greg puts down his tambourine and lifts two packages out from the sack he is carrying. He hands one present to Jafar and the other to Leroy. Jafar opens his to find a pair of binoculars. For Leroy, there's a Junior DIY solar panel kit.

'Those binoculars are so you can spot the swallows as they fly back to the UK next month,' Greg explains, as Jafar gives him a big hug. 'Did you know that migrating swallows fly over two hundred miles a day? They spend their winter in South Africa ...'

'Lucky bastards!' says Nat.

'Thank you, Greg.' Leroy also gives Greg a hug and rushes off to investigate his kit.

'I'm giving a talk next week at the Good Life about which wildlife to look out for in March and April,' Greg tells us. He sits down at the table to tuck into the large platter of cookies and fresh mint tea that Nahal has placed in front of us. 'For starters, we'll feature swallows and hares. Those hares, a funny bunch! This month is their mating season, and they get very excited ...'

'Mad as a March hare, and all that! Bit like the team here!' Nat chuckles.

Greg bites appreciatively into a cookie. 'The lot of you do look like you're at the Mad Hatter's tea party,' he laughs, as he points to Rich's hat. It's loaded with daffodils, a couple of cookies, and even a sprinkling of Nahal's fiery sumac. And he almost chokes when Old Spot waddles up to us wearing a pirate's hat made from Birdwatch magazine—his easter bonnet. Meanwhile, Sophia is lurking around the table, enjoying the scraps of food being offered to her.

'Rich, you can be the March Hare. You're mad, rude, and energetic,' Nat laughs. 'Deb, you can be Dormouse. You certainly look like you are about to drop off ...'

'I *have* been here since six a.m.,' I, Dormouse Deb, protest as I sit up straight. The mojitos have of course nothing to do with my tired slough.

Chef Chang chips in cheerily, 'Nahal, of course, will be the Queen of Hearts who made some tarts.'

'My mum and I saw you on the TV making chickpea cookies,' says Jafar. 'We copied your recipe to make our *nan-e Nokhodchi,* but we added cardamon and crushed pistachios.'

'Well, they're delicious, young man—much more creative than mine. Perhaps you will be a chef when you grow up.'

Jafar blushes, clearly delighted, while Chef Chang, the self-proclaimed Knave of Tarts, leans across the table to pick up another cookie.

'I think that Deb should be Alice.' This comes from GG, who has been very quiet until now. 'After all, she possesses all the right qualities: she's a heroine, sweet, playful, curious and intelligent.' He grins at me.

I think, but refrain from saying out loud, that that would leave GG to be the Cheshire Cat—all beguiling grin, and cunning, notorious for his exploits in misdirecting Alice. But, as much as I worry about why GG had still not answered my question about the curious twenty-thousand-pound donation, I can't help smiling back and staring into his deep blue eyes. They are as cloudless and bright as the cerulean sky above …

He lifts his glass to chink mine. I join in. After all, I am both Goddess Arachne and Alice, and must make the most of this wonderland. Around the table, there's much merriment as folks take a swig from the bottle of home-made hawthorn brandy being passed around. Any more questions can wait until another day.

Greg sighs in happiness, 'I love spring. I can almost feel the sap rising.'

'Well, something is certainly rising!' As subtle as ever, Nat's eyes are running down Chef Chang's body.

'With spring unfolding in a tide of blossom, it is a time of renewal,' says Nahal.

'Talking of renewal, it's time to exhume my pants!' Rich jumps up. 'C'mon everyone, let's do it!'

We follow Rich to a bed at the end of the garden and watch as he sinks his spade into the compacted soil. After digging away for a short while, he bends down and extricates a tiny piece of orange fabric from the bed.

'As I said in January, the best way to test the quality of our soil is to bury a pair of underpants for two months,' Rich explains to a bemused GG. 'If the pants are exhumed intact, then the soil is sterile and lifeless. But if only a small piece of fabric remains, it means the soil is thriving. As you can see here, hardly anything is left of my pants. There has been lots of microbial activity. We have great soil!'

'More like it means you have ants in your pants!' Nat laughs.

'Thanks for yet another of your redundant comments,' Rich shoots Nat a foul look. 'As I was saying, this is a spring rite of passage.'

'Certainly was the rites of some animal's passage ...' replies Nat.

Before Rich can react to another bit of 'Nattery,' Pippa comes running out from the church and cries out, 'Quick everyone! You'd better come and look. There's more than a hundred people queuing around the block. I think they're here for Chef Chang's workshop!'

APRIL

CHAPTER 19

Doughnut Economics

'So come on then, tell us about being a banker?!' Nat calls to Rich.

I lean forward, trying to prise an inch more space away from Nat. We have been squeezed together in the back seat of the Chip Fat Travellers van for two tortuous hours during our journey to the Bank of England headquarters. Rich, seated in the front between Mouse and Lucia, who is driving, continues to ignore Nat's barrage of questions.

The van lurches to another halt. Lucia jumps out and opens the bonnet. Our third breakdown of the ride is due to the waste vegetable oil biodiesel, and the way it freezes up in the cold. We discovered this hazard during the van's ill-fated trip to Knepps last November, when I was left without clothes. I wrap my scarf around me and shiver in the freezing cold. Winter has come again. The only spring glow that remains from last week's glorious *nowruz* meal is without doubt, the memory of GG calling me the goddess Arachne. Not only am I anxious about the content of Rich's talk, but I did sort of promise Stu, where I left him in Bristol last night, that I wouldn't join Rich and Nat in what he called Clive's preposterous 'we-can-change-the-world talks.' When Rich begged me this morning to come along for moral support, I didn't have the heart to say no.

'So, what did you do with the dosh then, Rich?' Nat changes her line of questioning. 'Or are you simply another rich kid playing at being poor?'

Rich sighs. 'If you're determined to know, Natalie, I'll tell you if it means you will finally leave me in peace. So here goes.' He takes a deep breath. 'When I decided to leave New York, my marriage fell apart. My wife Jo-Jo and I had been living together for eight years. As a native New Yorker, understandably she didn't want to leave the City ...'

Didn't want to leave the City? As Rich shares his sad dilemma with us, I realise this is something I can now identify with. The question of whether I am a 'city girl'—a native Kentish Towner—has been nagging at me. And there's a more worrying thought: What will happen to my marriage if I don't agree to move? Stu is expecting a formal offer next week and will have one month to decide whether to take the job in Bristol. It really is crunch time.

'We had bought a lovely Brownstone together in the West Village,' Rich forces the words from his throat. 'So, in answer to your question, Natalie, I signed over the deeds of the house to Jo-Jo ...'

'Blimey, talking about doing good deeds! Wish someone would hand *me* a house!' Nat's jokey words belie the look of concern in her eyes.

'Don't let our future go up in smoke.' The sudden call cuts through our thoughts as attention shifts to Lucia shouting a rousing anti-pollution slogan into her megaphone.

Mouse, who has jumped out of the van, joins in: 'Be part of the solution, not the pollution!'

They are ignored by the throng of people who push past her on their way to work in the busy road opposite Liverpool Street station.

'Join the green revolution to stop poll -'

'I'll give you two minutes to get your van off this double yellow line.' A warden taps Lucia on the shoulder, but then suddenly looks up to the sky as hailstones start to plummet.

Mouse slams down the bonnet and both he and Lucia jump back into the van. Lucia starts the engine, and, with a lurch, the van heaves off. We drive on in silence, the only sound that of hailstones pelting the van.

I turn to the internet on my phone to pass the time constructively by refreshing my knowledge of the classics—in particular, that of ancient goddesses. A while later, the van turns into Threadneedle Street—a street rather aptly named, I realise with displeasure. It appears that Arachne, the goddess GG said I was like last week, was not in fact Roman, but Greek. And worse, she was not the goddess of love: but a spider! I read on: *Arachne was a mortal who challenged Athena, the goddess of wisdom and crafts, to a weaving contest, and lost. Her forfeit was to be turned into a spider.* Great! GG sees me as a spider. I turn off *my* web, any interest in classical figures suddenly crushed.

'I'll just pull in here and drop you off,' Lucia shouts as she pulls into a bay in front of the Bank of England, which looms over us in all its formidable glory. I, er, spider-woman, sourly look up. Greek columns? Roman? Just old stuff to me.

'Did you know that the Bank of England is the world's eighth oldest bank?' Nat pipes up.

Oh yeah, I think grumpily. Just to cheer me up, we're hit by another barrage of hailstones as we get out of the van.'

We dash along the street and up to the fortress-like building, which, ominously, has no windows on the ground floor. Having been here lots of times to meet Stu, I know it is renowned, like a medieval monastery, for being walled off and self-contained. The Bank of England is one of the most powerful institutions in the world. I feel another rush of nerves. What on earth am I doing here?

We enter through the huge bronze front door to be greeted by the head of security, imposing in his ceremonial pink frock coat and tall black hat. Nat's question to him about whether or not it's fancy-dress day is received in stony silence.

Fancy dress, eh? As we walk along the ornate hall with its high ceilings and world-famous floor mosaics, I reflect on GG and Arachne-gate. Perhaps it was just a case of GG imagining me in a leather spider-woman costume? Vegan leather, of course.

'Apparently, one fifth of the world's gold is locked away in the vaults beneath our feet,' says Rich glancing down.

'While on the subject of a great kitty, wasn't Chef Chang's workshop fantastic?' says Nat. 'I can't believe over a hundred peeps turned up—or that we sold all fifty copies of the books Chef Chang donated. We made eight hundred quid. I must remember to tell Clive about how we're going to set up a bank at the Good Life.'

My spirits feeling as damp as my body, I follow Nat and Rich into a large conference room on the ground floor. The wooden-panelled walls and coffered ceiling add to the air of formality. A feeling of solemnity is enhanced by the dark suits of the men and women who sit around the horseshoe-shaped conference table. We are half an hour late, and judging by the impatient looks, our audience is already less than impressed. I smile nervously as I give Harold a little wave. He looks the other way.

'Welcome! Welcome!' Clive ushers us forward and encourages us to sit on the gilt chairs at the head of the table. 'Before we start would any of you like some mineral water?' He points to the plastic bottles of water placed all around.

'I hope you realise,' Rich says coldly, 'it takes at least three litres of embedded water to manufacture this one-litre single-use plastic water bottle?' He lifts a bottle and slams it back down on the table.

And bang goes any dream I might have had about my husbond-age's promotion at the Bank of England to persuade him not to leave.

'Well said, Richard.' Clive, in stark contrast to what I was expecting him to say, pats Rich on the back. 'That's why we've invited you here today to broaden our perspective!' He laughs. 'Without further ado, I would like to welcome you all to the latest of our "New Perspectives Series." As you know, these talks are aimed at looking into alternative ways of interpreting the economy and are an opportunity for different groups to ask questions. We're keen for them to challenge us here at the Bank of England, and to share views on the conditions businesses and consumers are facing.' He pauses to look around. 'Gathered in this room today are some of our finest researchers, economists, and analysts. They are very much looking forward to hearing what you have to say ...'

More interested in their Twitter feeds, I think, judging by the way these fine, upstanding bankers have their brainy heads bent over their phones.

Clive continues, 'So, today I'm delighted to welcome Rich, Deborah, and Natalie from the Good Life project. They are here to talk to us about designing a new economic system for the twenty-first century.'

Moi? Part of a group at the Bank of England to talk about a new economic system for the twenty-first century. Discuss! My cheeks burn with embarrassment. In truth, I don't even understand hus-bondage Stu's job. As Clive winks at Nat, and smiles at me, Rich bends down and pulls something from his rucksack. It's a box of Krispy Kremes. He lifts it up to show the room. 'I would like to pres-ent to you all, the future of economics: a doughnut.'

A doughnut? I'm struck by a wave of anxiety—and two thoughts: Firstly, for once, I am so relieved Stu is away. Secondly, am I really staring at a box of Krispy Kremes? There is a rumbling in my stom-ach. I knew I shouldn't have missed brekkie, but I was so nervous about today. I visualise the lustrous, naughty glaze; the light but airy dough that practically melts in your mouth. And, oh, the bite that oozes with caramel custard.

'Gross Domestic Product,' Rich continues in mock formal lan-guage, 'is measured as the market value of goods and services pro-duced within a nation's borders in a year.' Then he smiles. 'However, the future is not about GDP, but a doughnut.' He lifts the lid of the box. The Krispy Kremes contents have been replaced by some kind of home-made doughnut look-a-like.

'So what exactly is a doughnut?' he asks, as he hands the box of doughnuts around the table. Everyone apart from Clive and Nat refuses one. Clive bites into his doughnut.

'It's delicious, that's what it is!' Clive laughs.

'Scrummy!' Nat agrees.

'The doughnut to which I'm referring is a radical new mindset for addressing the economic challenges of the twenty-first century,' says Rich. 'It is a "doughnut" of social and planetary boundaries in which we can provide for every person's needs while safeguarding the living world.' He presses a button on the laptop he has clearly arranged to have set up. An image of a doughnut appears on the white screen behind him. He points to the words: 'Social Founda-tion,' that appear on the inner edge of the doughnut's circle. Another phrase, 'Ecological Ceiling,' denotes the doughnut's outer boundary. 'Between the two sets of boundaries lies the ecologically safe and socially just space in which humanity can thrive. That's the dough-nut,' Rich explains. 'The role of twenty-first century economics should be to help us enter the doughnut and stay there.'

'Would that be full of jam?' Harold calls out, nudging the man sitting next to him. They do little to hide their amusement.

Ignoring the titters of derision that break out around the room, Rich speaks up, 'By the way, Clive, don't forget the thengkai.'

Thengkai? Is this another twenty-first century financial term I need to remember? Or just something he's made up? Talk about Rich pickings …

'What the doughnut metaphor is really advocating,' Rich carries on, unperturbed, 'is that money, markets, taxation, and investment should be designed to conserve and regenerate resources rather than squander them. The question we should all be demanding of businesses is: How many kinds of value can you integrate into your company's design to make sure that you give value back to society and the environment?'

'Talking about giving value back to society,'—Nat stands up and speaks out to seize her moment—'we've got a great example of waste not, want not right here. These doughnuts are from a Southern Indian recipe. They're called *medu vadha,* and they're made from waste lentils and flour. They're part of the thirteen billion pounds worth of food the UK throws away each year.'

She dips her doughnut into a pot of something that Rich has placed on the table along with the doughnuts. 'This *Thengkai sambal*—or coconut chutney to you—makes them positively heavenly. Here … try one.' Nat forces a doughnut into the hand of the man sitting next to her. He reluctantly accepts it, then brushes away the coating of sugar that has appeared on his Savile Row jacket.

Rich puts his doughnut down and continues, 'As Epicurus said, there are two ways get rich: increase your financial wealth or decrease your desire. We simply cannot continue selling infinite growth to a finite planet.

'Bravo to that!' Clive calls out.

'Our ironically-named "free market economy" is driving ecological destruction and social inequality.' Rich raises his voice and continue, 'We need a new economic narrative for a shared economic future. One that meets the human rights of every person within the means of our life-giving planet. Instead of pursuing ever-increasing

GDP, it's time to discover how to thrive in balance. I say let's put humanity back at the heart of economic thought.'

'Hear, hear!' a woman shouts, whose place card declares she is: 'Director of Monetary Analysis.' Her contribution is followed by a round of applause.

'The Bank of England should consciously use money to create positive social, ecological, and cultural change. Build community wealth,' Rich continues.

'At our Good Life project, we are trying to build community wealth,' Nat butts in. 'We are going to open a community bank and -'

I hold my breath, praying that Nat doesn't talk about *our* stock exchange—a clothes swop shop.

Rich hurries on, 'We live in a monoculture of money. But money does not merely have to be a metal disc, a printed piece of paper, or an electronic digit. It is, in essence, a social relationship—a promise to repay that is based on trust. To Aristotle, money was a means of exchange. We need to find new means of exchange … this involves redistributing wealth and not just income: wealth that lays in controlling land, enterprise, technology, and knowledge. To quote my friend Kate Raworth's book, "Doughnut Economics," *It's time to draw the economy anew, embedding it within society and nature. Inequality is not an economic necessity: it is a design failure.*'

'But the Kuznets curve'—oh, I think, now they're all at it with the clever references!—'suggests that as countries get richer, inequality must rise before it will eventually fall.' This contribution comes from the sugar-coated jacket man.

'Kuznets curve is feckin' bollix,' Rich shouts

The only curve I'm aware of is Nat's derrière as she bends over the table to grab another doughnut. Judging by the gleam in Clive's eyes, he is more than aware of her curve too.

'Kuznets curve slows economies down by wasting the potential of folks who could be teachers, nurses, entrepreneurs, and actively contributing in their own way to the wealth and well-being of a community,' Rich continues more calmly. 'We have got to stop this relentless drive to minimise costs to maximise returns to investors. Mainstream twentieth century economics views enabled, endless, economic growth as a must, but nothing in nature stays the same, or grows for ever.'

He gets up and walks over to the window. 'I used to work in finance too, but I've spent the last ten years living under the philosophy of how much can I give, as opposed to how much can I get. Growth is one the stupidest purposes ever invented by any culture. Growth of what, and why, and for whom? How long can it last? How much is enough?' Rich opens the window and points to a man in the street. 'I mean, how much more do you think you need to earn than that street cleaner, Harold?'

'Really, this is going a little too far.' Harold rises from the table. 'Apologies Clive, but I have an urgent call to make.' He walks out of the room, followed by several other people.

My heart starts to beat frantically, although Clive still seems thoroughly absorbed in Rich's words. Rich continues, unflustered by more departures in the room. 'Currently, we have a GDP based on an economy that needs to grow whether or not it makes us thrive. We need to design an economy that makes us thrive, whether or not it makes us grow.'

Clive nods. 'An economy that makes us thrive whether or not it grows … Now there's a thought.'

'In summary,' says Rich, 'we need a dramatic new mindset if we are going to address the economic challenges of the twenty-first century. As Adam Smith, the founder of modern economics, said: "All money is a matter of belief." Well, I believe that we have to recreate a new narrative around money, and the first way to act like a twenty-first century economist is to change the goal: lose our fixation on GDP as a primary measure of progress. Second, stop treating climate change and nature as an "externality" to the British and world economy. Thank you for your time.'

The end of Rich's speech is met by a non-existent round of applause. The only sound is that of shuffling feet as people exit the room en masse. Clive breaks the awkward silence by standing up and patting Rich on the back. 'Well, I think that was a huge success. Thank you, Rich, for such a rousing speech. I, for one, would like to discuss some of your ideas further.'

Rich nods, trying to hide his disappointment at such little appreciation from a promising meeting and heads for the door.

'Perhaps you would all join me as my guests at a corporate day out next month at Sunningdale golf club?' Clive asks.

'Yes, er, thank you. That would be wonderful, Clive,' I butt in hastily, before Rich can respond with some golf-habitat-wrecking-stats.

'What fun!' Nat smiles. 'After all, you know what they say: it's not the size of your putter that counts, it's how many strokes you take!'

Clive burst outs laughing. 'And here's one for you Natalie—you wicked woman! What did the duck say to the golf ball? Nothing! It should have ducked!'

Offering a half-hearted laugh, I follow Rich, who has shot off like a four-iron. Or is it a putty? My interest in golf only extends as far as reading about the exploits of Tiger Woods in *Grazia Mag*. I'm thinking about the reports that Tiger had sex with over one hundred women—What? Really!?—when Clive says, 'Before you dash off, Deborah, do you have a few minutes to spare?'

'Oh, I don't want to hold you up any longer,' I reply. 'I bet you have a busy afternoon.'

'As it happens, I'm on my way to the House of Commons to attend a Parliamentary Task force on drones, he says. 'But I'd love a quick catch-up with you. Shall we walk out together?'

My heart pounds as fast as the steps Rich is taking to lead us out of the building. Because I wasn't planning to come on this trip today, I never thought to ask Stu what Clive knows about his forthcoming job offer.

'I hear drones are taking the UK economy to new heights,' Nat giggles, as the security man in his pink frock coat raises his hat in deference to Clive.

We exit to the street. The hail has given way to a damp, thick fog which makes it hard to see anything further than a few feet in front of us.

'While drone delivery is controversial, drones *do* have world-changing potential,' Clive explains as we follow Rich, who has not spoken a word since finishing his speech. 'Recent tests have seen drones delivering blood to rural hospitals in Rwanda, for example, hugely cutting wait times. They will potentially benefit everything from farming and building construction to search-and-rescue missions. It's estimated that drone delivery will create a one hundred-billion-pound market over the next five years.'

'Hmm,' says Rich, breaking his silence. 'But in the meantime, have you ever stopped to think about puddles?' He pauses beside a puddle in the street and crouches down in front of it.

Clive shrugs his shoulders and smiles. We gather round the tiny pool.

'The puddle's downfall lies in its humility,' Rich continues. 'It sits low, meek, and apparently motionless. But a puddle is evidence: there's a lot of water in one spot but nothing around it. Why is that? Why do we never stop to consider puddles?' He puts his hand in the murky water, which ripples.

I look over at Clive and offer an embarrassed smile. Natalie, the opposite of meek and motionless, comments on how the only water she's interested in is the fizzy type in a white wine spritzer.

Rich continues, 'I think twenty-first century living is all about slowing down and looking at the world in a new way—be it puddles, or global economics.

'Well said, my boy!' Clive laughs. 'While on the subject of looking at the world in new way, I wanted to ask you, Deborah, how you feel about Stu's job offer. The Economics futures course he is going to be teaching at Bristol sounds like it could really do with some input from Rich. How do you feel about moving to Bradford-on-Avon?'

'Moving to Bradford-on-*where*?' Rich and Nat call out in unison. They stare at me, wide-eyed with shock.

'I, er ...'

My embarrassment is relieved by the arrival of Mouse and Lucia, who come running up to us. 'Thank God we've found you guys!' Mouse cries out.

'Has anyone got a few quid that we can bribe this warden with?' Lucia points to the Chip Fat Travellers Van. It's hard to see much around us through the fog, but what is apparent is that the van is still parked in the bay where Lucia dropped us off over an hour ago.

A luminous yellow object, not exactly a ray of sunshine, is attached to the front wheel. We've been clamped. A warden standing by the van is speaking into her walkie-talkie.

'We took a quick walk around the hood to do some anti-idling campaigning,' says Mouse. When we came back, we found our van clamped and about to be towed.'

A tow truck turns the corner and pulls up beside the van. Clive looks at his watch and quickly flags down a passing taxi. With a friendly wave and promises to speak soon, he jumps into the cab. As it disappears into the misty distance, I try to calm everyone down.

Lucia and Mouse are shouting at the warden. Nat is shouting at me. And Rich is shouting at Nat. I fail miserably, beclouded in my own personal gloom.

CHAPTER 20

Swallow v Amazon

I t's the night of our church sleepover—or 'champing,' as we call it. After yesterday's bank-shenanigans, I'm not exactly champing at the bit for an evening spent with Nat shouting at me over my potential move to 'Brat'ford-on-Avon. Not to mention a sleepless night on the floor!

As I try to sneak into the Abundance Cafe, I can't help but smile at what looks like a cosy scene out of the Peter Pan nursery. The desks have been pushed to the side and replaced by blow-up mattresses. These beds have been covered with sheets and a patchwork of colourful knitted blankets care of Michael's Knit Wits group. Pippa is up a ladder stringing fairy lights all around, while Rich is busy lighting the candles placed here and there.

'I still can't believe it cost us four hundred quid to get the van back after it was towed yesterday,' Nat, who is reclining on her swivel chair, feet up behind her huge desk, calls out to Pippa. 'That's half our kitty money from the sale of Chef Chang's books.'

My efforts to reach Nahal in the kitchen without Nat spotting me are to no avail.

'Oh, look everyone,' Nat pipes up in a sarky tone, 'Lady Deb of Brat-ford-on-Avon has decided to grace us with her presence!' She glares at me, then pretends to bury herself in paperwork.

'Please don't call me that.' My eyes fill with the tears I've been trying to hold back since yesterday. My voice cracks as I say, 'The truth is I don't know who I am, anymore. Or where I belong …'

Rich walks over and puts his arm around me. 'Now come on everyone—and that means you Natalie—let's calm down and be a bit more supportive of each other.'

As Nahal joins us, Rich suggests that we have a group pow-wow. Nat tuts, but we follow Rich into the Daddy Day Share area. We crawl into the kids' tepee and sit in a circle facing each other.

I break the silence. 'I've wanted to tell you all for weeks about what's going on,' I sob through my tears flowing like a river bursting its banks. 'I just didn't know how to. But anyway, Stu has been offered a prestigious job at Bristol University to head a New Economic Futures teaching programme ...'

'Future Economics, a likely story!' tuts Rich.

'... And we've been to see a large house just outside Bradford-on-Avon. It's got lots of rooms and ...'—I sniff, a little embarrassed—'a tennis court. It's like the real good life I always dreamed of—the one I grew up reading about in rom-com books.' I wipe my eyes, but then break into a smile as Old Spot waddles over. 'I mean, who wouldn't want to live in a house with an acre of land?' I smile hopefully at Nat, who is sitting with her head lowered, refusing to look at me. 'Who wouldn't want to hang out in a garden with a formal parterre and cedar wood greenhouse—as opposed to a church in Kentish Town with a scrubby patch of land and a plastic bottle greenhouse?' I pause to stroke Old Spot who in return puts his head on my knee and grunts. 'But then I love it here. I love it so much,' I sigh. 'Nat, could you have ever imagined three years ago, that the woman you used to call the High-Heeled Gardener would be sitting in a tepee in a deconsecrated church, stroking a pig!' I laugh. 'The truth is that I'm in more of a pickle than your cheese sandwich, Rich ...'

Nat finally looks up, her eyes blinking. She seems to be holding back tears. 'Reminds me of a joke,' she says. 'What do you call a cheese that's sad?'

'Blue cheese,' Rich mumbles, biting on his sarnie.

'Or, as we are in an ex-church—What story did the cheesy Bible start with ...?'

Nat doesn't get to the punchline; instead, she bursts out crying. 'Please don't go, Deb. Please don't leave us. Yes, I know I've called you the High-Heeled Gardener, Dormouse Deb, and countless other names over the years ... but I *need* you, Deb. We all love you and need you.'

Everyone nods in agreement. As if to cover her emotion, Nat is looking around. Her eyes light on a book on the floor. It's 'The Canterbury Tales.' She picks it up and flicks through the pages, to land upon a chapter entitled: 'The Wife of Bath.' She points to a picture of a plump lady with a large smile, and even larger gap between her teeth. 'That'll be you soon, Deb, if you go—The Wife of Bath. Not that I'm saying your hips are as big as hers—although you have to admit you've put on a bit of weight recently. And of course, you don't have a gap in your teeth—but on the other hand, you clearly haven't had a hygienist appointment for a while. And even if you do have a teeny gap, in old days it was considered sensual and ...'

I take a deep breath and say, 'Nat, the decision to move is not mine alone. How can I ask Stu to turn down this job?' I swallow the lump in my throat. 'And if he takes it, am I meant to separate from my husband to stay here and ...'

Spend lonely nights dreaming about GG, or some such stupid middle-aged fantasy, I think to myself. Anyway, I love my husbondage, even though he's away more often than he's at home. Don't I? And if I remember rightly, didn't the Wife of Bath have five husbondages? I would prefer to stick to one.

Nat dabs her tears with a piece of kitchen roll that Rich has kindly offered—having used it as a wrapper for his sandwich. 'What you're really saying, Deb, is that you doubt that in four months' time—post August—the Good Life will still be going? So you're going to get out before then? You don't think we're going get an extended lease, do you?'

'I didn't say that Nat. I ...'

'You're right, we *are* going to need a miracle to keep it going.' Nat refuses to let me speak. The Gargoyles apartment block well is on its way to getting planning permission from Camden Council. Apparently, it's had the go-ahead from two out of the three local councillors.'

'Well,' says Rich, 'when you become a councillor in July, you'll be able to put a stop to it.'

'That's *totally* going to happen,' adds Pippa.

'Inshallah,' agrees Nahal.

'I can't do it.' Nat shakes her head. 'I'm giving up. I don't understand a thing about the issues Fred wants me to campaign on—social reciprocity, and all that. I pretend I do, but the truth is I'm not that brainy. On the other hand, Bradley has nothing to say at all. We went campaigning today and I stood for four hours in the high street and only two people talked to me. I can't do it. I just can't,' she blubbers. 'Who am I kidding when I think that I can oust Councillor Thornton—he's been in power for the last twenty years.'

'Twenty too many!' Rich shouts. 'You're not bloody giving up if I have anything to say about it. You're a pain in the arse, but a bloody natural. I will help you.'

He jumps up in such a fury that he bashes his head on a pole on the tepee. He takes off his battered fedora and looks at it. 'I'm the loser here, not you,' he sighs. 'My talk was rubbish. Everyone walked out.'

Pippa objects, 'You're no loser Rich. Look what you've achieved here. Everything you touch turns into good-life-gold. *You* should become Nat's campaign manager!'

'That's a great idea,' Nahal adds, before adding to the all-round misery by herself starting to cry.

I put my arm around her. 'Nahal, what's wrong?'

'Miss Stuart wants to test Jafar for autism.'

'Some of the smartest people I know are neurologically diverse,' says Rich. 'But why is Miss Stuart suggesting this?'

'She claims Jafar doesn't have any friends, and only responds to animals,' replies Nahal.

'That's 'cos he's a natural conservationist,' says Rich. 'I see a great future for him. And *Ms.* Stuart is too much of a shite teacher to see it.'

'And Jafar is one of the kindest, brightest kids I know,' I add.

Nat stands up, her eyes burning as brightly as the fairy lights. She dries her tears. 'I'm not going to let Miss Stuart dis Jafar. She's just a newly qualified teacher with little experience. NQT? That should stand for Newly Qualified Twat, like that Henry Smarmy Smythe. Did you hear that he's bringing Miss Stuart here to 'champ' tonight?'

'*Sah-wah-dee*, everyone.' A new voice cuts through our shock and fury. It's Pueng from Cuticles beauty parlour—our beautician for the evening. She pokes her head into the tepee. 'Can someone help me with heavy bag?'

'Listen, everyone,' says Rich, 'we've obviously all got some important issues to digest.' He looks at me. 'Why don't we carry on with this pow-wow later. Right now, we have an event to host. Let's try and have some fun tonight, eh?'

We all trudge out of the teepee, lost in our own thoughts. I link arms with Nat. 'For what it's worth, I do think the Good Life is going to be here for years to come,' I say. 'It's whether my marriage is going to. That's what I need to ponder on. By the way, what's the answer...?'

'Oh, the cheesy Bible thing? It's Edam ... and Eve!' Nat grins.

Whilst most folk would have thought I was asking if she still planned to run for councillor, Nat knew I was asking for the punch-line of her unfinished joke. But then, that's my relationship with Nat. We may be chalk and cheese—unprocessed, of course—but we *get* each other. I smile and place my hand to my mouth.

'And no ...' Nat shakes her head, anticipating my next question, 'your teeth don't need whitening!'

'Anyway, Deb,' says Rich, as we walk over to the beds, 'regarding your "Brat"ford move, why don't you talk to Father Guy about it tonight? 'See what wisdom he has to offer?'

'Oh, he won't be offering any wisdom at all!' says matter-of-fact Nat, fully recovered from her meltdown. 'He called earlier to say that he can't make it.'

'Typical,' I sigh. The two hours I spent selecting flattering flannel pjs was all for nothing.

'I saw Father Guy with old man wearing a blue coat full of holes in pub last week,' Pueng says, as Rich helps her unload her bag. 'Poor old man. Someone should buy him new coat.'

Hmm ... threadbare blue coat. My ears prick up. There's only one coat I've seen like that. 'He must have been with Father William, the Bishop of Edmonton,' I say. 'Just out of interest, who were they with?'

'That property man, Thomas Montjoy,' says Pueng. 'Now *he* knows how to wear a smart jacket.'

I turn to Nat, my heart racing. 'Don't you think it's odd that Father Guy and Father Bill were in the pub talking to Thomas Montjoy?'

'I can't talk now,' Nat snaps. 'I've got to go and get my slap on. I don't want my mascara to run in the night, so I'm planning natural eyes and scarlet lips. I'm so psyched that I'm going to be in the *Au Courant* mag!'

With all the drama around 'Brat'ford-gate, No-vote-Nat, Jafar and the NQT, I realise I have completely forgotten that Phoebe was coming to write a piece for *Au Courant* magazine.

As schlap-shtick Nat dashes off, I approach Rich, who is now preparing the final bed.

'Surely you must have heard that Montjoy and Father Guy were talking with …?'

But Rich is not listening either. His mind is elsewhere. He says, 'With Father Guy not coming tonight, we've got one bed spare,' he mutters. 'I'm gonna pop down to the high street and see if there's a rough sleeper who would like to join us. That would make thirteen …'

Thirteen? Unlucky for some … in this case, me! As Rich rushes off, I head for the beds … and, er, sort of swop two of the place cards laid on the blankets. Although my name is on the bed next to GG— or whoever is now going to take his place—I feel certain that Phoebe would prefer to be here. After all, the bed is positioned below the beautiful stained-glass window, which will flood with golden early morning light.

A tap on my shoulder makes me jump. It's Nahal. 'I've got to go and pick up Jafar and Chloe. Jafar is so excited that Michael has let us look after Chloe tonight,' she sighs. 'But he doesn't know that Miss Stuart is coming. Could you keep an eye on the taftoon bread for me? It's in the oven.'

And off she rushes. As I head for the kitchen, an unsettling thought hits me: For someone who's considering leaving the Good Life project, I do seem to be very concerned about its survival.

'Yoo-hoo, darlings, I'm here!' My reverie is interrupted a little while later, as Phoebe waltzes into the church blowing air kisses like a celebrity greeting her fans.

'Phoebe, sweetheart, it's so good to see you,' gushes Nat; all signs of her earlier self-doubt glossed over with pursed scarlet lips, which she points in Phoebe's direction.

Phoebe hands me her bag. 'You are so clever, Debo darling. Unlike others, I've never doubted you and always thought you were v. on trend. It's marvellous that sweet little churches like yours are opening their doors for champing-glamping nights. I don't suppose you're offering any spa facilities … like massage?'

'I can give you a massage, love!' The offer comes from a young man who staggers in behind Rich. His lined face belies the fact that he's only in his twenties.

'Er, John … let me show you where you will be sleeping tonight. Then we're going to serve a hot meal,' says Rich, as he leads the rough sleeper to his bed, placed next to an unsuspecting Phoebe.

As Chloe skips into the church and jumps excitedly on her bed next to Jafar's, Nat and I lead a scowling Phoebe to the Abundance Cafe. Pippa places a huge bowl of rice on the table.

'I've done the cooking tonight,' she smiles. 'I hope you are all going to enjoy my wild spring risotto.'

'Smells bloody delicious,' says John, as he and Rich join us at the table.

Phoebe shakes her head. 'Sorry, but I don't eat carbs after six.'

'What a shame. I'm sure I read about A-list celebs raving about a similar dish served in the Michelin-starred "Geranium" restaurant, in Copenhagen,' I mumble. I breathe in an aroma of roots and … er, soil.

'By eating wild plants I find myself becoming a bit wilder!' Pippa laughs, as she serves us each a portion.

As the kids scamper over to the table, the only people missing from this evening's guest list are Henry Senior … and Miss Stuart.

'The wild spring leaves in this dish are all cleansing herbs: wild garlic, nettles, cleavers, jack in the hedge and hairy bitter cress,' Pippa continues to wax lyrical. 'As I eat the local landscape, the ancient soil whispers through the wild leaves and settles in my bones. As I eat my plant supper I feel myself becoming more plant …'

As the kids giggle at the plant names, Phoebe agrees to taste the dish—just for research purposes. Nothing of course to do with my A-list Nordic nonsense.

We all happily chomp away, Plant-ripening Phoebe pausing several times to remove bits of soil from her plate. A while later, Nat and I are busily chopping up fresh mint, rosemary, and lemon balm for Pippa, who begins her herb workshop. Peals of laughter are coming from the beds where Chloe, plastered in bright blue eyeshadow, is star-jumping up and down with Jafar. John, oblivious to all the antics, is already asleep in bed.

Pippa adds a handful of salt to the chopped herbs and scoops the contents into a jam jar. She hands it to Phoebe. 'Check out this home-made aromatic kitchen scrub. All the herbs in this came from our garden! Isn't it fantastic?'

'I hope there's no parsley in this. I'm allergic to it.' Plant-Phoebe looks at the jar and offers a lacklustre smile. She's oblivious to the lump of mud lodged between her teeth.

'And there are no nasty chemicals or artificial fragrances in it,' Rich adds, as he stares at Phoebe's new shellac nails, which Pueng is now painting pink. In fact, the only artificial thing here is your ...'

'Did you know that tarragon helps speeds up digestion,' says Pippa, lifting another pot of herbs. 'It's good for swollen tummies!'

'You should try some, Deb!' Nat breaks off a sprig and hands it to me.

'As it's bedtime soon, I'm going to show you all how to make a fennel toothpaste,' Rich announces, as I place said swell subsiding sprig firmly back on to Nat's lap.

'You should write about this in your feature, Phoebe,' Rich continues. 'The UK spends over seven hundred million a year on oral hygiene products that are packed full of toxins. To make toothpaste all you really need is baking powder, mint oil and these fennel seeds I've saved from the garden.' He hands Phoebe a scoopful of tiny seeds which fall through her open palm. She closes her palm only for several seeds to stick to her nails which unfortunately have not yet dried.

'Feckin' fennel!' she yells. And storms off to the loos, bumping into Henry Junior on the way.

'There you are, Henry! Where's your dad and teacher?' asks Nat. 'I thought they were coming here tonight?'

'Dunno … I've been watching Love Island on my dad's phone,' says Henry, as he rushes over to Pueng's makeup box. 'They were in Rich's room jumping on the bed. It was making loud squeaky noises …'

'What the f…!' Rich gasps as Henry Senior and Miss Stuart—clearly having finished a riveting lesson—walk into the room. Their faces are as flushed as the red lipstick that Henry Junior is plastering all over his face.

'Hello, everyone, and, er … children.' Miss Stuart smiles at Chloe and Henry Junior, ignoring Jafar. 'I'm sorry I can't stay tonight. Henry and I have been discussing, er … Henry Junior's progress. Such a good student. Unlike others.' She looks pointedly at Jafar, whilst patting Henry Junior on the shoulder.

Henry Senior clears his throat and mutters, 'I'd better walk Miss Stuart home; you never know what shady characters are lurking about. Henry, you stay here with the chaps … You don't mind looking after him do you, Nahal? He's so excited about tonight's sleepover.'

'No, I'm not!' Henry Junior cries out. 'I want to go home.'

'If you're a good boy, maybe Miss Stuart will let you off homework tomorrow!' Henry Senior winks at his son and then heads for the exit door with Miss Stuart as she nods in agreement.

'That bloke's BS is as painful as root canal treatment,' Rich sighs.

'I think we should report Miss Stuart's conduct,' says Nat, choosing not to share what aspect of Miss Stuart's conduct she is referring to: the poke at Jafar, or the ... or that of another kind. She offers a half-hearted smile as she watches them leave. Then she continues, 'Did you hear the one about the dentist who planted his own garden? A month later he was picking his own teeth!'

'That's my girl!' Rich pulls her into a bear hug. He turns to face Henry Junior. 'C'mon matey, want to help me make a messy-magic tooth potion?'

Two hours later, it's midnight. Herby-Henry is covered in fennel seeds. Planty-Phoebe has been calmed down with the promise of joining me for a recovery massage that I've booked at a local salon. Chloe and Jafar, who have now cheered up, have been persuaded to trade star-jumps for stargazing in bed. Exhausted, we all head for dreamsville. My spirits are as deflated as my blow-up mattress turns out to be, but after this evening's hijinks, I suspect even Cinderella would have nodded off in her pumpkin coach. I pull my cover over me and fall into a deep sleep.

Hmm ... I'm having a nice dream. A fennel fantasy. Something to do with being tickled with downy fennel leaves by ... woah! What's that? There's an unwelcome prodding on my arm. It's Jafar who had been assigned the bed next to me. 'Wake up, Deb!' He prods me again. 'Did you hear that?'

'Hear what, Jafar?' I sit bolt upright.

'There was a giant bang on the roof of the church.'

'Oh, go back to sleep. It was probably just the wind,' I try to reassure him.

'Jafar! What is going on?' Nahal calls out from the bed next to Chloe. 'It's three a.m..'

'I heard a bang on the roof, maman.'

'I heard a bang, too, Nahal,' Chloe cries out. 'I'm frightened.'

'There is nothing to be worried about, children. It was probably just the wind,' says Nahal, getting out of bed. 'Try and go back to sleep.'

'But it was a *really* loud bang ...' says Chloe.

It's an hour and several cups of hot chocolate later before we manage to fall sleep again.

'Oo ... Oo ... Cock-a-doodle ...' I'm awake again. It's the crack of dawn—with the emphasis on 'crack.' It's 6 a.m.. The church is in darkness. The early morning light is just starting to filter through the ochre and blue stained-glass window. The colours seem to depict a piece of driftwood upon the shore. Never mind an alarm clock, this is more like an 'alarm cock.' The noise is coming from bloody Brutus, who is crowing away in the garden. I sneak out of bed, trying not to disturb Jafar and Chloe, who are breathing gently alongside each other as they share a pillow. In contrast, Plant-Phoebe, thanks to the Valium she took, is snoring loudly on the bed next to John. I tiptoe past, managing to avoid treading on Henry Junior, who is laying asleep on the floor, his arm in Pueng's beauty box. As expected, Henry Senior's bed is empty. In his place, Old Spot is grunting away. Nat's bed is empty too. Now that's interesting … I wonder where she could be.

I love early April, despite Brutus. The trees are starting to riot with their blossom of cherry, apple, and pear, in shades of cream and pink. My favourite, the hawthorn, or May Tree is a froth of white flowers. The one advantage of having been woken so rudely, and early, is that I will experience the dawn chorus in the garden. It always amazes me how many birds can be heard singing their hearts out even in the most densely urban surroundings.

As I creep past Pippa, who seems to be in a burning-thighs-of-hell, yoga pose, I can't resist peeking into Rich's room, through his slightly opened door. Nat is curled up in bed with Rich under his Thomas the Tank duvet cover. Rich's arms are wrapped protectively around her. A big, cheesy grin fills my face as I carefully pull the door shut. Knowing Nat was in a loving, supportive relationship would make my move to 'Brat'ford' much easier for me to come to terms with.

I sigh and walk into the garden, trying to muster up the joys of spring. I'm greeted not by the sound of carolling birds, but by a delivery man unloading a large spin-dryer.

'Stop! What are you doing?' I shout. 'Who said you could dump that here?'

'It's your Greener Properties delivery, love. As no one is usually here, we're told just to leave the stuff.'

'But we have nothing to do with Greener Properties,' I yell.

'You could've fooled me. We've been dropping stuff like this here for months!'

A bright-eyed Rich joins me to add an angry voice: 'What's going on?'

'This man says he's from Greener Properties and he makes deliveries here every week,' I tell him. 'This must explain the heap of useless items accumulating in the Daddy Day Share area.'

'Bollix Greener Properties! What the feck are you talking about?'

Rich places his hand firmly on the spin-dryer to stop the man from moving it any further.

'We pick up the stuff every week from Greener Properties' rental flats. It's from things folk have left behind when they move,' explains Spin Dryer man.

Just then another delivery man joins us. He holds up a clipboard and says, 'We're on the clock here, mate. Where do you want this?'

'We don't feckin' want any of it. Bloody take it away,' Rich hollers. He determinedly starts to push the spin dryer back onto the trolley and is helped by Nat, who has turned up, still sleepy-eyed. Clipboard Man looks at his watch, shrugs, and nods to his mate. They turn round and push the trolley back down the alley leading to the front of the church.

'Now hang on everyone, I'm sure there's a logical explanation for this,' I say, racking my foggy brain.

'Yes,' says Nat. 'That shady Henry Smarmy Smythe probably owns Greener Properties and is trying to derail the whole project by turning the Good Life into a junk shop. I knew he was up to no good.'

'I agree with, Nat,' Rich smiles at her. 'I think we should look into the company ownership to see what Henry has to do with Greener Properties.'

'I started studying law, until …' This comment from John who has joined us. 'If you give me the details, I could investigate at Companies House to research the company structure of this Greener Properties. The names of its directors, and so on?' he offers.

A loud cry cuts through our thanks to John for his help. It's from Jafar who has come shouting into the garden. 'There's a dying swallow in our front entrance,' he wails. 'Quick, everyone, follow me. Come quick …' He tugs at Rich's arm.

We all rush to the front of the church where Pippa is crouched down cradling a swallow in her arms. We crowd round her. The swallow has blood gushing out from its blue feathered wings which seem to have been sliced apart.

'Jesus Christ. Poor suffering creature,' Rich mutters, as he takes off his t-shirt to swab the flowing blood. 'It looks like some kind of blade has sliced the wings.'

Jafar strokes its head and sobs, 'The swallow's having trouble breathing. Quick we've got to do something.'

'Is everything OK, here?' A passer-by rushes over to us.

'No, it's not,' Jafar cries. 'We found this beautiful swallow laying here. I think it's dying. I don't know what happened, but I heard banging on the church steeple in the middle of the night.'

'My name's Sam. I'm a fireman from across the road—just finished my shift for the night. I thought I'd better come over and see what the problem is.' He bends down to appraise the swallow's condition.

'You're a fireman, Sam?' asks a trembling Jafar.

'Yes, I am.' Fireman Sam smiles at Pippa who carefully places the blanket Nahal hands her around the swallow.

'I think something may have crashed into the swallow.' Pippa smiles back at him through her tears. 'I don't suppose you heard anything strange during the night?'

'Actually, something very odd did happen,' Fireman Sam sighs. A drone came crashing down onto the top of our drill tower. Its vicious blades smashed all over the place. At the bottom of the tower, we found a crushed Amazon box, and next to it, a packet of mascara. We all considered ourselves lucky not to get hurt, but the same can't be said for this poor bird.'

'OMG,' Pippa gasps. 'Do you think Amazon are trialling night-time drone delivery and the blade got caught in the wing of this darling swallow?'

'It sure looks that way.' Fireman Sam shakes his head in disgust. 'I'll call my team and ask them to send out the Enfield Wildlife rescue ambulance.'

'This swallow might have been migrating back to Woodberry Wetlands,' Jafar sobs. 'You know the place we all went to?' He hugs Nahal as she wraps his trembling body in her arms.

'Did I hear something about a box of mascara going spare?' We are joined by Nat, who rubs her bleary eyes as if trying to process the scene that is taking place in front of her. 'Holy shite. What's going on?'

Pippa looks up at Nat, her eyes blazing brightly. 'What's going on is that I'm sure night-time drone deliveries are illegal in the UK. We need to investigate how drones are regulated.' She looks down at the swallow whose breathing is now very shallow. 'But do you know what this really is? It's the Good Life's very own Ecocide case: Swallow v Amazon.'

CHAPTER 21

Seedy Stuff

It is the last week of April and a gorgeous spring evening. As this could be my last spring in the area, I find myself exploring all the back streets of Kentish Town on my way to film night at the Good Life. Stu has one more week to decide whether to accept the job in Bristol.

As a likely soon-to-be-banished person, somehow the urban beauty all around me seems heightened and I'm struck by how glorious the area looks. The hedges are all puffed up in their new green coats. In the tree pits beneath the gorgeous white hawthorn blossom, umbels of cow parsley, frothier than a wedding dress, are starting to spring up everywhere. Not that all bridal wear is about meringue dresses, as … well, here's a confession: while taking a break earlier today from gripping eco-thriller, "There is No Planet B," I did glance at Vogue mag to spot an A-list celeb getting hitched in a white jumpsuit.

I sigh as I bend down to breathe in the gorgeous aroma of wild garlic. I walk on. In front of me, the beautiful bark of a cherry tree is lustrous in the evening sunlight. I stand beneath it and gaze up into a sky of pink. The wind rustles, and I am showered with a scattering of petals. I smile as I look around, and I realise that I'm standing in front of a church. The sign says: *St Margaret's*. But wait a minute … isn't St Margaret's the other church that Father Guy runs? Deciding on impulse to investigate further, I straighten my dress and walk inside.

The church is empty. Despite its faded grandeur, I'm struck by how clean and cared for it looks. The polished brass crucifix and candlesticks gleam on the altar in fading light. Pots of fresh flowers are scattered all around. It's obviously a much-loved church. I walk past rows of pews, with their neatly stacked cushions and prayer books, to stand beside the remains of what once must have been a grand organ. Its hundreds of pipes are now bent and buckled. A gaping hole has completely ripped out the centre of the organ. A notice above it reads: *'This magnificent pipe organ which was installed for the coronation of King George VI in 1937 has been silent since 1941. We are raising two hundred thousand pounds to buy a new one. For more information contact ...'*

Wow—two hundred thousand pounds! I can't imagine why on earth anyone wants to spend that kind of money on an organ, when Kentish Town has so many other regeneration issues. A row of flickering votive candles draws my attention to an engraved brass plaque on the wall: *"In memory of Father G. Mowbray, celebrated organ player who heroically gave his life to save this church on the last night of the Blitz: May 30th, 1941. Much missed by wife Carol, and son Arthur born the same night. May he rest in peace."*

What a tragedy. The parish vicar died trying to save his church during the Second World War. A tear runs down my cheek. He died the night his son was born. So he never got to meet his son? Nor did the son meet his father. How desperately sad; my eyes well up. It certainly puts my silly First World relocation problems into perspective. But hang on a mo ... G. Mowbray? 'G' couldn't stand for Guy, could it? I rack my brain trying to remember GG's surname. The image of a pork pie flashes into my mind. I'm convinced that all those months ago GG introduced himself as Father Guy Mowbray. But surely this is too much of a coincidence? After all, GG has repeatedly told us he is new to the area. Yet this new evidence seems to suggest otherwise. I shiver as a realisation creeps over me: If St. Margaret's Church is part of GG's tragic family history, wouldn't he go to the ends of the earth to protect it? And, if indeed it was his grandfather who was the celebrated organ player cited on the plaque, wouldn't GG be determined to restore the organ to its former glory?

If the answer to both these questions is, yes, wouldn't it be in GG's best interest to have the Good Life church sold off in order for church funds to be re-allocated elsewhere? Like St Margaret's? And what about the awful, but irrefutable proof of the twenty thousand pounds Thomas Montjoy offered to St Margaret's at the Gargoyles public meeting last month? At the time, I thought it was a bribe aimed at getting the Good Life closed, but now I think I know GG's motivations for taking it.

I rush out of the church. It's time to get to Team Good Life.

Fifteen minutes later, I arrive breathless at our Good Life church. I scan the room looking for Nat. In front of the altar, a spandex movie screen has been erected. Benjy-bard and Marg are attaching leads to the laptop and checking sound levels. I grin. There seems to be nothing Marg can't do! The rows of pews are filling up as guests arrive for the film.

I hurry over to the Abundance Cafe, where Greg is finishing his lecture on the decline in the wild salmon population and enjoying a hearty round of applause.

'Ah, Deborah, would you like to sponsor a smolt?' he asks me.

Nat smirks, 'Well, Lady-Brat-ford is a highly fishy girl!'

'Nat, you'll never guess what I've just discovered,' I race on, ignoring her sarcastic quip. 'I've just been in St Margaret's Church down the road, and ...'

'I'm too busy to talk now, Deb,' she snaps. 'I've got to find someone to serve the snacks tonight. Nahal can't be here, so it's down to me, muggins.'

'Where's Nahal?'

'A meeting with the headteacher, Miss Stuart, and Jafar at school.'

Making a mental note to call Nahal later, I entreat Pippa, 'Can I talk to you about something really important?'

But Pippa isn't really listening. 'Sorry, Deb, I don't know if you've heard but the swallow died. Sam and I are building a memorial outside in the back garden.'

'Oh no, that poor, poor swallow.' I place my arm around her.

'I'm serious about bringing the perpetrators to justice.' Pippa's voice is determined, and her eyes shine brightly. 'On behalf of the Good Life, I'm planning a legal case: "Swallow versus Amazon." The aim is to ban hazardous drone deliveries. Catchy name, isn't it?'

A memory of our recent event at the Bank of England pops into my head. 'I wonder if Clive Garney can help?' I suggest. 'Funnily enough, we were talking about drone delivery with him the other week at the Bank of England. I'm sure he said he was involved in some kind of Parliamentary Committee?'

'I'll ask him when I see him,' says Nat with a grin. 'I've got a date with him.'

'You've got a date with feck-wit Garney?' This outburst from Rich who glares as he walks up to us.

'I think Nat means we are all meeting him at Sunningdale golf course next week,' I say hastily. 'It's the Bank's corporate day out and we've all been invited to it. We can all talk to him about drones.'

I give Nat a kick on the shin. She can't be oblivious to Rich's feelings for her. And after all, she was in bed with him at the champing night—not that I've talked to her about that yet. The sad truth is that Nat and I are not great confidantes at the moment. And I miss her. The uncertainty around my move and 'Brat-ford-gate,' has taken a serious toll on our friendship.

'What's all this talk of golf? I've got a great stroke!' This comes from Henry Senior who has joined us.

'Bet you have. And very experienced at getting a hole in one,' Nat says with a tut.

'You're a right one to talk, Natalie,' mumbles Rich. 'It seems that you also like to frequent *multi-bunkers*.'

'I'm so pleased you've joined us, Henry. There's something we need to ask you about.' I change the subject, knowing full well that the new topic will do little to quieten the tense atmosphere. 'After your premature departure from the champing night last week,' I continue, 'early the following morning we discovered a load of useless items being dumped outside the back door. The delivery men claimed they were delivering "donations" to Daddy Day Share from Greener Properties—and they have been doing so for several months.'

'I don't know what you're talking about.' Henry shakes his head.

'Yes, you do, you lying fecker!' Rich shouts. 'Are you involved in Greener Properties?'

'I most certainly am not.'

'Why did you start Daddy Day Share, then?' Rich takes a menacing step towards Henry.

'I don't know what you're suggesting. And quite frankly, I'm insulted,' Henry vehemently shakes his head.

'Who gave Greener Properties permission to dump useless stuff there?' Nat joins in.

'I don't know,' Henry splutters. 'But what's all this got to do with me?'

'That's what *we* want to know,' Rich growls, raising his fists. 'If I find out you're in cahoots with Thomas Montjoy, and trying to close down the Good Life, I'll grab the useless steam cleaner that was dumped in Daddy Day share and shove it up your …'

I look around. The film night guests have all stopped talking and are staring at the fracas.

'I don't have to stand here and put up with this threatening behaviour.' Henry starts to walk away. 'I thought I would come by tonight to offer to help, as Nahal is having a few problems with Jafar, but I'm out of here.'

'I hate to say it, but I sort of believe him,' I say, as we watch him storm off out of the church.

'He's a wanker, but I agree with you, Deb,' Nat nods.

'Let's ask John later, what he found out about the Greener Property company structure,' Rich suggests. 'I think he's going to be a great addition to our motley team. I can't believe someone as bright and with so much potential as him, is a rough sleeper. What has society come to?'

I nod in agreement. 'Talking about fact-finding, I popped into St Margaret's earlier—Father Guy's other church. And you'll never guess what I discovered.'

This falls on deaf ears with Rich. He sighs as Nat wanders off and says, 'Didn't you hear what Nat just said. She's going on a date with feck-wit Garvey.'

'That's the first I've heard about it,' I say, determined to force Nat to have a proper chat with me tonight.

Rich says, 'As if the banking world hasn't fucked up enough of my life. I need to get some air …'

'But Rich, I found out that Father Guy is not new to this area. He's not told us the truth ...'

Rich cuts me short by bolting out of the door. If GG hasn't told the truth about this, what else is he lying about? My mind is in turmoil. It just doesn't make any sense. Why would GG claim he is new to the area? I rest my brain by taking a pew in front of the screen. I smile at Pippa and Sam who are sitting cosily together. Meanwhile, Food Critic Jim and his wife are reading the literature on GM seeds that Marg is handing out. There's a good smattering of thirty or so folk I don't know. The Good Life's reputation is clearly spreading. The last person I'm expecting to see is Father Guy. But here he is and he's taking a seat right next to me.

'Ah, there you are Dorito-Deborah. I was looking for you. I must say you're looking particularly lovely this evening.'

I can't help but notice how the golden April dusk-light glows on his flaxen hair. As he rolls up the sleeves of his linen shirt, he leans over me. The downy hairs on his arm brush across mine. I shiver. I can resist anything apart from ... a man wearing linen.

'We haven't, er, seen you for ... er ... a while,' I stutter.

'Ah, yes. I've been doing some important local work.'

To be honest, my first thought is: Am I really looking lovely? I must admit I did spend hours selecting my floral vintage dress and matching cardie. It's very difficult to get one's look right at this time of year. My second thought is one of more satori enlightenment, than sartorial elegance: just what kind of local work *has* he been doing? And important for whom? I've put wings on him. But is he really an angel?

'Actually, Father Guy, there's something I need to ask you,' I blurt out. 'On the way here tonight, I happened to walk past St Margaret's Church, and, er ... I decided to pop in. It's amazing your grandfather used to be the priest there during the war. You never told us about that. He was clearly an incredibly important local hero. I'm so, so sorry that he ... he ... tragically died protecting the church. I also read about your fundraising. How are you going to raise the two hundred thousand pounds for your dream organ ...?'

'What's this about a pipe dream?' Nat plonks herself down on the seat on the other side of me.

'Oh, goodness!' GG jumps up. 'I offered to go and help Pippa bring snacks in from the Abundance Cafe. Nahal's ramson spring rolls sound so tempting ...'

And let us not give into temptation ... GG rushes off, clearly not wanting to answer my questions. It leaves me more convinced than ever about the real temptation he is giving in to. And it doesn't bode well for the Good Life.

I turn to Nat. 'Please can we be best friends again? I miss you.' I take her hand, well aware that I sound like an over-wrought school-girl rather than a forty-something woman. 'Is there anything you'd like to confide in me about your whereabouts on champing night?' I wink at her.

'No, Deb.' Nat removes her hand. 'I mean, you haven't exactly been acting as a best mate or confiding in *me* recently, have you?'

'No, I haven't. You're right. And I'm sorry.' My eyes well up. 'I'm just so confused and don't know what to do. All I know is that Stu needs to decide about the new job by the end of next week. I don't want to leave here, but how can I ask him to turn down such a great job?'

Nat takes a tissue from her pocket. I smile through my tears as I notice it has a McDonald's logo on it. 'So, what's going on between you and Rich?' I sniff.

'It's purely professional.' The blush that fills Nat's face does little to convince me that it is. She continues, 'Fred has gone to Ghana to write a piece on corruption in the chocolate industry, and Bradley got a new job as area manager in a Nuneaton Lidl store for six months.'

'So, it's you and Rich, now, is it?' I smile. 'Just in the capacity of him being your Good Life campaign manager, of course!'

'It looks as if the Good Life won't continue much longer, anyway.' Nat lifts up a copy of the Camden New Journal. 'That's partly why I've been so down recently,' she sighs. 'Just look at this announcement written by *our* local councillor.'

She hands me the newspaper. The article by Councillor Thornton starts: "We are delighted to announce that planning application for The Gargoyles development along Kentish Town Road has been accepted as part of Camden's Community Investment Programme.'

'Community investment, my arse,' Nat tuts. 'Rich told me he saw Councillor Thornton in the pub with Montjoy the other day. Now I know what they were confiding about.'

'Talking about confiding,' I jump in. 'I've just found out the strangest thing about Father Guy. It turns out that his grandfather was ...'

'Sorry to butt in! I couldn't help overhearing ...' This from John, who is seated in the row behind. 'I'm still looking into Greener Properties company structure, but haven't found anything dodgy, yet.'

'Are you sure there's no mention of Henry Smythe on the list of directors?' asks Nat.

'No, definitely not,' John continues. 'Most of the Directors seem to be women. Just out of interest, have you girls thought of forming a community land trust—a Community Interest Company? Then you could buy this church and keep the Good Life going?'

'Now *that* is a bloody great idea!' This comes from Rich who sits down next to Nat. 'I've been talking to my chums who own the O2 Forum next door. No way do they want Montjoy's shite flats built here. They're worried that the monied residents would get the Forum closed down on the basis of environmental noise protection. The Forum loves the Good Life community hub, pig, and all! They want it to stay!' A loud announcement interrupts us.

'Welcome, everyone, to the Good Life's screening of: "Food, Inc." Marg's firm call commands everyone in the growing crowd to silence. From her perch atop the pulpit to the left of the film screen Marg continues, 'Before we start, I would like to introduce Sacha, who is going to tell you about a festival we will be hosting in June.'

'You hoo, lovely people!' Sacha greets us in her plummy voice. Her high stiletto heels click-clatter on the wood as she walks up to join Marg. 'What will food industry look like in 2030, and beyond?' she demands. 'This is what we are going to debate at our Pestival in June.'

'I do love a festival?' Critic Jim calls back.

'It's a *Pestival*, sir,' Sacha corrects. 'Pestivals aim to redefine humankind's relationship with the insect world. More and more people are exploring the idea of eating insects as a new sustainable protein source. To tempt you all, I've made some tasty snacks.'

As she totters back down from the dais, I giggle at the contrast between her Louboutin patent leather shoes and the scruffy brown paper bags she fetches out of her matching handbag. She hands the critter-crisps around the audience. The label on the paper bag handed to me reads: 'Crunchy roasted crickets in smoky barbecue sauce.'

'They're bloody delicious,' Rich says, leaning over and taking one of the, er … eat-grubs from my packet. He pops it in his mouth and crunches.

'I would like everyone to hand them round and talk to your neighbour about how it tastes,' says Sacha.

Before I can say chirp-chip, Nat shoves one in my mouth and laughs. I swallow it. The texture is dusty rather than crunchy. And there's a strong scent. But what of?

'The wings look the least appetising aspect, don't they, Deb? But they're more sustainable than pork scratchings!'

I swallow down the decidedly more creepy than crawly item and determine that my future relationship with the insect world would be left to the garden. Around the audience, some folks seem intrigued, while others are horrified.

'There's a very nice, nutty, sea-weedy, aftertaste that lingers,' Critic Jim pronounces. 'I'm going to write about this is my column next week.'

'Certainly brings a whole new meaning to Monster Munch snack!' Nat laughs. 'But then you wouldn't know that, would you, Deb? You're more a lentil crisps sort of gal!'

'And now for our main event,' Marg announces. 'Before the film screening, we are going to have a debate, which my good chum, Ben, will host.'

Ben strides into place in front of the screen. As he puts his arm around Marg, the sight of his muscular physique towering over Marg's petite frame makes me smile.

'We need to talk about the company, Bayer-Monsanto,' Ben begins. 'Combined, these smiling, damn villains control over thirty per cent of the world's seeds and pesticides market. The question I want to debate is how do we hold Bayer-Monsanto accountable for human rights?'

'In their case, more like human wrongs!' shouts Pippa.

'It's up to grassroots communities like ours to take action.' Ben stops to take a puff of his vape.

@NTS: Grass in all senses of the word.

'For thousands of years, farmers have saved seeds from one farming season to another,' Ben continues. 'But when Monsanto developed genetically modified—what they call GM—seeds and the glyphosate-based fertiliser "Roundup," it laid the groundwork for them to gain control of the global food supply.'

'They are just a bunch of pestitutes!' shouts Pippa.

'Hear, hear!' Fireman Sam echoes the punny statement.

'There are also other issues with genetic engineering,' Ben nods his head in agreement. 'This includes the contamination of organic crop varieties.'

Pippa interjects, 'Air and rain samples are also contaminated with glyphosate, and so are waterways in agricultural areas.'

'But most evil of all, there are also human and animal health effects that we're yet to fully understand,' says Ben. 'I believe that with genetically modified seeds, Monsanto is violating the self-organising, self-renewal capacity of plant life. Violating life itself.'

'A-feckin-men to that!' yells Rich.

I scan the audience looking for GG. There he is. Instead of returning to the seat next to me, he's sitting in the back row, his head down, and clearly lost in thought. Isn't there some kind of biblical quote about reaping and sowing? Ah, talking about sewing -

@NTS—must crack on with the Box-Clever orders. With all my brooding around Brat-ford-gate, I've taken my foot off the pedal, and have a backlog of two hundred boxers to make for Gordon Ramsey's Plant Shack new chain of restaurants.

I take a deep breath. Maybe it's best just to cancel the order and forget the whole Box-Clever idea? Just then, I notice Michael and his chums, who are sitting next to GG, busily knitting away. Maybe I could ask the Knit Wits for help? Well, I certainly can't ask GG. He's already on his toes. He has got to his feet and is now sneaking out of the church.

My attention is drawn back to Ben. 'Now, I don't wanna bring an even bigger downer to this chat,' he's saying, 'but the World Health Organisation has declared that Monsanto's Roundup probably causes cancer. It's like the death, as quoted by Shakespeare, which "sucks the honey of thine breath."'

Marg shakes her head. 'The streets and parks around here are sprayed with it each year,' she says sadly.

The debate continues for another half hour, the subject matter focusing on how the steady concentration of power into the hands of a small number of companies has already dramatically reduced the diversity of seeds used by farmers. I drift off on a quick power nap. It's all riveting stuff, but the thought of delicious woodsmoke is transporting me to our community garden last summer. All those bucolic evenings around the fire dish. The long tickly grass that is so perfect to frolic in. Wait a minute! I'm not imagining it—that smells like real smoke. I sit bolt upright as folk start coughing.

'Jesus, what the feck?' Rich gasps.

'There's a fire outside. Everyone evacuate the premises immediately!' Fireman Sam shouts, running up to the top of the pulpit. 'Everyone get out now!'

Some people are screaming as the church starts to fill with acrid smoke. Everyone rushes out, guided by Fireman Sam and Rich. Pippa helps some of the elderly folk out of the front door, while Ben lifts Old Spot, who has joined us and is refusing to budge.

Everyone safely outside, we gather in the street. We stand and watch as firemen from across the road attend to the fire. God knows how, but flames have somehow got from the smokehouse, which is on fire, and spread elsewhere. We're in shock. Our precious Good Life could have gone up in those flames.

A while later, Fireman Sam and his team pack up and head back to the station. The crowd disperse as the drama comes to what we hope is the end. Everyone and everything, apart from the Holy

Smoke filing cabinet, are safe. The windows in the Good Life have all been opened and no harm is done. Rich, Nat and I, huddle together in the Abundance Café, sharing a cup of fennel tea. 'The burning question is …' Nat, true to form, is the first one to speak. 'Did the Holy Smoke accidentally catch fire, or was it intentional?'

And the as yet, unknown burning answer: if intentional—at whose behest?

MAY

CHAPTER 22

Par for the Course

'They say golf is the Marmite of sports—you either love it or hate it!' Clive laughs as we walk over to the buffet table. It gleams with culinary delights piled on silver platters, more resplendent than the overhead sun. It is the first of May and boiling hot at the Sunningdale golf course where we have joined Clive Garney and his colleagues at the Bank of England's jolly day out.

'Well, I hate it,' Rich scowls as he surveys the spread that is groaning with all manner of meaty goodies.

Is it really such a jolly day out? I sigh as I watch bankers pile their plates from the bountiful buffet table, laughing as they knock back glasses of vintage claret. Their chatter is all about making mincemeat of the par 5—conversation befitting a bunch of carnivores!

'Do you have a handicap, Rich?' Clive asks as he places a guinea fowl filo parcel on his plate.

'The only handicap that matters,' Rich growls, is the catastrophic impact on ecosystems created from maintaining a golf course like this. And you shouldn't be serving these steak sausage rolls.' Rich grabs the roll I had picked up and was about to pop into my mouth. A mi-steak on my part, obvs Pun intended. He puts it back on the silver platter. 'Have you not heard how meat is responsible for fifteen per cent of all global emissions?'

Pippa points to the grass and says, 'And this manicured grass is completely free of any living organisms.' She wags her finger. 'Spraying it with fertilisers and pesticides are not only harmful to eco-systems, but also carcinogenic for humans.'

'Oh, how seasonal of you to have asparagus,' I add, quickly changing the subject as I spot a mini quiche on the table. I lift it from the platter but, spotting the crispy bacon glaze lustring with a smoky maple syrup, I put it straight back.

'You know, a UNESCO report says that an eighteen-hole golf course can use as much as two and half million litres of water a day, yet eleven per cent of the global population still don't have access to clean drinking water.' Rich bends down to feel the grass. 'It's bloody immoral.'

'What's all this talk of water?' Nat butts in, having just arrived. 'I'm bloody parched,' she grins. 'It's far too hot for May. Bloody climate change.'

More a case of clothes change, than climate change! I repress a grin at her diamond- patterned jumper and knee-high chequered wool socks. Are those tweed plus-fours that she's wearing? Very natty, Nat! *Not!*

'Ah, there you are, Natalie.' Clive gives her a smacker on the lips. 'Try some of this chilled Muscadet. It'll cool you down.' He hands her a crystal glass.

Accepting it, Nat says, 'Sorry I'm late, but I got this great golfing gear from …'

Clive raises an eyebrow. 'It's … very, er, fetching, m'dear …'

Rich snorts, 'More retching than fetch …'

'There's only *one* wretch round here!' Nat snaps at Rich. 'Anyway, pleased to find *you* still here, Deb.' She turns to me. 'Did you hear, Clivey? Lady 'Brat'ford here may well be leaving us for pastures new.'

'Yes, I've been meaning to ask you how you feel about the proposed move, Deborah.' Clive places his hand reassuringly on my shoulder. 'I believe Stu is in Bristol right now reviewing the contract. I'll be very sad to see him—and you—go.'

I take a deep breath but am unable to answer him. Nat's face fills with a smile more mocking than the stares of bankers strolling by, whilst Rich's red face suggests it's not just the temperature that's making him heat up. The sight of Nat cosying up to Clive maybe? I grab the bottle and pour myself a large glass of wine. It's going to be a long day.

'Anyway, time to stop peeing each other off and start teeing off! Shall we?' Clive chuckles. 'I've taken the liberty of hiring a bag of golf clubs for you all to share. I reasoned you environmentalists wouldn't want a buggy to drive around in! Perhaps you can take turns carrying it.'

'Yeah, we wouldn't want to drive a wedge between us! And that's no joke.' Nat grimaces at me and links Clive's arm.

As they stride off towards the first hole, Nat strips off her diamond jumper to reveal her 'May Contain Prosecco' T-shirt. She pushes down her knee socks, bemoaning 'the buggering heat!' I know she's disappointed in me, quite rightly, but I can't help but smile at Nat. I love her eccentricity. She really is one in a million.

We follow Clive past Sunningdale's iconic grand oak tree to walk on grass more heavily striped than the pressed trousers of fellow golfers who pass us. Several golf carts whizz by while caddies call out tips for approach shots and fairways.

'Did you know that King Edward VIII used to be a captain here?' asks Clive, as he selects a wooden club from his bag. From the elevated tee-off he looks to where the first hole is concealed beyond bunkers and a thicket in the distance.

'Have you told Clive about the fire at the Good Life?' I ask Rich, before he can add an unfavourable republican comment.

'Yes, how is it going with the Good Life?' asks Clive, as he swings his club and takes a shot. The ball shoots off into the distance.

'Shite,' Rich replies. 'We had a fire. The place almost burned down.'

'We think it was arson,' says Nat with a grunt, as she tries to yank her clearly uncomfortable plus-fours further up her legs.

According to *Country Life*, (which I obvs only read for Good Life research ...) plus-fours, which were introduced in the 1920s, got their name because they were made four inches longer than knickers. I smile at Nat and her plus-twos!

'But why on earth would someone do that?' Clive asks, beaming with satisfaction over his first shot.

'To shut down the Good Life, of course, Clivey,' says Nat. 'There have been some very odd things going on.'

'That someone, Clivey,' Rich glowers, 'is a wanker called Thomas Montjoy.'

He takes a shot. The ball curves to the left and disappears into a copse.

Pippa 'chips' in, 'He's a property developer who wants to build a posh block of flats on the Good Life site.'

'I still think it was that shite Henry Smarmy Smythe, who's in cahoots with Montjoy,' Nat says, as she places her ball on a tee. 'Remember how he stormed out of our film night last week?' She swings at the ball, only to miss.

'Great shot, Nat!' Rich winks at her. 'And I reckon Montjoy's got the council in his pocket,' he continues. 'Last week's local rag reported how The Gargoyles development—the name Montjoy has given to his folly—has been accepted as part of Camden's Community Investment Programme.'

'But this is awful—particularly when the Good Life is such an important and noble project,' says Clive, greeting two golfers who are walking past smoking cigars. They give Clive a curt nod. 'It sounds as bad as the corporate world.'

Rich says, 'I haven't told you all yet, but I found out yesterday that Montjoy already has a relationship with the Land Director of the diocese. Apparently Montjoy bought a church in Birmingham from the diocese only two years ago.'

I add, 'And *I* found out that Father Guy is not new to our area, as he told us. But *au contraire*, his family have been involved in the area for nearly one hundred years.'

I tell them how I discovered that GG's grandfather was the vicar and celebrated organ player, who died trying to save St Margaret's Church on the last night of the Second World War. And now Father Guy is its parish priest. It would therefore seem to be in his interest to have the Good Life site sold off in order for church funds to be re-allocated to St Margaret's. I explain how Father Guy was trying to raise two hundred thousand pounds to restore his grandfather's grand organ.

'What? Why didn't you tell us, Deb?' Nat yells. 'Guess you're not bothered about the Good Life anymore!'

'I *am* bothered! And I … *did* … try to tell you.' I burst into tears. 'I've also tried to talk to each of you about the twenty grand Montjoy offered to St Margaret's at the Gargoyles meeting in March, which I thought was suspicious.' I look around in a silent plea to Rich and Pippa, my eyes urging them to believe me. They all look away. 'None of you would listen to me.'

'Father Guy. You are feckin' kidding me!' Rich kicks the grass with such a force that he displaces a large tuft.

Using his club to repair Rich's Doc Martin divot, Clive also tries to smooth things over and says, 'Look, this all sounds highly suspicious, but it's a beautiful day and you obviously all have a lot to digest. Why don't we play a few holes, then go and have a proper chat? I'm sure there's an innocent explanation. After all, the Lord does work in mysterious ways.'

'Good one, Clivey!' Nat tries to laugh, as if it's the first time she's heard that joke. But her lacklustre smile suggests that for once she is unable to find anything positive to say.

The yellow buttercups, still green with late spring promise, shine out in the hedgerow around us, as we walk on in silence, and attempt to play the first hole. Half an hour later, Clive has managed to finish the hole in three shots, but it's taking the rest of us as many attempts as my age to get to the elusive hole. We are all in the rough, in more ways than one. As Nat might quip, if we weren't all so downbeat, we can't see the wood for the trees.

As we walk over two the second hole, I'm sure Clive must be regretting his invitation. Our golf is as bad as our news. Rich breaks the silence. 'It was suggested to us the other week, Clive, that we buy the Good Life property ourselves.'

'Yes, our ... er, legal adviser, John, suggested we—that is, the Good Life team—set up something called a Community Land Trust,' I say, aware that after the call I'm expecting from Stu, I will no longer be part of the team.

'Now *that's* a marvellous idea,' says Clive. 'What's your chap's name? Who is he with?'

'Er, he's just starting up ...' I reply.

'Oh, cut the bullshite, Deb,' Rich snaps. 'It's time you were straight with people. And straight with yourself.' He turns to Clive. 'John, our *so-called* legal adviser, is currently a rough sleeper. Life has cut him a raw deal. He started studying law, got married at nineteen, and then his parents were tragically killed in a hit-and-run car crash. He tried to bring the perpetrators to justice but was too inexperienced and he failed. He dropped out of uni and turned to drink. And if that wasn't enough ...' Rich pauses for breath, 'his wife bunked off with some other bloke and kicked him out of their council house. So now he can't get another one. A few months ago he moved here from Glasgow to try to get work. And failed at that too.'

'Oh, how simply dreadful.' Clive shakes his head.

'I tell you what, mate, he doesn't need your patronising pity,' Rich growls. 'He's a bright lad. Why don't you sort him out with an apprenticeship, or a job? I know you think of the Good Life as your little pet project, but perhaps you could extend your charitable concerns and do some real good?'

Clive looks down and then nods. 'I appreciate your honesty, Rich.' He pats Rich on the back and says, 'Send him in to see me. I'll see what I can do.

I smile at this, but's it's a bittersweet emotion. Why didn't I know this about John? I'm so wrapped up in my privileged, first-world life problems that I hadn't even bothered to find out his story. How brilliant it would be if Clive did offer John a job. The Good Life was really helping sort out people's lives. All apart from mine. My good old husbondage's insatiable ambition was doing that for me. My fingers start to fiddle with my diamond wedding ring. Is Rich right? Am I not straight with myself? Who am I? Dormouse-Dorito Deborah? Ex-fashion designer? Soon to be redundant Wife of Bath?

'How about it, Deborah ...?' I look up, startled, realising that Clive is talking to me. 'Why don't you tee off? It's a par five hole.'

I reluctantly take the club that Rich is offering and stand over the little ball nestling on its green tee—pun intended. I take a deep breath and angrily swing out at GG 's probable duplicity. I swing out at the unfairness of John's life; the insecurity of my marriage; my sadness at losing Nat's friendship, and ...

@NTS: Why are tees made of single-use plastic, not wood?

Amazingly, the ball soars way into the distance.

Clive shouts, 'Well done, Deborah! If you carry on like that you might get a birdie.'

'What's a birdie?'

'It's one under par.'

'Ha!' Nat sniggers, 'That's not the under-par Deb's feeling!'

'Talking about birdies,' says Pippa. 'Clive, we would really like to talk to you about a swallow.'

'A swallow?' Clive stops mid-swing, raising his eyebrows along with his club.

Pippa continues, 'Yes, this poor swallow was killed by a drone's rotary blade. It plummeted to its death on the roof of the Good Life.'

As we walk on to look for our balls—Nat and Rich giving up any pretence of trying to play golf—Pippa continues to tell Clive about how the swallow—on its migratory home run—somehow got mangled in the drone's blades. And how, judging from the packet of mascara and delivery note that we found by the body, it appeared that the drone was part of an Amazon trial delivery service.

'We were hoping you might be able to give us some advice,' Pippa goes on. 'I'm a law student—like, er … John. I'm interested in climate justice and ecocide, so I want to launch a case: Swallow versus Amazon.'

'Swallow versus Amazon! The name certainly has a ring to it!' Clive laughs.

'Deb told us you're involved in a group looking into drone regulation. I know we're probably not worthy of your group's attention, but …'

'Far from it, m'dear.' Clive pats Pippa on the shoulder. 'Deborah is right. You *should* all listen to her more.' He smiles at me and looks at each of them in turn. 'I've just been invited to join a Parliamentary task force looking into drones and their application in business delivery. It's going to be big business. There are several grey areas regarding their regulation, and there does seem to be a number of trials going on in London as we speak. You might have uncovered one of them. Leave it to me to see what I can do.'

'Thanks, Clive.' Pippa throws her arms around him and gives him a hug. 'You're so not a banker wanker! I'm going to go and start digging.'

Clive laughs as Pippa rushes off. He says, 'In the meantime, you might all like to all start using your considerable energy to drum up some publicity.'

'Oh, do stop *droning* on, Clivey,' Nat interjects. 'Let's go and get a drink. I'm …'

Her entreaty is interrupted as a caddy cart pulls up beside us and a man jumps out.

'Ah, I thought it was you, Garney,' the man says, offering his hand for Clive to shake.

'Afternoon, Mikey,' Clive responds.

Mikey has a snub nose and razor-sharp grey eyes that even his thick black rimmed glasses cannot obscure.

'Good to see you, Garney. On form today? No fried eggs, eh?!'

At the mention of fried eggs, my stomach lets out a loud rumble. What with the meat only buffet I wouldn't say no to a nice egg sarnie.

'I'm pleased to report no lost balls yet!' Clive laughs. 'Let me introduce you to my new friends.' He motions to us. 'They're running a very interesting new social enterprise called the Good Life. It's a project encouraging climate action and social responsibility. The team recently popped into the bank, where Rich …'—he pats Rich on the shoulder—'delivered a brilliant lecture to senior staff on our relationship with money and new economic thinking in these times of climate and ecological emergency.'

I stare at the man standing in front of me. Not that I'm the most politically savvy, but isn't that …?

'Oh, how interesting. Perhaps you could explain it to me in a nutshell?' Mikey asks Rich.

Rich scowls and tenses his fists. But he speaks with surprising calmness. 'I'm interested in advancing the richness in human life, rather than the richness of the economy. The monetary economy is not the only type of economy we can choose …'

'Are you a politician? I'm in politics, too,' Nat butts in. She seizes

Mikey's hand and shakes it. 'I'm gonna be the UK's first Good Life local councillor by July. Richard is my campaign manager.'

'I never bloody agreed to …' Rich doesn't get to finish his sentence.

'Perhaps we could do lunch?' Nat takes a crumpled flyer out from her plus-twos and hands it to Mikey who reads its message: 'Vote Nat. A Good Life vote.' He gives it all of half a second before jumping on his electric cart and driving off.

Rich can barely contain himself: 'Tory bastard … You do know who that complete arsehole was, don't you, Nat? It was feck-wit Michael-Mikey Gove. He was responsible for …'

Clive chuckles, clearly amused by Nat's lack of political savvy.

Nat shrugs, nonplussed. 'We politicians do have to stick together. And you know what they say …' She raises her fist in defiance. 'Good Life local councillor one day: DEFRA Good Life minister the next!'

Rich rolls his eyes. 'Bet you don't even know what DEFRA stand for?'

'I most certainly do. It's Department of Education and, er …'

Clive interjects, 'So what else is going on at Team Good Life?'

'Well, we have a fabulous May Day Fest this weekend, which we have spent yonks planning. We even have a May queen—not that I'm saying who it is!' Nat winks at Clive. 'And big news …'—she glances at me—'I wasn't going to tell you, Deb, until I knew what decision Stu had come to today about the job, but last night I had an exciting phone call. The RHS wants us … wait for it! … to design a Chelsea Flower Show Garden.'

Design a Chelsea flower Show garden? The absolute pinnacle of my High-Heeled Gardener daydreams! I'm struck by visions of a gold medal being presented to me amid a glorious native wildflower garden that just happens to match my floral haute couture gown.

@NTS: Check whether Chelsea Garden designers wear heels on site? Sinking stilettos is not a good look.

I can already hear the clink of my champagne glass as it connects with Monty Don's. I sigh. Shame I probably won't be here next year …

'Did you hear what I'm saying?' Nat's high-pitched voice brings me back to pesticide-sprayed earth. 'Some community group has had a fight and pulled out. Do you remember that Delia Arundel from RHS who helped finance our community garden two years ago? She's the one who called me. It's only a tiny space—five square metres, but we've got three weeks to get this show garden ready.'

'What! It's for *this* year?' I gasp. 'We've been asked to design a garden for this year's show?!'

'Yup. The build starts in two weeks, so you'd better not go all Wife of Bath on me yet. It's our luck that somebody's argy-bargy has let us in. I guess not all community groups can get on as well as we do!'

Rich raises his eyebrows and laughs. I'd do the same expect my phone suddenly rings. And it makes my heart start to race. It's the call I've been expecting from Stu. Clutching my phone, I dash off and nip behind a nearby tree to answer the call. I listen in silence as Stu tells me his news. No gap in the conversation to share our exciting Chelsea news. I can barely say goodbye as the call ends. I sit down on the grass. I need a minute or two to collect my thoughts. These are disturbed by a man's voice: 'Yes, who *are* those oddballs Clive is with?' There's a sniggering tone as the speaker chats with his friend in front of the tree that I'm hiding behind. The horrible smell of cigar smoke drifts over with his words.

'His latest pet project, yes. You know he loves his charity cases.' I recognise the second voice. Its Harold from the bank. 'Don't know why he's bothering with that fantasist, Rich—you know, the one who gave that stupid presentation at the bank about Krispy Kreme economics.' Harold tuts. 'The only doughnut around here is Clive for entertaining their ideas.'

As they walk off in the opposite direction, I sneak out from behind the tree to re-join my friends. In the centre of the group is Nat, doing a strip. Well, removing her plus-twos anyway.

'Oh sod it. It's too hot!' she says, revealing the bright blue Box Clever boxer shorts underneath the trousers.

I stand tall; I clear my dry throat and speak calmly. 'That was Stu on the phone. He's accepted the job. We are moving.'

'Can't you help find finance for Deb's Box Clever, brand?' Nat asks Clive as she twirls around showing off her boxers which gleam in the sunlight.

'Well, I'm sure we do have contacts in factories in India …'

Rich interjects, 'Feckin' India? Have you not listened to a word about what the Good Life project is about?'

'More importantly, have none of you listened to a word I've been saying?' I raise my voice as I twiddle my wedding ring. 'I'm moving! It's too late!' I take in a deep breath and turn to Nat. 'You'll love it there,' I say hopefully. 'You can come and visit and … er, play tennis.'

'They're not the backhanders I'm any good at,' Nat mutters. 'Come on Clivey, you must have a job for Stu? Can't you give him a promotion at the bank?' That's Nat for you. My truly tenacious, positive friend is still trying to come up with a handy solution.

'Look, I don't know the timing, and …' My resolve to stay positive cracks as I spot a tear forming in Rich's eye. And suddenly the dam bursts on my own tears despite my best efforts to hold them back.

Rich kicks out at a golf ball. It lands with a thump on the grass a few feet away.

'Bad luck, old chum. Bit of a dribbler there!' Harold and his cigar chump have joined us.

'There's only one dribbler round here,' snaps Rich.

Harold puts his hand on my shoulder. 'No need to cry, Deborah. I'm sure your game isn't as bad as you think.'

'Oh, sod off, Harold,' I yell. My calm deserts me. 'You and your sodding perfect wife and children.'

'Well, there's no need to for that kind of language, Deborah.'

'I simply must protest, Clive,' adds Cigar Chump. 'We do have standards around here.'

'I'll shove your feckin' standards up your arse!' Nat bursts in. 'Don't you dare talk to my best friend like that!'

Best friend, I hear. I lean into Nat's shoulders and continue to sob.

Harold and Cigar Chump walk off, muttering how the membership fee of three thousand pounds a year is meant to deter people like us.

'Your three grand is not worth the paper it's written on,' Rich shouts after them. He turns to draw us all, and, surprisingly even Clive, into a group hug.

'More bad news, I'm afraid.' Our moment of mutual consolation is interrupted by Pippa who re-joins us. 'I've just had a call from Michael. Chloe found Sophia Loren, our lovely chick, with her head chopped off. And there's more …'—Pippa takes a deep breath—'A pipe has burst and is flooding through a manhole cover on the pavement perilously close to our Peoples Fridge.

'Someone's so out to get us.' Nat shakes her head and smiles at me, mascara starting to run down her eyes. 'Maybe we should just accept that the Good Life was a lovely dream, but it's over now?'

Good old Clive now reacts as the voice of hope. 'Now come on, Team Good Life, that's enough of this gloom and doom! When starting any business venture—be it a multinational corporation, or a small start-up like yours, there will always be a few mountains to climb—or in this case, bunkers to get off. It's all just par for the course.' He lifts an iron golf club from a bag and waves it in the air. 'Let's grab our "sand-wedges" and come up with a plan.'

'Ok, Clive. Must say I *am* a bit peckish,' says Nat, giving him a hug. Her smudged mascara leaves a mark on his cheek.

Rich looks at me, and we burst out laughing. Nat seems to be thinking Clive is referring to a snack rather than a golf club.

'That's the spirit everyone!' Clive claps his hands. 'Now, I know we are only at the third hole, but perhaps we should skip a few, and head straight to the nineteenth …'—he pauses—'I'm talking about the club bar—of course!' He laughs. 'It's time for restorative G&T's all round.

CHAPTER 23

May Day . . . May Day

It's the day of our Beltane festival: day of revelry, fire and ... passion.

I'm doing my best to join in with the fun and help get the Good Life ready for our big May Day parade, but my body feels weighed down with sadness. Stu has handed in his notice at the Bank of England and has started preparing for his new job at Bristol Uni. We're going to Brat-ford next week for a final viewing of the house that Stu wants to put an offer on, despite my reservations.

Yet, I can't help getting caught up in the Good Life bustle. I'm excited to see how beautiful our May queen looks in her gown, which I've upcycled. Everyone is rushing about in a flurry of preparation in the forecourt around me. A banner has been made from several sheets tied together; not my stuff for once—my laundry cupboard is now guarded with a Nat-proof lock on it. The slogan: Swallow v Amazon, has been painted on the banner which is now being hung across the church roof by Rich. Somehow, he has managed to climb onto the roof without a ladder. Only a few slate tiles have been dislodged in the process, narrowly missing a grunting Old Spot, who is trying to snooze in the early morning sun.

The centre of all activity is a giant maypole that Rich has built. It stands tall and proud in the centre of the action. The multi-coloured ribbons attached to the top of the pole are flapping around in the gusty May breeze like the arms of excited children, welcoming all to our May Day festival.

As I dig my spade into a wheelbarrow of compost and continue to fill our new raised bed before transplanting pea plants into it, I look around at my lovely friends, who I will sorely miss. Mouse and

Lucia are giggling behind the counter of their Chip Fat Travellers van as they prepare for their *secret* workshop. Jafar is helping Pippa lay out leaflets on a stall to promote our Swallow v Amazon campaign. Next to him, Nahal is laying kindling onto a large campfire dish which Rich has borrowed.

'Michael, you really are a nitwit!' Nat yells, as a bunch of her leaflets—'Vote Nat: A Natty Vote,'—fly off her desk, which a grimacing Michael is trying to carry out into the forecourt.

Nat aside, I feel a surge of pride as I take in the scene. As I put down my spade and glance at my fingernails, which are caked with compost, I realise I'd swop a Bristolian spa for a spade in Kentish Town any day! Not only have Team Good Life's high spirits returned, but they have been joined by others. And a spirited bunch they are. Or should I say spirited shoal? Because the place is suddenly filled with a mass of newcomers all dressed in fish costumes.

What a spectacle! An inflatable dolphin glides through the crowd in the forecourt. A lady strolls by sporting a fascinator with a fabric goldfish pinned onto it. She's holding hands with a male seahorse. There's even a bloke wearing a T-shirt adorned with a tin of sardines!

@NTS: Must design a top with fin-like sleeves. Scales 'n all.

The scene gets even odder, when some fish in the growing crowd form a circle and hold hands. The focus of their attention is the large hole in the ground they gather around, peering over the red and white safety tape the council have installed.

It transpired that the burst pipe, and flooded manhole cover that subsequently cut the electricity supply to our People's Fridge and ruined all our food, was not just any rush of water. It was from the subterranean River Fleet, which for centuries has flowed in pipes below us, for the most part unseen, from Hampstead Heath to Blackfriars and into the River Thames. The River Fleet—one of London's great lost rivers, is alleged to be one of Europe's most ancient sites of Christian worship. Without wishing to visualise it, word has it, that a *fatberg* had blocked the effluvial flow downstream, causing it to burst through the submerged pipes and manhole cover, and out into the fetid stream that now surrounds our ex-People's Fridge. On the upside, social media word spread like wildfire. This resulted in brilliant publicity for the Good Life and the arrival of the river spirits who have come to share their blessings.

My smile is suddenly and painfully wiped from my face when a heavy webbed foot stamps on the charity shop azure sandals I'd bought to match my aquamarine top. I wince in pain, as a merman—I *think* that's the name for a male mermaid—tries to lumber past me. As Merman waddles off, a man sporting an orange and white striped costume rushes up to me.

'Well met, sister.' He throws an arm around me, clearly having judged from my unintentional ocean-colour themed outfit, that I am a fellow believer. The odour from his armpit, sheathed in a costume several sizes too small, is almost as rancid as the People's Fridge. Never mind finding Nemo, someone should tell this character it's more about finding deodorant!

I nod politely, retrieve my arm, and walk over to Rich, who is now bolting the maypole to a pallet to secure it.

'Beautiful isn't it, Deb?' Rich looks up at me. 'Happy Beltane.'

'It really is.' I give him a hug. 'The blue ribbons are gleaming as brightly as the sky.'

'They were donated by the bead shop down the road, and the pole is made of coppiced wood from Hampstead Heath.' Rich slides his hand up and down the mottled wood. 'A perfect example of the gift economy in action!'

Nat sidles up to me. 'I assume you know the ribbons on a maypole symbolise female energies wrapping themselves around the male form?' she says. She grabs a ribbon and shoves it between her legs. 'Blimey, this pole looks a bit phallic!'

'Well, Beltane is the day to embrace our sexual nature,' Rich says, his brow furrowed as he watches Nat demonstrate her version of maypole dancing. 'And Beltane does means bright fire. In the old days the fire was blessed by people dancing around it naked.'

Dancing naked around the maypole? An image of Father Guy flashes into my head: his golden hair gleaming as he weaves through silken ribbons; his torso tantalisingly revealed as it slides past the pole; his soft hands scattering daisy petals as he …

'Lighting the Beltane fire is all about rubbing and grinding until sparks fly,' Rich explains, suggestively rubbing his hands together.

Nat coughs, 'We've got so many great activities happening today. What do you fancy, Deb? Bet you're looking forward to the dwile flonking!'

I sigh. A few weeks ago, I would have fancied hearing GG's may-day blessing, however clothed; but today, I'm just expecting to hear another of his lies. It's probably time to change his nick name from gorgeous Guy to guileful Guy.

I fake a bright smile and ask Nat, 'Dwile … what?'

'Dwile flonking is the old East Anglian pub sport where a soggy dishcloth is fished from a bucket of old beer and lobbed at a circle of players. And wait till you see our version of Morris dancers!' Nat chuckles.

'Yep, it's all going to be great fun. The one downer today was having to bury Sophia in the back garden this morning.' Rich shakes his head.

'I think it was another case of foul play!' says Nat. 'Get it? *Fowl*, as in chicken!'

'I've got a good mind to put you over my knee and give you a good spanking, but you'd probably enjoy it!' The grin on Rich's face fades as he surveys the crowd. 'It's great that the rediscovery of the River Fleet flowing under the Good Life has attracted a big crowd, but I hope that those fishy folk don't ruin our May Day parade.'

'They do seem to be getting well "tanked" up!' Nat points out the hip flasks being passed around the crowd. 'Every watery pun intended!'

She giggles at her own nattery joke, and rich laughs along.

'You two seem to be getting on well.' My face breaks out into a genuine smile this time. There can be no doubt about the growing the chemistry between them. 'Have you agreed to be Nat's campaign manager?' I ask Rich.

'Well, we've been outdoor-knocking every night over the past week, and we did stay up all last night having er … a planning meeting,' Nat says quickly. 'You know what is said: "*The fair maid who on* the first of May goes into the fields at the break of day, and washes in dew from the hawthorn tree, will ever after handsome be." Do I look younger, Deb?' Don't know about younger, but her face is glowing with happiness as she smiles at Rich. 'In fact, you're not gonna see much of me during your last few weeks here. Rich and me have got a lot of campaigning to do for the local election in eight weeks.'

Last few weeks, I sigh; kicking off next week with Stu and I getting to know our new area by staying at a boutique hotel deep in the Somerset countryside. Or is it Wiltshire? All I know is that I'll be missing the planning of our dreamed-for Chelsea Flower Show Garden that Nat is working on with Rich and Pippa. They are understandably being very secretive about it. The first I will know anything will be at the Chelsea build in two weeks' time.

As Rich disappears off to get ready for his part in our May Day parade, I walk over to Nahal. She is stirring the ingredients in a giant cast iron pot that is hanging from a tripod above a blazing fire dish. I crouch down beside her and stare into the embers.

'I am cooking this *Ashe-e post-e pa*, thick vegetable soup, for you; to mark a farewell.' Nahal hands me the ladle. 'In Iran, we cook this ceremonial soup to pray for the shortening of a sojourn. Would you like to stir it?'

I take the ladle with a grateful smile. Somehow, Nahal always has the right words, but also knows when to be silent.

My eyes well up. Nahal puts an arm around me, and we gaze into the pot. I continue to stir the ingredients; to invoke her words. As Nat would say, I really feel in the soup.

Our silence commune is broken by Jafar, who rushes up to us carrying a bundle of leaflets. He hands one to me. I read: *'Swallow v Amazon. Do you feel that local folks like you and me are too insignificant to make a difference? At the Good Life, we are going to prove this idea wrong! Join our campaign to regulate Amazon's drone deliveries. Together, ordinary people like us can change things.'*

While I remain unconvinced that there's anything we can realistically do to influence big corporate business, I smile at Jafar, who gushes: 'Our #SwallowVAmazon campaign now has five thousand followers on Twitter and Insta!'

I'm just about to remind Nahal what a bright boy Jafar is and ask for an update on the school meeting with the horrid Miss Stuart, when a booming voice intrudes. 'Fellow dowsers, our ceremony is about to begin.' We look over to see that a man in a long brown cape with a pointed hood is doing the bellowing.

Jafar takes both Nahal and me by the hand and leads us towards the manhole cover. Someone has removed the red and white safety tape. We join the ever-growing crowd. I'm careful not to stand too close to Merman or Nemo, who are leaning over into the exposed manhole cover.

'Welcome to our new site of worship,' Cape Man calls out as he lifts a large Y-shaped wooden stick into the air.

'Hold on a minute, matey, this is not your site!' The words of censure come from Nat, as she pushes her way through the crowd, parting the blue sea. 'This site belongs to the Good Life.'

'You don't understand, sister,' says Cape Man. 'We are the Kentish Town Urban River Diviners. This sacred site will allow us to connect and interact with beings beyond our spectrum of perception.'

Nods of agreement all around. Several fish-folk start waving something in the air. A closer examination reveals they're metal clothes hangers.

Nat says, 'Town Urban River Diviners? T.U.R.D, eh? Well I'm interacting with you TURDs, right now, to tell you that our May Day Parade is about to start. If you could hold back on being divine until later and join in our fun, we'd appreciate it.'

'There's no need to be sarcastic, sister ...'

'I'm not being sarcastic, just factual,' says Nat firmly. 'You can chose the initials!'

Turds, indeed! Perhaps they should have remembered that this latest River Fleet kerfuffle is the result of a build-up of effluvial waste downstream in Kentish Town. I don't know how Nat manages to look poker face at Cape Man, but I look down to stop the fit of giggles which threatens to burst my banks.

'There's no bloody Kurds here,' the man wearing the sardine can T-shirt calls out. He takes a swig from a silver flask and passes it to Cape Man.

'Maman, that man is being racist,' Jafar mumbles, as he stands nestled between Nahal and me.

'Everyone is welcome here,' I cry out.

'Yes, they are,' says Nahal, her voice newly strong. 'Everyone and anyone are welcome here, from Kurds and Sunnis to Hassidic Jews and Sikhs ...'

'Apart from you, Sardine.' Nat walks over to the man. 'Both your words and T-shirt are pickled in brine! You're banned.' She grabs the hip flask from him. 'And furthermore, this is not a bring your own event.'

'Listen here, sister, we drink this magic potion to transport us to other realms,' Sardine shouts back at Nat, and waves his metal coat hanger in the air with such force that it bends. 'With dowsing, we are measuring the change in vibrations and energy fields.'

'If you ask me, you could do with a good dousing of cold water,' Nat snaps back.

'Give me back that flask!' Sardine tries to wrestle the container from Nat's hand. In doing so, he drops his redundant divination tool to the ground.

Nat and Sardine's altercation is stopped by a sudden piercing scream, followed by a loud wooden thwack. We turn round. It's Cape Man. He has somehow managed to tumble backwards into the middle of *my* new raised bed. He now lies there silent and soiled, mid compost. A bunch of us gather round the bed where Cape Man lies deadly still. Nat looks at me with concern, while Nahal shields Jafar's eyes. The only sounds are gasps of distress from the crowd. I'm wondering about calling an ambulance when Cape Man's wooden stick starts to twitch. It's followed by his arm, which (unlike my now squashed peas) shoots out from the bed. His whole body starts to writhe about, following his twitching rod.

Cries of joy erupt from the fish-folk at the sight of their chief diviner, not only returning to this life, but apparently connecting with spirits on another spectrum. Hip flasks are handed around as the coat-hanger crew start to sway, their metal 'rods' aloft. A loud pulsating drum starts up, stopping Nat in her angry stride as she charges up to Cape Man.

'Let the revelry begin,' Rich calls outs, striding into the forecourt. His almost naked body, protected only by a painted-green loincloth with additional decorative orange swirls on his face. His green hair is crowned with a garland of ivy.

'Welcome, citizens of Camden and beyond …' he shouts, winking at Nat, who is all too happy to switch her attention away from Compost-Cape Man to this Incredible Hulk.

Rich, our Beltane King, strides over to the Maypole and looks around the large group of people who have gathered and now outnumber the fish-folk. He calls out to them, 'Friends and neighbours … all you lovely people, welcome to the Good Life's May Day parade.'

I'm happy to see that the Good Life is attracting people of all ages. There's a bunch of older folk, who are sitting on deckchairs they have bought along. A crowd of hipsters are laughing as they check out the Chip Fat Travellers secret workshop. Several families with kids are already dancing around the maypole. There's even a dog caught up in the ribbons!

Our Beltane King continues, 'Would you all please put your hands together to welcome our May Queen, Flora, Goddess of spring …'

There's a loud roar of applause as Marg—the May Queen!—saunters in. Her silver hair gleams with a crown of woven cow parsley. She looks beautiful in a long white satin sheath gown, (donated by dry-cleaner Hari), to which I have added long green velvet scooped sleeves. My eyes are wet with pride, as the long train attached to the back of the dress which I made by sewing four rows of net curtains together—froths along the cobbled forecourt.

Behind her, Pippa, dressed in a green velvet dress, giggles as she tries to stop the trail from flying off in the blustery wind.

'Wait for us!' cries Chloe, skipping alongside them, a posy held in one hand and Old Spot's lead in the other.

They circle the forecourt, the crowd continuing to applaud them, until Old Spot, who looks very cute with a pink ribbon tied round his neck, decides it's time to stop. He lays down. Time for his afternoon snooze! At the sight of him rolling on to one side, refusing to budge, and Chloe trying to coax him into action with a belly rub, the crowd roar with laughter.

'I now call upon Goddess Flora to share her May-Day blessing.' Beltane King Rich takes a deep bow in front of May Queen Marg, who now stands beside the maypole.

'We bless you, God of Seed and Harvest,' Marg cries, throwing her arms into the air, scattering the ribbons. 'And we bless each other for the beauty of this world and the love that created it.' She casts her arm around the crowd. 'As the sun shines down upon our land, we offer thanks for the gift of life each spring. From the seeds that spring forth ...'

Springing seeds? For some reason, that makes me look over to Cape Man, who is extricating himself from the raised bed and dusting himself off, before disappearing down the High Street. Whilst several of his fishy-folk have followed him, others have chosen to remain, and now stand enraptured by Marg's pastoral, non-T.U.R.D words.

'It's time to rejoice in the Earth's fertility, with music and dance,' announces the May Queen, as she's approached by two blokes strumming ukuleles, and Pippa jauntily playing a violin.

Rich takes Marg's arm, and they start to dance. Shrieks of laughter break out as her trail gets entwined with the limbs of some in the crowd—me included—as we all start to dance around the maypole. Leroy, Chloe, Jafar, and other kids dart amongst the adults, weaving the ribbons together. In a blink of my eye, as Nat spins me round, I see that absolutely everyone, fish-folk included, have joined in the fun. As the music gets faster and faster, so does the dancing. It's more Maypole knotting than dancing, but it's great, exhilarating fun.

After a good hour of music and mayhem, a breathless Beltane King Rich and completely unflustered, May Queen Marg—her train amazingly still intact—manage to extricate themselves from the maypole.

'Ladies and gents,' announces Rich, 'please form a circle and give it up for the premier performance from our very own Kentish Town Morris Dancers!'

There's a huge round of applause as an accordion strikes up. The crowd form a large circle around the group that has made its way into the centre of the forecourt. The dancers turn out to be our friendly neighbourhood firefighters. Dressed in full uniform and wearing their yellow helmets, the firemen have elastic bands tied around their knees and calves, with spoons clenched between them!

The crowd roar with laughter as the Kentish Town Morris Dancers, Fireman Sam among them, prance around, clanking and jangling their knees together. It's a musical movement in several parts, and definitely on the sharp side! This Kentish Town troupe might not win any national Morris dancers of the year awards, but they are completely on fire, and the crowd cheer their every clang of spoons and stomp of boots.

Nat dances up to me, clapping her hands: 'What do you call it when spooning leads to sex?' she giggles. 'Forking!' She whacks me on the back. 'Hilarious, eh?!'

I smile as I stare at her face, now imprinted with green smudges and orange swirls. Funnily enough, it's exactly the same design as on Beltane King Rich's face. Ah-ha … gotcha, Nat! Been 'spooning' with Rich, eh?'

'You've gotta come and have a go at Lucia's workshop.' Nat grabs my hand and pulls me through the crowd to the Chip Fat Travellers van. It's flanked by a queue of millennials who are dancing to the Morris dancer's music.

'Deb, I hope you're going to have a go at making a burlesque pastie!' Lucia calls to me, leaning out of the van.

'And before you tell Lucia you're not hungry, take note, it's a nipple tassel workshop!' Nat chuckles. 'Mind you, Deb, this workshop might be more suited to me with my full rack, than to you!' She looks down at her breasts, their generous shape barely concealed by her 'Good Life: Vote Nat' T-shirt in bright pink. Then she glances at my more modest décolletage. Pushing her way to the front of the queue, Nat grabs a couple of glittery felt patches. She sticks them on her T-shirt, twirls her boobs around and grins at me.

@NTS: Must chat with Nat later, about the *kind* of Good Life message her T-shirt is proposing/suggesting, apropos her election campaign strategy.

Promising Lucia to have a go at the workshop later, I walk on. I come across Greg, who is showing a group of young families how to turn an old broom into a hobby horse. He explains how it's customary to make 'obby horses on May Day. He lifts a pair of tights from a selection of hosiery laying in a box, and stuffs it with straw. Attaching his panty ho(r)se head to a broom handle, he puts his 'obby horse between his legs and gallops off.

As his audience laugh, I notice the pair of gorgeous Fogal Sensuelle tights, still in their wrapping, which are now laying on top of the box. They cost over fifty pounds. I'm just wondering whether I should rescue them when Henry Junior beats me to it. He grabs them and rips open the packaging. Placing the tights over his head, off he trots, trampling on several courgettes placed on the ground next to Leroy, who is manning the adjacent stall.

'Oi, watch out,' Leroy cries, as he picks up a squashed courgette 'This is part of our vegetable orchestra.'

Clippity-clop Henry Junior ignores Leroy and charges off towards the maypole. 'Are you coming to join our orchestra, Deb?' Leroy looks at me hopefully.

'Let's make some swede sounds!' says Leroy's father, Francis, waving a bunch of carrots in the air.

I join the large group gathering around Leroy and Francis, as they hand out carrots and courgettes.

'We are going show you how to turn this courgette into a flute, and the carrot into a recorder,' announces a grinning Francis.

'And turn this green pepper into shaker,' says Leroy, cutting the pepper in half. He hands it to me. I sit down and start to scoop out the seeds. Yep. It's time to 'turnip' the music!

The next few hours disappear into a blur of magical, non-stop, fun. I don't know where the time has vanished, but it's now 8 p.m. The grin on my face is as big as the bowl of *ashe-e post-e pa*, veg soup, that Nahal now hands me. I giggle as I reflect on the afternoon of magical mayhem: from floppy courgettes and twirling tassels to worm-chanting and hobby horse races.

After a particularly robust session of dwile flocking—tossing beer laden dishcloths—I'm sopping wet and happy to be warming myself at the campfire among the remaining revellers. I tuck into the yummy soup, which Leroy is quick to remind us of is partly made from the leftover vegetable orchestra.

Nat plonks herself down next to me and stares at the fire. Her face is glowing as brightly as its embers, as she hands out her campaign leaflets and starts to speak. I look around at the crowd who sit absorbed in her every word as she talks about what her vision of a Good Life is for Kentish Town. I've never really believed she has a chance of winning the local election and becoming a councillor but watching the enraptured reaction and nods of agreement—Rich included—I'm beginning to think twice.

I sigh in the knowledge that even if by some miracle it *does* happen, it's something I won't be here to enjoy. Or more likely, come to dread! All I do know is that I will miss Nat terribly. I can't help wondering that if only Stu had turned up here today—as he promised to—he might have seen what fantastic fun it has been, and how the Good Life really is starting to build a community of …

'Oh my God, Deb, you'd better come quick …' The hissed words of distress come from Pippa, who is leaning over me whispering into my ear. 'Marg's just woken up from a nap to realise that Old Spot's disappeared once again. And worse still …'

Pippa doesn't get to tell me what is 'worse still,' as there's a sudden blast of beeping cars. I jump up. We run out of the forecourt onto the main road where a big queue of traffic is piling up. A bus driver leans out of his window to see what the problem is. Several car owners are shouting in anger. The sound of beeping cars is joined by a chorus of wolf whistles. And then I see why there's a traffic jam in Kentish Town Road at 8 p.m. on a Sunday night. In front of us, several female T.U.R.Ds have taken off their tops and are now dancing semi-naked, in a circle, in the middle of the road. Their nipple tassels are not the only thing now moving in the street!—apart from Cape Man and Sardine. They've clearly consumed a huge quantity of their magic potion, and the now drunken dowsers are fighting each other with their 'obby horses. Henry Junior appears from nowhere. He rushes into the street brandishing his headless horse, only to spear a passer-by, causing her to drop her bag of shopping.

The lady starts shrieking, 'Police! Police! Someone call the police.'

As the nipple tassel dancers rush over to the aggrieved woman, she shrieks even louder. '*Heeeelp!* There's a dead pig in the street!'

All eyes turn to the spot where the T.U.R.Ds had been dancing. Old Spot is laying there motionless. Besides him on the ground is the T.U.R.D's silver hip flask, now empty of its magic potion. It has clearly taken Old Spot to another realm. We all hurry to his aid.

May Day! May Day!

CHAPTER 24

Bloom and Bust

4:30 a.m. It's Chelsea Flower Show press day. Yippee! Press day!—an event I've dreamt about for many years. I may have spent all night with Team Good Life, filling countless old Amazon delivery boxes with soil and planting them with wildflowers, and even the searing pain in my back has not diminished my excitement.

Alongside me, Pippa, Greg, and Marg continue to place the newly filled boxes around a giant spandex screen that has been erected in the middle of our 'concept' garden. Well, I say *our* concept garden, but Nat and the 'design team' are being secretive about what's going to be shown on the screen, and how the planted Amazon boxes fit in. All I know is that Nat has told the RHS that our garden is an homage to protecting wildlife.

I stand up with a wince, but I'm soothed when I admire the Amazonian mountain. The variously sized boxes of wildflowers do look pretty. What a lovely assortment: red campions, ox-eye daisies, scabiosa with their lilac pin cushion flowers … a tapestry of wildflowers towered over by pale pink foxgloves, whose pollen-rich flowers are abuzz with gratefully guzzling bees. The overall effect is a lovely haze of pastel colour that contrasts well with the buff-brown boxes. All that's needed now is the screening of the mystery film of wildlife cuties and our concept garden will be ready to open for press day.

Though it's the middle of the night, it's boiling hot. I sigh as I roll up the soggy, long sleeves of the green T-shirt I'm wearing over heavy denim dungarees. The patches of sweat don't exactly reflect the stylish 'build' outfit I'd carefully planned. Cambridge-Kate didn't have this problem with her dungaree look at last year's Chelsea! But then who could have imagined it would be twenty-four degrees in the early hours of the morn? And as I only got back from Brat'ford yesterday at 5 p.m., and had to rush straight to Chelsea, I had no time to go home to re-style.

As I stretch out to relieve my stiff back, my loud yawn joins the serenade of nature's choristers who are heralding the daylight creeping into the sky: There's the high-pitched trill of the robin as well as the *chiff-chaff* call of the chiffchaff. I smile at Greg, who is still artily placing the last few planted boxes around the screen. It's thanks to him that I now recognise bird calls. A year ago, the only chafing in my vocab would have referred to the rubbing of sweaty dungarees on my legs.

The birds continue singing to one another from tree to tree around the gardens, perhaps choosing their own favourite show garden. I gaze over the neighbouring concept gardens, where stall-holders are anxiously racing around adding the finishing touches … Which is *my* favourite?

Could it be the #6G garden facing ours? Its mass of tangled tree roots is a rather sinister symbol of the interconnection of everything. The group of Chinese stallholders stand nodding their heads with satisfaction at their sign: 'Huawei. Welcome to the Wood Wide Web.'

Or how about the 'No Mow' garden,' next to ours, with its Astro-turf striped lawn. A striped, yellow deckchair placed in the centre is the sole accessory. How this illustrates the message that a plastic lawn encourages wildflowers is beyond me, but then that's a 'concept' garden for you.

Finally, on the other side of our Good Life offering is a garden called, 'Can't see the wood for the trees.' It's a thicket of trees with a clear metaphor. What's not so clear is why the team has waited till the last few hours to place the last tree which is currently being lowered by crane into the middle of the site. The designer is shouting crazed directions to the crane driver.

Ah, yes—Chelsea Flower Show press day! *Yippee!* I close my eyes and breathe in the fragrant air. It's redolent of elderflower jasmine and … fried bacon. The stallholder walking past me is trailed by the aroma of his bacon sarnie. I'd almost swop my coveted press day stallholder's pass for a rasher!

'Not flagging are you, Dungaree Deb? Or should that be Dung Deb!' This smarty pants observation is so Nat. She approaches, pinching her nose at the sight of my muddy outfit. She's in a pretty, pristine, vintage floral dress, accessorised by the matching bow tie worn by Old Spot, who waddles alongside her.

'I didn't think animals are allowed at Chelsea,' I hiss. 'How'd you sneak him in?'

'In that TV delivery box, of course!' Nat replies, pointing. 'Since Spot-gate on May Day, Marg understandably doesn't want to leave him on his own. I still crack up at the thought of Old Spot lying dead drunk in the middle of our High Street. A plastered pig's a new one on me!' She giggles as she releases Old Spot's lead and lets him wander off.

'So, changed your mind about Brat-ford, yet?' Nat puts her arm around me. 'You seemed to spend more time last week texting me about how much you hated it there than you did hanging out with Stu.'

I look down at my wedding ring and sigh, 'We never seemed to get over our row on the first night about Stu not turning up at our Good Life bash for May Day. I hoped that if he saw what the Good Life was achieving, he would …'

'What the …! Why d'you bring *that* rag here?' Nat yells, cutting me short, as she spies Rich heading our way. He's carrying a food parcel—but it's covered in a copy of the Camden New Journal.

'We had to wrap our grub in something,' Rich replies, as he opens the parcel and hands the contents to me. 'Deb—unlike others—has been working hard all night and deserves some brekkie.' He winks at Nat.

'I'll have you know that a show garden designer's work is never done.' Nat tries to shoot Rich a stern look, but her sparkling eyes betray her affection. She turns them to her phone. 'Anyway, I can't chat now. I've got to prep for my TV interview at nine a.m.. Grub's up, Dung Deb!'

TV interview? A story as flaky as my vegan sausage roll, I figure, as Nat dashes off, with Rich in tow.

Sitting down to munch my surprisingly, tasty Quorn roll, I unfold the crumpled newspaper to re-read the CNJ article about our May Day fiasco, which Nat is so affronted by.

Beneath the opening line, 'Piggy In The Middle,' the article lists the alleged atrocities that took place during our May Day event. It includes an eyewitness quote from none other than, Thomas Montjoy: 'Hosting a pagan festival in an ex-church is a travesty. I witnessed topless women dancing in the middle of Kentish Town High Street. Feral children were throwing spears ...' I skim over the article, not wanting to dignify Montjoy's ridiculous comments, but can't help giggling when I read, 'Viewers were relieved when what was thought to be a sacrificial pig lying dead in the middle of the road wagged its tail, got up and waddled off.'

On that happy note, I shove the paper into one of the Amazon boxes and jump up to re-join Pippa, Greg, and Marg. It's time to put the finishing touches to our garden and then get glammed up for the Chelsea press day—the fulfilment of my high-heeled gardener dreams! And what an outfit I have planned!

8 a.m.—Our garden is ready and, surprisingly, looks quite professional in an artsy sort of way. It's a glorious day, not a cloud in sight. The temperature is rising as rapidly as the frayed tempers of the team from the neighbouring, 'Can't see the Wood for the trees,' concept garden. It turns out that you *can* see the wood. And it's bent in two. The overly dry conditions have caused the trunk to split. Apart from that little catastrophe, the gardens around us are all gleaming and waiting for the all-important judges visit.

'Time to get changed, Dung Deb,' Nat orders. She hands over an over-sized black T-shirt sporting a white logo: 'Swallow v Amazon,' and a pair of my Box Clever black shorts. 'Here's your uniform for the day.' She pats me on the back.

'Uniform?' I stutter. 'But I've planned an amazing outfit.' I look down at the shorts, which are several sizes too big for me. 'I made these boxers for a school basketball team.'

'Well, I've appropriated them for Team Good Life. My design concept is that the team dresses in monochrome, leaving the wild-flowers to represent our burst of colour.'

But what about my primrose yellow Erdem dress with its layers of floral chiffon …? I'm about to sink into a major sartorial sulk when Greg and Marg appear, dressed in their uniform. While Marg's T-shirt and boxers swamp her tiny frame and hang down to her knees, the drawstring on Greg's boxers sits below his bulging belly, revealing the perished elastic of his greying Y-fronts. Trying not to give in to a fit of giggles, I grab the uniform from Nat, and stomp off.

Half an hour later, Team Good Life are gathered around our garden. Nahal looks very pretty in a cornflower blue headscarf, black T-shirt and long black skirt tinged with violet. Pippa has hitched up her shorts to reveal long shapely legs, her cropped T-shirt tied into a knot to show off her flat tummy. Even Miss-bloody-Stuart, whom Henry has brought along, is wearing a bright pink dress and hat. They match the colour on her cheeks as she gives Jafar, who is cowering next to her, a good telling off.

I'm fuming too. While Nat gets to wear a designer dress, I look like a blob of ink, no matter what fashionista tricks I have used to makeover my uniform. The only saving grace is my pair of gorgeous—some might say unpractical—strappy high-heeled sandals with five-inch wedges decorated with alpine strawberries. I'm doing my best not to topple over in them. Must remember today's mantra: *Teetotallers don't totter.* (Try saying that when you've had a few.)

Talking about saving graces and all things godly, I cast my eyes around the team. There's still no sign of Father Guy, who is supposed to be bringing Father William today. I haven't seen GG for weeks. Along with my Stu, he was another *no show* on May Day. It's almost as if the guileful-Guy has been avoiding me. But today I'm determined to confront him about his relationship with Montjoy, and the bribe to St Margaret's church.

'Welcome, Team Good Life, to the launch of our Swallow v Amazon, garden,' Nat announces, interrupting my machinations. 'Before we play the film,' she points to the screen, 'I'd like to thank Pippa, Greg and Jafar for all their hard campaigning work ...' She pauses as we break into a spontaneous round of applause. Greg, who is standing in front of me, takes a bow. I flinch at the sight of his large bottom being flashed in front of me. Turn the other cheek, Greg.

Nat continues her pep talk: 'I'm so proud of how far the Good Life project has come. It's hard to imagine that it didn't even exist eight months ago! Yet here we are about to open a Chelsea Flower show garden. Wow! Then next week we are presenting a deputation to a Parliamentary task force on drone deliveries. And, yes, I will stop droning on eventually!'

Greg roars with laughter, Nahal giggles, and Marg and Pippa shout a *'hear-hear.'*

Nat turns up the volume in rallying style: 'I believe that when a determined bunch of folk like us come together, we can change the world.' She winks at me. 'Just think back, Deb, to that misty day last September when we first went to visit a grotty church in Kentish Town Road. Who knew where it would lead us?'

It would lead to bottom cracks and belly laughs, exasperation and education, lots of fun, and delicious new food. I smile as I look around at Nahal, guffawing Greg, and the motley group of new friends. I would give anything not to leave them. Count me in to sponge down a community fridge five times a week, or clean out a chicken coop. I wipe my eyes on the baggy sleeves of my monstrously large T-shirt, and wink back at Nat, my beautiful, courageous best friend.

Nat lowers her head and speaks less confidently: 'As you know, next month I'm standing in the local elections to become a councillor. I probably won't win but ...'

She is silenced by Rich, who strides up to her and plants a smacker of a kiss on her lips.

We all cheer.

'Let the show begin!' Rich calls out, as he presses a button on his laptop and the screen bursts into life.

But when I say 'life,' what we are presented with a is a parade of death. A series of images flash before us showing birds and animals crashing into drones and falling to their death: an eagle flies into the blade of a drone; a colony of seals are chased into the sea by a drone—several pups being crushed in the process; nesting birds are panicked and plummet off the cliffs into the sea. There are images of wildlife running in distress from a low flying drone; a baby bird is sliced in two.

The film ends with a heart-breaking close-up shot of Jafar cradling a dead swallow in his arms in the Good Life forecourt. Lying a few feet away is the drone blade, an empty Amazon box and a packet of mascara. The end title reads: '#swallowvamazon: We call on the government to regulate drone delivery. Stop drones from killing wildlife.'

The images are horrific and moving. The short film ends, but soon restarts on a loop. We all stand in silence—until Henry Junior starts to laugh and shoots a pretend air rifle at the screen.

'You need to get your son under control,' shouts Rich, turning to Henry Senior.

Jafar stares at the screen and starts to sob. Nahal puts her arm around him.

'No one likes a cry baby, Jafar,' snaps Miss Stuart.

'You can feck off for a start, Miss Stuart,' Rich growls at her. 'I don't know what you're doing here, or what your problem with Jafar is.'

'There's no need to be so rude, Richard,' Henry Smarmy Smythe says loudly. 'Miss Stuart is here for research purposes.'

'Well, there's no more important research than on the screen in front of you. You and Miss Stuart, who looks like a feckin' jam tart, can …'

'You-hoo! Have we come at a bad time?' The lady who interrupts is carrying a clip board. She introduces herself. 'I'm Hatty, one of the flower show's TV producers. I hope you're all excited and ready to be filmed?' She looks around at the boxes and wildflowers which have already started to droop in the heat. 'Your garden looks very … er, interesting.'

'Not at all, it's a perfect time!' Nat replies in her most plummy voice, as she shakes Hatty's hand. 'Just pre-show jitters!' She forces a laugh.

Filmed? For TV? Strike that comparison I made earlier about the comparative flakiness of Nat's story with a sausage roll. I'm desperately trying to locate the lippy in my bag, when a man holding a camera strolls into our garden.

'Let's set Joe up over here,'—he looks at the script on his clipboard—'and Natalie and Jafar to the right of him.' He stops to smile at us all. 'Morning all, I'm Nigel, the cameraman/director.'

Nahal gives Jafar, whose teary eyes now shine with excitement, a hug of encouragement; and Hatty escorts him and Nat to the spot chosen by Nigel. Their every move is watched wide-eyed in disbelief by Miss Stuart and both Senior and Junior Henrys.

'Perhaps one of your workers could be seen planting the wildflowers in a box,' suggests Nigel. 'How about you with the great shoes?' He points at me.

Me and my great shoes? On TV? This lift is followed by a rock-bottom thought: doesn't TV make you look fat? My derrière bent over in basket baller boxers is not the look I would have chosen for my debut appearance on telly.

I totter over and bend down in front of a box as, unbelievably, Joe Swift walks in!

'Hi everyone, great to meet you. I'm Joe,' he says, rolling up the sleeves in his pale blue linen shirt and tilting his signature trilby hat.

'Nice to meet you, Joe. I'm Nat, the designer.' She gives him a hug.

'Take a look at this, mate,' says Rich, as he hands Joe a #swallowvamazon leaflet which summarises the concept of our garden, and the campaign.

Joe quickly reads it. 'Important issues you're raising here, guys.' He nods his head.

Even with my back to the camera, I'm aware of the large crowd that has gathered around us. I can't believe Nat and Jafar are being interviewed by Joe Swift for TV.

'As we *are* a bit pressed for time, shall we get cracking?' says Nigel.

'Roll cameras, sound speed,' I want to shout, as the interview starts. But all I do is take a deep breath and squeeze in my buttocks.

'Thanks for being here, Natalie,' says Joe, as he starts the interview.

'Well, thank you for interviewing us, Mr Swift. You've got near enough the right name for our "Swallows v Amazon," garden!"' Nat speaks confidently, then howls with laughter.

'I'm not sure "Joe Swallow" has the right ring to it!' Joe joins in the laughter. He then turns to Jafar. 'And what's your name, young man?'

'Jafar,' our shy boy mutters, looking down.

'Well Jafar, would you like to tell us about the idea behind your fantastic garden?' asks Joe.

Nat takes Jafar's hand and gives it a squeeze. He takes a deep breath, looks up into the camera and speaks out in a louder voice: 'British swallows spend their winters in South Africa and migrate back to the UK in April and May. There's been a big decline in the swallow population since 1970. The world can't afford to lose any more.' He pauses to look at Nat, who gives him a nod of approval. 'That's why I was so upset when a swallow got its wings caught in the blade of a drone over the church in Kentish Town.' Jafar's eyes start to well up again. 'It turned out that it was part of an Amazon delivery drone. The poor swallow died in my arms.' Jafar turns to point at the screen, which is showing the dead swallow cradled in his arms. 'I don't think this should be allowed to happen again. The government need to set up rules.'

'You should be very proud young man. What a confident and expert speaker you are.' Joe pats Jafar on the shoulder.

Then he turns to Nat. 'And what is the reason for this mountain of wildflower boxes?' he asks.

'The empty boxes symbolise our consumption-obsessed, throw-away culture, while in complete contrast the wildflowers represent the importance of protecting our planet.' Nat leans across to grab a box from my hand. I turn to smile into the camera, but find my eyes and lips are crusted by a mix of lip gloss and soil.

'For example,' Nat continues, 'how often do you think a drill like this is used in its lifetime?' Nat asks Joe, while indicating the Bosch label on the outside of the box.

'I, er … don't know, Nat.' Joe looks perplexed, this question clearly off script.

'It's eleven minutes, Joe. The "must-have" drill, purchased by millions of us all around the country, is, on average, only used for eleven minutes during its *entire* lifetime.' Nat shakes her head. 'Most drills just rot away, unused. We all need to start sharing more stuff. It's not only good fun, but will help cut down on unnecessary, polluting deliveries.'

Jafar eagerly jumps in: 'At our Good Life project, to stop stuff being wasted, we've set up an equipment sharing library called 'Daddy Day Share.'

Nat looks to camera. 'Yes, ladies, you heard right. There are lots of single dads in Kentish Town, London. Come and nab a fella, while you're borrowing a fondue set!'

Joe bursts out laughing. 'I can quite honestly say, Nat, that in all my years of TV, this is a new one on me!'

Nat continues, 'We've also been invited to talk to a parliamentary committee about the regulation of drone delivery. I know many of your viewers will think that there's nothing ordinary people like us can do to change the law, but *we* think we can.'

Jafar pipes up again: 'Please support our campaign. It's "hashtag Swallow 'V' Amazon." We're on insta and twitter.'

'It's the only tweet that matters!' Nat winks into the camera.

'Well, this interview has been a complete pleasure,' Joe wraps up with smiles at Nat and Jafar. 'I think your concept garden is fantastic. It's disturbing, but important.' He looks straight at the camera. 'All you people out there, I urge you to get involved.'

'Thanks, Joe. Before you go, I'd like to tell you about another of our Good Life projects. It's aimed at our throwaway culture …'

I gasp when Nat lifts a pair of Box-Clever shorts from my Chloe bag. She hands them to Joe. 'These boxers were made from upcycled curtain lining, by our designer, Deb.' She points to me. I try to stand up, only for my wedged shoe to have other plans. It turns ninety degrees causing my foot to twist and land awkwardly on the ground. A pain shoots up my leg.

'It's bloody hot. Why don't you nip behind the screen and put'em on!' Nat laughs with Joe, unaware of my agony.

'They do look great … maybe later.' Joe holds the boxers up to camera. 'One final question. What's the symbolism behind this bra?' He points to a giant bra, which someone has stealthily laid across one of the boxes. Its generous cups are planted with wildflowers.

Nat laughs, 'A-ha! That's no symbolism, just a bit of fun. After all, gardening and environmental action should be all about having fun, don't you agree? *Bloom and bust!*'

CHAPTER 25

Busted and Bloom

4:30 p.m. It's still Chelsea Flower Show press day. Yippee … yawny! I can't remember the last time I slept; or how much of Rich's homemade elderflower champagne I've drunk despite regularly reminding myself that teetotallers with throbbing ankles don't totter. But not even my swollen ankle or the constant pain shooting up my leg can dim my excitement.

After Joe and the production team left, the popping of corks started—even though it was only 10 a.m.. The popping hasn't stopped since. The judges came round and asked probing questions about our garden, which Jafar answered brilliantly. Since then, the stall has been packed. All kinds of celebrities have come and gone, having stood for selfies. Hundreds of campaign leaflets have been handed out. The last few hours have vanished in a blink of an eye. In my case, more of a blink-*less* eye. It turned out, post TV interview, that in my haste to put on lip gloss I had managed to smear a layer of soil across my lips and eyes. Compost-coated eyes and a baggy black outfit is not an image I want to see on primetime telly tonight!

Beauty concerns aside, I can't stop grinning as I gaze around our garden, which is buzzing with people. There's a long queue winding, like bindweed, around the outside. Bartender turned bouncer, Rich, is busily checking names on his guest list before letting people in.

'Congratulations, m'dears …' This salutation comes from Clive, squeezing his way to us through the crowd. He gives Nat a loud kiss on the lips. 'Your show garden is an absolute triumph,' he cries. 'Just the publicity we need before your presentation to the parliamentary task force next week.'

'Thanks, Clivey!' Nat hands him a large helping of bubbly served in one of our recycled jam jars. 'I've also just had an update from Leroy, our social media manager. He tells me our campaign now has thirty thousand followers on Twitter. At this rate we might go viral.'

@NTS: Our social media manager—an eleven-year-old schoolboy!

'*Viral?* Sounds nasty!' Clive chuckles as he knocks back his drink. He turns to me. 'Shame Stu couldn't be here to see your triumph today, Deborah. But exciting stuff that he's in Bristol to sign off on the new house, eh?'

Stu ... Bristol ... new house. The smile is wiped off my face.

Marg walks over and hands Clive a leaflet, before leading him off for a tour of the garden. I giggle to myself as she starts to lecture him on the Bank of England's policy on fossil fuel divestment.

'Praise be to God! You've arrived.' Nat greets Father Bill who has turned up still dressed in his pale blue raincoat despite the searing heat. 'Look at the success of our Good Life, garden of Eden.' She flings her arms wide despite the jam-packed crowd and pulls him into a bear hug, hitting several people in the process. 'And more good news, dear Father William—I've been filmed for telly,' she excitedly bubbles on. 'We're going to watch it here together at eight tonight. I hope you will stay and join your flock?'

'A television interview? How wonderful, Natalie. Of course, we will stay,' Father Bill says, turning to nod to Father Guy, who has sidled up next to him, his face downturned.

'Wonderful!' Nat claps. 'Now, let me give you the grand tour. And as it's so hot, do have a libation. This refreshing elderflower elixir is homemade.' She hands Father Bill a large drink, takes his arm and leads him off.

A surge of new guests enters the garden, pushing GG and me just a few inches apart. 'Hello, Dorito-Deborah,' he mumbles. His shoulders are stooped, his face still lowered, his eyes unwilling to meet mine. *Au contraire,* my face is very much raised, and active. My eyes are scanning his body. His beige linen suit is crumpled in all the right places. His crisp white shirt is opened at the neck, revealing a tanned neck glistening with beads of sweat. He finally looks up at me, but even the golden sunlight cannot lighten the black rings around his steely blue eyes. He sighs. 'We need to talk ...'

'Yoo-hoo, Debo! Caught you in the act!' Phoebe interrupts. She and Fliff are pushing their way over to us.

'We've been trying to talk to you all day,' says Fliff, churlishly, 'but your stall has been packed with all kinds of 'B' list celebs.'

'For some reason, your stupid bouncer didn't have our names on his guest list,' tuts Phoebe, pointing at Rich.

'But might have known we'd find you here with the hot vicar!' Fliff giggles.

GG's cheeks turn a shade more scarlet than the brim on Fliff's ludicrously large hat.

'What *are* you wearing, Debo?' Phoebe's eyes widen in frock-shock horror as she stares at my uniform. 'Gosh, you've put on quite a bit of weight.' She straightens out the non-existent creases of her blue chiffon Erdem dress which highlight her flat tummy. 'But I guess that happens when you work in a café.'

I instinctively cover my tummy with my hands. Hmm ... maybe I have enjoyed a bit too much of Nahal's irresistible nosh.

'Deb doesn't just work in a cafe, you cow!' Nat butts in, leaping to my defence. 'Unlike some I could name, Deb's a community activist and fashion designer whose Box Clever brand is going to be huge. We've even had an enquiry from the RHS. They want to sell a range of Debo Designs at their shows next year.'

Did I really just hear Nat mention a huge order from the RHS? Phoebe's gritted teeth and wide-open mouth seem to suggest I did.

Nat explains further, 'The RHS want Deb to come up with a range of Box Clever shorts, made from upcycled remnants including horticultural fleece. Isn't that bloody amazeballs?' She hugs me. 'Initial order around five thousand pairs!'

One thousand pairs of boxers made from ... eh? Horticultural fleece? What *is* that exactly? I grab the bottle of bubbly Nat is holding and take a swig. Teetotallers don't twopple be damned.

Just then, there's another astounding comment. Chef Chang comes striding in. He cheerfully calls out, 'Yes, at the Truffle Hog, we all *love* Deborah's Box Clever shorts ...'

The gawping crowd parts to allow their idol through. Everyone seems to recognise him. Could my day get any better? Yes, it could! I look up to see GG's eyes are flooding with brightness and warmth. He smiles supportively at me.

'Allow me to introduce myself, ladies.' Chef Chang takes Phoebe's hand and gives it a kiss. Gasps can be heard from the crowd. This is the Changster after all!

'*Chef Chaaaang*! May I just say, I'm your biggest fan,' says Phoebe shrinking back in shyness.

'Father William, have you met Chef Chang?' Nat asks, pulling Father Bill next to us. 'You're probably too busy to watch MasterChef on telly, but …'

Well, has *she* got it wrong! Father Bill is practically licking his lips at the encounter. 'Ooh! You're Chef Chang,' he says. 'Could I have an autograph, please? But, er, hang on … what have I got for you to sign it on?' He ferrets around in his pocket and finds a cutting of the Camden New Journal about the damning May Day feature. 'Could you sign it on this?'

Chef Chang takes the cutting and scribbles his name above the headline. 'Pagan festival in ex-church.'

Father Bill looks excitedly at the autograph. Then he takes in the heading and looks sternly up at Nat. 'We do need to talk about this article …'

'Apologies, Father. I'm afraid the crowd were a little too enthusiastic at our multi-faith event the other week. But, as the good Lord says, "Forgive us our trespasses as we forgive yours." Not that *you* have anything to forgive … Holy shit!' she cries out, changing the subject. 'Isn't that Daniel Craig posing in front of that tree? Look, it's James Bond, Father Bill! God, he's short in real life, isn't he? Shall we go and ask him for his autograph?'

Father Bill puts the CNJ cutting back in his pocket and off they traipse.

'Dorito-Deborah, we really *must* talk.' A strong hand grabs mine. I tingle and my throat feels dry as GG leads me away. I'm no longer aware of the pain in my ankle, just the warmth of his hand on mine as he pushes his way through the crowd.

We walk on in silence past the #6G garden. It's web of tree roots and branches look as tangled as my mind, as I try to remind myself of all the questions I need to ask GG. Leaving the crowd behind, we arrive at a steep woodland bank. A blanket of pretty white cow parsley and ox-eye daisy flowers send out a glow from the dappled shade. GG lets go of my hand and bends down. He slowly starts to unwrap the straps on my sandals. 'You won't be needing these,' he smiles. His eyes now clear pools of bright blue sky, stare searchingly into mine.

Having helped to remove my shoes, he carries them in one hand, and puts the other hand around my waist to guide me up the embankment. Umbels of frothy cow parsley and long stalked daisies tickle my legs, as he leads me into temptation. We reach clearing under a hawthorn tree, its white blossom petals tinged with pink. 'Let's sit here,' he says.

'We haven't seen you for a few weeks, Father Guy,' I murmur, as he takes off his jacket and ushers me to sit on it.

'It's Guy, Dorito-Deborah. As you well know.' He speaks softly, his eyes still fixed on mine. He takes my hand, turns over my palm and starts to trace his finger along it. My heart line: my line of questions tremble, as he lets out a deep sigh. 'I'm so terribly ashamed of what I've done,' he whispers.

'Why did you say you're new to the area, when your grandfather was the priest at St Margaret's during the second world war?' I blurt out the question I had been dying to ask for weeks. 'I popped into to St Margaret's by chance one evening and read all about your grandfather's untimely death, and how he didn't get to meet his son … I assume his son was your father?' I pause to look at him, but he hangs his head.

I continue to speak, but more slowly, 'I've been racking my brain since the Gargoyles meeting at the school in March, as to why you would accept … what was obviously a bribe for your other church. But now I know all about your tragic family history, I can understand why you would want to protect St Margaret's. And why the fundraising to bring your grandfather's organ back to its former glory is so important to you. But sadly, I also know what this means for the future of the Good Life. And it's not good …'

'I've been such a fool, Deborah.' GG removes his hand from mine and shakes his head. 'I feel so ashamed and guilty …'

'Oh my God, Deb! Here you are!' A shriek comes from below our feet. It's Nat, who has somehow found us. She clambers up the bank, treading on several ox-eye daisies as she swigs from a bottle of bubbly. 'You're not going to believe it,' she cries, 'but the RHS have just given out the awards, and we've only *bloomin'* well won a silver gilt medal.' Nat holds up a certificate.

I stare at it in disbelief, but sure enough I see the embossed RHS silver gilt coin stamped in the middle of the certificate. I try to process how the conversation has suddenly switched from guilt to silver gilt in the flapping of a certificate, while GG, the guilty man himself, is still not offering an explanation.

'The last time I won anything was a dart board at a school fair,' Nat giggles, hugging me.

'Many congratulations to you both,' says GG in a cheerless voice.

'We've won silver gilt at Chelsea!' Nat whoops. 'We are Chelsea silver medal designers. We are sooo gonna aim for a gold medal next year, aren't we, Deb?'

As Nat stresses the word *we*, I can't help but smile. But it's bittersweet emotion. Next spring, the only garden I'll likely be designing will be a row of lonely carrots in Brat-ford. Nat grabs my hand and jumps up. The daisy stalk she has just trampled proves a resilient survivor by springing back to life. It inspires me. I jump back up, too. 'Gold medal? Bring it on!' I cry.

'That's the spirit,' Nat laughs. 'Talking of which—c'mon Dung-Deb and Father G, let's go *partée* …'

8:30 p.m.. It's *still* Chelsea Flower Show prize day. What an amazeball day—the most golden of days, which can't be dimmed by my stinging eye or throbbing ankle. Yes, the Joe Swift Gardeners World TV interview, which we've just finished watching, might have displayed my compost-coated eye and encrusted lips; it might have even shown me toppling over in strawberry heels—much to everyone's amusement. But today is not about me. It's about my wonderful

Team Good Life. I couldn't be prouder to be part of it. Today is about celebrating a delighted Jafar, who everyone is currently squashing in a group hug; it's about Nat, Rich, Marg, Pippa, Greg, and the rest of the Good Lifers, who have been partying with as much passion as they put into developing our #swallowvamazing garden.

I take another swig from my bubbly-filled jam jar, which magically seems to have been constantly topped up over the past few hours. While guilty Guy had made a hot-footed escape as the silver-gilt celebration started, the same can't be said for Father Billy. He's dancing and singing along with us all, word perfect, to Abba's greatest hits.

'The winner takes it all!' Father Billy croons as he takes another glug from one of the bottles being passed around.

'The loser has to fall ...' I giggle, looking down at my bare feet and remembering my rather ungainly high-heeled fall, in full glory on national TV.

Nat and Rich tango up to us. *'Money money money,'* Nat sings out at the top of her voice as the playlist changes to another Abba classic. *'It's a rich man's world!'*

'It certainly is!' Rich silences Nat by pulling her into a passionate snog.

Even Marg, who is still lecturing Clive on the perils of capitalism, joins in with the group cheer.

'Hashtag update, everyone!' Pippa calls out. 'You're not gonna believe it, but we've had another twenty thousand retweets and likes for #swallowvamazon. *We're going virrrrall!'*

Greg, who is limbo-dancing in front of me, fist-pumps the air, bestowing me with an extensive view of his sweaty bottom crack. Amid the general mayhem, I feel a vibration in my boxer shorts pocket. I take out my phone and see Stu's number come up. I hurriedly answer it but can't hear what he's saying. The line goes dead. I send Stu a quick text saying I'll call him back. I make my way out through the packed crowd, trying to redial Stu's number, as I stand beside the Good Life's neighbouring garden, our 'Can't see the wood from the trees,' rival. What I *can* see, unbelievably, through the thicket are Jo Swift and the Changster, wearing my Box Clever shorts and clinking glasses. And I also see red. Flapping around them is Fliff, in her monstrously large, red-brimmed hat, and Miss 'Jam Tart' Stuart.

I still can't get a phone signal, but what I do get is a text from Stu ...

I rush off to find Nat. She's not in the 'No Mow' garden, but Marg and Pippa are. They're busy trying to coax Old Spot awake. He's fallen asleep on the yellow stripy deckchair, much to the scowls of displeasure from the stallholders. I quickly move on to the #6G garden where Nat is chatting away. 'There you are, Deb,' she slurs her words. 'Come and have shum tea with our new friends. This man is called Hugh-wee.'

I give Hugh's hand a hasty shake, and pull Nat away. 'Nat, Nat ... I must talk to you! You're not going to believe it,' I burble. 'I've just had a text from Stu. The house in Brat-ford has dry rot, which means we can't buy it! The house has fallen through. I'm so happy! I never thought I'd love dry rot so much!'

'Deb, that's amazeballs!' Nat pulls me into a crushing hug. 'Brings a whole new meaning to *what rotten luck!*' She guffaws and turns back to Hugh. 'Here's to dry rot!'

'Dry lot?' Mr Hugh-wee clinks his teacup with Nat who shouts, 'Could this day get any better?'

'Actually, it seems only likely to get worse ...' This comment from Rich, who marches up to us. 'I think you'd both better follow me,' he says. 'We need to, er ... rescue Father Bill.'

We hurry back to our garden where Father Bill is lying down splayed among the boxes of wildflowers. Much to the amusement of the crowd, and clicks of phone cameras, he cradles the giant bra, now empty of wildflowers. 'Oh, this bra is rather jolly!' Father Billy cries out. 'Reminds me of dear mama before she passed on.' He sings at the top of his voice, '*Mamma Mia, how can I resist you ...?*'

As Rich dashes round the crowd trying to stop people from taking photos, Nat and I move in to rescue Father Bill—busted and bloom.

JUNE

CHAPTER 26

Fondue 2

I t's one week later. I'm hobbling around the Good Life back gar-den feeding the chickens and feeling more than a little sorry for myself.

I still have a hangover from the Chelsea press show day: more like Chelsea piss day. My headache may have abated, but now I'm being punished with a painful eye infection and swollen ankle. I try to resist rubbing my throbbing eye as I scatter feed into the chicken coop but must cut a sorry sight as even Brutus is keeping his distance. His beady eyes seem to have taken in my bandaged ankle and weeping eye as the blustery June wind whips matted hair across my face. A sight for sore eyes indeed.

Feeding time over, I close the gate and blearily admire the new meadow surrounding the coop. The transplanted wildflowers from our Chelsea show garden are rooting nicely. That's more than can be said for me. Once again, I feel completely *up*-rooted. The house in Brat-ford might have fallen through, but grrr … Stu's already lined up another three properties to view. I walk slowly back inside. A giant papier-mâché bird, created by Greg and the kids, hovers above the Daddy Day Share area. As I close the back door, its giant papery wings flutter in the draught. I smile as I'm reminded of Nahal's Sufi story about Huma, the mythical bird that flew around the world in search of a magical land. And here she is, now settled in our cosy urban nest.

Huma's wings shadow me as I explore the Daddy Day Share area. It's been completely remodelled in the week since I was last here. A new row of shelves made from pallets are piled high with toys. Daddy Day Share is now a Toy Swop Shop. All broken VHS machines, 1950s salon hairdryers and other rubbish from the Greener Properties scam are long gone. I giggle—*ouch!*—at the sight of the one remaining item—a fondue set. I guess it's in response to Nat's tweet that went viral, following her TV appearance, that people can come to the Good Life to 'borrow a fondue set and nab a fella!'

I walk on, trying carefully not to step on Leroy's designs for a football pitch lit by bike pedal power that are scattered across the floor. I'm equally careful not to disturb Marg, who is deep in concentration sorting through her new 'Meatless Marg plant recipe' cards.

Next to her, Sacha is busy on her phone. 'Insects are a sustainable food source. They have a significantly lower carbon footprint than meat production,' Sacha enthuses, in her plummy voice. 'We'll be showcasing a selection of edible insects at our Good Life Pestival on June twentieth. It would be soo marvellous if *Vogue* could come along and ...'

While I admire Sacha's PR puff in trying to get Vogue to come and feature our Pestival in two weeks' time, I can't quite picture a Vogue headline, 'Critter Canapés—the next "bug" thing!'

Giving Sacha a quick wave, I go over to Nat's campaign desk. The local election is just over a month away, but according to the sign-ups on a clipboard stuffed with sheets of paper, a staggering six hundred people have already pledged their support for her 'Vote Nat: A Good Life' campaign. I'm amazed. And more than a little proud. At the same time, I feel ashamed of how little support I've given Nat. I've been completely self-obsessed with Brat-ford-gate. Some friend I am. *Not.* I pick up the clipboard and scan the names. Could Nat really become a local councillor? Didn't she say she only needed a thousand votes to get elected? But the three councillors have been in power for ever, including Cllr. Thornton who I recall was cosying up to Thomas Montjoy at the Gargoyles meeting back in April. How *are* they connected I wonder? @Detective Deb. Time to get digging? And thankfully, for once, I'm not talking about compacted, back-breaking clay.

But let's be realistic, while six hundred people have signed a form, they have yet to cast a vote. I'm just thinking how unlikely it is that Nat will win, bar a miracle, when something bright catches my eye. There's a beam of light coming from the top of the pulpit. It's a reflection from our Chelsea silver gilt medal, which someone has proudly placed up there. It makes me smile—and I reflect: three years ago, Nat didn't even know how to grow a cabbage. If she can win a Chelsea flower show medal, why the hell couldn't she become a local councillor? Nat doesn't *need* a miracle; she *is* a miracle!

Around the room, there are so many examples of the projects that Nat's boundless energy and enthusiasm has helped create. A new banner above the kid's teepee invites guests: 'Learn how trees talk to each other through the Wood-Wide Web.' A pile of colourful knitted scarves and beanie hats are spread across the pews where the Knit Wits group host their weekly sessions. On the barter board, Nat has placed an offer for an hour of 'Vote Nat' campaigning time, in return for a jar of 'Rich's raunchy ramson pesto.' Raunchy Rich indeed! As if I could forget Nat and Rich's passionate snog at Chelsea … And Nat's craziest project of all—Box Clever. I sigh, staring at my now boxed up singing sewing machine. It's been silent for several weeks, yet the Box Clever orders keep coming in …

Michael scuttles over to open the front door, signifying the magic opening hour of 11 a.m.. A smattering of people walk in and start exploring the Good Life. A Sikh gentleman signs up to Nat's campaign—that's six hundred and one names and counting! Marg explains to two teenagers how 'eating less meat is one of the best ways you can help tackle the climate crisis.' She hands them each a recipe card. 'We are serving this aubergine *mirza ghasemi*, at our Abundance Cafe today,' Marg says, pointing to where John, the cafe's first paid, part-time employee, is laying the tables.

Over at the Toy Swop a line is quickly forming, people eager to borrow items. 'This is such a good idea,' a bloke wheeling a pram says to his friend as they walk past me clutching a Lego bricks set they are clearly here to exchange. There's no doubt that the Good Life has become a thriving hub, despite all the efforts to close us down.

I notice a photo of Father Guy that someone has pinned to the dartboard. Everyone was shocked when I told them about my chat with GG at Chelsea. *'I feel so ashamed and guilty for what I have done …'* he had started to admit before Nat interrupted us with the news of the award. During the frenzied hours of celebration that followed, I didn't get to find out what GG was admitting to, and he hasn't returned any of my texts ever since. Now coincidentally, he's away on another 'retreat.' I'm guessing its far from a spiritual one.

I cup my palms, remembering the warmth and softness of his hand on mine, the lightness of his touch as he traced his finger along … *Hang on a mo!* I give myself a little kick. My life isn't a TV show. And this isn't an episode of *Fleabag* featuring the hot vicar. I'm no fictional damsel. And GG, it seems, is far from a hero.

I take a deep breath and think of all the things that have gone wrong at the Good Life: the Daddy Day Share scam, the burned down smokehouse, the vandalised People's Fridge, the constant bad press … Surely GG couldn't have been behind all this? The imaginary chimes of a celestial pipe organ now disrupt my thoughts. Every note tolls a reminder of the twenty thousand pounds bribe offered to St Margaret's Church for the restoration of GG's grandfather's organ. I bend down to stroke at the pain now shooting up my leg and wipe my eye. There's so much to think about. Perhaps I could nip into the kid's teepee for a little lie down and …

@NTS: How *did* it pan out for Phoebe Waller-Bridge in Fleabag?

'There you are my dear,' a distant voice floats into my daydream. I'm lying naked in a bed of wildflowers. It's sweltering hot. Pearls of sweat coat my body. A butterfly flutters down upon my flabdomen. A strong muscular hand covered in fine blond hairs reaches to gently caress the butterfly's iridescent wings. The hand moves down to … 'We were worried about you,' the voice persists. 'We didn't know where you'd got to.'

I sit up and grab my phone. I can't believe it's midday. I'm in the kid's teepee where I've been asleep for two hours. Never mind a dream about a quivering butterfly, I've metamorphosed into an inert caterpillar.

@NTS: *Flabdomen?!*

Marg pokes her head into the tent. 'Is there room in here for us?' She crawls in, closely followed by Nahal, carefully holding a cup. Marg puts her arm around me. 'How's our brave eco-worrier feeling?'

I nestle my neck into her shoulder. 'Thanks for asking, Marg. I must admit that my ankle's still throbbing, and my eye's so sore.'

'I've made you a cup of turmeric tea,' says Nahal, handing me a steaming cup. 'It will help soothe you.'

I smile gratefully and take a sip. My mouth tingles with a delicious burst of peppery sharpness and velvety sweet honey. As I savour the rest of the cuppa, we sit in silence and stare out through the giant web that Greg and the kids have made from recycled rope. Shafts of sunlight stream in through the stained-glass windows onto a latticework of coppiced tree branches that have been placed all around.

Nahal closes her eyes. 'We could almost be in the Jangal abr forest in northern Iran. I used to visit it as a young girl. I still dream of the huge tree trunks covered in moss, ferns carpeting the forest floor and clouds so thick that you couldn't see an arms-length in front of you.'

'It sounds magical, Nahal,' I whisper, closing my eyes and trying to conjure up Nahal's dream.

'My friend, Wangari Maathai, once said, "When you plant a tree, you plant a seed of peace and hope."' So saying, Marg places a warm hand on mine. 'Talking of hope, my dear, I have a feeling that it's not only your eye and ankle that are paining you.'

My eyes snap open. 'Have you ever been married, Marg?' The question pops out before I can stop it.

'Oh yes, my dear, I certainly have,' Marg replies. 'But not all marriages work. Back in 1973, when we were living in Kenya working for the Red Cross, my husband, Stanley, wanted to move back to England. But I didn't. So, I stayed. I can tell you it caused quite a rumpus at the time!'

So he moved and she stayed … Marg has voiced the very scenario I've been dreading having to contemplate.

'I look forward to telling you both the full story over a glass of Rich's homemade gin,' she continues, 'but in the meantime—talking husbands—I can't help noticing that we've never met your Stuart. Does he not support your endeavours here?'

I look down and twiddle with my wedding ring. 'Stu's been so busy planning his new job at Bristol University. He'll be heading a whole new module. It's called Economic Futures.' I realise I'm trying to sound convincing. But just who am I trying to convince? 'Also, now we are empty nesters, he *wants* to move. Stu thinks it'll be nice for me to be nearer our son, James. He's studying at Exeter University and ...'

Marg sighs, 'My dear, I'm sure as much as your son loves you, he's enjoying his freedom. Don't make that your reason to move. If it's about rekindling your relationship with your husband, then that's another thing.'

'Of course I love Stu, but ...'

'My Ahmed hasn't been around here either,' Nahal interrupts, jumping in to defend me. 'It's not that he's unsupportive, he just thinks this project is mine. *My* sense of purpose. *My* new friends. We talk about it all the time at home. Do you talk to Stu about the Good Life at home, Deb?'

'If I'm honest, Stu and I don't talk about it much,' I say, looking away, 'but I guess with the house move and his new job ...'

'But what about your job here, my dear?' presses Marg. 'Your Box Clever brand has such potential. You talk about Stuart's new course ... what was it, "Economic Futures," but maybe the economic future that Rich is creating here is just as valid. After all, it's one based on developing a sharing economy as opposed to constant growth.'

'I don't want to move,' I blurt out, bursting into tears. 'Stu's found more houses for us to view. I know I lead a privileged and charmed life ... but ... I'm dreading telling Nat. I just don't know what to do.'

Nahal takes my hand. 'There is a famous Persian saying, Deb— One finger cannot lift a pebble. We are here for you now.'

'Talking about someone needing support,' Marg eyes me sternly. 'Nat really needs your help, my dear. There are so many issues a local councillor must apply themselves to. Are you aware how many hours she's spent locked away, swotting up on the local issues, case-loads, council structures and all that formality malarkey? She's even turned down going to the House of Commons today to present to the Select Committee, she's so loaded down. Did you know that?'

'I didn't know that,' I say, dabbing my wet eyes. 'I feel so ashamed that I don't even know what a local councillor does.'

'We've all been out campaigning for Nat, and ...'

'You are totally right, Marg,' I admit. 'I've been selfish and preoccupied. But that's going to change from now.' I wipe away my tears. 'Do you really think there's a chance that Nat could win?'

'Crazier things have happened, my dear,' Marg smiles.

Nahal chimes in, 'Yes, look at my Jafar. Six months ago, he wasn't even confident enough to speak to the kids in his class, and now he's presenting a petition on drone regulation at the House of Commons.' She nervously taps her watch. 'Rich, Pippa, and Jafar should be halfway through their presentation right now. I do hope Jafar's OK?'

I squeeze Nahal's hand. 'Jafar is a fantastic kid—you should be very proud of him.'

'Don't forget this!' Marg points to the screen on her mobile. Our Swallow v Amazon social media campaign has eighty thousand likes, according to my latest Snapchat story. Plus, there's been countless snapstreak emojis!'

Nahal and I giggle as our octogenarian social media whizz-kid scrolls through her 'likes' at breakneck speed. Go Marg!

@NTS: Snapstreak?

'And what about the RHS ordering five thousand pairs of your Box Clever shorts?' says Nahal, giving me a prod.

I look away again, unwilling to admit that I didn't believe the RHS order was real and not just another example of Nat's kind, wishful thinking, to protect me from Fliff and Phoebe's derision.

'Even crazier,' Marg presses on, 'who'd have thought that my Meatless Marg campaign would have us hosting a "Pestival"—a festival promoting edible insects for goodness sakes!'

Pestival. Here. In two weeks' time. Same date as my birthday. Something I would prefer not to be reminded about—the bugs or my age.

Nahal throws her arms into the air. 'When a passionate community comes together—there's no stopping us!'

But then, stopped we are ... 'Excuse me ... sorry to interrupt you ...' The voice is followed by a woman's head, pushing into the tent. 'Someone called Michael told me you might be able to help me. I've come for a fondue set.'

We burst out laughing, and cheerfully tumble out of the tent to join the blushing woman. Since Nat's piece with Joe Swift aired on telly, we've had lots of women popping in to ask for a 'fondue set,' as if it's a code: Borrow a fondue set ... and nab a single dad. Two for the price of one. A gift set.

We apologise that it's not currently available and invite our nervous visitor to stay for lunch. This, we explain, will soon be served by the single dads from Daddy Day Share. Red-faced woman thanks us and heads hurriedly to the Abundance Cafe.

A powerful aroma of garlic and cumin wafts from the kitchen. 'Lunch smells yummy, Nahal,' I say. 'I'm on washing up duty today and I intend to create lots of dirty dishes to clean up!'

'Pleased to hear that, Deb!' Nahal replies, looking at her watch. 'But if I don't get the *mirza ghasemi* out of the oven now, there will be nothing but cinders to eat!'

As Nahal and Marg rush off, I walk over to my sewing machine and run my hands through the overflowing box of fabric remnants. If by some miracle the RHS order *is* real, and not just another bit of Nattery, what kinds of designs could I come up with? Gardener shorts? The ideas start taking root: Bermudas? Hot pants? Deep pockets? How about shorts tied with a jute garden twine belt? Patches of recycled hessian potato sacks and horticultural fleece stitched into the shorts? I imagine a catwalk showcasing models with runner-bean legs disporting Box Clever shorts and dungs, wearing horti-couture milliner, Philip Treacy plant pot fascinators on their heads, their faces caked in mud.

But how could we scale up production? And most importantly, could I oversee it from Brat-ford? Feeling some of Marg and Nahal's positivity wash over me, I take my phone and send Stu a text message Then another to GG. There's no response from either, but there *is* a response from my singing sewer when I put my foot down on the pedal. I select a length of fabric and glance up at Huma, the Iranian magical bird. I, too, start flying, as my hand glides across a silken turquoise sky.

Two hours pitter-patter by. Suddenly, the front door bursts open. It's Jafar. He dashes in, quickly followed by Rich, and heads straight over to the Abundance Cafe where Nahal and I are bringing out teacups. 'Oh Maman, it was so amazing! The House of Commons was so big and filled with so many …'

'Tory wankers!' Rich butts in. Nahal gives him a playful slap.

'But Jafar did really well,' says Rich, fist-bumping Jafar. 'He spoke with the confidence and authority of a teenager.'

Jafar jumps onto the chair and opens his arms wide. 'I told them Maman! They say that drones and those whatsits … er, yes, Unmanned Aerial Systems are great for delivering medical stuff and cutting down pollution, but they fly dangerously close to breeding birds and animals. We need laws to make sure this doesn't happen!'

Rich gives him a thumbs-up of encouragement.

Jafar continues excitedly, 'I told them how twenty-six per cent of wildlife species that drones harm are under threat. And we showed them our film, and I told them how our poor swallow was killed by Amazon.'

Rich growls, 'I also reminded them how a bill regulating drone delivery failed to pass in the Commons last year. They need to get their Tory story shite together.'

Nahal coaxes a revved-up Jafar down from the table. I pour everyone a cuppa as we calm down for the rest of the story. Rich shoves a slice of heavily-frosted carrot cake into his mouth, licks his fingers and laughs: 'You should have seen the frost on the Tory MP's faces when Pippa shoved Ecocide posters at them! More frost than on this cake!'

'So what happens next?' asks Nahal.

'Jafar will fill you in on the rest,' says Rich jumping up. 'I gotta dash.'

'And where are you off to?' I ask, winking at Rich.

'I've gotta go and help Nat with some … er … swotting up.'

Swotting? Or sweating? I don't say it out loud. Besides, Rich is in too much of a hurry to listen. Off he goes, with an eager spring in his step.

Jafar picks up the thread: 'Maman, the building was so fancy, it was like a palace. The room we talked in had wooden beams and a painted ceiling like out of a fairy tale. Clive told us that the committee we spoke to will use some of our evidence in an environmental report. And that will then be presented to all the MPs in the House of Commons.'

'What an amazing story!' I clap my hands.

'Talking about stories,' says Nahal, 'Jafar, your Headteacher emailed me. He wants you to present your story of today at a school assembly next week.'

Before Jafar can respond, there's another interruption. A middle-aged lady walks up to us wearing a slinky black skirt. 'Excuse me, is this the Good Life? I'm, er … looking for a …'

Jafar beats me to it with his instant, innocent, and passionate response: 'No! We don't have any more fondue sets! But I've been asked to talk to my whole school about my trip to the House of Commons, and how we need to project animals. So there!'

Nahal and I look at each other and smile.

'I love the Good Life, Deb,' says Nahal, pulling me into a hug. 'Just look how it's brought my Jafar out of his shell.'

'I couldn't agree more,' I reply. 'I'm kinda fondue it. And you are too!'

CHAPTER 27

Simply the Pest

I return from the field with gypsy feet. Soil crumbs between my toes, I dance on earth, my long skirt filled with sky ...

Then reality kicks in. When I say, 'return from the field,' it's more a case of return from having to field off complaints from disgruntled residents. I've spent the morning—as I have every morning this week—campaigning on behalf of Vote Nat. Who knew there were so many potholes in our borough. And gypsy feet? Perhaps door knocking in strappy sandals, having just recovered from a swollen ankle, wasn't my greatest idea. Particularly when making an escape from an over-enthusiastic guard dog. As to my long skirt ... well, it now has a couple of extra ruffles in it, having been gnawed by said terrier. Sartorial woes aside, I'm really chuffed that I've managed to get a hundred more sign-ups to Nat's campaign. I'm also happy because it's my birthday. And it's shaping up to be the best one ever.

Husbondage Stu apologised this morning for being too wrapped up in himself to buy me a gift, and then he gave me the news that was better than any pressie: he's decided that we're not going to move. We're going stay in Kentish Town. *Yippee!* On the upside, it's bye-bye Brat-ford-gate, *partir* posh parterre, and *ciao* ex-church and scrubby patch of land in Kentish Town. The downside is that Stu is going to commute—he will stay in Bristol three nights a week. Stu assured me that the time will pass quickly, but I'm feeling nervous about it. I'm still getting used to being an empty-nester, with James at uni—and now I face life without my hubby for half the week.

This starts to sink in as I walk into the Good Life forecourt. It's an outcome I've never imagined. The truth is I haven't lived by myself since leaving home, aged nineteen. I've always been someone's live-in-girlfriend, wife, or mum. Three nights alone each week. What will I do?

'Ah, finally! The birthday girl has arrived,' Nat shrieks, dashing up to me. 'Amazeball news about you staying.' She throws her arms around me. 'Just think what we can get up to on your Stu-free nights. The two of us plotting world domination for Box Clever and the Good Life over lots of wine—not you on your own *whining!* Or moping around indulging in more carnal clergyman dreams!'

'Yep … it'll be great to spend time with you,' I reply. But I'm rattled by Nat's thought-reading ability. The truth is, I'm still waking most nights in a hot sweat over a certain vicar. 'But in case you haven't noticed,' I cough to clear my dry throat, 'the clergyman I assume you're alluding to only seems to be interested in *screwing* the Good Life.'

None of us has been able to get hold of him for three weeks, though to get the facts straight—not that I'm counting—I realise what I'm letting slip, and cough again. 'Anyway, there's no chance of any other screwing being on the table,' I add, fiddling with my wedding ring.

'How about in the pulpit? Nat laughs. 'But look, as to anyone screwing over the Good Life, it won't happen. We'll get our extended lease, birthday girl, just you wait and see. Also, if I become councillor, I'll need an assistant!' she grins. 'BTW, thanks for all the campaigning you've done this week. I've got over a thousand pledges now.'

And three weeks before Election Day, someone will need to turn those pledges into votes. I keep the thought to myself, not wanting to dent my best friend's enthusiasm. It's been weeks since we've had such a lovely bonding chat—Council dogsbody job offer aside.

'I'm soo going to be the next *bug* thing—get it, bug as in insect!' Nat laughs. 'Talking of which, it's time to get the Pestival going, as well as your birthday party.'

She takes my arm and yanks me towards the stalls, which are laid out in a semi-circle around the forecourt. There are already queues of people, and the stalls are a-buzz, probably quite literally, with buggy parts and chefs busy prepping ingredients. Rows of sofas made from discarded pallets have been placed behind a stage made of other pallets nailed together. At the far end of the forecourt, Rich is chopping wood to fire up our new tandoor cob oven. Greg, meanwhile, is drawing chalk lines across the length of the forecourt for the 'World's Annual Snail Racing Championship,' which is taking place here this afternoon. A big group of kids are chalking pictures of creepy crawlies all around. A giant banner, erected across the front of the church, towers over all the action: *'Welcome to Pestival ... Simply the Pest!'*

'Don't the stalls look brill?' says Nat, pointing to a stall where Mr Pang is tossing spring rolls in a wok. A giant jet of flames catches them as they fly up, then tumble back into the wok. Nat licks her lips. 'Hope you're feeling hungry, Deb. There are six edible insects on the menu for you to try.'

I'm saved from having to respond by the sound of Sacha calling out through a megaphone: 'Welcome friends and neighbours to Pestival—Kentish Town's very own Glasto of the edible insect world.'

Now, even though I'm a fully committed member of Team Good Life, I don't do insects. I hate creepy crawlies. I'm even allergic to bite stings. I shiver as I remember an excruciating horsefly bite last year when my arm swelled up bigger than ... WTF, I've just noticed the stomach protruding from Cllr. Thornton's jacket, as he swaggers onto the Good Life forecourt.

Nat has seen him too. 'What's that bastard doing here?' she cries, and chases after him.

'Eighty per cent of the world's population regularly consume insects,' Sacha continues, her plummy megaphone voice increasing in pitch. 'Forget your kimchi; edible insects are the original super food. Do try the delicious critter cuisine our chefs are cooking. And today, let's redefine our relationship with the insect world.'

I can define my relationship with insects in one word: mothballs. I'll never forget finding my best cashmere covered in moth larvae last winter.

Sacha ends her welcome speech, everyone claps, and the music starts.

'You're simply the best ..." Tina Turner's vocals are drowned in a

fuzz of distorted bass through the archaic amplifier that Rich procured from the local music shop in exchange for a pallet deckchair. But the crowd aren't put off. People start to sing along, many replacing the word 'best' with 'pest.'

I approach Mr Pang's stall, which has a long queue in front of it.

'Ah, Deborah,' Mr Pang waves me over. 'Come and try my spring roll. As a birthday gift, I offer you two for the price of one. They have real *spring* to them!' he laughs.

There's a loud crunch as two young blokes next to me bite into the batter, and chomp away on … 'Grasshopper spring roll with crispy veg and lime peel. Very tasty,' beams Mr Pang. 'As eaten, all over China. Can one and a half billion Chinese people be wrong?'

'Yes, they bloody well can,' newcomer Rich butts in. 'China has the most appalling human rights record.'

But Mr Pang carries on with his spiel, 'Chinese people enjoy eating over one hundred and seventy-nine insect species. In Beijing night market, a big favourite is edible scorpions served with …'

There's a rumble in my stomach. And it's not from hunger. I wave at Mr Pang and move swiftly on. Out of the corner of my eye I notice that, while Nat has been distracted talking to a group of potential voters, Cllr. Thornton is taking the opportunity to rifle through the sign-ups on her Vote-Nat desk. I head briskly towards him, but John beats me to it.

'Can I help you with anything, sir?' asks John, grabbing the clipboard away from Cllr. Thornton, whom he clearly recognises. 'Are you interested in signing up? Can I add your email address?'

'No, you cannot,' snaps Cllr. Thornton. He storms off.

'Well, thanks for showing an interest in our campaign!' John calls after him. 'Join the thousand others who have pledged to elect our first Good Life local councillor.'

'I can't believe you managed to keep a straight face,' I giggle, as John places the clipboard firmly back on the desk. 'Do you have time for quick a chat about Cllr. Thornton?'

'That bloke's a snake!' says John. 'Why don't you guard the desk while I go and grab a mealworm taco from the Guac Attack stall. We can share it while we talk?'

Snakes … and now mealworms? I reluctantly sit down behind the desk to await John's return.

@NTS: Re topic of beastly creatures—check husbondage's inbox to see if he's received a reply to my email to Greener Properties expressing an interest in the Gargoyles block. Hmm … maybe it was a bit naughty to send an email from Stu's Bank of England address.

John returns with the taco. He bites into the crunchy shell, which is squirming with guac, and goodness knows what else.

'Bloody good this, Deb. Have a bite?' He offers it to me.

'Thanks, I've eaten,' I reply. The truth is, I've even lost my appetite for the 'Pret' tuna sarnie stashed in my Chloe bag.

John notices Marg approaching and says, 'We should cook these at home, Marg. They're made from waste food advos, cheese, topped off homegrown coriander and edible …'

'I didn't know you were living at Marg's, John?' I interrupt, glad to change the subject from whatever John is now biting into.

'Oh yes, dear. John's been my roomie for a couple of months now,' Marg replies. 'Old Spot and I have a spare room, and John makes a mean curry!'

'Living with Marg and Old Spot is brill fun, and I'm psyched to have been accepted to go to City Uni in October to finish my law degree,' says John. 'Since I met you guys and got involved in the Good Life, everything's turned around for me.'

'That's such amazing news, John,' I smile.

'Yep, I'm here to stay.'

'Me too!' I add.

'So I hear, my dear,' says Marg, putting her arm around me.

'Now all we need to do is make sure that the Good Life stays open. We've only got three months to get a new lease, and I really don't trust that Thomas Montjoy.'

I take a copy of the *Camden New Journal* from my bag and turn it to a page featuring an interview with Cllr. Thornton. A key quote: '"When I'm re-elected, my first priority will be to launch an action plan to regenerate our high street," pledges Cllr. Thornton.'

'Like building the Gargoyles apartment block?' John snorts.

'Exactly,' I nod in agreement, and continue to read out loud.

'"There is huge potential for property developers like Greener Properties to help both our high street and local community groups flourish."'

'Community groups, excluding us at the Good Life,' says Marg.

'But including St Margaret's Church, which he offered the bung to,' says John. 'Have you spoken to Father Guy about it yet, Deb? I still can't believe he'd try to get the Good Life closed. He seems such a nice bloke.'

'Father Guy's still away,' I sigh. 'He sent me a text confirming that he'll be joining us on our road trip, next week. I'll confront him then. But talking about dodgy men, do you think we should check out Cllr. Thornton a little more?'

John nods. 'After I've tried the smoked paprika crunchy critters, I'll go online and take another snoop around the Greener Properties company structure.'

'And I'm going inside right now to see what Cllr. Thornton's up to,' says Marg.

They set off. 'By the way, do either of you know where we're going on our road trip?' I call out to them. Both shake their heads.

So where *are* we going next week on our team bonding outing that Nat is organising? I imagine a nice day out in Brighton, mixing a bit of retail and Father Guy therapy. GG's intense blue eyes are burrowing into mine, his strong hand gripping me as he reassures me that he's had nothing to do with getting the Good Life closed down ... Or maybe it could be a picnic in a wildflower meadow, GG peeling pea pods, popping Good Life peas that explode with sweetness into my mouth, then reaching out to reclaim any errant petit pois that might make their way down my body ...

No! Think Birds Eye frozen peas. It really is time to cool down.

I set off to find Rich, confident that he'll know all about the team bonding outing. I come across him peering into a giant wok at a stall signposted, 'Choc-cocks.'

'American cockroaches!' the stall holder calls out in a French accent.

'You couldn't be more right!' Rich responds. I get the idea he's referencing certain sections of the American populace more than the sizzling contents in the wok.

The stallholder licks his lips. 'These are deep fried twice in hot oil to make sure their shell remains *croustillant*, leaving their innards to remain soft and succulent.'

'Is it true that a cockroach can live for a month without a head?' asks Food-Critic Jim, who is standing next to Rich.

'*Bien sur*,' says Chef Cockroach, lifting the frizzled body parts out with a spatula and dunking them in a pan of gooey chocolate. 'We coat zem with fair-trade chocolate. *Et voila: les Choc-cock-Critters.*' He dangles his delicacy in front of me. 'Do you have a sweet tooth, madame?'

I shake my head. Time to move on. And I do, but even the thought of a Lion Bar now fills me with horror.

I walk past Sacha, who is chatting with someone busily scribbling notes. A journalist, I deduce—her snake-shaped bracelet and bug earrings, which are dive bombing around as if after some prey, suggest that she's from a fashion mag. Has Sacha managed to coax *Vogue* mag here?

'Yes, ant eggs are often compared with caviar,' Sacha enthuses. 'After my presentation we must go and try some divine honey and miso fried locusts.' She points to a stall. 'Did you know that some people refer to honey as bee vomit?'

The journalist's face turns almost as pale as the diamonds on her dragonfly broach. Sacha raises her megaphone and blasts, 'Ladies and gents, girls and boys, it's time for a bit of *ento-tainment*! *Ento* as in, entomology—the study of insects. Geddit? Please take a seat and our presentation will start in five minutes.'

There's a ripple of laughter as people rush to the rows of pallet sofas.

'Deb! Over here!' Nahal calls out to me from one of the sofas. Jafar is with her.

'How did your school assembly go yesterday, Jafar?' I ask, as I take the seat they've saved for me.

'It was *brilliant*, Deb,' says Jafar. 'My headteacher said it was one of the most interesting assemblies she has ever heard. She's asked me to join a school conservation club she's setting up.

'I'm the proudest mum ever,' Nahal grins.

'Can I go and help set up the worm championships with my friends, mamam?' asks Jafar, jumping up.

'To think that six months ago, Jafar had no confidence, no friends, and his only connection was with the animal world. Just look at him now.' Nahal points to Jafar as he dashes off to join the kids drawing chalk insects on the forecourt.

'Oy, budge over!' Nat squeezes into the tight space vacated by Jafar. 'Have you seen the latest on Jafar's #swallowvamazon twitter campaign? It's bloody well started hundreds of chats.' She scrolls through a twitter feed on her phone. 'For example, I dunno who this bloke who's picked up on the twitter story is, but he's got over half a million followers.'

I read @GeorgeMonbiot: '#swallowvamazon aside, here's a real-life Swallow and Amazon hero! Seven-year-old schoolboy, Jafar Karimi, urges select committee to re-consider drone regulation and protect our birds from UAEs.'

Nat raises an eyebrow. 'Wonder if this George bloke would retweet my "Vote Nat for a Good Life" campaign?"'

Sacha's voice gets our attention again. 'Relative to their size, insects may be the most powerful creatures on earth,' she starts her presentation. 'But there's another way in which insects can play a key role in our future, one that I hope you're enjoying here today? And that's on our dinner plate.'

'Waiter, waiter, there's no fly in *my* soup!' Nat cries out to a chorus of laughter.

'*Sssh!* Nat, behave.' I dig her in the ribs.

'Whereas traditional meat production uses seventy per cent of our planet's cultivable land,' Sacha continues in her plummy voice, 'rearing insects uses less resources, like water and feed. Two billion of us around the world regularly eat insects.'

'How do most fleas travel around the world?' Nat says loudly. 'They *itch-hike!*'

Nahal and I burst out laughing much to the annoyance of Sacha.

'They are most commonly eaten in Africa, Asia, and South America. That's eighty per cent of the world's population. Caterpillars, termites, crickets, and mopane worms are common fare. In Thailand, street hawkers flog scorpions, crickets, or giant water bugs.'

Half an hour later, and I'm bugging out. Leaving the Q&A session during an emotionally charged debate over whether vegetarians can eat insects, I head over to the tandoor oven that Rich has fired up. It's pizza time. Rich, Anousha, and the Power Ranger ladies are busy rolling out dough for bases, and a table of toppings has been laid out. I dread to look. My imagination is running as riotously as creepy crawlies on the pizza bases. But all that is on the table are gooey slabs of mozzarella, slices of ripe tomatoes, and lashings of our homegrown rocket. It's a Good Life Margherita.

Anousha hands me a rolling pin, and I get stuck in. There's an outbreak of giggles, as our clothes, faces and headscarves become coated with flour. We toss and turn the dough, flicking the odd puff of flour over each other. It's late afternoon and the sun is beaming down. We roll countless bases of the delicious mushroom-scented dough. Everyone roars with laughter as I try to spin a base into the air, only for it to splatter down all over my Chloe bag. Our hijinks are witnessed by a gathering crowd.

Over at the World Annual Snail Racing Championships, there's a round of applause as the winner is declared. Rocket—the name the kids have given to the victor—completed the thirteen-inch course in two minutes, thirty-eight seconds.

Two hours later, we've made and served more than a hundred pizzas. The crowd has dispersed. Anousha and the lovely Power Ranger ladies have left, but we've arranged to meet for tea in couple of days. My brow might be soaked in sweat, my face caked in a gluey paste, but I've loved every minute. A final pizza comes out of the tandoor and is passed around for us to finally try a slice. My tummy rumbles as I bite into the dough which is light and crunchy … Wait a minute …! *Crunchy?*

'Tasty isn't it, Deb?' asks Rich, shovelling a whole slice into his mouth. 'It's the bug-based dough. Adds a nice nutty, earthy flavour. Did you know that the flour is made from ground-up crickets?

'No, I didn't!' I slam down the slice of pizza. Crickets? *Yuck!* And cricket the sport, equally yuck, now I think of it. It just so happens to be the start of the cricket season today. Hence Stu is at Lords Cricket Ground instead of being here with me on my birthday. As if …

'Why don't you finish mine?' I suggest to Rich. 'I have to save my appetite for dinner.'

'So, which poncy restaurant is Stu taking you to tonight?'

'Nobu. For sushi.'

'Just take off the letter, "U!"' Rich grumbles.

Sacha wanders over, carrying a covered tray. 'Did you know that insects are tipped to rival sushi as fashionable food of the future?' She lifts the cloth on the tray to reveal a plate of flapjacks. 'They're just missing something …' As if by magic, Nat appears with a lit candle. She plonks it in the middle of a flapjack.

'*Happy birthday to you … happy birthday to you …* ' Nahal, Jafar, Sacha and Rich all sing along.

'Don't forget to make a birthday wish,' Nat cries, as I blow out the candle.

I smile in gratitude as I look around my lovely friends. I close my eyes, and wish for …

JULY

CHAPTER 28

Root 66

I wish ... I wasn't in the middle of our high street, knee-deep in sand.

It's Sunday morning, the day of our team-bonding road trip. We are not hiking along dappled country lanes in the search of a nice old pub and a Pimms, nor toe-dipping in the sea at a balmy Brighton. We *are* on a beach ... but it's in the middle of Kentish Town Road.

Nat's so-called 'road trip' has not gone much further than our own doorstep. It's an expedition to 'reclaim the street,' and visualise what it could look like once it's car-free. Nat's secret plan was to turn a stretch of the tarmac outside the Good Life into a beach. However, according to her unlikely story, she made out the order for the sand without wearing her glasses. Which explains a huge truck has tipped countless tonnes of sand in the middle of the high street.

It's now only 9 a.m. on the hottest morning of the year. Nat, Rich, and I, have been here for two hours, forty-three minutes and ten seconds, shovelling sand from the middle of the street into the Good Life forecourt. Unsurprisingly, no one else was available at 6 a.m. when Nat was ringing around for help. Her hammering on our front door did not make for the greatest start to the day between Stu and me, my workaholic husbondage, who'd claimed to have been up into the early hours working.

'I still can't believe I managed to get tins muddled with tonnes!' Nat proclaims for the hundredth time. An equal number of cars are angrily hooting as the congested traffic is reduced to one lane.

Rich laughs, 'Save your fictitious stories for the voters! Or better still, I know a way to shut you up.' He throws down his spade and pulls Nat into a passionate snog. While it's great that they've made their relationship public, one can't help wondering if it's a little *too* public, as the driver of car one hundred and one yells, '*Get a room!*'

'Get a feckin' life!' Rich shouts back. 'The pollution caused by the nitrous oxide belched out by your car is three-hundred-time times more warming than C02.'

'Or come and sunbathe on our beach!' Nat chips in. 'And remember—"Vote Nat for a Good Life!" Local elections in two weeks!' So saying, she turns and grabs Rich's crotch.

Ooh! Playa del Good Life, eh! The powder white sand of St Barts might have been replaced by the coarse grain of a UK quarry, but the summer bonkbuster taking place amid gridlocked traffic is just as steamy. I take a deep breath as a wave of longing washes over me. Jealous …? *Moi?* Can't remember the last time Stu and I …

'I'm so psyched about today's road trip,' says Nat, finally extracting herself from Rich.

'Yep,' Rich agrees. 'Particularly Mouse and Lucia's Community Assembly on clean air.'

'After all, reducing air pollution isn't an easy task, but it's a mission. Or should I say *emission*!' Nat laughs.

'And just wait 'till you taste the cocktails young Leroy will be shaking up with his bike-powered smoothie maker.' Rich licks his lips.

Nat nods. 'Just add gin, eh, Daiquiri Deb!'

'The only thing I'll be knocking back anytime soon, is a pain killer. My back is killing me.' I prove it by wincing, as I stretch and put my shovel down. I wipe my hand across my hair, which is streaked with a mix of sweat, grease, and quarry sand.

'Better not be late for your hair appointment,' says Nat, with a wink. 'We don't want you looking anything less than irresistible for …'

'I don't know what you're talking about, Natalie.' I blush a shade redder than the widget on my phone that beeps to remind me about my hair appointment at ten a.m.. 'But I might just go and …' With one last look at the huge mound of sand still to be shifted to the forecourt, I hurry away.

@NTS: Must Nat-proof the password on my phone diary.

Several coiffured hours later, I have no grey or gritty roots, just long tresses of hair as chestnut-coloured as the branches on the tree I'm now walking past. And my nails are as pink as the pretty flowers in Café Renoir's window box on the high street. Perhaps it was a mistake to drop into Cute-icles to invite Pueng to our road trip. I shouldn't have let her talk me into staying for a quick manicure. It's now 2 p.m., and I'm really late.

I dash past a row of cars that are plastered with parking tickets. Who knew wardens worked on a Sunday? Not that I, of course, would ever be an eco-baddy who drives to the High Street ... There's a tap on my shoulder. 'Miss, will you help us elect Councillor Thornton for another four years?' A young man wearing the skimpiest of shorts hands me a leaflet.

@NTS: Did this boy really call me, Miss? And why are his shorts so tight?

I divert my gaze to the campaign stall, where a large crowd is gathered. Volunteers sporting rosettes as red as my burning cheeks are confidently handing out leaflets. There's no sign of Councillor Thornton. I guess he's so certain about winning back his seat, he thinks he doesn't need to be there.

It doesn't look good for Nat, or the Good Life. But what looks even worse is the vision ahead of me up the street. The Playa del Good Life has been shifted to the forecourt, but it's been replaced by what looks like a living room, set up in the middle of the road. Young people deep in conversation are lounging around on a vintage maroon sofa and matching armchairs, while others are laying on scattered Persian rugs. Behind them, several teens are studying leaflets displayed on a pine dresser. Others are sitting on chairs around a large pine kitchen table, busy writing notes and drinking mugs of tea. Further along, Mouse and Lucia seem to be hosting their Community Assembly from the comfort of ... a double bed. It's a *pied a terre*, quite literally. Although this *terre* is concrete.

'Bloody move this shit out of the way!' a passer-by shouts. Road rage has turned into room rage. Mouse pushes his Thomas the Tank Engine duvet cover aside and jumps out of bed. 'So let's turn our ideas into reality and clean our air!'

'Let's make every other street pedestrian only,' Lucia chimes in.

'Let's share cars, and put the *park* back in *ex*-parking spaces,' a girl cries out.

'And use more cargo bikes,' another voice calls out from the sofa.

'Let's get delivery vans banned during the day!' Mouse bangs on the window of a Lidl van stuck in the traffic. The driver leans on his horn, hooting away like mad. He's soon joined by the rest of the vehicles.

Nat manages to bellow through the cacophony: 'Vote Nat for A Good Life! And, er ... clean air!'

I can't believe my eyes. Nat is floating in a pool made from a giant jam vat, which has been placed in the street outside the Lidl store. She's dressed in a Day-Glo pink bikini. While it makes me wonder just what kind of good life she's offering, my BF looks hot! The excited expressions on the faces of passers-by confirms it. I'm just wondering if this day can get any more surreal when a voice I've been waiting to hear for four weeks, two days and five hours, pipes up, 'Dorito-Deborah! Over here!'

It's Father Guy. Finally.

My heart races as I straighten my dress which is sticking to me in all the wrong places, and affect a nonchalant stroll into the Good Life forecourt. To my left, some people are pedalling like mad on static bikes connected to smoothie-makers, churning up cocktails—shaken and stirred. I'll probably need one soon. On my right, people are relaxing on garish pink deckchairs laid out around our re-located beach. These carry signs bearing the slogan, 'Vote Nat for a Good Life.' Bossa Nova music is blaring out, the sun is beaming down ... the Playa Del Good Life really is an idyllic sight. And to cap it all, I'm heading over to GG.

'Hello, Dorito-Deborah. I've been saving this chair for you.' He pats the chair next to him. As I sit down, I notice the dark rims around his eyes. They're almost as red as the swirls on his Hawaiian shirt. He rubs his hand across the bristles of his unshaven chin as his teeth bite his chapped, lower lip. There's an embarrassed silence.

I break it by asking, 'How was your retreat?'

'I wish I was more like you,' he blurts out.

'Like me?' I blink in surprise.

'Yes, like you.' He looks into my eyes. 'You're such a positive person. I've watched you over the last year always putting an optimistic slant on things.'

@NTS: *Me?* Always positive? Are we talking about the same person?

He continues, 'I know how tough it's been for you with your, er ... changing fashion career. I've seen the way your so-called friends, Fluff et al, try to put you down ...'

@NTS: This alleged glass-half-full gal could do with a snifter right now. He's right about Fliff and Phoebes. The question is how come he's noticed it, and I haven't?

'You are also so resilient. Just look at Box Clever. You've even managed to launch a great new brand.'

'This is very kind of you,' I reply hesitantly, 'but I think Box-Clever is more a case of *Nat's* brilliant positivity ...'

He interrupts full flow, 'You're so self-deprecating. And talking about Nat, you don't mind how often she ribs you! You take it with such good grace. You're also not afraid of getting stuck in, doing your bit. You're clumsy and so funny ...'

@NTS: *Me?* Funny? At dinner parties with Stu and friends, I've always come home feeling a bit of a bore.

He smiles, 'You're also so kind to others. You've really bonded with Nahal, and have helped boost Jafar's confidence ...'

I can't believe what I'm hearing. All the time I've been noting every little detail about him, like the way his eyes turn a lighter shade of blue when he smiles, he's been doing the same about me. The question is, *why?*

GG continues, 'You're the first to admit how privileged you are, and not afraid of being taken to task for it by Rich and others. You're not afraid of leaving your comfort zone and ...'—He pauses to push his long bare feet through the sand and move them closer to mine—'You're a gorgeous, sexy woman—even though you don't think you are. From my perspective, you don't seem to get the attention or appreciation from your husband that you deserve.'

I look away. I don't know what to think about first: GG's

worrisome observation about Stu, or, second: the fact that GG thinks I'm sexy.

@NTS: Me, *Sexy?*

I cross my legs to hide the varicose vein snaking down my calf like an errant stocking seam. If only. I have to say something. But all I can force out is, 'Did you set fire to the smokehouse?'

'Of course not.'

'Did you kill our chick, Sophie Lor-hen?'

He shakes his head.

'Did you get the power turned off at the Good Life several times?'

He blinks in surprise. 'No, that wasn't me. I would never have let that happen.'

'Did you give permission for Greener properties to dump all their ex-rental stuff here?'

He takes a deep breath. 'I might have suggested that some of their unwanted items might be useful for ...' A tear rolls down his sun-kissed cheek.

'Oh, Guy ... no ...' I look down. 'You must have known that turning the Good Life into a dump would harm our credibility.'

He sighs. 'The "donation" for the organ was just so tempting. And to be honest, the Good Life was so disorganised at first, it didn't seem like it could work. There was a constant barrage of public complaints; it was all so chaotic. And there were genuine health and safety concerns. It was suggested to me that in the short term, it might be kinder to point out these shortcomings to Father William ...'

'Suggested by a certain Thomas Montjoy?'

GG nods. 'But the trouble is, after Father William was given a bowl of soup by Mouse and Lucia at the Souper Van back in January, he became a Good Life convert. And six months later, who can disagree with him? I mean, just look around ...'

He points to Jafar and the other kids who are handing out homegrown peas in their pods to the guests sitting on deckchairs; then he points to Leroy and his dad, Francis, who are setting up their bike-power energy workshop. A faint smile crosses GG's face as he watches Mouse and Lucia write up the recommendations of their

People's Assembly on blackboards. He sighs, 'The Good Life is such an inspiring place. It's really turning people's lives around.'

'Including mine,' I add.

'I just wish it had turned mine around, too.' Tears start to appear in GG's eyes. 'I totally regret my actions.'

'Oh, Guy … surely it's never too late to …'

He cuts in, 'I don't think my father ever got over the loss of not meeting *his* father. It was always his aim to restore his father's organ. But his dream got put aside after he met and married my mother. They moved to Rugby and had a happy life. And then last year, he made me promise that I'd restore the organ to its former glory. But he died unexpectedly—and the same year, my divorce came through. I needed a fresh start. The opportunity came to return to my family parish, so …'

@NTS: Did GG just say the 'D' word? He's divorced!

I give myself a little kick and carry on listening. His baby blue eyes flood with tears. 'Anyway, Dorito-Deborah, I'm going to resign. I'm going to admit everything to Father William.'

I grab his soft but strong hand and say: 'I'm so sorry about your dad. But maybe you won't need to resign. Surely the bible tells us: "Forgive us our trespasses as we forgive those who …"'

I look away, unable to summon up any more of my school-girl words from the Lord's Prayer, as I meet his gaze. But I add gently, 'After all, we are all sinners.' Or would like to be, as Nat would say.

GG wipes his eyes. 'I guess I'll just have to wait and see what Father William says. But talking about sinning, do you fancy … er … a drink? I think we both need one.'

I slowly let go of his hand. We walk over to the bike smoothie-maker where several people are listening to Leroy and Francis' workshop, and where Old Spot is rooting around in a box of fruit.

'As you can see, it takes a lot of work to generate electricity!' Leroy explains, as he pedals his bike furiously. 'A recent experiment showed that it took twelve cyclists pedalling for seven minutes to create enough power to boil one cup of water!'

'And thirty cyclists pedalling as fast as they can, to power a kettle!' adds Francis, pointing to some kind of dynamo attached to the rear wheel. 'What a waste when most of us boil a whole kettle of water for just one cuppa.'

'Yikes! *Mea culpa*,' I mumble. 'Or as Nat would probably say, *mea cuppa!*'

GG chuckles, 'Why do you never take credit, Dorito-Deb? That was funny. And you said it, not Nat.'

Leroy continues, 'And did you know that the average person boils a kettle one thousand five hundred times a year? Yet many of us fill them to the brim, instead of only adding the amount of water we need.'

Francis adds, 'By boiling less water, we not only waste less energy, but we also save money on our energy bill!'

There's a tap on my shoulder. It's Nat. Her bikini bottom is now covered by a pair of shorts, but she's still in the Day-Glo top that is struggling to contain her impressive boobs. 'Did you hear the one about how I used to date an electrician, but he was shocking in bed!' She roars at her own joke—as usual.

GG looks down, trying not to chuckle or stare at her vivid décolletage. Then he turns away and wanders off.

'It's going so well today, Deb, isn't it?' Nat enthuses. She picks a carrot from one of the veg beds. 'Just look at our road trip. We've created our own Root 66! Geddit? "Root" spelt like the veg ...'

I would laugh along with Nat, but for an ominous new presence—a police officer. And he's heading for Nat.

'Excuse me, madam, are you the Good Life candidate?' he asks in a stern voice.

'I certainly am, officer,' Nat smiles and offers him the carrot. He refuses the carrot, but hands Nat a parking ticket. 'Perhaps you would like to explain this?'

Nat blushes and passes it to me. On closer inspection, I realise that it's not a valid parking ticket but a look-a-like. The words 'Parking Violation' have been replaced by 'Pollution Violation.' A copy line has been added: 'What's thicker—the air, or our politicians? Vote Nat: A Good Life vote.'

Mr Police Violation turns to me. 'Someone has placed these on all the cars along the high street. Would you care to comment, madam?'

I glare at Nat, who's completely lost for words … for once. I take a deep breath, but don't know what to say.

'Hello there, officer. What seems to be the problem?' GG has come to our rescue. Gorgeous Guy—with Old Spot. It may be more a case of a priest with a pig, than a knight with a white horse, but never was there a better saviour. My heart soars. GG takes the ticket from my hand and studies it. 'I'm Father Guy Mowbray—local priest in charge of the Good Life. Officer, I'm so sorry about this. It must have been the kids! They've been a little bit over-enthusiastic. But isn't it fantastic that young people care so much about air pollution? I'll get these removed straight away.'

Mr Police Violation hesitates, then he says, 'Right you are, sir. Well, thanks for the explanation, father.' He takes a little black book from his pocket. 'But would the several tonnes of sand dumped earlier today in high street, for which we received forty-two complaints, also be a bit of *kiddy* fun?'

Guy shakes his head. 'Ah yes, that sand was due to be delivered to the fire station across the road. They've donated a small patch of spare land for a children's playground. Isn't that marvellous, officer? It's being moved there tonight.' Old Spot, now nestled against Guy's leg, grunts in agreement.

Nat and I look at each other and grin. The Lord really does work in mysterious ways.

CHAPTER 29

Midsummer Magic

'I know a bank where the wild thyme blows, where oxlips and the nodding violet grows,' trills Nat in a loud theatrical voice. She leans forward to give Rich a good look at Titania's décolletage, which, in all senses of the word, is bursting out from her tight-fitting bodice.

'Thou art as wise as thou art beautiful … and look bloody sexy in that costume!' leers Rich. He pushes back his donkey ears and pulls Nat into a passionate snog.

'Hang on, that's not in script,' shouts director, Benjy-bard. 'Remember Nat, you're playing Titania, the fairy queen. You live in the wood and infuse the play with your magic. And you, Rich, are Bottom the weaver, disguised … and acting, like a right arse.'

I suppress a giggle and return to sewing the final embellishments on the costumes I'm making for our production of Midsummer Night's Dream. We are in the Good Life back garden where the performance is taking place here next week. Tempers are rising as high as Rich's blood pressure as he caresses Titania's neck. I'm particularly proud of the giant donkey's ears I've made for him. Who knew that an ex-potato sack would make such flappy ears.

Marg, aka Peaseblossom fairy, twirls past me in the green tutu I've made for her. It matches the French beans which she picks and hands to the Power Ranger ladies building our makeshift stage. She skips over to the lettuce bed where young Leroy and Jafar are attaching solar powered fairy lights to a giant wooden crescent moon. They are joined by Snug the Joiner, played by Mr Pang, who offers them a voucher for the launch of his new range of edible beetle bhajis.

Queen Nat pulls away from 'arse-acting' Rich. She takes out a costume from her Lidl carrier bag. 'Look Deb, I've made a cape,' she says, wrapping the carmine velvet cape around herself and Rich. They disappear into its voluminous folds in a fit of giggles.

@NTS: Must check the confession box curtain is still in place.

'Titania,' shouts Benjy-bard, 'you need to be professional and remember it's Midsummer's Eve ...'

'And you, maestro, need to remember that it isn't just Midsummer's Eve, but it's also election eve,' Nat barks back. 'I need some stress relief before voting opens tomorrow morning.'

Rich grabs her hand, and they disappear off. Doubtless to 'vent' some of that stress.

Election eve, eh? I know how nervous Nat is about the outcome tomorrow. But I also know we've done all we can. Every team Good Life member, bar Henry Smarmy Smythe, has spent the past two weeks campaigning. We've been leafleting and postering. We've set up stalls and handed out hundreds of snacks from the Abundance Cafe.

'Enter stage left, Michael and Anousha,' calls Benjy-bard. 'You two are playing the lovers Hermia and Lysander.'

Anousha, wearing a garland of yellow summer wildflowers over her purple headscarf, walks in with Michael holding hands. It's such a lovely sight.

Benji-bard continues, 'Remember, the play's theme is not only about love, but about how sometimes things are not quite what they seem, and we fail to see situations as they really are. People pretend to be something that they are not, hiding their true selves.'

@NTS: Appearance v reality. You can say that again, I think, as I watch Guy enter.

Whilst I'll never really come to terms with the harm he tried to inflict on the Good Life, or his motivation that led to it, or even get know what kind of person he really is; what I do know is that over the last two weeks he's been completely contrite. He's pitched in seven days a week to help with Nat's campaign, endlessly door knocking, preparing food, cleaning the community fridge. He's even taken Old Spot on daily walks.

'Ah, Dorito-Deborah, there you are.' GG walks up to me. 'Lidl's got a new flavour: Truffle temptation!' He hands me a giant packet of Doritos and sits down next to me. I smile and rip open the bag, only for an arrow to whizz past me, knocking it from my hands. The tortilla chips scatter all over the floor. Of course, it's Henry Junior, who is rushing past us firing his slings and arrows of misfortune.

GG sighs as he starts to pick up the crisps. 'By the way, Father William and I are having "the chat" when he comes to the Good Life today. I'll just have to wait a bit longer to hear my fate.'

I nod in agreement, knowing there's nothing really left to say. I hand him a needle and I start to teach him how to sew patches of sparkly fabric remnants onto Peaseblossom's fairy wings.

An hour later, our silent endeavours are interrupted by a fresh-faced Nat. 'I'm so nervous about the election, Guy,' she rattles on. 'I really need a touch of midsummer magic. Any chance of you asking your boss?'

'Father William will be here soon,' Guy smiles at me. But it's a bittersweet smile. 'We've got a lot to talk about, and ...'

Nat looks up to the sky. 'No, not Billy boy, silly. I'm talking about the big guy up there!'

'Or woman,' adds Marg, dashing past us with her basket of harvested veg.

Nat grabs a sprig of rosemary from it. 'Here you go, Deb—rub this into your forehead. It will help get rid of your wrinkles. It's my bit of my fairy magic.'

'Yes, well ... I'd better go and help Nahal prepare lunch,' says GG, and takes off.

'Hello team!' calls out a loud voice. It's Henry Smarmy Smythe. He wanders in wearing a striped boating blazer.

'Oh, it's you, Henry,' snarls Nat. 'We haven't seen you for weeks and you've done bugger all to help with my campaign.'

'Sorry, but I've been busy, with ... Ah, Michael, just the man I wanted to talk to.' He turns round to shake Michael's hand. 'Thanks for looking after Henry Junior. I know he's no trouble, but ...'

'You're welcome, Henry, but actually it's you I should thank,' replies Michael. 'I've wanted to say this for a while ... As a result of you dragging me into Daddy Day Share, I've made such lovely new friends.' He smiles at Anousha who is standing beside him. 'And also, Henry, I owe you an apology.' He pulls him into a hug. 'For a while I thought you were in cahoots with Thomas Montjoy trying to close the Good Life. I now realise the only mounting you wanted to do was ...'

'Ah, there you are, darling ... ' This from a blonde woman who walks in wearing an oversized blue and white straw hat, a pale blue suit, and matching shoes. She walks over to Henry Senior and gives him a kiss on the lips. 'I thought I'd surprise you.'

'Oh, Annie, how ... er ... wonderful,' Henry splutters.

'And here's my darling boy,' she says to Henry Junior who comes running into the garden. He tries to give her a hug, but she backs off, keeping him at arm's length. 'Do be careful, Henners, and don't mess up mummy's hair.'

'Do come and meet the ... er ... charity team I've been helping.' Henry Senior, for once almost lost for words, looks down and mutters, 'Team Good Life, meet Annunciata ... my wife.'

'Your *wife?*' Nat roars.

'What the ...' Michael raises his normally timid voice. 'I thought you were a single ...'

Old Spot saunters up grunting in displeasure, as much at the unfolding conversation as with the lion's mane costume which someone has put round his neck.

'Henry Junior, I have your blazer here,' says Annunciata, taking out a boating blazer from her Harrods carrier bag, seemingly unaware of the drama around her.

Henry Senior continues to stare intently at the lettuce by his feet as if it's the most interesting thing he's ever seen.

'How lovely to finally meet you,' I shake Annunciata's hand. 'We've heard all about you.'

'*Not,*' retorts Nat.

'Yes, about those *knots* ...' I quickly add my terrible segue. 'We must go and finish making breeches for Oberon's costume.' I link Nat's arm before she can throw another punch—verbal or otherwise.

'Yes, we've also got to hurry along.' Annunciata bends down

to stuff Henry Junior into his blazer. He looks as squashed as the worm he deposits on her hat. 'We've got to get to Henley for two,' she enthuses. 'You know I hate to miss the first race, Henry. Cheerio all.'

Like two peas in a pod, she marches the submissive Henrys—Senior and Junior—out of the garden.

'*Annunciata*? What kind of name is that? Sounds more like a Catholic mass to me!' Nat bursts out laughing. 'I always knew there was something fishy about him. Oh well, plenty more fish in the sea.'

'What, *my* cod piece not big enough for you?' winks Rich, walking up to us.

'I'd better check!' replies Nat, grabbing his crotch. 'By the way, Deb, talking of all things fishy, I was thinking that we should host a sustainable fish festival next summer. Call it "Fishstock" instead of *Woodstock!* Hilarious, eh?'

'It'll be a load of pollocks!' laughs Rich, as he extracts himself from Nat's firm grip and trots off to finish building the stage.

Nat and I walk inside the Good Life and over to my sewing machine.

'Blimey Deb, these sample pieces for the RHS are looking fab.' She picks up a waistcoat I've made from an old potato sack.

'Thanks,' I smile. 'I've been experimenting with lot of different designs. I still can't believe that the five thousand order is for real. I thought it was one of your "fabrications,"' I wink.

'Hey, save the "fabricating" for Debo designs,' she smiles. 'And here's some more news that'll make you happy.' She races on, 'Remember Toby, who helped set up our community garden last year before disappearing off to run an eco-farm in Devon?'

@NTS: Toby. As if I could ever forget the sexy ex-councillor who taught me, ex-High-Heeled Gardener, how to suck nectar from a flower, and the joys of mud. I blush as I cast my mind back to the other things I wish he'd taught me ...

Nat races on, 'Well, he's coming to visit us. Bet *that* will bring a smile to your breeches.' She grins at the baggy oversized trousers I've just tried on. I've made them for Oberon, who Greg is playing. Even though they are meant to be knee-length, they hang down to my ankles. Nat continues, 'I remember you fancied him like mad.'

'Ooh, Debo, who are you fancying now?' It's Phoebe. She walks in, blowing us air kisses. 'Mind you, with Stu away three nights a week and no job, you must have lots of spare time on your hands.'

'I … er … don't have *any* spare time.' I look down as the breeches fall to my ankles revealing the pink tutu I'm wearing underneath. As I've made it for Mustardseed Fairy being played by Chloe, it's obviously several sizes too small for me. I know I look ridiculous, but calmly continue, 'I'm actually really busy working on …'

Nat throws her arm around me, looking at Phoebe, and says, 'I'll have you know that Debo Designs is now officially supplying the Royal Horticultural Society,' she grins. 'She's replacing your planet trashing Haute-Couture with eco Horti-Couture. And I couldn't be prouder to be her friend.'

Phoebe lifts the sackcloth waistcoat and sighs, 'Sounds unlikely, but thought I'd drop by to wish you all congrats for getting a line about your buggy event in this month's Vogue. Unbelievable!' She takes a copy of Vogue from her Burberry bag and reads: '*On trend: The buzzin' Pestival of bugs at the Good Life community hub in Camden.*'

@NTS: Do I need earwax removed, or did I just hear The Good Life named trendsetter in Vogue? How come I haven't read Vogue this month yet?

'Talking of being on trend,' Phoebe continues to snigger, 'I must tell you, Debo, that those thin spaghetti straps on your silk vest are not the most flattering look with your now generous sized arms. You're more tagliatelle girl now!' she laughs. 'And as for the breeches, is there anything you'd like to tell me?'

'Actually, Phoebe, there *is* one thing I'd like to tell you …'—I tenderly trace my hand along my shoulder strap—'and that is to feck right off,' I shout. 'I'm sick and tired of the way you always make fun of me. You've been putting me down for years, making feel shit about myself and …'—I pause, stunned by my outburst; stunned by the vitriol that I can't believe is spewing out of my mouth. But my home truths are met by a big round of applause. Everyone in the Good Life downs tools and claps.

'Bloody well said!' Nat slaps me on the back. 'Our Deb is the kindest, most creative person I know. And so what if we've both got bingo wings.' She raises her arms and flaps them.

'How rude,' Phoebe manages to mumble.

'I'll escort you out,' says Rich, linking her arm and practically dragging her to the front door. Phoebe lets out a loud shriek as his giant donkey ear flaps across her face giving her a good slap.

'I'm so looking forward to a bit of theatrics. Hope I haven't missed anything?' says Clive, as he walks in.

'Nothing at all,' I add proudly, expecting to burst into tears, but laughing instead. I turn round to Nat. 'Gosh, that felt good.'

Jafar runs up to us. 'Hi Clive! Leroy and I have designed a crescent moon with a solar panel on it as a stage prop for our Shakespeare play. Shall I show it to you?'

'That sounds great,' smiles Clive. 'And *you* are just the young man I want to talk to. I come bearing good news. I've found an MP who has agreed to present our bill in parliament. It will review the rules on Unmanned Aerial Systems and drone delivery, and all because of *you* and the Good Life.'

'Oh, thank you,' says Jafar, throwing his arms around Clive.

'Wow! That's amazeball news, Clivey,' adds Nat.

'Hey, the world's a stage and us dudes are merely players,' drawls Benjy-bard, as he grabs Nat's hand. 'Titania, I need you to hasten back out into the garden for rehearsals.'

'Before you disappear, I've also got some really interesting news to share,' John calls out as he comes rushing into the Good Life. 'It might even affect the outcome of the election.'

'No way?' Nat shrieks.

'What kind of interesting news?' I calmly ask, although my heart is racing.

John takes a deep breath and explains: 'I've managed to uncover the fact Cllr. Thornton seems to have an undeclared vested interest in Greener Properties.'

'How the hell did you friggin' find that out?' Nat yells.

John continues, 'His wife is A. Stuart. She appears to be a Director of a Greener Properties company offshoot called ...'

'How do you know his wife's name?' I ask.

John grins and opens his phone. He scrolls through his photos. 'Just look at these screenshots I've saved. They're from photos of them glamming it up at flashy restaurants and luxury holidays. I found them on Facebook.' He hands us his phone.

Nat and I quickly scan the pictures. 'You're a bloody genius,' Nat squeals, giving John a smacker on the cheek.

'Stuart?' I ponder, in Detective Debo mode. 'I wonder if she's any relation to Miss Stuart?'

'I thought that too,' John adds, 'so I dug a little deeper, and found out that Miss Stuart, Jafar's teacher, is actually Cllr. Thornton's niece!'

'Oh my flipping God,' shrieks Nat. 'This means that Miss "Jam Tart" Stuart probably misused school premises for personal reasons to host those Greener Properties meetings and that's ...'

'... a sackable offence,' I finish Nat's sentence.

'Sure sounds like it,' says John. 'Anyway, I called the editor of the Camden New Journal. They're going to publish the story online within a couple of hours. I also contacted Cllr. Thornton's team for their reaction. They had no comment but are apparently going to issue a statement any time now.'

'Oh my flipping God,' Nat bursts into tears.

'This means that Cllr. Thornton might pull out of the election,' I gasp, 'and you would have a really good chance of winning. *Councillor Nat!!! Yeeeees!!*' I grab Nat's hand and we dance around in a circle.

'That's my gal!' Rich walks up to us dragging the giant wooden crescent moon. It's bigger in size than Jafar, who is pushing it from behind. 'Let's see what unravels in the next few hours,' he suggests. 'Meantime, how about breaking into a bottle of my new plum wine to celebrate?'

'*Nooo!*' Nat and I call out in unison.

Clive walks up and pats John on the back. 'You're going to make a fine lawyer one day. When you finish University, I want to you get in touch with me.'

'Thanks. I will,' John replies with a big smile spreading across this face.

Rich and Jafar place the crescent moon next to Clive.

'This is a fine piece of construction,' says Clive, tracing his hand along the crescent moon. 'The pieces of recycled wood have been so carefully glued together.'

'Thanks,' replies Jafar excitedly. 'Leroy and I added a mini solar panel and battery to help it shine in the dark. In my faith, the moon represents life, light, and good luck.'

'And in my faith, we say, "Let your light shine that they may see your good deeds,"' adds Father Bill who walks up to us wearing his blue raincoat despite the glorious summer weather. 'As I'm feeling a little weary, could you remind me, Natalie, is this a quote from Matthew 5:16 or 5:17?'

Nat stops dancing around. Of course, dear Father William … it's from … er …'

'Matthew 5:16,' GG answers for Nat, and winks at her. 'In fact, Natalie has just finished holding, er … a circle of communal prayers here. It's the local election tomorrow and she's standing as an independent to become a Good Life councillor.'

'I've always thought of you, Natalie, as an upstanding citizen,' says Father Bill. 'I'm sure you will do very well.'

'There's only one thing upstanding in here,' Rich mutters, as he looks at Nat's breasts which her boisterous dancing have hoisted further up her costume.

'Anyway, I'm pleased to find you all here,' continues Father Bill. 'Especially you, young man.' He pats Jafar on the shoulder. '*You* are responsible for many good deeds, including the well written, passionate letter you wrote to me telling me why the Good Life should be granted a long lease. The diocese was also very impressed by your entreaty for us to grant permission for solar panels to be installed at the Good Life project. We agree with you that we all have to play our part to address the climate crisis, no matter how big or small our actions.'

'Let there be light, and all that. Amen, dearest Father William,' adds Nat.

Father Bill smiles, 'So, I've come here today to give you the good news that the diocese has decided to grant the Good Life a lease for five years.'

'Whaaat?' yells Nat. 'We've got the lease here for five flipping years. *We've done it, Deb, we've bleeding done it!*' Nat throws her arms around Father Bill.

'That's absolutely amazing,' I cry, and without realising what I'm doing, I throw my arms around GG. A giant cheer goes up around the room as Clive, Marg, Jafar, and Rich all come and join us in a group hug squashing Father Bill and Nat in the middle.

Father Bill comes up for air and continues, 'I must also give praise to the whole of the Good Life team. You have worked wonders here.' He pauses to look around the room brimming with desks full of activities: At the Abundance Cafe, people are enjoying lunch; there's a scattering of kids and carers over at the Daddy Day Share Toy Swop—someone has even changed the image on the centre of the dart board. It now contains a photo of Henry Smarmy Smythe! Father Bill continues, 'Ten months ago, this place was a soulless, dilapidated ex-church, and now it's a thriving hub, a place which has renewed my faith in the power of community, and frankly, humanity.'

I'm just wondering whether the day could get any sweeter when Nahal walks out of the kitchen carrying a tray piled high with my favourite sesame and pistachio Zaban cake dripping with syrup.

'*Mobarake.* Huge congratulations to us all,' she laughs. 'Let's sit down and enjoy a cup of Persian tea and cake.'

As we walk over to the Abundance Cafe, GG continues, 'And no matter what you decide about my future, Father William, I'll be giving the twenty-five thousand pounds donation back to the Good Life … As you know, my, er … misplaced intention, was to buy an organ for St Margaret's Church. But how about using part of it to buy some instruments to set up an after-school kids rock or rap band here at the Good Life?'

'So the memory of your grandfather's music lives on, but in a different way,' I quietly add. GG squeezes my hand and smiles at me.

'*Love* that idea,' says Nat. 'I'm actually a great drummer.'

'Yeah, right!' scoffs Rich, but his eyes are full of love.

'And I'll be yon master of revels,' says Benjy-bard.

'Well, there's a lot more to discuss,' says Father Bill, 'But after tea, Father Guy, I'm afraid you and I need to have that chat.'

In a slightly more sombre mood, as everyone sits down for tea, Nat grabs my hand and drags me outside to the front of the church. The sun dazzles me as we step out into the beautiful, warm afternoon. There's giggling coming from the Chip Fat Travellers van, whilst over at the People's Fridge, a man and woman are helping themselves to some goodies. Nat bursts out laughing as she reads the words on a giant banner above the front door which Rich has erected: "*Vote Nat: A Good life campaign. Get up and get voting tomorrow morning you lazy buggers.*"

Whilst I'm not sure it's the election eve message *I* would have chosen, I can't help but admire Rich's passion. Even the gargoyle below the banner seems to be winking in agreement.

'I'm so proud to be your friend,' I say to Nat as I pick up a bundle of 'Vote Nat' flyers. 'I can't believe what we've achieved here, mostly because of you and your amazing, effervescent energy.

'I feel same way about you, too,' says Nat, hugging me.

'I can't believe you're not more anxious, waiting to hear about what Councillor Thornton does next?' I race on, 'I know I have a posh restaurant booked tonight, but I'm going to cancel it. It's election eve– it's now or never. Let's spend the whole night leafleting. Just think, you could be a councillor tomorrow night ...'

'Deb ... whatever will be, will be,' Nat answers in the calmest voice I've ever heard her speak in. 'But do you know what I'd really like to do with you tonight? Let's go home to our community garden. Just you and me, back to the place where our adventures began; our crazy, fun adventures which turned you from being a High-Heeled Gardener to a High-Heeled Eco-Worrier; from being a stranger to my best friend. Let's go and pick some salad and make ourselves a feast.'

I smile in agreement as Nat links my arm and we walk onto the Good Life forecourt. 'And you're right about another thing, Deb,' she continues, 'Councillor Nat *has* got a nice ring to it.' She smiles. "But better still, *Prime Minister Nat* in a couple of years' time!? You could be my campaign manager ...'

'Naaaaatalie -'

Acknowledgments

Once again thanks to the love of my life, my eco-lover, Wooly.

And my son, Lu. Check out his beats: insta: lucid_productions

Ahoy there, Captain! Thank you, Mike Sumner, for your editing and contributions to this book. What an amazing wordsmith you are. And a very funny bloke.

Eli, *grazie mille* for another beautiful book cover. www.elisabettagiordana.com

In solidarity with all you High-Heeled Eco-Worriers around the world. Have fun and keep on going!

If you are new to the world of climate action, want to get involved but don't know where to start, check out the Transition network: www.transitionnetwork.org

Huge thanks to Dickie, my publisher, and the team at Malchik Media.

Debbie Bourne
Head of Imagination Think&Do

thinkanddocamden.org.uk
@ThinkDoCamden
@HeeledGardener
@tkentishtown

About the Author

Debbie Bourne, author of the Eco Romance Series, lives in Camden, London, UK, with her hubbie and son.

A few years ago, there was a knock on her door ... that changed her life forever. You'll have to read the first book in the series, *The High-Heeled Gardener,* to find out about her big "growmance."

It could happen to you!

Debbie also co-runs Think&Do, an environmental and social action organisation based in Camden, London.

For Debbie, homemade sloe gin and elderflower bubbly are her cocktails of choice.

She can now appreciate the difference between a hedgerow and a hedge fund. And green is very much the new black!

FOR FURTHER ADVENTURES
IN THE ECO ROMANCE SERIES:
Book 3: High-Heels & Tight Briefs

@tkentishtown
@ThinkDoCamden
@HeeledGardener

For all book enquiries:
richard@richardlynttonbooks.com
www.richardlynttonbooks.com

Printed in Great Britain
by Amazon